THIRSTY CREEK

BY

JENNIE BRICKER

Unsolicited Press
Portland, Oregon
www.unsolicitedpress.com
info@unsolicitedpress.com
619–354–8005

THIRSTY CREEK
Copyright © 2025 Jennie Bricker
All Rights Reserved.
Printed in the United States of America.
First Edition.
ISBN: 978-1-963115-65-9

Distributed by Asterism Books
https://asterismbooks.com/

For wholesale orders:
Asterism Books
568 1st Avenue South, Ste 120
Seattle, WA 98104
(206) 485-4829
info@asterismbooks.com

Cover Design: Kathryn Gerhardt
Editor: Summer Stewart

For my folks, Pat and Sterling,
who taught me to love being outside.

THIRSTY CREEK

Wednesday, September 15, 2004

Another body in the water, floating face down, wrapped around a piling of the old sawmill wharf. It wore a red T-shirt that billowed as the lake rippled.

Mike stowed the oars and knelt in the dory. He worked his fingers under the waistband of the jeans. Heaved the body upward. Got the head and an arm and a leg over the gunwale and, gasping, rolled him onto the boat. The face of the out-of-town scientist stared up at him, skin the color of granite, hair plastered to his forehead in three spikes. Mike shuddered. He thumbed the eyelids shut on the staring eyes and nudged the chin to close the gaping hollow mouth. Better. He sat up on the bench to ease his back, scratched at his goatee, and let the jagged mountains draw his gaze away, across the lake.

That was that. Fletcher was gone.

Wednesday, September 22, 2004

1.

Jess MacKinnon frowned at her fingernails. They were ragged and decorated with black crescents of grime from working on her motorcycle. She went at them with her teeth, but Darrin had summoned her to his office. It sounded urgent.

Darrin Woodruff, president of Columbia Environmental Consultants in Portland, Oregon, was a grim man, and he sounded more grim than usual as he nodded Jess into a chair and offered her coffee. "There's been an accident at the Still Lake site," he told her.

Jess burned her tongue on the coffee. She balanced the cup on her knee, tucking her dirty fingernails away from Darrin's view. The tiny town of Still Lake sat nestled in Oregon's northeastern corner, high in the Wallowa Mountains. C.E.C. was consulting on a fish restoration project there. "What kind of accident?" she asked. Shit happened. The year before, a C.E.C. employee had driven his backhoe into the side of a greenhouse.

"The biologist that the feds sent up there."

"Is he okay?" Her heart made a fist. Ben worked for the U.S. Fish and Wildlife Service.

The lines on Darrin's face deepened and drew the corners of his mouth downward. "Depends on how you look at it. He's dead."

"Dead!" Jess gulped the coffee. It scalded all the way down. "Who? Who was it?" *Not Ben*, she thought.

"Ben Fletcher. Are you okay? Here."

He handed her a tissue from the box on his desk. She stabbed at the coffee that had sloshed onto her pants, keeping her eyes down as the stain bloomed across her thigh. She took in a long breath, shaky, the tissue a ball in her fist. She squeezed it and pressed her knuckles into her thigh. The room seemed to slide around her. Everything had come unfastened.

Ben and the Kid were points on her compass: They oriented her. She'd seen Ben at the Kid's seventeenth birthday. The Kid would be eighteen next month. She bit her lip hard, and focused on that small pain. She composed her face and raised her head. Darrin was watching her.

"You knew him?"

She stared at the cleft in Darrin's chin, his lips, his nose, his hazel eyes, which bored into hers. His close-cropped gray hair. Darrin was a point on her compass, too.

"Yes." She looked out the window, at Lownsdale Square and at the tops of the ginkgo trees. What else was there to say about Ben? The ginkgo leaves had turned yellow—all at once, as they did. They waved their hands at her. She wanted to let Darrin know she was all right, that he could carry on with whatever he had to say, because she wanted this meeting to be over so she could be alone. "We weren't that close," she said, watching the trembling leaves. In truth, she'd never been closer to anyone.

"Well, I'm sorry," Darrin said.

Jess turned from the window. Her lips wanted to shake. She pressed them together. She spidered her fingers across the rim of the half-full cup. Set it carefully on the floor. Lifted her hand away. Folded the hand in her lap. When she thought she could trust her voice, she asked, "How did he die?"

"Drowned in the lake. The autopsy showed he was drunk."

Her body gave a little shudder as though it felt the cold plunge into darkness. "That doesn't sound like Ben," she said, but she could understand how it had happened. Ben liked to drink. He didn't always think things through.

Darrin said, "I don't know the details," and the silence swelled between them. The ginkgos waved their yellow hands.

"Is that everything?" she asked. She shifted in the chair, crossed her legs, and uncrossed them. She remembered Ben's tanned, freckled face smiling into the sunlight and her mind wheeled like a bird over the water, no place to perch.

"I need someone at Still Lake," Darrin told her. The lines across his forehead narrowed. "I think you could handle it."

Jess looked down and tried to gather herself together. She picked up the coffee cup and took a swallow, tepid and harsh. The part of her brain that still functioned registered this as a career breakthrough, exactly what she'd been waiting for. "Why me?" she asked. "Why not another scientist from Fish and Wildlife?"

"C.E.C. is taking over the project." Darrin bounced a little in his chair. In his quiet way, he was excited. "It's a huge opportunity for us, kind of a one-shot deal. Because of this accident, the feds are finally out. The tribes want C.E.C. to take over, and the governor's office is on board, at least for now. This is our chance to show the Consortium what the private sector can really do." Jess nodded. C.E.C.'s fifty-two scientists and engineers referred to the client—an alliance of tribes, state government, and federal agencies—as "the Consortium," capital C. The Consortium was C.E.C.'s most important client. Darrin smiled, a little half-smile with his lips closed and his mouth pulling up on one side. "We need a P.M. Interested?"

Project manager of a cutting-edge fish restoration project. There was no way she could turn that down. Ben had asked her, at the Kid's birthday almost a year ago, how work was going. Like her, Ben was a fish biologist. He was the reason she'd chosen her career. She was still hoping for a major project, she'd told him. This was it.

She had to stop thinking about Ben. She drained the bitter coffee. "Of course," she said.

"You'll have to go up there right away."

"When?" Jess dropped the balled-up tissue into the empty cup and squeezed the cup between her hands.

"Monday." Darrin picked up a map and rifled the folds with his thumb. "You'd be back here on Friday, we have a meeting set up to brief the Consortium. It's not much time."

She nodded and met Darrin's eyes. "I can do that." Her gaze slid over to the photograph on his desk—Darrin and his wife, their four smiling daughters sorted by age, descending like a staircase from their father's outstretched arm. They wore ski clothes, with snowy mountains behind them. Jess had never been skiing.

"Still Lake is a weird little town," Darrin said. "You'll need to tread lightly. For some reason, whatever happened to the native fish population, the locals are sensitive about it. Fletcher didn't do well with public relations, apparently. In fact, he made a mess of it. You'll have to do some damage control."

Jess pinched the bunched-up skin between her eyebrows. "Damage control?" she asked.

"You'll do fine." He opened the map and slapped it onto the desk. "The main thing is the fish. What happened to them? We need to understand the place and its history, way back to the first settlement. Why was the fish population decimated? Is the population extinct, or can we bring it back? If we bring it back, is it sustainable?"

Jess stood up and tried to look curious. "Okay, so the first question is, are there any fish left?"

"Right." He smoothed the map flat. Jess stood beside him, smelling his aftershave. He planted a forefinger in the center of a lake.

"Here's Still Lake—the town is named for it. Sits in a glacial scour. Two inlet streams, Old Chuck Creek, and a smaller one, North Creek. No outlet. Creeks are fed by snowmelt, primarily, and springs. There's a lot of flow variability, some flooding. Catastrophic flood this past March. One person died. Fletcher had been up there for a week in February, but he wasn't there for the flood. The basin is small, remote. There's one hotel, sort of a fishing lodge. Not much going on."

Jess bent over the map and pushed her fingers into the wrinkled contours of the mountains that ringed the lake, where Ben had drowned.

"You should try to get buy-in from the local government. Talk to the city council. Talk to the mayor. Tell them there's funding available. Small towns are usually strapped for cash."

This was starting to sound like a lot of politics. She preferred science. She was a scientist, like Ben. Because of Ben. She folded the map and crammed it into her back pocket.

"Another thing. There's a Nez Perce family in Still Lake, last name Branch. Mike Branch is the local fishing guide, the one who found Fletcher's body. The Branches have no official role in the project, but the Nez Perce are one of the lead tribes in the Consortium. So you should find these folks. They could be allies."

"I can do that." She edged toward the door. She wondered how Ben's parents were taking the news. She wasn't close to them—far from it—but still, they'd lost their son. She would see them, and the Kid, on October thirteenth. The Kid's eighteenth birthday. Alone, without Ben. Everything had changed.

Thursday, September 23, 2004

2.

Riley Bishop, Private Investigator, found three people waiting on the landing outside her office door at eight-fifty-seven on Thursday morning. They did not have an appointment, and the gangly-limbed teenager was grinding the toe of his cowboy boot into a hole in the carpet, with the apparent goal of enlarging it. These two details vied for top billing in the list of reasons for Riley's irritation as she pushed past them to unlock the door. She addressed the rust-colored mop that passed for a hairdo on top of the teenager's head. "Would you please stop doing that?" A very tall man stuck out his arm. Riley pocketed the key and shook hands. She was five feet, three inches tall; he had to be pushing seven feet. His hair was the same rusty color as the boy's, white at the temples. From the deep lines on his face, he looked old to be the kid's father, but maybe he spent too much time in the sun.

"Dr. Rex Fletcher. This is Becky, my wife." The plump woman chirped a little greeting. She smiled, but her eyes looked bleak, her face tense. "This is Moses." The teenager stared past her, said nothing. Charming. "Could you spare a few minutes for us?" Fletcher's tone was polite, but commanding—he was used to getting his way. Half because of that, and half on general principle, Riley almost refused. But she recognized the name Fletcher from the newspaper, and as per usual her curiosity held sway. She swung the door open and gestured them inside.

She got them seated and took her place behind the desk. The kid, Moses, threw himself into the armchair in the corner, propped his boot heels on the ottoman, and let his hair fall into his eyes until Riley wanted to sweep it out of the way, grab the scissors from her desk, and whack his bangs off, or scream. Possibly all three.

Riley Bishop's office in Enterprise, Oregon occupied a cramped, low-ceilinged room above an East Indian restaurant. At all hours, odors of ginger and cumin wafted through the ventilation system, and the office's single window opened only three inches. Bookshelves lined two walls, sloppy with ragged stacks of paper, three-ring binders, books, and dusty mementos—wooden totems, wildly painted animal figurines—from Riley's travels. Some of the piles had escaped to the floor, where they waited like small pets for her attention.

"Nice office," said Rex Fletcher, face expressionless. Riley was trying to figure out whether he was being sarcastic when Moses snorted and gave it away. She decided not to offer them tea.

Becky Fletcher leaned forward. Her eyes were red and her lips trembled. "It's about our son, Ben. He drowned in a lake up in the mountains, just a week ago." She ducked her head.

Riley laced her fingers together and set them on the desk. Becky Fletcher's grief seemed to seep from her pores and fill the room with an empty smell, the smell of water. Riley waited for the rest. But Becky covered her face and wept, shoulders jerking. Riley scanned the room for a box of tissues but could produce only a wrinkled paper napkin from a desk drawer. "Happy Birthday," it said, in rainbow colors. Riley gave herself a moment to acknowledge the irony.

Rex scooted forward, scraping his chair on the threadbare carpet. "They said an autopsy was standard procedure, so we agreed," he told her. His voice was gruff, either full of emotion or from anger; Riley couldn't tell, but she liked him better for it.

"Yes," she said.

"They said he was drunk. Went for an evening swim. Drowned."

Becky scrubbed her eyes with the napkin. "Ben was not a drinker," she said. "Not like that. He wouldn't have done it——gotten drunk, gone swimming. He just *wouldn't*."

"The coroner found something else, a 'blunt force trauma' to Ben's head." Rex slid a folder onto the desk.

Riley opened it. The autopsy report. She lifted an eyebrow. Moses stood up. "I'm starving," he announced, as though they'd been discussing the weather. "I'm going to get something to eat." He shuffled toward the door.

Rex held up his hand. "Just hold on there," he said. "First tell Miss Bishop what your brother said to you." He turned toward Riley, who hadn't been called "Miss" in two decades. "This was less than one week before he died."

The three of them watched the mop-headed teenager as he continued to sidle toward the only exit. "But I'm *hungry*," he whined. "We didn't really have breakfast."

There was something underneath the whining, Riley realized as she watched him—like the smell of blood. Fear. Moses hadn't let Ben Fletcher's death sink in yet, and he didn't mean to let it. He was trying to escape. As he and Rex argued, Riley did the math. The kid was skinny; his bulk hadn't caught up to his height. The fur on his cheeks told her he hadn't started shaving yet, but needed to soon. At most, he was eighteen. Probably closer to sixteen. She flipped to the summary page of the autopsy report. Ben Fletcher had been thirty-six. Interesting. She interrupted the squabbling, which had become unbearable; Becky was actually covering her ears. "Were you and your brother close, Moses?" she asked loudly.

The bickering ceased. She waited out the silence. "Yeah, sure," Moses said. "I guess."

"Do you have other brothers or sisters?" She looked up from the autopsy report and willed him to make eye contact.

His gaze brushed her face and quickly swooped away. "No," he answered. "Just Ben."

Without looking away from Moses, Riley fumbled in the drawer where she'd found the napkin, produced a candy bar, and tossed it across the room. Moses caught it easily. Good reflexes. "Eat that," she told him. Becky was watching, her expression darting between surprise and amusement; the napkin had made a mess of her make-up. Moses ate the candy bar in two bites. Riley relaced her fingers on the desk. "Now. Tell me what Ben said to you."

Moses started to hand her the candy wrapper, then reconsidered and stuffed it into his pants pocket—faded blue jeans, both knees ripped out. "He said the people at Still Lake had committed a 'crime against the environment.' Then they hushed it up. There's some Indian guy who knows all about it. An old guy. Nez Perce. Ben was ready to expose everything. They didn't like that, the people up there. He thought they were going to run him out of town." Moses sagged against the wall.

"Is that it?" Riley asked. Moses nodded. "All right. There's a market across the street if you're still hungry."

When the door closed, Becky mumbled something in a low voice that shook with intensity. "What did you say?" Riley leaned across the desk.

"We think they killed him. The people in Still Lake." She raised her head, her eyes fiery and her mouth hard. Riley shrank back, purely on instinct. The lingering blood smell turned sharp and metallic. "We believe Ben was murdered."

3.

Jess's cell phone rang as she flew down Interstate 84 toward the Wallowa Mountains. She took the next exit, leaning deep into the turn. Her front wheel hit a spray of gravel and the bike shimmied. She throttled up until it steadied, feeling the bike's raw power beneath her.

In her C.E.C. interview, Darrin had asked her why she liked motorcycles. "There's no reverse gear," she'd answered. "It only goes forward." He'd offered her the job at the end of the interview.

She pulled into a gas station. An old man in greasy blue coveralls shuffled over, tipping his John Deere baseball cap. His shaggy sideburns, white as sun-bleached bone, caught the sunlight.

"Yessir?"

She tugged off her helmet. Her braid fell down her back.

"Excuse me. Ma'am?"

Jess offered up a smile. "Restroom?" she asked him, when the tank was full.

"Round back," he answered, pointing, his voice roughened by decades of smoking. She saw the red and white package peeking from his chest pocket, the streamer of cellophane. She shaded her eyes from the broad bright sky.

"There's something you should know," said Darrin when she called. "Ben Fletcher's parents hired a private investigator."

"Is that right?" Jess pictured Ben's father stomping around, demanding explanations. She walked to the edge of the asphalt, to the seam between desert and sky. "To investigate what?"

"Apparently they do not think he drowned accidentally. They think somebody up there did him in. You with me?"

"Murdered, you mean?" The big sky pressed down on her. A bank of clouds stretched over the sun, dropped her into shadow, then moved on.

"Yes. Well, they're his parents. The coroner and the sheriff say he was drinking and went for a swim and drowned. Of course they don't want to believe that."

Jess knew Rex Fletcher—hated him thoroughly, as he hated her. He did not indulge in fanciful thinking. If Rex thought his son had been murdered, it might be true. "What do *you* think?" she asked Darrin.

"Here's what I think: Pay attention. Watch your back. First sign of trouble, you're back in the office. Game over. No project is worth that kind of risk, not even this one."

"Got it." Her eyes followed the jagged line the mountains made under the sky. Ben had been here, had traced the same horizon. He might have stopped for gas, right here. How odd death was, how final. As heavy as the blank desert dirt and sky.

"Me? I think he got drunk and drowned. His blood alcohol was point-one-three."

Jess turned a slow circle: Dirt. Sagebrush. Through the greasy front window of the cinderblock building, she saw the attendant playing solitaire at a card table.

"You there, MacKinnon?"

She started. "Yes! I mean, yes. I'm here."

"You should stop in Enterprise and talk to this P.I. What time can you be there? I'll call ahead."

4.

Riley needed to get out of town. Every time Enterprise, Oregon became too stifling, she bought a plane ticket. Bali, Burma, Egypt, Wales. She turned to the world map tacked up under the window. For her last trip, she'd picked her destination by throwing a dart at the map, had ended up in Norway. Not a bad method. She found the dart in her desk and hurled it, but her throw was high and the point ricocheted off the window. Before she could retrieve the dart, someone knocked at her door: That would be the fish biologist from Portland.

They shook hands and Riley sized her up: a small woman, thirty-something. Blue jeans, chunky black boots, motorcycle helmet under one arm, gigantic duffle bag hanging from the other. "Traveling light?" Riley couldn't resist saying.

Jess MacKinnon shrugged but didn't smile. Her dark brown hair was pulled back into a braid, unruly wisps of it framing her face. Her face was heart-shaped, not unpleasant, but she had a worn look, a pinch of tension between her eyebrows, and a hard blue light in her eyes. *Rode hard and put away wet,* Riley thought, smiling at her cowboy metaphor.

MacKinnon perched on the chair seat, duffle bag between her feet. Riley offered her some tea—a side benefit of her lease from the restaurant. MacKinnon sipped the tea, frowned, and sipped again. Her fingers tap-danced around the rim of the cup. Her movements had a delicate, feline quality that Riley found at odds with the boots and the leather jacket and the way MacKinnon planted her elbows on the desk like a pair of howitzers and said, in a bossy voice, "So. Tell me what happened to Ben Fletcher."

In lieu of answering, Riley smiled behind her teacup, inhaling the steam that fogged her glasses. Today's batch was heavy on the cinnamon. "Where are you from?" she asked.

"Chicago." MacKinnon's lips twitched into a little smile. "How about you? New York?"

"Brooklyn." Riley nodded to acknowledge their kinship. What the *hell* were the two of them doing out here in B.F. Nowhere? She glanced at the map and allowed herself a pang of longing. She set her cup down firmly on the desk. "As for Fletcher, who knows? Maybe he died accidentally. Maybe he had help. I'm looking into it."

"Help? Is that what his parents think?"

Something in her voice made Riley's eyebrows snap upward. MacKinnon leaned back in the chair and crossed her legs in a gesture Riley interpreted as feigned nonchalance. Picked up her tea. Set it on her thigh. Threaded her fingers through the handle and wrapped them around the cup, all the time looking down at her lap and her hands. "That's right," Riley said slowly. Riley had a tendency to mix up sensory information, a trait she'd first identified in kindergarten, when a child psychologist informed her parents, Mr. and Mrs. Larry S. Bishop, that their daughter was "non-neurotypical." Sometimes she experienced strong emotions and personality traits—other people's— as odors. Rex Fletcher, for instance, had given off a stink of arrogance, sour and caustic, like battery acid. MacKinnon's scent was sharp, like citrus: The smell of pent-up bright yearning. As MacKinnon lifted the teacup to her lips, Riley smelled the effort of will it took her to sit quietly, to rest against the back of her chair, to keep her fingers still. Riley inhaled: Cinnamon, the tea. Ginger and cumin, the air in her office. Just-sliced wedges of lime, Jess MacKinnon. "Why do you ask?"

MacKinnon met her eyes, then looked down again. "Just curious," she answered, with the same forced casual tone.

Riley put it together then, as though the two odors mingled in her non-neurotypical brain. Under the cinnamon, the sour pungency of Rex Fletcher and the sharp, sweet scent of limes. She spread her hands on the desk and leaned toward MacKinnon. "You know them, don't you? The Fletchers."

MacKinnon's mouth made a circle of dismay, but then she smiled. Her teeth were crooked and the effect was oddly charming. "How did you like Rex Fletcher?"

Riley's crooked teeth had been straightened by braces in the eighth grade, courtesy of Mr. and Mrs. Larry S. Bishop. She supposed that Jess MacKinnon's people had lacked the means or the interest to sponsor orthodontia. This fact made MacKinnon more interesting, so Riley returned the smile. "He's a fourteen-carat asshole," she answered. "Not to speak ill of a client. How do you know him?"

"Ben and I were . . ." MacKinnon waved a hand around, as though trying to capture the right word. "Close. A long time ago."

"How long ago was it?" The other pieces of the story were sliding into place. MacKinnon's pointed, dimpled chin helped: She had seen it before, just last Thursday, on Moses Fletcher's face.

"What?" MacKinnon looked alarmed.

Riley was about to commit the sort of social infraction that made people dislike her, but as per usual she couldn't help herself. "Moses is your son, isn't he? Yours and Ben's?" Oh, shit. Tears flooded MacKinnon's eyes, as though Riley had peeled off her clothes, then her skin. "Would you like more tea?" she asked cheerfully. A lot of people sobbed in her office. She had never gotten used to it.

"No. How did you—" MacKinnon bit her lip. "Only five people in the entire world know that. Now Ben's dead. So, only four."

"And Moses is not one of them, is he?" Good: She was not going to cry.

MacKinnon shook her head. "No, he doesn't know. Did Rex tell you? Or Becky?"

"I just figured it out. Sorry." Riley lifted her palms in apology. "Why doesn't Moses know you're his mother?"

MacKinnon looked away and Riley thought she wasn't going to answer. "Rex and Becky raised him. They wouldn't . . . They didn't approve of me."

"Why is that?" The lime smell sharpened. Instead of answering, MacKinnon looked at her watch, then out the window. Riley waited her out.

When MacKinnon turned, her face wore a bitter half-smile. "I was a shitty little tramp from the projects," she said. She was quoting someone; the words had a meter, old and ponderous. They had their own scent, too: garbage burning. "The deal was, I could see Moses once a year, on his birthday. If I kept the secret. So, I gave up custody. I was sixteen. I didn't know I had a choice."

MacKinnon's anguish rolled across the desk in waves, and with it the foul burning smell. "That's rough," Riley said. "You and Ben. Were you still together? When he died?"

MacKinnon looked startled. "Oh, no," she answered. "Definitely not." She touched the teacup to her lips, then tipped her head and tossed the whole thing back like a shot of whiskey. "He sided with his parents. I hated him for that, and I still hate him. Even though he's dead."

She snorted and slammed the cup onto the desk, for all the world like a shot glass. Maybe MacKinnon was a hard drinker. Which would fit with the rest. Outstanding.

"But I used to love him. In a weird way, I still do."

"Even though he's dead?" Riley finished the thought.

"Yes. Why am I telling you all this?"

"I asked." Riley shrugged. She fostered over-disclosure, useful in her line of work. One of her superpowers.

"Ben and I were going to tell him the truth, together, on his eighteenth birthday."

"Which is when?"

"October thirteenth. Less than a month from now." Abruptly, as though she'd just remembered something, MacKinnon stood and leaned across the desk. Brackish swamp, burning garbage, fresh limes. "Can you help me find out what happened to Ben? It's important."

"Of course. Those are my marching orders." Riley got up and shrugged on her coat. "Come on, I'll follow you up to Still Lake. I want to take a look around."

"I don't know what happened, but I have a bad feeling about it." She pushed past and out onto the landing, bumping Riley with her helmet, failing to notice or apologize.

Riley locked the door behind them. "As do I," she muttered, but MacKinnon was already halfway down the stairs.

5.

Jess tore up into the mountains from Enterprise, leaning hard into the switchbacks. She beat Riley to town by ten minutes and, because she was angry at the nosey P.I., felt smug when she pulled into the parking lot of Still Lake Lodge. By the time she had stashed her helmet and duffle at the front desk, Riley's battered Subaru was turning onto Main Street. She shrugged her orange backpack onto one shoulder.

Along Main Street, a row of storefronts gripped the eastern shore of the lake. Riley parked outside a building whose planks had weathered to silver. "Still Lake Outfitters, est. 1962," read the sign above the door. Riley pulled herself out of the car. "Welcome to the wild, wild West," she said, spreading her arms.

Jess laughed. She hated to admit it, but there was something likeable about the P.I. "Where is everyone?" she asked, spinning around. A sidewalk connected the storefronts. Beyond it, the lake, a round green mirror.

"Hiding from us, maybe?" Riley pointed to the Still Lake Outfitters sign. "Let's go talk to Mike Branch. He's the one who found the body."

The body. Jess walked to the edge of the sidewalk and looked between the buildings to the water. Riley was talking about Ben. She and Ben had a child together and somehow Riley, a stranger, knew. One twenty-minute conversation, and her life's grand secret was laid bare. How had that happened? She felt as naked as the mountains that rose across the lake, spreading their rubble into the water. They were the biggest things she'd ever seen up close, taller than the skyscrapers in Chicago. They made everything else small: The little clapboard town. The trees on the grassy slope of the shore. Her. She tugged her cell phone from the backpack. No signal. A wind gust rippled the lake, flattened the grass, and turned the sweat on her throat to ice. She shivered. The lake looked dangerous, the water that had swallowed Ben Fletcher. She sensed movement, as though the mountains, riding on their tectonic plates, were closing in.

"Are you coming?" Riley called.

Three steps led up to the Still Lake Outfitters' green front door. Jess waited on the bottom step, not ready to share the narrow landing with Riley Bishop. The P.I. was neither young nor old, neither thin nor fat. If she had a shape, her loose sweatshirt and baggy blue jeans kept it hidden. Her black hair hung straight, past the square frames of her glasses, down the sides of her face like a set of curtains, partly closed.

Riley tapped her foot and pretended to check a nonexistent wristwatch, but Jess did not let herself smile. "Wait a minute," she said. "Look. About Moses." Riley dropped her fingers from the door handle and turned. "You can't tell Rex and Becky that you know about Moses. They'll think I told you." She fixed her eyes on the railing that led up the steps. Her gaze slid up the railing and landed on Riley's face, which wore no expression that Jess could discern.

"But you didn't. I guessed." Riley put her hand back on the door handle, poised over the thumb latch, and lifted one eyebrow.

"Rex won't believe that." She imagined Rex's face, hot and thin-lipped with anger, his ruddy neck swelling over his collar. She'd seen plenty of it, that face. She spread her hands and lifted her shoulders. "Why does it matter? Why do they even need to know I'm here?"

"I don't usually keep things from my clients." Riley bent her head. The curtains of hair fell over her face. "All right, tell you what, Cowpoke. I won't say anything unless it becomes directly relevant to the case."

Jess supposed that would be enough. She clomped up the steps. The mannequin angler in the window display stared at her with beige eyeballs. They went inside.

Still Lake Outfitters burst with merchandise and seemed to teem with activity, though Jess saw only two customers browsing through a rack of plaid shirts. She and Riley crossed to a glass counter packed with fishing flies. Behind the counter a young man stood nodding as an older man talked to him, waving his arms. The older man's crew cut was black and gray and he wore a goatee, which he scratched with his left hand whenever he paused in speaking. Jess saw that he was the source of the bustle that permeated the store—his animation filled every corner. She felt herself swept up in it as he glanced their way and paused in mid-sentence, rubbing his chin before letting his hand fall to the counter. "Can I help you?" he asked, smiling.

The smile opened his face and set Jess at ease. Riley had stepped away to study a wall of photographs, so Jess stuck out her arm and shook hands. "Jess MacKinnon. I'd like to ask about fishing on the lake."

"Mike Branch." Still smiling, he clamped a brown hand on the younger man's shoulder. "This is Scott. He can book a fishing trip for you tomorrow morning."

"Actually, Mr. Branch, I have more of an academic interest. Do you have time for a few questions?" She pulled her clipboard from the pack. The smile dropped from Mike's face and tension crept into the room. She felt it lift the hairs on the back of her neck. When she looked up from the clipboard, she found Scott staring down at the counter and Mike's dark eyes filled with suspicion. *Shit.* What was going on?

"You from the government? Fish and Wildlife?"

"People out here hate the government and can't stand any regulation," Ben had told her at the Kid's last birthday. "I try to tell them I'm just doing my job, but they hate me, too."

Jess had been half listening, half watching Moses demolish a second wedge of chocolate birthday cake. As a teenager, the Kid had turned sullen and the birthday visits were hard. But when she left the Fletchers for the long ride back to Portland, Moses had hugged her at the door, said, "It was great to see you, Aunt Jess." She'd shoved on her helmet so he wouldn't see her eyes tear up.

"I'm not from the government," she told Mike Branch. Scott flipped through a notepad next to the cash register, his lower lip trapped beneath his teeth. "I'm a private consultant." She looked around for Riley: It would be nice to have some back-up. Jess spotted her behind a rack of postcards. She appeared to be hiding.

A telephone on the counter trilled. The tension broke, sending ripples through the room. Mike and Scott both reached for the phone; Mike was faster. As he answered, "Still Lake Outfitters," the front door opened and a small and very old man came in. He wore faded jeans, white running shoes, and a long-sleeved shirt buttoned at the cuffs and neck. His silver hair hung down his back in a braid, as long as Jess's. He stood beside her at the counter and rested his elbows on it, looking over at her with eyes that were dark like Mike's but crackled with— what? Amusement, Jess decided as they stared at one another. He was no taller than she was, five foot five with her boots on.

"Great, I'll see you down at the dock at six in the morning. It'll be colder than you expect, so wear layers," Mike said into the phone. He set it down, bounced once, scratched his beard, and fixed the old man with a stern look. "Papa. I told you I would pick you up." So this was the fishing guide's father—a possible ally, according to Darrin.

The old man lifted his shoulder. "No matter," he said. "I'm here." He placed a square hand flat on the counter in Jess's direction but his eyes stayed on Mike's face. "Who is your visitor?"

"This is—Jess?" She nodded. "Jess MacKinnon. She has an academic interest in fish. And your friend?" Mike waved toward Riley, who was trying on cowboy hats near the front door. "Is she also academically interested in fish?" Mike's voice had turned flat, his lips hard.

Riley joined them at the counter. She glanced at Jess and didn't answer Mike's question.

Mike laid his hand on the old man's shoulder. "This is my father, Jack Branch." The telephone rang and he snatched it up.

"Fish just want to be left alone," said Jack. He locked eyes with his son. Mike frowned back. But when Jack turned to Jess and Riley, his expression was warm. "You want to study the fish?" he asked her. "Which ones?" He wasn't smiling, but Jess thought his face looked kind. There was something wild and gentle in the creases that ran down from his cheekbones, his eyes lively.

Mike hung up the phone and checked his watch. "We're late," he said to Jack, wheeling around the counter. "We've got to go."

"The kokanee," Jess answered.

"Then you'll have a quick time of it," said Mike. He brushed past Riley and strode to the door. "The kokanee are gone."

"Really?" Jess knew her dismay must show. Jack patted her hand, where it rested on the counter. The touch felt reassuring. He kept his hand on hers until she met his eyes. Then he smiled, a little smile with his lips closed that deepened the creases on his face.

"Maybe yes. Maybe no," Jack said. When he lifted his hand from hers, she felt strangely bereft. He followed Mike outside. The door started to swing shut but then Mike's head and shoulders popped back in. "Scott can show you around," he said. Jess felt the sense of breathlessness empty out of the room as the door closed behind him. She slid her hand off the counter and tucked it into her pocket.

"Are you staying at the Lodge?" The voice startled her; it belonged to Scott. She turned and found him watching her. He looked friendly enough.

Jess nodded. "Yes. The only overnight accommodation in Still Lake, I'm told."

"Both of you?" Was that a hint of excitement in his voice? He was wondering whether she and Riley were a couple. She almost snorted: The very idea!

"No!" she answered, too loudly. "Just me."

Riley put out her hand. "I'm Riley Bishop."

"Cleveland Scott Kittridge. I go by Scott." He blushed. "That's obvious, I suppose."

Jess watched Riley explain who she was and watched Scott. He was about Moses's age. A sweet kid.

"Are you in high school?" Riley asked. "A . . . Wildcat, right?"

Scott told them, yes, he was a senior at Still Lake High, home of the Wildcats.

From outside, an incongruous urban noise broke into their conversation: The grind of a skateboard. Jess laughed to herself and Scott turned intent. The sound crescendoed into a scrape and a squeal, then Mike's voice, shouting, "Goddammit, Jon! Watch where you're going with that thing!" Scott giggled and shot around the counter to the front door. Jess and Riley followed.

On the sidewalk, Mike helped Jack to his feet. Jack tried to shake him off. A tall man with a pile of curly black hair stood holding a skateboard, sheepish. Mike took his father's elbow but Jack darted down the sidewalk, Mike in pursuit. The skateboarder nodded in their direction. "Hey, Scott."

"Hey." Scott's voice had climbed an octave and he was blushing. He cleared his throat. "Oh. Uh, Jonathan. I should introduce you." Some intensity passed between them. Had she stumbled upon a scandalous liaison? Scott looked at her helplessly; he had forgotten their names. No, she decided, they weren't lovers. Scott had a crush. Riley rescued him, stepping forward to shake Jonathan's hand.

"I'm Riley Bishop."

"Jess MacKinnon." She tapped the end of Jonathan's skateboard. "May I?" Jonathan surrendered the board and she dropped it and hopped on, took a few tacks, and landed a perfect kickflip. Scott and Jonathan applauded. Riley laughed.

Jess did another kickflip, flew down the asphalt, and ollied back. She was showing off. It felt glorious to be on a skateboard again. Why had she ever given it up?

6.

At fourteen, Jess took the bus down Diversey to Lincoln Park every Saturday. At the skate park, she would balance her board on the lip of the deepest bowl. *That* was the best moment: right before she tipped down the wall, right before the plummet, the swoop in her gut. She'd smoked weed with her mother's boyfriend. This was better.

Sometimes she fell at the bottom. Last summer, she'd broken her arm. The danger was part of the enjoyment in a way that didn't make any sense, at least not to her mother.

A boy had watched her from the other side of the bowl. When she looked up at him, he smiled. She tipped the board and flew.

"I like your style," he told her later. They stood close, beside the edge, boarders careening all around them. He dipped his head and laughed as though struck by sudden shyness. "Sorry. I just had to say that."

He had a sprinkle of freckles beneath his eyes that matched his brown hair. When he smiled, Jess's stomach felt like a helium balloon. He offered to buy her ice cream and took her hand when they walked across the park to the soft serve stand. They sat at a picnic table and talked for an hour. Ben Fletcher was in Chicago to start college in September. He would study biology and then go to medical school. When he told her he lived on a ranch in Oregon, she asked if he was a cowboy, which he found hilarious. After that, Jess concentrated on not saying anything stupid. No one in her family had ever been to college. The high school counselor, Mr. Schoenfeld, said she was smart enough, but her mother had snorted at such a "high-falutin' notion."

Monday, September 27, 2004

7.

On the Main Street of Still Lake, Oregon, Jess spun the borrowed skateboard and tacked back to her audience, flipped the board up, and caught it. She proffered it to Jonathan with a ceremonial bow. "Very cool to meet you," he said. He dropped the board and hopped on, waving his arms for balance. "I've got to get going. Oh, hey. Scott. I finished the canoe. You want to come with me tomorrow for its maiden voyage?"

Scott nodded, beaming. Jonathan pushed away. Jess liked this boy, Scott, his Norman Rockwell haircut and clean looks, the red blotches on his blushing cheeks. A young gay man, from the looks of it, stuck out here in the mountains. She started to touch his arm, then pulled her fingers back. "Well," she said. "That was silly."

"You're good." He turned away from the now-distant figure of Jonathan. "How did you learn to do that?"

"Lots of practice," she said. "When I was a kid. Including a couple of broken bones."

"Very impressive," Riley said, so curtly that Jess wondered whether Riley thought cavorting around town on a skateboard was undignified. "Scott, can you show us where Mike found the body?" Riley asked, all business.

Jess knew it was important to act professionally. She didn't always pull it off. Often, the professional–unprofessional line remained mysterious until it was too late, until she saw in someone's expression—Darrin's, Riley's—that pinched look that exposed her as an imposter in the professional world. Like right now. Shame inched up her neck to burn her cheeks. She let herself loathe Riley, fucking uptight bristly New Yorker, and the burning subsided.

Scott turned businesslike, too, smoothing down his hair. "Right. Mike said I should show you around." He gestured to the lake. "Over here's our dock." They walked down the grassy slope between the Outfitters and a restaurant, passing a miniature shingled shack on a ledge of rock halfway to the water. Jess asked about it and learned it was the kiosk where Mike had started his fishing guide business more than forty years before. He had purchased the Outfitters building, Scott told them, with a loan from the town.

A deck spanned the rear of the Outfitters, stretching out into the lake on pilings. A gangway carried them down to a dock where fishing boats and canoes were moored. Jess walked to the end of the dock. The air tasted of wood smoke. The lake held a perfect reflection of the high gray mountains with the sky at its center.

Ben had been here, in this town. Maybe, probably, he'd stood where she was standing. Was part of him still here? She wanted to call to him, across the green water: *Ben!* As though the lake were the bowl at the skate park, as though he might be watching now from the opposite shore, where the mountains parted in a forested canyon. That was Old Chuck Creek. To her right, a smaller canyon ended in a waterfall that tumbled into the lake. That would be North Creek. Beside the waterfall, the ruins of a stone foundation rested on a bulwark, fronting the lake. The skeleton of a wharf poked its stray bones out of the water.

Scott and Riley joined her. Scott pointed to the remnants of the wharf. "Over there's where Mike found the body, up against one of those pilings."

"Early morning?" Riley asked, and Scott nodded.

"Was he wearing a Fish and Wildlife shirt?" Riley wanted to know, but Scott couldn't tell her. Jess watched the North Creek waterfall tumble into the lake and tried not to picture Ben as a watery corpse. As they hiked back up the grass to Main Street, she asked what they fished for in the lake.

"Lake trout. Our biggest fish was twenty-one pounds."

Riley climbed into her Subaru and waved goodbye from the open window. Scott returned the wave. Jess did not. She pulled her clipboard from under her arm and turned her back on the P.I. "Mike said there were no kokanee in the lake," she said to Scott. "For how long? Do you know?"

"I don't know. But then Mike could tell you. He has catch records that go way back." Scott rocked, heel to toe, and blew out a long breath. "I wish I knew how to skateboard. I wish I lived in Portland. Do you like it?"

"I do." Jess wrote "catch records" on her clipboard.

"All types of people, right?"

Beneath the casual question, she caught his urgency. So he must know he was gay, but maybe no one else did. *I know how you feel!* she wanted to tell him. *I'll teach you to skateboard!* But it wasn't professional. "Right," she answered. "Every variation." Just a few months before, Multnomah County had started issuing marriage licenses to same-sex couples. The pairs stood in a line that wrapped around the block between Hawthorne Boulevard and Southeast Madison Street. She had seen them on her way to work, huddled under umbrellas. On the third day, March fifth, she'd pulled over to donate a box of donuts to the folks waiting in line to get married.

"Mike's father didn't seem so sure about the kokanee," she said to Scott. She'd lost him; he was staring down the street. She touched his arm, tried again. "It sounded like Mike's father thought there might be kokanee left. Do you know why?"

"No, sorry. Jack Branch can be kind of mysterious."

Jess wrote "Jack Branch" on her clipboard. Tomorrow she would talk to him, and she would talk to whoever was running this town. Scott told her Jonathan's father, Paul Monticola, was on the city council. He pointed down Main Street to a big log building.

"My mother would know all that. She runs the museum and the library and she publishes the newspaper. It's all over there in that log building." Scott glanced at his watch. "She'll be there now."

"What's your mother's name?"

"Rill. Rill Kittridge."

8.

Rill Kittridge pushed open the door that separated the print shop from the museum proper. She snagged a blue apron from a hook and ducked into its loop, adjusting the chain that held her reading glasses around her neck. As fluorescent lights flickered and caught from the open rafters, she tasted the sharp scent of ink and fresh newsprint that she associated with the shop, her father, and her grandfather—really with Still Lake itself. She hugged herself then and spun around, trying to dispel the panic that swelled in her throat, warning of an impossible grief. Her father, dead only six months, still lingered here in the print shop, like a scent; she could be comforted by it if she could only shake loose the panic. She brushed her fingers together as though grief were dust and crossed to the cast iron clamshell press bolted to the floor. She had work to do and not much time.

The press was a 1908 Chandler & Price jobber with an eighteen-inch inking disk turned upward at the angle of a face expecting a kiss. Rill believed (like her father and her grandfather) there was no better way to print a newspaper. She set out two cans of ink on the marble counter opposite the Chandler press, pried their lids off, and plucked a sheet from a bin of scrap paper. She dipped a putty knife into one of the tins and smeared red ink across the paper, wiped the knife, then added another red smear from the second tin. The second ink was a brighter, bolder red—the color of blood—while the first tended toward maroon. She capped the first tin and returned it to the cabinet.

From the other, she swiped a smear of bright red across the inking disk and switched on the motor. She watched as the press came to life, four rollers lifting to cross the disk, which rotated an eighth turn each time the rollers passed, spreading the ink evenly across its face. She turned back to the counter and the chase, in which she had already fastened the plate that would produce the paper's front page. The first page would sport a two-color banner title, Still Lake Gazette, with Thursday's date underneath, then three columns of black type separated by thin red lines and frilly corner accents replicated from the paper's original 1910 edition. She lifted her glasses to her nose and examined the plate, then switched off the motor and clipped the chase into position beneath the inking disk. Back on with the motor, and the rollers again began their movement through the ink. Rill eased a sheet of scrap paper onto the platen. Then with the lever to her left she pushed the press into gear. The rollers inked the plate, then lifted onto the inking disk as the platen closed to meet the plate. Rill pulled the gear lever back and switched off the motor. She took the paper off the platen and nodded once. "That'll do," she said aloud.

Rill slit open a new box of paper and set a one-inch stack on the oak tray, tidying the corners. She switched on the motor, slid the top page onto the platen, put the press into gear. She pulled back the gear lever but left the motor running as she removed the first sheet from the platen and studied the results. It looked good: square to the page, centered, and crisp. The red was almost too light but would work. The maroon might have been better after all.

Too late for the maroon. She slid another sheet into place and pushed the gear lever. While the rollers swung down across the chase, she replaced it with a fresh page. She worked quickly but held to the rhythm: Feed, remove, stack, repeat. The stack of blank pages dwindled. She smiled at her dance partner, the old Chandler & Price. Wasn't it odd, she thought, and a little tragic that humans could build machines with longer life spans than their own?

Rill planned to finish printing five hundred sheets in red, clean up the press, and begin setting type for tomorrow. Tomorrow she would switch to black ink. In three columns of Times Roman, she would tell the town about itself. Today she had a five o'clock appointment—pleasure, not business—that she intended to keep.

A bell tinkled at the front, signaling that someone had opened the door to the museum. Rill pulled the printer out of gear but left the motor running. Any local visitor would know to find her here. "I'm back in the print shop!" she called. The print shop door swung wide and a nimbus of bright yellow hair shot into the room. Inside it was her sister's face, decorated with cherry lipstick. The hair color was new, but Rill recognized one of her sister's favorite going-to-town outfits: Tent-sized purple tunic, tight faded jeans with red knee patches, and the blue cowboy boots that meant Birch had ridden to town on her mule.

"Birch! What brings you to town?" Rill kept her tone cheerful but covertly glanced at her watch: Four-ten. Birch lived across Old Chuck Creek from Rill on the last parcel of private property before the headwaters. She relished her remoteness, cultivated eccentricity, and rarely ventured into town. But once she found herself among humans, it could be difficult to extricate oneself from her unrelenting stream of witty repartee.

"Apparently there's someone else poking around about the fish!" Birch sounded angry rather than witty. She stomped to the end of the marble counter and planted two indignant fists on her hips.

"Oh? From the Fish and Wildlife Service?" Rill turned off the motor and shifted the stack of printed sheets to the counter. She remembered Ben Fletcher, his easy, little-boy grin, and the puckers at the corners of his eyes when he laughed.

"Mike says no, she's from an environmental consulting firm. And she had a private investigator with her! What the hell?" The bell at the front door tinkled again. Birch shot a look through the open door into the museum. "I wonder if that's her now?"

Birch started for the door, her boot-heels cracking on the hardwood floor, but Rill pushed past her. "Just calm down," she whispered. No one had come in all morning, and now it was Grand Central Station. Rill checked her watch again, four-fifteen, and peeked around the door jamb.

A small, dark woman examined the photographs in Rill's "Building the Town" exhibit. Its centerpiece, mounted right onto the logs of the far wall, was the sixty-inch circular saw blade from the old Luder mill. The woman reached out for the jagged edge.

"Careful! That's sharp!" Rill hurried across the room. All she needed was a claim on her insurance.

The woman snatched her hand back. "Sorry!" She offered the hand to Rill and introduced herself as Jess MacKinnon. Her thick, gathered hair made a frame around her triangular features, and crooked teeth gave her smile a quirkiness that was not unattractive. She hoped to learn about Still Lake's history, she said, waving at the saw blade.

"That's the blade from the sawmill at North Creek. You might have noticed the waterfall? You're not here for just the day, I hope?" Rill stole another look at her wristwatch, then back to the print shop. Birch filled up the doorway like a bird of prey scanning for rodents. Rill lowered her voice. "Because the museum is closing a little early today, I'm afraid."

"When did the sawmill operate?" The woman scribbled notes on a clipboard with a no-nonsense intensity that made Rill uneasy. She raced through the essentials—the Luder sawmill, the early settlement, the log drives down Old Chuck Creek. Under the window, a pair of mannequins in red flannel shirts and suspenders balanced on a section of old growth Douglas fir. One held a peavey pole against the log, but the other mannequin's hands were empty. Jess MacKinnon wrote furiously: She was interested in the log drives.

"I wonder where the other peavey pole went?" Rill said. She tried to remember if she'd seen it there on Friday.

The woman squatted down to examine the pole's hickory handle, the spike end with its iron hook.

"One of your boys probably made off with it," said Birch from the doorway. "They seem to think they're entitled to anything in the museum." Rill did not like the edge in her sister's voice. True, Scott and Brian might have taken the pole. But it was none of Birch's damn business.

"My sister, Rosemary Stukel. She goes by Birch."

Birch swooped into the room, boots snapping on the wood floor. "I legally changed my name twenty years ago, as you well know, *Rylene*."

Rill tried to look apologetic, but the "Rylene" made her stiffen with anger. After all, it was Birch who had bestowed her nickname. Their mother, God rest her soul, called them all by their first and middle names, too many syllables for little Rosemary Louise. So Rylene Michelle became Rill and the oldest, Rachel Cecilia, became Race. As for Rosemary, she'd ducked out of Still Lake for the Bay Area at twenty, studied software engineering, and acquired a modest fortune, as well as the new name. She had also acquired, ever so briefly, a husband. He had a tree name, too—Oak? Alder?

Colby Stukel had shrugged it off. "What's in a name?" he asked, raising one palm into the air. Their father was a student of literature, ready with a line of verse for every occasion. "A rose by any other name would smell as sweet!" Then, because Shakespeare straight up had to be diluted, he'd quoted Gertrude Stein: "A rose is a rose is a rose." Rosemary–Birch had taken offense and launched into such a tirade that their mother went to lie down.

Birch looked furious now as the new woman held out her hand. Instead of shaking it, Birch folded her arms. "Are you here about the fish?" she spat.

"That's right." The woman wrote something on her clipboard. "Can either of you tell me who's on the city council, besides Paul Monticola?"

"I am, for one. I'm the newest member." Birch looked like a crow in that tunic, or some freakish tropical bird with a curly, banana-yellow head. Rill again looked at her watch: Four-thirty. Damn.

"Excuse me," she said. "I've got to clean off the press before the ink dries." She cut past them into the print shop. Obviously the paper would not get printed today in the red ink. She scrubbed the disk with a rag that quickly turned crimson.

The voices in the museum remained pleasant. Birch was explaining Still Lake's politics to the fish biologist. Tradition divided the power of governance among the four families who had first settled here in the nineteenth century: The Stukels, the Monticolas, the Luders, and the Branch family, of the Nez Perce tribe. Colby Stukel had been mayor for forty-six years. When he died in March, Sammy Branch took his place and appointed Birch, a Stukel, to the city council to fill his vacancy. Karl Luder and Paul Monticola had served on the three-member council for a decade or more. Rill dabbed at the platen with a fresh rag. Her father, a true statesman, had been reelected every four years, without challenge, by a town that adored him. She capped the tin of blood-red ink and stowed it in the cabinet.

"Is that your pony tied up outside?" asked Jess MacKinnon. Rill groaned. That was sure to set Birch off. She tossed the red-stained rag into the trash bin.

"He's a mule, not a pony, City Slicker. You can tell by the ears."

A trickle of tense laughter welled into the print shop.

Birch's voice got louder. She said something about Mike's business, Still Lake Outfitters. Jess MacKinnon replied in softer tones; Rill heard her mention the Nez Perce tribe, and Birch's shrill response: "There are three generations of Nez Perce right here in Still Lake, and they think leaving the ecosystem alone is a fine idea."

It was four-forty-five. Rill hung up her apron and, holding her breath, ventured into the fray. Birch swept the air with broad, emphatic gestures, purple tunic flying. Jess MacKinnon clutched the clipboard across her chest as though to shield herself, but she wasn't backing down. "Outside, both of you!" Rill spread her arms as though herding chickens. "Come on, shoo!"

"What's the harm in keeping an open mind? You haven't even heard what we're proposing." MacKinnon's voice was low but fierce, a match for Birch's intensity.

Full of passionate intensity, Rill thought—half a line from a Yeats poem, in her dead father's voice.

The arguing women shuffled out the museum door, locked in a clumsy two-step. Rill trailed them down to the sidewalk, the sting of her memory bowing her neck.

Birch's mule tossed his head and brayed when he saw her. Birch hooked an arm over the mule's neck and swung onto his bare back. She held a rope in one hand and used the other to point at Jess MacKinnon's chest. "I understand perfectly. We've already been through this once before, remember? You're wasting your time here."

Rill's sounds of parting went unnoticed. She walked to the intersection of Main and Fourth Streets, where the pavement ended and the dirt trail began.

9.

Rill followed the North Creek trail to the old sawmill site. All that remained was the stone foundation; the timbers of the building had tumbled into the lake in March, in a spring flood, taking her father with them. On the flat stretch before the trail veered north, against her will, Rill's nimble imagination offered up the details: Colby Stukel in the sheeting rain, his rust-colored field jacket whipped by the wind, calling for his dog from the rotten planks of the sawmill wharf above the choppy black lake. "Rascal! Here boy!" Hands framing his mouth for a funnel against the wind. North Creek raging over its banks. The waterfall became a tsunami of froth and debris, and the sawmill blew apart like a matchstick house and burst into the water. Colby Stukel was standing in the way.

Rill turned her back on the sawmill and followed the trail into the forest, breathing hard with the uphill climb and the images of her father's death, which faded to black in the shade. She, Rill, was alive, and young—a long way short of fifty. She felt it in the blood that squeezed through her heart, the burn of the muscles in her thighs. The trail turned west along the north boundary of the Branch property and the grade leveled at the top of the Old Chuck Creek canyon.

Her father's death had affected Rill strangely. She hardly knew herself. Two weeks after the flood, on the Spring Equinox, she'd emerged from a torpor to take up a diet and exercise regimen. She cut her cotton underpants into dust rags and buried her old lady bras at the bottom of the kitchen wastebasket. In Enterprise, she bought lingerie and a tight black leather skirt. She wore this to a bar. A young, clean-shaven man in a blue silk shirt tried to buy her a drink. She had recognized him: He was the scientist from the Fish and Wildlife Service who came to Still Lake about the fish.

They joined a line dance when the band played "Cotton-Eyed Joe." He was graceful and knew the steps, holding her fingers high as they kicked and turned. In a corner, they drank beer. Rill held the bottle against her hot face. "I like your style," he'd said, and then looked embarrassed. She started to ask how old he was, but instead she let him kiss her and slip his fingers under her skirt. He came back to Still Lake in May and June. They had carried on a bit, nothing serious.

Another young man had sidled up to her in this forest one morning in August, had pressed her into the trunk of a hundred-year-old Ponderosa pine with its scent of vanilla in the sunlight. She laughed, unafraid: She had known this man his whole life. He tickled her ear with his whispery breath: "I want you, Rill. No one has to know." The creek's chuckle was the only sound sneaking through the trees.

Now Ben Fletcher was dead. It was complicated. She'd taken a lover as an antidote to mortality. She headed west toward the Monticola place, turned onto a spur path to Paul Monticola's property, her skin quivering. The path ended in a gravel yard before a massive shop building where Paul kept wood stored for his Millworks business. The right half of the shop's double doors stood ajar, a blue bandana knotted around its handle. She freed the bandana, pulled on the handle, and stepped inside, where the air was dim and thick with the aroma of cut pine.

"You made it."

"Sorry I'm late." She moved toward the voice. A leanly muscled figure began to take shape as her eyes adjusted to the dimness. He wore plaid boxers and black high-tops without socks. She tucked the blue bandana into his waistband, then ran her palm along his smooth torso to the patch of black hair between his nipples. She felt her own nipples harden as he bent to kiss her, and they pressed their bodies together fiercely.

10.

Rill hummed to herself and kicked a pinecone along the trail as she followed it from the Monticola property to her own house. Cleve's pickup was in the driveway. Why was he home early, today of all days? Thirty minutes ago she'd been rutting about on the concrete floor of the woodshop, her sweaty body breading itself with boot dirt and sawdust. She crept in through the back door, fighting an impulse to run away. Inside, she heard the voices of her husband and their youngest son, Brian. She paused in the doorway, itchy all over. Were they arguing? They were both hotheads, quick-tempered, while she and Scott were calm and did their best to avoid conflict. She listened for anger in their voices but heard only emphasis, something about Dallas. Good: They were arguing about football, or some other sport—safe territory for both of them and possibly enough cover for her to escape upstairs for a shower. She crossed to the stairway. They stood in the living room. A game played soundlessly across the television screen. She started up the stairs, her steps silent on the carpet.

"Rill!" Cleve called. She stopped and peeked over the banister.

"Hi, guys!" She forced as much cheer into her voice as she could summon. "Watching football?"

Cleve crossed the room, his square jaw set and his lips a hard red line under the bushy black moustache. "Where have you been? I thought you'd be home by now."

"I took a longer walk than usual." Rill felt her heart pounding, clear to the roof of her mouth. Why in God's name should she have to explain herself? But as she tried to feel indignant she heard her voice continue. "Oh, and a biologist from Portland stopped by the Museum this afternoon with questions, so I was late leaving."

Cleve's eyes narrowed. "Biologist? What did he want?"

"She. We didn't get that far." Rill took another step up the stairs. "I want to take a quick shower before supper. Tacos okay?"

"Sounds good." Cleve smiled—his smile was disarming, always, with its gold front tooth, the dimples that made him irresistible. Or had, twenty years before. Rill felt the tension dissipate. She glanced at Brian, standing in the middle of the living room. He had been listening and watching them warily but, like her, he had felt the tension slacken and she saw his posture relax.

In the shower, she let the spray sluice dust out of her hair, cooling her skin. Musky odors of sex drifted to her nostrils as she lathered her body and scrubbed it red. She pinched her soft belly and flexed her biceps. She'd lost thirteen pounds on her diet and could, for the first time ever, do three pull-ups. She was forty-two and supposed she was having a mid-life crisis. She felt as though she were executing the choreographed steps of a dance, powerless to do otherwise. She used her fingers, slippery with soap, to massage her face. If Cleve found out about her affair, he would kill somebody for sure—her, most likely. Or him. It was slightly exciting to think about that. Rill shook her head in equal parts amusement and horror. She had become a puzzle to herself.

In August, her back against the rough bark of the Ponderosa, she had pushed her would-be paramour away. "I'm married. You know that."

Wildness glittered in his eyes. It was sexy. "I saw you kissing that scientist." He pressed against her.

She squirmed away, freeing herself from the tree. "What? Where?" Her hand darted to her mouth. Her lips trembled and parted.

"In his truck, by the museum. Next to the Millworks. Relax. No one else saw."

"Are you sure?"

"Relax," he said again, bending to kiss her neck.

She pulled back. "This is crazy," she said.

"Does he mean something to you, is that it?" His wild dark eyes searched her face.

"None of your business."

He put his hands on her shoulders, gentle. "Did you sleep with him?"

"Also none of your business." But she let him lift her face and kiss her, his lips light as summer.

She turned off the water, turned off the pictures playing in her head, stepped onto a bath mat, and pirouetted into a towel. Three curly wood shavings were trapped in the shower drain. She plucked them out.

"Rill?" The bathroom door swung open, and Cleve blocked the doorway.

Rill's left hand flew to her throat; her other hand made a fist around the wood shavings. "You startled me."

"Sorry." Cleve braced his hands on either side of the door frame and leaned into the bathroom, toward Rill, who stepped back. "Dinner tonight, just the two of us? Maybe that steakhouse in Enterprise?"

Rill wrapped the towel more tightly around her breasts and held it there. The wood shavings bristled against her palm. "What's the occasion?"

Under the black moustache, Cleve's lips stretched into a smile. "Does there have to be an occasion?"

She turned away from Cleve and ran her hand down the outside of her thigh, past her knee, testing for stubble. "Not tonight, okay? I'm a little tired." In her right fist, the wood shavings prickled. He'd asked her to have dinner on Friday, too, and she'd turned him down. She knew better than to provoke him. The affair made her reckless.

"What the hell, Rill? When then?"

Under the towel, Rill started to sweat. "Leave, please, so I can get dressed."

"What if I feel like watching?" Cleve's hands fell from the door frame and he stepped forward.

Rill's gut clenched but she met his eyes and squared all one hundred sixty pounds of her sweating body to his. "Leave. Now."

He flinched at her tone, a twitch at the wrinkled corners of his eyes. He held up his hands and stepped back with a laugh. "Guess you're not in the mood?"

"Like I said, I'm tired."

He put a hand on the doorknob. His other hand compressed into a fist, then opened. "Maybe later tonight, Rill? It's been a long time."

"Maybe." She tried to smile, willing him to leave the room. He pulled the door closed. She locked it. "Maybe in another lifetime," she muttered, stepping to the toilet. She brushed the wood shavings off her hand, flushed, and watched the pieces swirl into oblivion.

11.

Before she left the Museum, Jess extracted an invitation to lunch the following day, and a concession that Birch Stukel would "make a reasonable, good faith effort" to consider the merits of the fish restoration project. Now she stood at the door of City Hall, which was locked. A paper clock in the window promised that city business would resume at nine o'clock in the morning.

She took stock. Local politics ran strictly on nepotism. The fishing guide, Mike Branch, was hostile. The locked door felt like a symbol: The town itself was shut against her. She scowled at the door and raised her fist to pound on it when someone called to her from the street.

"Admiring my handiwork?" A dark-eyed man climbed the steps, hand extended. At last, a friendly face. Jess felt calluses on his palm. He introduced himself as Paul Monticola. He pressed his right hand flat against the speckled oak grain of the door. Half his ring finger was missing.

"You're the woodworker. Father of Jonathan, the boat builder."

"That's right." The creases at the sides of his mouth meant he smiled easily. He smiled at her now. "And you're the fish scientist and expert skateboarder."

"Yes." At the memory of her indiscretion, warmth seeped into her cheeks. She turned away and rattled the door handle, a big brass affair to go with the big door. "Going in?"

"Not today." He patted the wood. "I'm looking for my son, actually. I need his help at the Millworks." He shaded his eyes from the low sun, looked up and down the street. "You can walk with me, if you like. We can talk on the way."

"So," he said, "you're here to take over for the fellow who drowned? Ben Fletcher?"

The fellow who drowned. He could have been making an observation about the weather. At once, she was furious. So when she answered, "Right. And you hold the Monticola family slot on city council," it came out sounding snarky.

Paul stopped walking, held up a hand. "Whoa there. Guess you disapprove."

Why had she said that? She'd told Riley Bishop the truth: She hated Ben and also loved him, nothing in between. Paul's friendly face had turned as impenetrable as the locked oak door. She looked at the sidewalk, at the scuffed toes of her boots. "I didn't mean nothing— I really didn't mean anything by it." Great, now she couldn't even talk. She walked on with her head down. He fell into step again beside her.

"Maybe the town just isn't that friendly to outsiders," she tried, watching her boots measure off the distance to Monticola Millworks.

"Ben Fletcher came on pretty strong. A real know-it-all." He had his head down, too, and wouldn't look at her. "That doesn't go over well here. Nothing to do with friendliness."

"So it was a personality problem." This was no time to defend Ben Fletcher. Anyway, it was true. He was—*had* been—pushy. When he wanted something, he moved right in. How else had she ended up in his college dorm room at the age of fifteen?

"More than that. It was the project. Save the native kokanee! But no one's seen a kokanee in Still Lake for thirty years. What makes you think there's anything worth saving?" Paul walked faster. "We're a little tiny town, with a little tiny budget. We can't go off chasing fantasies."

Jess half walked, half jogged to keep up with him. "I can answer that question, if you're looking for an answer," she said. At Monticola Millworks, she trailed him up the steps to a porch, where he stopped abruptly and she ran into him.

"What question?"

Jess backed away until she collided with the porch's railing. "Why I think the kokanee might still be worth saving," she answered. From the edge of the porch, she could see the shop's bay doors and a yard stacked with logs and milled lumber. Three huge logs—each one more than a yard in diameter—reclined along a blue tarp, black and glistening. He shoved his hands in the pockets of his jacket and raised his eyebrows. "The answer is a principle of biology," she told him. "The goal of any species is persistence. A species will adapt. It will always create mechanisms to ensure its survival."

"Okay," he said. He shifted from one foot to another. The porch's planks creaked under his work boots.

Jess pointed to the stack of three black logs. "I wanted to ask you about the log drives," she said.

"Well, those are log drive artifacts." He waved at the door. "Are you coming in? Or is this conversation over?"

Once inside, he turned to face her. "Okay, we got off to a bad start. Just one more thing I want to say. Our positions are elected. Anybody who wants to run can do so. We have eighty-five percent turn-out for local elections."

She turned to look around as Paul switched on the lights. Monticola Millworks smelled of turpentine and cedar, its showroom crowded with chairs and tables, dressers, and wagons. She followed him into the back, which seemed to be a workshop. She stepped gingerly around a bright, freshly painted canoe on the floor. She *would* watch her step. She would have to compensate for Ben's mistakes. "I didn't mean to imply any wrongdoing," she said.

"Yes, you did." He ushered her into a small office. "Have a seat. Ask me what you want to ask."

But Jess stopped to examine a wall covered in cork, pinned with drawings and diagrams—hundreds of them. Some were sketched in fuzzy pencil on torn paper fragments, others inked on sheets of graph paper. She moved closer. She read the names on some of them. Some had dates. One drawing showed two square platforms, with a ladder in between them and another ladder descending from the second platform, into nothing. At the top, in block print, were the words CAP BRANCH, and a date below, March 1902. The papers were windows into the town's past; standing before them, she felt the tug of memory, could almost hear the whispers of ghosts. "What's the story with all those drawings?" she asked Paul, who was standing behind a desk, waiting for her. She sat down across from him.

Paul slid out of his wool jacket and hung it over the back of his chair. He sat down, pushed his rolled-up sleeves higher, crossed his arms. His forearms rippled with ropes of muscle and his hands wore a Braille of scars: his body's record of the things he had made, the saw blades and chisels he had wielded. Jess found herself staring as he rested his elbows on the desk and made a gable with his fingers. "Those sketches? Part of this place's history. The history of what we've made. My father. His father." He tapped his fingers together. Jess noticed, fascinated, that Paul's right ring finger tapped its mate in the air, as though the missing half remained. "If you want to understand this place—even what happened to the fish—then you need to understand history."

"You mean the history of what happened to the kokanee? What *did* happen?" Jess leaned forward.

"No. History, meaning our place in the world. Don't you have people you belong to?"

After her morning with snoopy Riley Bishop, Jess was not about to launch into her life story. "Sure," she said.

"Who are your people? Where do they live?"

For fuck's sake, Jess thought. "My mother lives in Chicago. Why?"

"Is that where you belong? Chicago?"

In their flat with its faded checkered curtains and cracked linoleum, Jess and her mother would clean up after their dinner. Priscilla washed; Jess rinsed and dried. She had a school assignment involving her "family tree" and she asked about her grandparents. She must have been twelve. "You never met them," Priscilla said, handing her a soapy plate. "They both died young." Jess rinsed the plate under the tap and rubbed it dry with her towel, the white one with daffodils. "We wasn't fancy people. We wasn't even *from* here." Priscilla felt through the dishwater for stray silverware. "My folks, they come from Appalachia. My sister, Jessica—the one you're named for—she died, too. You already know that. Ain't no one left now. Just us." She blew out a breath and swiped absently at the forks she'd gathered. "Makes me sad to think about that, my girl. Still. Those were your people. That's who you are."

"What about my father?" she asked, rinsing the forks.

Her mother waved her hands, sprinkling Jess with soap. "Oh, Kevin MacKinnon!" She unplugged the drain. "That's a story for another day, my girl."

"Definitely not Chicago," she answered Paul Monticola.

"When's the last time you were there? When's the last time you saw your mother?"

She laughed. "I'm struggling to see the relevance here."

"Come on, how long has it been? I'm trying to make a point." Paul's fingers stopped tapping and made two fists.

"I don't know." She really didn't. "Years."

"How often do you call her?"

Jess folded her arms. Why were they having this conversation? "Once in a while," she said. She glared, daring him to disapprove. "What about the log drives? You said those logs outside were artifacts."

Paul Monticola stared at her, his clenched fingers hiding his mouth, until the silence grew heavy. Jess waited him out. "Sure enough," he finally said. "Jon and I fished those out of the bottom of the Big Sink. That's a pool halfway up the creek. They've been down there in the water for a hundred years, speaking of history. The wood's still as good as the day it was cut."

"The log drives were a hundred years ago?"

"Started in 1900. I know that because Charles Stone—that's the "Old Chuck" of Old Chuck Creek—came to town that year with my grandfather, man by the name of Albert Monticola. He was a timberman from Minnesota. Chuck Stone and my grandfather just about cleared the old-growth forest along Old Chuck Creek, and they chuted the logs into the creek and drove them down to the lake to Luder's sawmill. The Big Sink is so deep the logs would get stuck there. This whole town is built out of that timber."

The door flew open and Jonathan rushed in.

Paul stood. "You're late!"

Jonathan leaned into the office doorway. His face glistened with sweat. "I'm sorry."

Paul cuffed his son on the side of his head, then guided him into the work area with a hand across his shoulders. They bent over a workbench together. Apparently, the interview was over. Jess followed them out. "Are the log drives what decimated the kokanee population?"

"Don't think so," Paul answered. "That was later. Nineteen-sixties, nineteen-seventies, thereabouts."

Jonathan switched on a table saw and fed a blond plank into the blade. A piercing whine filled the room, then the scent of pine. Jess stepped around the canoe and opened the front door. "Call your mother!" Paul shouted after her.

12.

Paul Monticola had told Jess that everything in town was made of wood. In the restaurant next to Still Lake Outfitters, a polished redwood slab separated the kitchen from the dining room. Jess hitched herself onto a stool and slid her fingers along the grain.

"Hey, Jess!" Scott Kittridge waved from across the room. He sat with a plump man whose gray hair was pulled back into a ponytail. Jess had hoped for a quiet meal but braced herself for more mingling, maybe more hostility. But she and Scott had bonded, and the plump man was not hostile. He stood and took her hand, bent, and kissed it. "Sammy Branch." His voice was resonant, an old-time radio voice. He pulled out the chair next to Scott. "Will you join us?"

She was having dinner with the mayor of Still Lake! Her excitement waned as Sammy Branch plied her with questions through dinner and dessert. He disarmed her with his wide, kind smile, reaching across the table to pat her hand, chuckling in delight at each bit of information. Before the dishes were cleared, he had learned she'd grown up in Chicago, had moved to Portland at sixteen and started college at twenty-two; had no pets, no hobbies, no husband or boyfriend. The interrogation paused when the server collected their plates, and Sammy leaned back and adjusted his bolo tie. He wore a white dress shirt, gold ring on his right hand, none on his left.

Jess felt stunned. The men she worked with talked about themselves and the few questions they asked her, she easily deflected. Sometimes they asked whether she had children. Every time she answered "no" the word stung her like a wasp of betrayal. "I'm sorry, Kiddo," she would say to Moses in her head. Thankfully, Sammy hadn't asked about offspring once she'd told him she'd never been married.

Jess turned away to look outside. They sat next to a bank of windows beside the lake, its surface deep silver at twilight. The mountains on the opposite shore loomed black, the last glow of sunlight behind them. Jess pulled her gaze back into the room and found Sammy and Scott watching her. She smiled. "Is it my turn to ask questions now?" She felt the mountains behind her, the silver lake.

Sammy held up a hand. "One more question only. Are you connected to the young man who drowned recently—a biologist, like yourself?"

She was connected forever to Ben Fletcher. Even death couldn't change that. "The project is the same," she said, "restoration of the native kokanee. But the focus and leadership have changed." Sammy leaned toward her. The mayor. She needed to sell this project to him. "I should mention there's funding available. A grant for local government to participate." Sammy's eyebrows lifted.

"But the kokanee are gone now." Scott looked out the window, as though searching for fish. "Aren't they?"

The front door swung open. "Mike's here," Scott said, pushing back his chair. "Hey, Mike!"

Mike dropped into a chair beside Sammy. He nodded to Jess—curtly, it seemed to her. "Nice to see you again, Ms. MacKinnon." She squinted at Mike as though to bring him into focus. When he wasn't smiling, his square jaw and close-cropped hair and beard made him look jagged, like the lacerated mountains. He fidgeted constantly, twirling a spoon in his fingers, glancing all around the room. Beside him, placid, Sammy patted Mike's arm.

"Scott and I have been learning about the fish restoration project. Apparently, it has changed since the gentleman from the Fish and Wildlife Service drowned."

Mike grunted. "Gentleman. That's generous."

Jess picked up her fork and clenched it, along with her teeth. She wondered what it would feel like to plunge the fork straight into Mike's eye.

"Not to speak ill of the dead." Sammy gave their server a wave. "You look tired, Mike. You should eat. Things did not go smoothly at the doctor's office?"

"No, things did not go smoothly at the doctor's office." The spoon leapt from Mike's hand and clattered on the table. All four of them watched it for a moment. Jess set the fork down. She remembered what Darrin had said in their briefing: Ben made a mess of public relations in Still Lake.

Sammy frowned. "Is Jack all right?" Jack was Mike's father, Jess remembered, the old man she'd met at Still Lake Outfitters.

"There's not a single thing wrong with him. Except his attitude." A loaf of sourdough arrived. Mike tore off the heel and threw the rest back onto the plate. "He's as strong as ever. The doctor could not believe how old he was. I thought he was going to make us show a birth certificate."

"How old *is* your father?" Jess asked.

"He's a hundred and two."

"A hundred and two!" Jess looked from Mike's face, to Scott's, to Sammy's.

Sammy gave them a solemn nod. "The Ipsootchuck," he said. Mike snorted. Sammy frowned at him again, his chin puckering with his brow. Scott looked back and forth between them.

"The Ipsootchuck?" Jess asked.

Sammy started to reply. Mike interrupted. "The Ipsootchuck is a natural well on the Branch property. The house has plumbing now, but our family has a tradition of carrying water from the Ipsootchuck to drink with supper every evening. They never put a pump in it, so they used a bucket. My grandfather and grandmother claimed it was some kind of health tonic."

"'*Ipsootchuck*' means 'secret water' in Chinook jargon, which is what our mother mainly spoke, along with English," said Sammy. He gave Jess another wide smile. So Sammy was Jack's brother. She leaned forward, silently urging him to go on.

But Mike had picked up the spoon again and was tapping it into his palm. "Enough of the folklore, Uncle Sammy. Seriously."

"When did the Branch family settle here?" Jess leaned further over the table toward Sammy, avoiding eye contact with Mike.

"My mother and father came in 1885. Calm yourself down, Mike! For heaven's sake."

Mike had been tipping his chair back as if to distance himself from the conversation. He let it snap forward with a crack. "What difference does it make? Why is everyone suddenly so interested in these fish?"

Sammy patted Mike's hand, wrinkling his forehead into a stern look. "Let me remind you, dear nephew, that as mayor I have a responsibility to learn about this project and be helpful where I can."

Mike grunted. Scott's voice cut through the tension like an easy breeze. "My grandfather was mayor before Sammy."

"Oh, was he?" Jess pulled her eyes and her attention away from Mike Branch. What an asshole.

"Colby Stukel." Sammy patted Scott's hand. "Scott lost his grandfather in a big flood we had this spring, I am sorry to say."

The flood in March, Jess remembered. *One person died*, Darrin had said. Beside her, Scott's face was grave. "Grandpa was with my mom at the Museum and his dog ran away. Grandpa went after him and my mom didn't notice for a while that he was gone. They were putting sandbags around the building in case the lake overflowed, but then, it never did. We think Rascal fell in the lake and my grandpa jumped in to save him. The sawmill fell down." Jess saw that he was close to tears. She looked at the table. He cleared his throat. "Anyways, we found Grandpa's body in the lake two days later. The coroner from Enterprise said he was crushed by some of the timbers from the sawmill and then drowned. We never did find Rascal. My mom still can't talk about it." Scott blew out a breath and bent his head.

Mike stood and looked at his watch. "I've got a fishing trip at six in the morning, folks."

Jess scooted free of the table and stood next to Mike. "How *is* the fishing?"

He took a step backward. "So-so."

She edged closer. He wouldn't meet her eyes. "Scott said you have some fishing records?" she started, but Mike brushed past and led them out of the restaurant as though he hadn't heard. Outside, darkness and the high mountain chill had arrived together. In her thin sweater, Jess shivered, regretting the jacket she'd left in her room.

"Mike, all the kokanee are gone now, right?" Scott asked.

"Right, Scott." Mike paused on the sidewalk to wait for Sammy. "There are no more kokanee." He hung his hand on Sammy's shoulder and Jess saw a long look pass between them. Was it true? Mike's hand fell, Sammy nodded to her, and the two of them turned and started down the street. It was late. A full moon blazed a path across the lake's dark water.

Jess stepped into the shadows at the edge of the sidewalk, traced the shimmer of moonlight across the lake. "Are you there?" she whispered to the fish, and maybe to Ben. He would have come to the restaurant, he would have ordered food at the polished counter. He would have asked these same questions. What had happened to the fish? What had happened to Ben? Did anything linger? She folded her arms against the cold.

"What?"

Jess spun. Under the streetlight, Scott rocked heel to toe with his hands in the pockets of his letterman's jacket.

"Oh!" She flattened her hand on her chest. "I didn't—"

His teeth flashed white. "I didn't mean to startle you."

"It's okay." She stepped toward him, away from the shadowy edge of the sidewalk. Returned his smile: What a sweet boy he was. Too tender for the wild, wild West.

Scott yanked his hands free of his pockets and waved toward the lake. "I asked Uncle Sammy about the fish, the kokanee. He told me how they used to turn red and swim up the creek in the fall."

"That's right. Have you ever seen salmon migrating?" Jess bounced up and down, hugging herself.

"I never have." The brown leaves of the maple trees in the park rustled and broke free as a wind blew down from the mountains. "Here," Scott said. "You're cold." He pulled off his jacket and hung it around her shoulders. "Do the fish really go back to the same place they were born? How do they do that?"

"They do return to the same stream," said Jess. She drew the jacket closed and smiled her thanks. "Not the exact spot, necessarily, but the same reach. They imprint to their natal water, we think based on scent, and they return at maturity, which is—or rather, was—four years old for the Still Lake population.”

“They only live four years?”

“Generally speaking.” They turned together to look out across the dark water, its river of moonlight. The maple leaves hung quietly on the branches and their fallen comrades lay scattered across the grass. The silence felt solemn between them. Jess was thinking about death: Ben’s, her own. She wondered whether Scott was thinking about his grandfather.

When he spoke again, his voice was low. “Is that how long other types of salmon live? Only four years?”

“It varies.” Four years, the length of high school. The length of college. It had taken her six and a half years to finish her degree, working full time.

“And they live that whole four years in the lake? Or I mean, they used to?” Another wind passed through the trees and the piles of leaves pitched across the park.

“Right, except when they spawn. The spawners lay their eggs in the inlet stream, which in our case is Old Chuck Creek.” Jess threw her arm out toward the dark water, then drew the jacket around herself again. The chill was deepening.

“How do the eggs stay in one place? The current is so fast.” He stepped closer. They were still turned toward the lake.

She chuckled at his curiosity. He ducked his head as though he thought she was laughing at him, so she pushed her arms into the sleeves of his jacket and touched his shoulder. “Aren’t you cold?” she asked. He shook his head. He was acclimated; she wasn’t. She remembered the first winter after she moved from Chicago to Portland, how she went about in a T-shirt, waiting for the weather to turn cold.

She made a swishing motion with her right hand, brushing her left arm. "The female uses her caudal fin, or in other words her tail, to scoop out a depression in the stream gravel, or small cobbles—any place the water will be able to circulate. Those nests are called redds. The male deposits sperm over the eggs, and then the female covers them by churning up the gravel on the upstream edge of the redd. She might do this several times, until all her eggs are gone." Jess watched his face as he took this in. She could tell he was imagining the bright red bodies digging in the gravel.

He cleared his throat, tucked his hands back into his jeans pockets. "Then she dies?" he asked.

Jess nodded. "Then she dies."

Tuesday, September 28, 2004

13.

Scott Kittridge woke on Tuesday morning, his eyes gritty and his head throbbing as though he hadn't slept at all. When the sawmill crashed into the lake, it knocked his family askew. He knit his fingers behind his head and stared at the ceiling. His grandfather was dead; his mother was a nervous, jumpy freak job; his father was even more of an asshole than usual. He and Brian were the only normal ones left. Well, *Brian* was the only normal one.

When he was twelve, he'd had a boil on his butt cheek, angry under his skin. And growing. When he'd finally told his mother, it hurt so bad he couldn't sit down. She'd hauled him to the doctor, who distracted him with questions about baseball statistics while he unwrapped something sealed in paper—something sharp and metal— and stabbed the nasty thing. Scott couldn't stop himself from watching as yellow pus burst out. "Scotty," his mother said, as he limped to the car, bandaged and relieved, "you have to tell me when something's wrong. I'm your mother. I need to know."

The butt boil had been embarrassing. Being queer, though—that was beyond mortifying. What could he say? "Mom, I'm homosexual." No. He hated the H-word. Five syllables of overkill. "Mom, I'm gay." Lighter. Too light, really, but it would have to do. His mother would not freak out. His father was another matter. He couldn't think about that.

He swept off the covers and pitched himself out of bed, digging at his eyes. He would tell his mother. Today. This morning.

But when he plodded downstairs from his room, late, he found her sitting by the window staring over the top of her book in the direction of the creek and the forest, her reading glasses perched low on her nose, still in her pajamas. The Still Lake Museum opened at nine-thirty, sharp. Rill always rose early to fix breakfast and a sack lunch for his father, who drove to his job in La Grande each day and had to leave by seven-thirty, in good weather. "Mom!" He blocked her view out the window. "What are you doing?" She sprang from the chair in a panic. Everything was askew. He ate a handful of dry cereal while she ran around like a spooked horse. Her glasses swung on her neck as they rushed out of the house, down the North Creek Trail towards town.

"Why are you so jumpy?" Scott asked as they hurried along the top of the canyon past the Luders' place. He had been rehearsing his opening lines for this conversation that had to happen.

"What? This morning? I was reading."

"No, you weren't. You were staring out the window, practically in a coma."

"Well, I suppose I was thinking about what I'd just read, Scott."

"What were you reading?"

"I don't remember."

"Mom!"

"What?"

"It's impossible to talk to you! Why are you so edgy all the time?" This was not going the way he'd planned.

"I've got things on my mind." Rill quickened her pace as though fleeing the conversation.

"What things?"

"Things." Scott brushed his hand across the ferns that grew in the seams between the rocks. *Homosexual. Gay. Queer?* Maybe "homosexual" *was* the word to use. It sounded like a medical condition. An affliction. Which was how it felt. They turned south. Walked downhill through the forest in silence.

"I need to talk to you, Mom." Exasperated, Scott halted in the middle of the trail as it veered east from the Luder sawmill, just a pile of hewn stones now and some rotting planks out in the water. Rill kept walking, and he realized she didn't want to stop here; it reminded her of how his grandfather had died. He ran after her. "Mom!" he shouted. "I really need to talk to you!"

They reached the pavement. Finally, she stopped, faced him, put her hands on his shoulders. He was four inches taller and could see the top of her head, the hanks of gray hair mixed into her curls. "I'm sorry, Scotty. What is it? What's bothering you?" She scrutinized him. "Is it a girl?"

He felt like shouting, *No! It's a guy!* But he caught her sneaking a look at his watch to see what time it was. It was nine-thirty-five. His courage flew off, a startled little bird. "It's okay, Mom. You're late. We'll talk later." He pulled away. After she disappeared into the museum, he made up a song and a skipping step to keep time with his throbbing headache as he continued down Fourth Street: "I'm gay, I'm queer, ho-mo-sex-u-al." He'd always liked the idea of tap dancing. He tried a few steps. "I'm gay! I'm queer!" he sang under his breath. He could be a dancer, a hairdresser, an interior designer. "Ta da ta da ta da!"

"Scott! What are you doing?"

Scott froze, mid-tap. He was in front of Monticola Millworks. Jonathan had opened the bay doors of the workshop and was dragging a canoe outside. Scott pushed his hands into his front pockets and bounced on his toes. "Hey, Jonathan," he squeaked.

"Hey yourself. Nice moves, there." The postage stamp beard under Jonathan's lower lip bristled. He was trying not to laugh. He waved at the canoe. "You ready for a test run?"

"Well, sure. I've got school, though." Jonathan looked disappointed. He set the canoe down.

Scott stared out over the lake, where black-bottomed clouds mustered on the mountains. "It might rain. I guess we should get out there. While the weather holds." *What the hell?* he told himself. Canoeing with Jonathan, or chemistry class? It was an easy choice. "Yeah, let's do it. I'll skip first period."

"Great!" Jonathan lifted the canoe's prow. The muscles in his forearm writhed like a dancing cobra and Scott could not move his eyes away. "Give me a hand, would you? This thing is heavy."

14.

The canoe rose into graceful scallops at bow and stern, the thwart low and narrow. Scott and Jonathan carried it to the lake and launched it off the Outfitters dock. "I'll take the bow," said Jonathan, stepping into the boat. "You're better at steering. Watch out—it's kind of tippy."

"You're not going to dump me in the lake, are you?" Scott sidestepped off the edge of the dock and sat on the aft bench. The air felt warm for September, and heavy. He threw his jacket onto the dock. Jonathan peeled off his T-shirt and passed him one of the paddles, a solid piece of blonde wood. "Beautiful," said Scott. "Is it ash?"

"Yeah. How does it feel for weight?"

Scott dug the paddle into the lake, moving the canoe into the open water. "Good. Light. The canoe feels like a fast one." He watched Jonathan's profile, and saw his smile. Scott felt his heart pounding, sweat on his palms. He wiped them on his shorts, one at a time.

"I built it for speed." Jonathan turned forward and dipped his paddle on the port side. "Let's see what she's got! Ready? All the way across the lake!"

Scott moved his paddle to the starboard side. "Ready!" he shouted. "Go!" They whooped once and paddled hard. Scott matched his paddle strokes to Jonathan's, long and even. They were the same strength, same size. The canoe sprang forward and cut through the quiet water like a fin. Scott could not stop grinning. His breath quickened and sweat beaded on his forehead. He kept the canoe's high prow in line with a stone pillar that grew from the scree on the far shore, where the mountains glittered in the sun. He watched Jonathan's brown arms, the muscles in his back and shoulders. Jonathan switched sides and Scott followed, hardly breaking rhythm. He added an arc to the end of his stroke to keep the canoe on course; Jonathan wasn't as strong on this side.

As they neared the west shore and the mouth of Old Chuck Creek, a crane rose from the sedges. Jonathan's brown back glistened. "Let's come around!" Scott called. "Ready?" Scott planted his paddle in the water, then sculled it backward as Jonathan pulled hard on the other side. The canoe turned and tipped.

"Whoa!" shouted Jonathan, leaning to compensate. The canoe righted; they kept paddling, both of them laughing.

"I love living dangerously!" Scott yelled.

In the middle of the lake, Jonathan rested his paddle across the bow. Scott used a J-stroke to keep the canoe tracking back to the dock.

"I can't keep up with you," Jonathan said. "It's like you've been rowing around the lake all summer or something."

Scott laughed. "Well, as a matter of fact . . ."

Jonathan laughed, too. Scott's insides tingled. Jonathan turned around on the bench to face him. Clouds had cleared the mountains and were blowing in from the west, darkening the moss-green water.

"Are you going to keep working at the Outfitters now that school's started?" Jonathan asked.

"Some. I'll keep doing tours until it freezes. Mike'll need help."

"Aren't you playing football?"

"I didn't sign up, but then, Brian is pressuring me. It's not that fun to be on a team where your kid brother is showing you up all the time."

"Oh, man. No shit." Jonathan rested his elbows on his thighs and let his hands dangle between his knees. "Brian's a junior this year, right?"

"Yeah."

"He's basically the star of the football team, isn't he?"

"Right. Since he was about twelve." Scott laughed.

"That's great for him, kind of a bummer for you," Jonathan said. "But you're not all that into it, are you?"

Scott shook his head.

"I wasn't, either. I played every year, but it wasn't my life. You know?"

"Yeah. Do you miss high school?" Scott studied Jonathan across the boat, eight feet away. He wanted to memorize the color of Jonathan's eyes and the angles of his face.

"Sometimes, a little. I like working with Dad."

"Are you still going out with that girl, Gwen?"

"No. She went off to college. We broke up before she left, sort of."

"How do you sort of break up?" Scott's palms were sweating again. He pulled the paddle into the boat and dried his hands on the tail of his T-shirt. He could say, *You know, I have these feelings about you.* Which was crazy.

"She said, 'Let's keep in touch,' and I said, 'Sure, as friends,' and she said, 'That sounds perfect,' and then she left and we never called each other."

"Were you in love with her?"

"I don't think so."

"Did you—you know?"

"Sleep with her? Sure. What, are you her father?"

Scott laughed, but tension drifted down into his stomach. "Just wondering." He could say, *Well, if you're between girlfriends* . . . Crazy. There must be *something* to say. The pressure of everything unspoken pounded behind his eyes.

"How about you? Do you have a girlfriend?"

"Nope." Scott dipped the paddle back in the water. Suddenly he wanted to get back to shore and out of this conversation. "You seeing anyone now?"

"Yes."

Yes? "Who?"

"I can't talk about it." Jonathan stepped his feet to the forward side of the bench and picked up his paddle.

"What do you mean, you can't talk about it?"

"She's married, okay?"

"Really? Geez. Do I know her?"

Jonathan paused without turning around. "Believe me, Scott, you don't want to know any details. Just drop it, okay?"

"Oh, come on!" Scott paddled harder. "Fine. Whatever." So they both had secrets. They slid to the dock and Scott pulled them alongside. Jonathan ducked into his T-shirt, stood, and jumped onto the dock. The canoe rocked and heeled and went over and Scott, with a yelp, was in the lake. He thrashed to the dock. Jonathan knelt and offered a hand. They clasped wrists. Jonathan pulled him up. "You did dump me in the lake!" Scott wiped his eyes.

"Sorry about that." Jonathan smiled. Scott's stomach flipped. The clouds blanketed the sky, low and leaden, the lake pewter, the wind picking up.

Scott shuddered as the breeze caught his torso. Jonathan turned to go. "Oh, man," Scott whispered, clothes dripping on the dock. He picked up his jacket. The first gust of hail hit him in the face like buckshot. "Jonathan! Wait up!" he shouted.

15.

Jess MacKinnon checked her watch. Prickly as her spiked blond hair, the clerk at City Hall, Maggie something, had been steadfastly unhelpful for twenty-six minutes. From behind her thick glasses and the counter that separated them, she stared Jess down as though daring her to complain. She had already fired off one round of bad news after another: No, councilor Karl Luder was not available. No, she could not give out his telephone number. Nor could she provide a phone book; someone had made off with it the week before.

Jess's pleasant countenance began to feel forced, but she kept it stuck on her face. At last she hit upon the right question: The clerk would show her files with the minutes of city council meetings. The files dated back to 1910 and were grouped by decade: Which decade would she like to see?

"How about all of them?" Jess laughed merrily, as though they were sharing a joke. The woman smirked. Jess had already established that there was no one but Maggie to deal with.

"One decade at a time, Ma'am."

Jess looked out the window. Paul Monticola thought the kokanee had disappeared in the sixties or seventies. "Nineteen-sixties, please." She widened her grimace and then let her face go slack as she watched the clerk's plump retreating backside and fantasized about planting her boot there. The clerk's midsection spilled over her tight jeans; she had a serious case of what Jess's mother used to call "sidesy fat." At last, she returned with a brown accordion pouch and thumped it onto the counter.

Inside were ten manila folders labeled with years. No, nine: 1962 was missing. Jess flipped through 1960 and 1961. No mention of the fish or the lake. The clerk retreated to a stool and picked up a paperback novel. She threw it down in a pique when Jess asked about 1962. She flounced to a library-style card file on the far wall, producing an index card with something paperclipped to it that looked like a driver's license. "It's checked out," she announced.

"Checked out? Who has it?"

The clerk studied the card in her hand. Jess guessed she was trying hard to think of a reason not to answer. "Colby Stukel," she finally said.

"Colby Stukel?" That was Scott's grandfather, who had died in the flood. "But he's dead."

The clerk shrugged and turned back to the card file. The front doors opened, light burst into the lobby, and with it came Sammy Branch and Birch Stukel. Jess explained the missing council member, the missing file.

"I am confident we can locate Karl Luder, at least," Sammy said.

"Just go out to Karl's farm and talk to him there. He won't mind." Birch pointed her finger across the counter. "Maggie Turner. Aren't you supposed to keep a record when someone checks out a file?"

"I do have a record!" Maggie brandished the driver's license.

"Who has it then?" Sammy asked.

"Colby Stukel."

Birch opened her mouth to speak, but a strange dark consternation swept over her face, and a muscle spasm stretched her lips taut and squeezed her eyes shut.

Sammy glanced at her, then at Jess. He stepped up to the counter and held out his palm. "Hand it over, Ms. Turner."

The clerk shook her head and backed up.

"For pity's sake. Colby is gone," Sammy said. "He is not going to come in here asking for it."

"How about the file, then?" asked Maggie, backing up another step.

The muscles in Birch's face went slack. "I'll look for it. I promise," she told the clerk. "Don't make me pull rank, my love. Or turn you over to the mayor." She hooked her arm through Sammy's.

"As mayor, Maggie, I hereby order you to relinquish that license," Sammy said.

Scowling, Maggie jerked Colby Stukel's license free of its clip and slapped it onto the counter.

"Thank you, dear," Birch said. She held the card by its laminated edges. Her face gripped again, then relaxed.

Sammy asked Jess how he could help with her research. Jess held up the accordion file. "You were on the city council in the sixties."

"Yes." He squinted over her shoulder at the pouch of folders. He wore a freshly ironed slate gray shirt that matched the stone in his bolo tie. "We convene a city council meeting once every ten years whether anything is afoot or not. Usually, not."

Birch laughed, the shadow dropping from her features as she stowed the license in her handbag. "The Luder farm is up Old Chuck Creek, halfway to my place. You'll pass some orange markers by the side of the road. Karl's driveway is half a mile further, but it can be hard to spot. If you come to a footbridge over the creek, you've gone too far."

"Thanks." Birch's face was placid. Jess almost thought she had imagined the contortion.

"Please be cautious on that canyon road," Sammy said. "The place marked with cones in particular—watch for a sharp bend. A car went off the road there."

Jess nodded. Birch slid the pouch out of Jess's hands with a proprietary air that made Jess's eyebrows shoot upward. Birch tucked the 1960 and 1961 folders back into their places and tapped the pouch on the counter to settle its contents. She spoke to the pouch. "I'll see you later today, won't I? For lunch at my place? Are you finished with these files?"

"I'll come back tomorrow." Jess grinned broadly at the clerk, thinking, *Won't that be fun, Maggie?*

"Here, Maggie," said Birch, strumming the folders with her thumb. "Better take care of this. You don't want any more files to go missing." Maggie took the pouch and vanished in a huff.

16.

As Jess crossed the Still Lake Lodge parking lot, the front desk clerk ran outside and called to her. The clerk, whose bronze name tag said, "Bethany C.," passed her a slip of paper. Riley Bishop had called.

Jess wanted to leave for Karl Luder's farm before the rain picked up. Clouds hung low and they were darkening. "Was it urgent?" she asked, but Bethany C. did not know. Jess trotted upstairs to her room to return the call.

Riley picked up on the second ring. "Glad you called. Nothing conclusive yet on Ben Fletcher. But I can tell you, there's definitely more to the story than a drunken swim in the lake."

Jess stood at the window and wrapped her forefinger in the telephone cord. A wind gust blew a furrow across the lake, and a bristle of hail. "What does that mean?"

"It means he may have been killed deliberately. *May* have been. It's still possible it was an accident."

Jess dropped onto the bed, her hand tangled in the phone cord. Hail gusted against the window like machine gun fire. She couldn't

70

take her motorcycle up the narrow canyon road in this weather. Anyway, what was the point in finding Karl Luder? If Ben had been murdered, nothing else mattered. "Keep talking," she said. "Tell me why you think that."

"One week before he died, Ben Fletcher told his— uh, Moses that what happened to the fish was a big secret, and he was going to expose it. Apparently some folks in town didn't take kindly to his interference. He also said an old Nez Perce man knew all about what happened."

Old Nez Perce man? Sammy? Jack? Jess jumped up and looked out the window at the dark sky. How could Ben get murdered over some fish? That was a lot more than a public relations problem.

"That's the first reason," Riley continued. "Second reason: The autopsy showed a blunt force trauma to the head. The coroner said Fletcher hit his head as he was drowning, or after he drowned, possibly on the pilings where they found him. I read the report and I didn't think so. So I sent the data to a *real* coroner, in Seattle, and she agrees with me. His lungs were only partly filled, and the trauma is consistent with a blow to the head *before* he entered the water."

"You think someone hit him over the head?" Jack Branch with a club? Colonel Mustard with the candlestick? Absurdly, Jess wanted to laugh. Her head felt light. Her throat kept tightening. Maybe it was Jack's son. Moses would think of Mike as old, and Mike was hiding something. But what?

"Not necessarily, but that's one possibility. Third reason. There are flaws in the toxicology report."

"Do you not think Ben was drunk?"

Jess had seen Ben shit-faced only once, at the Kid's third birthday. He'd arrived at the Fletcher ranch two hours late, in a Mustang packed with loud college friends. He smelled like whiskey and his words ran together. He took her aside in the evening, after cake and presents and forced merriment. The Kid had fallen asleep and Becky carried him to bed.

"I want you to know I'm sorry," Ben said, thickly, as though his tongue were swollen. They sat alone in the Fletchers' living room, with the day's last light at the windows. "I let my father push me into this." He swept his hand around the room, at the scatter of paper plates, plastic forks, crumpled wrapping paper. "I should have listened to you instead."

"Whatever." She was still angry that he'd been late, had left her alone with his parents, who despised her. "It's done."

"Can you forgive me?" His eyes moistened. "Please?"

She snorted, rose from the sofa, and began stacking the paper plates. "You're drunk," she said, without looking at him. She carried the plates into the kitchen, where she licked a smear of too-sweet frosting off her wrist.

"He was drunk, no question." Jess heard irritation creep into Riley's voice. "The trouble with the coroner in Enterprise, he's a little lazy. I think he stopped at the blood alcohol and looked no further. He stopped his examination when he got what he expected." Jess heard a slurp and guessed that Riley was drinking tea, courtesy of the Indian restaurant downstairs. "Anyway, it happens all the time. People drown, good swimmers, when they've been drinking. So the coroner jumped to a conclusion. In my humble opinion. Goddammit, I wish they'd go easy on the cinnamon! This tea is actually making my tongue go numb."

"What are you going to do?" Jess asked.

"About the cinnamon?"

"No!"

"Oh, yeah. Well, I'm going to try to get the toxicology redone by an independent lab. That's what his parents want. I mean, you know, Rex and Becky."

"Then what?" Jess sank down on the bed. Her shoulders sagged. Hail flew against the window. It was a mess out there. "What happens then?"

"Then we'll know more about how he died, and whether a crime took place. If I were you, Cowpoke, I'd get the hell out of Dodge."

"Seriously?" Jess pulled her finger free of the phone cord. Maybe that *was* the best thing to do. She could leave in the morning if the roads were dry.

"You could be in danger."

"I'll think about it." Jess stood up. "Let me know what you find out."

"One other thing. A high school kid told the police there was a white pickup parked by the lake the night Fletcher drowned. That's all we've got, besides the autopsy."

The hailstorm had blown itself out. Jess didn't scare easily, but the image of Ben being clubbed on the head and dumped into the lake made her feel as cold as if she were the one falling through water. She looked at her watch. Eleven o'clock. She still had time to visit Karl Luder, then keep her lunch appointment with Birch Stukel. "I'll be careful," she told the P.I.

The road along Old Chuck Creek wound into the mountains, hugging the canyon's lip. Patches of hailstones gathered in the deeper shadows the trees made across the road. Jess took it slow, kept the bike in low gear. There were no guardrails. She passed a row of orange stanchions that stitched the road's shoulder as it bent over the precipice. That was the corner Sammy had warned her about.

She stopped to look. The stanchions were nailed into the asphalt, which had broken away to leave a jagged edge cutting straight down to the water. She left the motorcycle in the middle of the road—there was no traffic—and leaned out over the edge. At the bottom spread a huge round pool, fifty feet across. The little creek jumped into it from a twenty-foot waterfall, flying into froth. The pool boiled foamy green—a scour pool carved by the waterfall, what geologists called a "high-energy environment." Then it spread into a long skirt of shade and lapped at its mossy shore. Downstream, at a mound of cobbles, it dwindled back into a modest creek. This must be the place Paul Monticola had rescued his hundred-year-old logs, stranded in the deep water. What had he called it? The Sink? The Big Sink.

The acoustics in the canyon were strange. Two crows called and the sound ricocheted across the rock walls, multiplying their voices into a chorus, caustic treble to the bass of the waterfall. Then, from down the hill, the growl of an engine and the whine of a transmission, shifting down.

Shit! She sprinted to the bike, grabbed the handles, swung her leg at the kickstand, then over the seat. A truck pelted up the road, horn blaring. She turned the key, popped the clutch. The truck tore past, missing her by an inch, the driver leaning on the horn. The bike lurched, hit a pile of hailstones, and she was down and sliding.

She ground to a halt less than a foot from the road's edge.

As she pried herself loose from the motorcycle, she saw the truck make a three-point turn and barrel back in her direction. A white pickup. "Fuck! Fuck! Fuck!" she chanted. She burned her fingers on the tailpipe, fumbling for a grip on the fallen bike. She could lift it—barely—but her muscles were trembling and her boots slipped on the wet pavement.

The pickup skidded to a stop and a man vaulted from the cab. He was Jess's exact stereotype of an eastern Oregon redneck: muddy work boots, blue jeans, a belt buckle the size of Texas. She'd landed hard on one knee and stayed down, panting, fingers cemented to the bike, bracing for another try.

"Need some help, Ma'am?" He swaggered across the road with his droopy black moustache, wavy salt and pepper hair, square jaw. He smiled: gold tooth. Perfect. He *looked* like someone who would hit Ben Fletcher with a blunt instrument and then throw him in the lake. And he was driving a white pickup.

"No, I've got it." She strained against the bike. Her boot slipped.

He laughed, cruel. Crouched next to her and hoisted the motorcycle upright with a little grunt. She flipped down the kickstand. "Thanks," she said. *Asshole*, she added silently.

He tipped an imaginary hat. "Happy to help. Name's Cleve Kittridge. Did you hurt yourself?"

"I'm fine." She started to hold out her hand and then wiped it on her pants instead. "Jess MacKinnon. I appreciate your help." Cleve Kittridge? This must be Scott's dad. Jesus H. Christ with a rainbow flag. What a bad draw for a father.

"What brings you up this way, Jess MacKinnon?"

"I'm here for work." She ran her fingers over the bike. Her hands were shaking. The chrome was scratched but nothing looked bent.

"This here's not the best weather for a motorbike. Where you headed?"

She didn't want to answer, but what difference did it make? "Karl Luder's place." Though when she checked her watch, she saw that it was nearly noon and time for lunch with Birch Stukel.

He pointed a finger. "I know who you are. You're the fish scientist." It sounded like an accusation.

Jess turned the ignition. The bike rumbled under her hands, which were still shaking. She threw her leg over the seat. "Yes. Thank you again for the help." She tried to look grateful. The bike's vibration steadied her.

"You're just here to cause trouble, same as that guy who drowned."

"Just doing my job." She tightened her grip on the handlebars.

"Oh, yeah? '*Just doing my job*.'" He mocked her and stalked to his truck.

She gritted her teeth. Anger made her face hot and laced her voice with sarcasm. "You have a job, right? You understand the concept?" Beneath her the bike grumbled. She bumped it into gear and felt it surge.

He turned from the open truck door and took a step toward her, eyes cold as steel. "What does that mean, you brainless bitch? Of course I have a job." He climbed into the cab, slammed the door, hard. Poked his head out the window. "You wasted a trip. Dinged up your motorbike for no reason."

She was so angry she didn't trust herself to speak. She scanned the road for hailstones and pulled on the throttle, inching forward.

"Karl's gone until tomorrow night," Kittridge called from the truck cab, gleeful. "Livestock auction in Pendleton. Maybe you should head on back to the city." His tires chirped as he sped away.

17.

By the time Scott pushed open the museum door, he'd been dunked in the lake, drenched in cold rain, and peppered with hailstones. Worse, he felt cold inside beyond any threat of hypothermia. Was there no way to tell Jonathan the truth?

"I'm back in the print shop!" Rill called.

From the doorway, Scott watched his mother feed sheets of paper to the ravenous exoskeleton of the Chandler & Price letterpress. "Hi," he said. She pushed the lever that stilled the press's iron arms.

"Scotty! Why aren't you in school?" Rill switched off the motor. Wiping her hands, she looked him up and down. "You're a drowned rat! What happened?"

"Are there any dry clothes here?" Scott's whole body was quaking. "Or a blanket?"

"Come over here. Take those off." She sat him down next to the pot-bellied stove and tugged at his jacket sleeve.

"I can undress myself, Mom!" He jerked his arm away.

"Don't be an ingrate. I'll find something for you to put on." She vanished into the storeroom.

Scott peeled off his clothes and hovered over the stove in his briefs. Rill returned with a folded stack: gray slacks, white undershirt, cream-colored dress shirt, suspenders, socks, boxer shorts. He held up the boxers: red and green plaid. Seriously? "Mom. I don't wear boxers. Where did you get this stuff?" He dangled the suspenders on the hook of one forefinger: gray and black pinstripes.

"Those were your grandfather's." Rill shook out the pants. "You can't wear those." She snapped the waistband of his briefs.

"Mom!" He jumped out of reach. Snatched the clothes away and ran to the storeroom to change.

He pulled the undershirt over his head. It smelled musty, and underneath he caught the faint scent of Colby Stukel's pipe tobacco.

Rill waited for him by the stove. She'd spread his wet clothes across a chair to dry. "Okay, Scott." She folded her arms. "Why aren't you in school? Why are you soaked to the skin? That isn't just from the rain." He sat down and pulled on the socks, handed her the suspenders.

"I'm definitely not wearing *those*. I fell in the lake. I was messing around on the dock." Partially true. He buttoned the shirt and tucked it in. Looked down at himself. The pants were too short. He looked ridiculous.

"Oh, Scott." His mother's eyes turned misty. She spun him around. "You look just like the old pictures of your grandfather when he was young! Same hair, same eyes. Same build—those clothes fit you perfectly!" She threw her arms around him. Her shoulders shook. He patted her back. She pulled away, dabbing at her eyes. He bent over the counter and picked up a freshly printed page of the *Gazette* while his mother pulled herself together.

"Paper looks nice." It did: crisp red and black. Words in even columns. A pleasing symmetry. Something that made sense, for a change.

"What were you trying to tell me this morning?" Rill took the page from him, added it to the stack, and tidied the edges.

"Nothing important." Which was a complete lie. Whatever being gay meant—mental illness, sin against God, or just another "lifestyle" (a word he hated more than "homosexual")—it was definitely important. He needed to tell her. About being gay, about Jonathan. She would know what to do.

"O love is the crooked thing!" she said, as though she'd heard his thoughts.

"*What?*"

"Yeats. 'Brown Penny.' Your grandfather loved that poem. It's about a young man in love."

Scott ran his finger along the stack of newspaper sheets. "Have you set the type for page two yet?" he asked her. "I could help you." He pictured the two of them bustling around the shop, as they sometimes did. Imagined himself bringing it up casually, maybe as he arranged letters in the chase. *I don't mean this to sound like a big deal, Mom*, he would say. He'd be leaning over the chase, his fingers stained with ink. *But you should know.*

She shoved him toward the door. "Off to school, you truant!" She swatted him as he ran past. "Hey, wait a minute! Did you and Brian take off with that peavey pole?" She pointed at an empty-handed mannequin in the logging exhibit.

"Haven't seen it."

18.

Riley's dart was stuck in the middle of the Pacific Ocean. She scanned the map. Was it close enough to Hawaii to count? She didn't like islands that much, nor cruises. All that monotony of green-smelling water! No, thank you. She plucked the dart free and threw it back into her desk drawer. She was about to go find some lunch and was reaching for the doorknob when the door swept open and nearly smacked her. The rude teenager, Moses, occupied the door frame, his face hard with anger.

"Sure, come on in," Riley said loudly as he shoved past her, but he was too agitated to appreciate her sarcasm.

"My brother was *murdered*," he not-quite-shouted. "And no one is doing anything!" Riley didn't tolerate being yelled at. But the kid was close to tears. She pulled out a chair. He took his fists off his hips and folded his long body into the seat, hitching up his blue jeans and unbuttoning a denim jacket lined with red flannel. Then his face folded, too, and he started to cry.

"It's okay," Riley said in her most soothing tone. "I'll get us some tea." She gave his shoulder a pat and fled the room. She fetched the tea and then she paced around at the bottom of the stairs, giving the kid a minute.

He was still sniffling and gurgling when she set the mug on his side of the desk. Since his mother's (or grandmother's, she corrected herself) outburst of weeping the week before, Riley had intended to stock up on tissues. But she hadn't done it. As she searched the desk in vain for a stray napkin, the kid pulled a white handkerchief from the

79

front pocket of his jacket, crisply creased and folded, shook it out, and blew his nose into it. She'd never seen anyone so young with a hanky; maybe she should get one. She pictured herself drawing out the bright scrap of fabric and offering it up with a flourish. But then Moses inspected the hanky's contents, balled it up (snot and all), and shoved it back into his pocket. Revolting. She would buy tissues.

Moses had finished his crying but now he looked embarrassed. His embarrassment smelled briny, like a shanty town on the sea. "Why do you think Ben was murdered?" She spoke softly as though to a nervous horse.

"Don't *you* think so?" he said, his voice cracking. His face hardened again while the blush of embarrassment traveled down to his collar and grew fiery. Bonfire sparks. Ocean spray. "My parents said someone hit him over the head and then threw him in the lake." He jumped up, waved his arms around, but couldn't find any more words. He flopped back into the chair. "I can't even stand to think about it!" His scent surged and the brine grew foul, rotten fish. Old blood. "My folks are paying you! Why aren't you investigating?"

Riley sipped her tea. She knew the steam would fog her glasses and make her inscrutable. "What'd you have in mind?" she asked him. The tea was molten. She slurped it. Good batch, just an *implication* of cinnamon. "What kind of investigating should I be doing?"

"You know. Like James Bond." The red faded from his cheeks and the fish smell with it.

Riley nodded, not bothering to point out that James Bond was a spy, not an investigator. "I should be jumping around on top of speeding trains? Getting shot at?"

He looked uncertain.

"What I do is ask questions. A lot of questions." The lower half of his face was a copy of Jess MacKinnon's, with peach fuzz added. How did no one notice it? "Let me ask you a few, okay? How long have you known Jess MacKinnon?"

"Aunt Jess? My whole life, I guess. What's she got to do with any of this?"

Riley decided her promise not to mention Jess's presence in Still Lake did not extend to Moses, only to Rex and Becky. "She's up in Still Lake," she told him, "doing her own biologist-type investigation. Probably jumping on trains."

It was the wrong thing to say. Moses popped out of the chair again and her office smelled like a fishing village. In the restaurant downstairs, someone turned on the meat grinder. The floor began to vibrate and one of her bird masks did a nose dive off the bookshelf. Moses shot out a hand and caught it before it hit the floor. Impressive.

"What *is* that?" Moses held the painted beak in front of his face as though the bird might speak to him.

"It's a ceremonial bird mask. From Panama."

He slid the mask onto the desk. "No, I mean the noise."

"The restaurant's meat grinder. Makes the whole building shake." She stroked the bird's head that sprouted with bristles——some sort of Panamanian grass.

"You were in Panama?"

Riley nodded. "Have you been there?"

"No. I want to go there. I want to see places like that." He tucked his hands into the pockets of his jacket and hunched his shoulders.

The meat grinder stopped. Moses sat down. Both of them looked at the mask. What if it *did* begin speaking? Riley would not have been surprised. The Emberá woman who'd given it to her had implied the mask held special powers, a personality, that it had selected her, Riley, to be its human consort.

"I've never even been outside Oregon. My Mom's super, super over-protective." He picked up the mask and held it in his lap. "It's tough for her to lose Ben," he said to the mask. "Very tough. She lost a baby between me and Ben, a little girl."

"What happened?" She remembered Becky Fletcher, in tears, the smell of empty water.

"SIDS. Sudden Infant … Death something."

"Syndrome?" Riley offered. So Becky's sadness was deep.

Moses nodded. He ran his forefinger down the smooth wood of the beak, yellow and orange triangles, a green line.

"Is Aunt Jess your mother's sister?" Riley asked, just to see what he'd say.

His head snapped up. "Aunt Jess—hey! She could be in trouble up there!" He set the mask down. "She's not really my aunt. I just call her that. She's an old family friend." He said this by rote, Riley noticed. That's what he'd always been told.

"I talked to her this morning," she told him. "She's all right. She'll be careful."

He stood and brushed his large hands together as if dismissing the entire conversation. "Well, I'm going to go check on her," he announced. "There's going to be another storm tonight, and she only has her motorcycle."

Riley intercepted him. "Do your folks know where you are?" She put a hand up to block the door as he swung it open.

"Kind of. Excuse me." He wedged himself past her and out to the landing. With his flight path clear, he turned back to her and pointed an accusatory finger. Riley was sure she'd seen Rex Fletcher make the same gesture. "And I'm going to find out who killed my brother, too! And I'm going to make sure he gets what's coming to him." He pivoted and leaped down the stairs three at a time.

19

Jess's legs wobbled as she climbed off her motorcycle in front of Birch Stukel's cottage. Thwack! Birch was splitting wood in the front yard. The wedges flew away, scattering chickens.

"Well, well," said Birch, burying the blade in a log round. "If it isn't Jess MacKinnon, champion of the environment. Give me a hand with this firewood." The chickens settled back into the gravel, pecking and scratching.

Jess picked up an armload of pine wedges and followed Birch to the far side of the cottage. Five feet of mossy ground separated the house from a barn. For thirty feet down the side of the barn, the wood stack was as flawless as the interlocking cogs of a machine. Jess both admired it and found it disquieting. The edges of the wood pinched her forearm. "Does your mule live in the barn?" she asked.

Birch nodded. Jess handed her the wedges of pine and she placed them, one by one, at the top of the stack, fitting each piece.

"Is that how you get around?" Jess asked. "By mule?" She was half joking, but there was no car in Birch's driveway. Birch was taking forever to stack the wood. Jess's arm ached.

"Yes. Or I walk." Birch's voice held no trace of humor, as she took a step back to study her wood stack. She adjusted one of the wedges and Jess handed her another. "I've never owned a car. Never learned to drive." She stacked the last piece. She pushed past Jess through the narrow tunnel between the wood stack and the cottage. "Just my modest contribution to the planet's well-being," she called over her shoulder.

Jess followed her down to the creek. So, Birch had an environmental ethic. Why didn't she like the project, then? They crossed a meadow to a stand of aspen, and stood together at the lip of the canyon with the sound of rushing water all around. Jess braced her hand on the trunk of an aspen and she gazed down at the creek. "I have a question," Jess said loudly, over the sound. "Old Chuck Creek is named for Charles Stone? Is he the founder of Still Lake?"

The muscles of Birch's face contorted and tightened in the same strange spasm Jess had seen that morning in City Hall. Jess looked away, uncomfortable, her eyes following the canyon downstream. "Three hundred million years ago, this was all ocean," Birch said. Her face had stilled. She wasn't answering the question; Jess wondered whether she had heard it. "After that, volcanoes. Right here, a seam in the earth's crust." Birch swept her arm in a circle. She twisted toward Jess and smiled. "Old Chuck was a prospector who came here looking for gold in 1882," she said. "Instead of finding gold, he cut down the entire forest. No one thinks of him as the founder of anything."

"Paul Monticola told me about the log drives." Jess returned Birch's smile, relieved that the conversation made sense again.

Birch led the way back to the cottage. She kept talking, and Jess hurried to walk beside her. "Yes, the log drives were a big deal," she said, brushing at the spikelets of hairgrass. "The Branch family objected to them. Mary Riffle Branch in particular. Jack and Sammy's mother."

At the house, Birch disappeared inside and Jess perched on the edge of a purple Adirondack chair. From a window into the kitchen, a yellow and white striped curtain swelled in the breeze. Birch kicked open the cottage door and set a tray on a table near Jess's perch. She poured tea from a flowered teapot into matching cups and pointed to a plate of dainty sandwiches. "Please help yourself," Birch said. She sat on a bench beside the porch rail. "Mary Branch is the one who named the creek, actually."

The tea was dull green and afloat with specks of brown and orange. Jess sniffed it and smelled menthol. She took a sip. It wasn't bad. She bit into one of the tiny sandwiches: cucumber and hummus; lots of dill and something spicy. "Is that right?" she said. She took another sandwich. She heard the creek's rush, across the meadow.

"It's a matter of record. The first edition of the *Still Lake Gazette* quoted her as saying, 'The creek is Old Chuck.' I believe she was speaking metaphorically. Perhaps she was being ironic. After all, the Nez Perce lived here long before Old Chuck Stone or any other European." A chicken raced across the yard, two others in pursuit. Birch refilled the teacups. "It's herbal," she said. "My own recipe. I grow all the herbs here, in my garden. Out back." She leaned against the porch rail and crossed her legs. "So, the fish. Why should the city council support your project?"

"There are lots of reasons. A healthy ecosystem. For the town, economic development." Through the tea's menthol steam Jess scrutinized Birch Stukel. Her green eyes, like her wild yellow hair, darted every which way. She was intelligent, eccentric, a recluse, an environmentalist. She should like the idea of saving a threatened fish population. "The project is cutting edge," she began, watching Birch's reaction. Birch's face remained impassive, her gaze flitting to the chickens, the meadow, the aspens. "The goal is to restore natural, baseline conditions in a discrete watershed. Here, that would mean bringing back a sustainable population of native kokanee." Jess set her empty cup on the tray, helped herself to another sandwich. She settled back into the Adirondack chair, which swallowed her like a giant purple mouth.

"What if the kokanee are gone?"

"We'll look at other options." Jess tried to wriggle free of the chair's clutches. She pulled on the arms and hauled herself up.

"You'll try to find out what happened to the fish, years ago?"

"Yes." Wind blew down the canyon and carried the smell of heather. The porch grew sunny between the shadows of the fir trees in the yard. Despite this, Jess shivered.

Birch sipped her tea and peered over the porch rail at one of the chickens, a rust-colored hen that appeared to be sleeping. "You'll find out who was to blame for killing them off?"

Interesting question. Birch's features had hardened. "This is not about blame," Jess said. She picked up another tiny sandwich; this one stuffed with smoky, soft cheese.

"No? That's what it was all about for Ben Fletcher. Blame and shame. Shame on us, the town of Still Lake, for eradicating a fish population." Birch rested her cup on the table and stood up. "My father was mayor of this town for more than forty years. Fletcher tried to destroy his legacy."

Ben Fletcher. Again, it seemed he'd made himself unpopular, had been pushy and tactless. Jess, at fourteen, at fifteen, had loved his take-charge ways. He knew how to make things happen. He knew how the world worked. "I'm gathering historical data only with the goal of restoring a sustainable fish population," she tried, but Birch did not seem to be listening.

Instead, Birch bent over the porch rail and poked at the sleeping chicken. "Fortuna has taken ill. She stopped laying a week ago." Birch scooped up the hen and cradled it on her lap. "She's gotten into something. She has no sense and will eat anything she finds. Well, it's unfortunate. Pun intended." Birch picked up the chicken's head with gentle fingers and stared into its eyes.

Jess drained her tiny teacup, noticing for the first time the tea's unpleasant aftertaste. "What do you think happened to the kokanee?" she asked.

Birch stroked the chicken's untidy feathers. Wind bent the grass in the meadow and a sage grouse rose, wings clapping. The storm clouds closed ranks and the sun disappeared. "Mike Branch poisoned the fish. It's common knowledge." Birch closed her fist around Fortuna's head, stood, and held the hen at arm's length. Fortuna's pale wattle spilled from the back of Birch's hand as she clomped down the porch steps and into the yard, scattering the other chickens. Jess could not make herself look away as Birch twirled the animal at the end of her arm, faster and faster until the body separated from the head and, to Jess's astonishment, jumped around on the ground like a decapitated marionette before collapsing. Jess struggled out of the chair and stood, light-headed. Birch stroked the severed head and kissed the beak, crooning, "There, my love. That's better." She tossed the head into the trees and wiped her hand on her pants. She saw Jess's expression and laughed. "What's the matter, City Slicker? Weak stomach?"

Jesus H. Christ on a raft. What the fuck? Jess wasn't sure she could speak. "I'd better get going," she whispered. But leaving seemed impossible. Her feet were glued to the planks of Birch's front porch.

"So soon?" Birch kicked the headless bird aside and crunched across the gravel to the doors of the barn. She pushed them open. "Come here a minute. I have something for you."

Jess descended numbly into the gravel yard. She wanted to sprint to her bike and tear down the canyon back to the Lodge. In fact, she was ready to hightail it out of Still Lake, out of the Wallowa Mountains, and back to civilization. She looked up at the low dark clouds. In the morning, first light. She nodded to her motorcycle as though making a pact, and she joined Birch at the barn doors.

"How did Mike Branch poison the fish?" Inside the barn, five ceramic crocks were arranged—in perfect symmetry—around a drain. The air was thick with the smell of rotting fruit.

"He wanted to make Still Lake a trophy-fishing destination. He introduced an organism for the fish to feed on, to make them bigger. Killed them instead."

Birch slid a bottle from near the bottom of a wine rack on the wall and brushed the dust away.

"Do you know what it was?" The odor in the barn was overwhelming. Jess took shallow breaths through her mouth. Her head got light again.

"Can't recall." Birch presented the bottle. "Here. Wild berry wine, my own recipe." Jess stared at the label, a woman with long, flowing tresses, her breasts bulging from a low-cut red gown. Her hands felt heavy at her sides. She didn't think she could lift them. "Come on, my dear, it's a peace offering. I'll vote to support your project." Jess knew she should be happy to hear this news, but Old Chuck Creek seemed to be roaring inside her head. Through the barn doors, she saw the rust-colored lump of Fortuna in the gravel, two of the other chickens pecking at it. It was only a bottle of homemade wine. Jess wiped the sweat from her palms and took it.

20.

In his college dorm room, Ben Fletcher had converted the wastebasket into an ice bucket for two bottles of wine. They drank from paper cups. Jess didn't like the wine—it was too sour and left the taste of glue in her mouth—but Ben kept refilling her cup. He toasted their relationship. "To us!" he said, smiling. He reached out to unbutton her shirt. Everything felt fuzzy and distant: his fingers, the narrow bed, the trees out the window blowing in a hard February rain. He eased her onto the pillow. She could not close her eyes for more than five seconds, or the room started to spin like a carnival ride. As though she were a spectator in the last row of seats, she watched him pull off her jeans, then her underpants. He rubbed between her legs. She shut her eyes. The room lurched. Groping, she found his head on her chest. Felt his hair, fine like feathers. He nuzzled her breasts. He was naked. He ground between her legs with his hips, groaning, and pushed her thighs apart. Her foot hung off the bed. The ice in the wastebasket shifted. She heard the wind, running at the window, tossing the trees, grabbing at the tender leaves. Sharp sensations traveled up from her pelvis: pain and pleasure, then a rhythm she recognized—the tempo of her mother's bed creaking when a boyfriend spent the night.

Afterwards, he swaddled her in a blanket and helped her down the hall to the bathroom so she could vomit, the alcohol searing her throat. For the rest of her life, the smell of wine washed her with vertigo, as though she were a new leaf buffeted by the wind.

21.

The clerk at Still Lake Lodge waved to Jess as she walked by the front desk. "Sammy Branch came by looking for you. Said he'd stop by later." Jess offered her the bottle of wild berry wine. "I don't drink wine," said the woman, Bethany C., with her perfect teeth and shoulder-length blond hair. "But I'm sure I can find a home for it." She tucked the bottle away.

22.

In the spring of 1986, when she was fifteen, Jess MacKinnon was seized with nausea after breakfast, every morning for a week. On the two days her mother fried eggs, the smell alone was enough to send her running to the toilet. Her mother pulled a box of powdered cocoa from the cupboard. "A hot drink, my girl." She filled the kettle with tap water. "You got to put something in there, settle your stomach."

At the table, Jess put her head on her arms. Her mother set the cup down beside her and took the other chair. Jess lifted her head. She had to tell her mother. "I think I know what's wrong with me," she whispered. How could she say it?

"Well, spit it out, by golly!" Priscilla patted her arm. On the counter, the coffee maker gasped. The smell almost made Jess run to the bathroom again.

"I have cancer."

Priscilla tipped her head back and laughed.

89

"I'm serious, Mom!"

"Sorry, my girl." More arm patting. Then the smile fell from her face and she stood up, poured a cup of coffee. "I got a different idea what's wrong," she said to the coffee maker, which hissed in response. "But you got to tell me the truth, Jessica." Her mother sat down, stared into her coffee, clearly uncomfortable.

"What?"

"Have you been with a boy?"

Priscilla stood outside the bathroom door while she unwrapped the white wand that would tell her whether she was pregnant. She showed her mother. Two blue lines. "Well, goddamn," Priscilla said. Jess had been buoyant with relief that she would not die of cancer, but now another heaviness rooted her to the bathroom floor. She would have to tell Ben.

23.

There was a tentative knock on the door of her room. She opened it to find Sammy Branch. Sweat beaded on his forehead. He shushed her when she greeted him and crept into the room after looking up and down the hallway. "What's going on?" she asked when the door was closed.

He thrust a file folder into her hands. "Some of the city council minutes were missing." He was whispering. "I have kept my own set of files over the years. I think this may be helpful to you."

"Sammy, why are you whispering?" she asked. "And why are you so nervous?"

He gave a little laugh and smiled at her, his chin crinkling. "I *am* being silly, skulking about!"

"Why are you helping me? Not that I don't appreciate it." She set the folder on the desk. So far, Sammy and Scott were her only allies.

Birch had promised to vote in favor of the project, but the image of the headless hen, Fortuna, danced into her consciousness. She pushed it back into the darkness where it belonged.

"I hope you will succeed, and that you can bring the kokanee back." He was still whispering.

"Is that the only reason?" She couldn't make herself tell him that, fish or no fish, she planned to head back to Portland in the morning.

"That is enough. There is more at stake than just the kokanee." He opened the door.

"Like what?" Jess said, but he scurried for the stairs.

The folder was labeled "1962." She flipped it open. The first sheet wore lengthwise stripes from a mimeograph machine, blocks of crowded blue type. She unfolded a dog-eared corner and pressed it flat. "STILL LAKE CITY COUNCIL," the page proclaimed, then "Meeting Minutes, January 24, 1962." She scanned the fuzzy type but found no mention of the fish or the lake. She checked her watch: Almost dinnertime.

She shuffled through the minutes for February. Nothing. What a day. She'd nearly tumbled into a canyon and she'd watched a chicken get decapitated by a looney winemaker. Ben could have been murdered, and his murderer could be right here in Still Lake—driving around in a white pickup truck. Like Cleve Kittridge. Too risky.

She squinted at the Still Lake City Council meeting minutes for March 1962, but the blue type swirled into an eddy and her stomach grumbled. She shrugged on her backpack.

24.

"Somebody's looking for you," said Bethany C. when Jess returned from the restaurant. "A guy." Her blonde hair swept across the front desk as she bent over it, propped on her forearms.

Jess frowned. "Not Sammy Branch?" she asked.

The clerk shook her head. "A young guy. I didn't know him. He's waiting for you upstairs."

Jess had a momentary urge to run for it. Who could be looking for her that Bethany C. did not recognize? She trudged up the stairs, wary but resigned.

He sat in a ball with his knees pulled up and his back against the wall next to her door. "Hi, there," she said to the rusty top of his head as she turned her key in the lock. He lifted his chin and unfolded his arms and legs.

"Aunt Jess!" Moses jumped up and grabbed her into a hug that squeezed all the air from her lungs.

"Kiddo, what are you doing here?" she asked when she had gathered enough breath to speak. She held his elbows and looked up. His face was thinner than she remembered—it had been nearly a year since she'd seen him—and his eyes were red as though he'd been crying.

As usual, she was elated to see him, all out of proportion to the occasion. Her delight bubbled into her throat and stung the back of her eyes. She always felt close to tears when she first saw his face. His unruly curls, sky-colored eyes, perfect lips, pointed chin: Every time she looked at him she saw him at every age, from the moment of his birth. His face was screwed up and purple, his toothless mouth preparing for a good squall; and it was quiet, his eyelids drooping as he fell asleep. He was five, riding Ransom, his pony. He was thirteen, embarrassed about his acne. It made no sense but there it was. He was hers.

$$25.$$

At the hospital, October 13, 1986, Ben squeezed her hand while she grunted and pushed. She saw on his face the reflection of her own terror. Moses came out coated in a waxy white sheathing that the nurse wiped away. Then the nurse wrapped him up like a burrito and handed her the bundle. Her throat closed; she wanted to hand it back. She rubbed her thumb across his cheek where a trace of the coating remained. She looked over the baby's head at Ben, who stared with wide eyes, his freckles dark and the rest of his face drained of pigment. "Oh, fuck," he whispered. She frowned at him, shook her head, and tightened her grip on the burrito. But the words bounced off the walls of her skull: Oh fuck oh fuck oh fuck.

$$26.$$

He had his big, heavy hands on her shoulders. "Aunt Jess! I was so worried about you!" She steered him backward into the room and sat him on the bed. She listened while he talked, jumping to his feet and sitting back down, bouncing on the mattress, jumping up again.

Ben had told him there was a "Nez Perce old-timer" who knew all about the fish. Moses was sure he'd meant Sammy Branch, actual *mayor* of Still Lake. Did Jess know that Mayor Branch had been on the city council since *1958*? That meant that whatever had killed off the fish, Mayor Branch knew all about it, and maybe was responsible. Of course he would try to cover it up!

Moses was disgusted with Riley Bishop, who wasn't doing anything except making phone calls. So he, Moses, had been following Mayor Branch all afternoon. And Mayor Branch was looking for *her*, Jess—at the hotel desk, he'd asked where she was and when she'd be back! Moses was sure the mayor was after her. He was *positive* that Mayor Branch had murdered Ben.

Jess straightened the corners of the Still Lake City Council meeting minutes, 1962, and tucked them in their folder. She did not believe for a minute that Sammy Branch had murdered Ben, but Moses was on a roll and she knew better than to try to stop it. Moses paced in front of the bed, a route that took him to the window, where he peered into the darkness as though straining to see what lurked there. "Kiddo, do your folks know where you are?" she asked him. "Do they know you skipped school today?"

He spun from the window, throwing his arms out. "This is more important than school!"

"That wasn't my question." She tapped her fingers on the manila folder, waited him out. She held a unique but precarious position in his life: He acknowledged her as an adult but confided in her as a peer—or a sibling. Like Ben.

"Guess what?" he had asked her on his fifth birthday. The presents were open, the cake eaten.

"What?" she answered, knowing what was coming.

"Chicken butt!" he shrieked. She laughed and slapped her thigh, not to disappoint him.

"No, really. Guess what? Ben is not my real brother!"

"What?" Jess spread her hand against her chest, felt her heart thumping as though it would jar itself loose. Someone had told him— but who? Did he know who *she* was, then? Her eyes careened around the room. They were alone. Moses grinned madly. Was this all a big joke to him?

"Ben told me himself."

"Is that right?" Her voice came out in a croak.

He nodded, emphatic. "He's a space alien!" A blue balloon floated down from the open rafters and he bolted off the sofa to capture it, hooting with laughter. Jess collapsed against the throw pillows, grabbing one for support and clutching it to her stomach.

"My parents think I'm at a study group," he told her now. "I'm supposed to be home by nine-thirty."

It was eight-fifteen. Baker City was a three-hour drive. "Okay," Jess said.

"I can't stop thinking about Ben!" he cried. He sat down and put his head in his hands. Jess sat on the mattress beside him, slid her arm across his shoulders.

"I know, Kiddo. Me, too." She rubbed his back. "But remember, we don't know for sure that it wasn't an accident." She stroked his hair where it fell over his collar. "And I think you might be wrong about Sammy Branch. He's one of the few people who've tried to be helpful to me."

He grabbed her forearm. "He's playing you! Don't you see that? You should have seen him today, sneaking around outside in the parking lot, waiting for you!"

"I suppose it's possible." Jess said, though she didn't suppose it at all. Still, Sammy knew something. *There is more at stake than just the kokanee*, he'd said. Jess stood and picked up the phone. "Let's get you a room for tonight. It's too late for you to drive home. I'm leaving in the morning. We can have breakfast and then head out together. I'm going back to Portland." There was no answer at the front desk. She set the phone in its cradle.

"You're leaving? You just got here!"

"I know. But it's starting to feel like too much to deal with." She called the front desk again. The clerk picked up and assured her there were plenty of rooms available. Moses could have 214, right across the hall.

Moses had his arms crossed. He stared at her, lips tight.

"What's the matter?" she asked. "I got you a room."

"Fine. Because I'm not leaving this town until the mayor answers for killing my brother."

"Kiddo, that's crazy. This isn't your responsibility." She could see in the set of his chin that he wasn't going to let this go.

"Well, I think it *is* my responsibility! Somebody's got to do something. My parents hired Riley Bishop, but she just reads reports and makes phone calls. And now you're leaving. It's all on me, obviously." He bent his head, but not before she saw his lips tremble.

He'd worked himself into a frenzy and, what's more, he was exhausted; it was there in the slump of his shoulders. "All right, I'll stay," she told him. He lifted his head and gave her a big smile, the kind that made her insides escape to the ceiling like a blue birthday balloon, bursting with helium.

27.

Scott stared at the blank sheet of paper until his eyes watered and the lines jumped on the page. Outside, the wind hurled the rain around and tossed the boughs of the fir trees. Eleven o'clock. If he went to sleep right now, this very minute, he'd have six hours before he had to wake up and help Mike get ready for a fishing trip. He twirled the pencil in his fingers.

He thought about the Still Lake kokanee, how they had hatched in the creek, swam to the lake, grew up, had their babies: all of it, a complete lifetime, in four years—only that! He thought about his grandfather and that poem, "Brown Penny." "Wherefore I threw a penny," he whispered, "to find out if I might love."

"Dear Jonathan," he wrote. "We've known each other since we were little kids." He groaned and spread his hands and raised his eyes to the ceiling. No. "Ah, penny, brown penny, brown penny," he chanted as he crumpled the page into a sphere and airballed it across the room to join the others. He slid a fresh sheet onto the desk, hunched over it. "Dear Jonathan: I hate how people talk and never say anything real. I know you agree. So I have decided to tell you how I feel."

A tree branch scraped the house. Scott looked up. Then he bent again and wrote, the rasp of the pencil on the paper vibrating through all his bones.

Wednesday, September 29, 2004

28.

Jess's dream began with an image that always recurred: A baby in dark water, drowning, the surface closing then becoming smooth over the plump face and rounded lips. And Jess, always wading in too late, waving her arms through the water and feeling nothing.

This time the scene shifted and she was kneeling beside Old Chuck Creek, Mike Branch beside her. Everything in the creek bed had been worn smooth by water, the slick mossy cobbles with their green hair trailing, the glistening gray stones, the tangles of wood, the gravel and the sand. Flecks of mica flashed in the sand as the afternoon sunlight wandered through the shade and onto the sparkle of the water. Mike's lips moved, but there were no words in this dream, only the voices of the water that sheeted over the stones. When she looked into the creek again a ruby necklace of eight red fish draped itself across the streambed, holding position against the current, sleek tails waving. A ninth fish arrived at the base of a dam of branches, gathered itself into its bright body, flung itself to the top of the barrier, and then slithered clear to rest in a pool of green shade. Jess raised her head to lock eyes with a raccoon on the opposite bank. Like her, like Mike, the raccoon watched the fish with its curious face, then it ambled into the forest. Jess awoke to find she'd overslept. She and Moses had stayed up talking until past midnight.

It was time to make another run at Mike Branch, local fishing guide.

29

Alone in Still Lake Outfitters, Scott tidied a display of baseball caps and, for the hundredth time, drew a folded sheet of notebook paper from his back pocket and read it over. The creases were fuzzy from overuse. If he wasn't careful, the thing would disintegrate before he could give it to Jonathan. He looked out the back window. The wind had swept the sky clean after last night's storm but mist hovered on the water. He refolded the letter and slid it back into his pocket. Tired as he was, he felt like running out onto the dock and throwing himself in the lake.

He went through the back door and onto the deck. Someone stood on the end of the dock, right where he'd imagined launching himself into the water. He trudged down the stairs, down the gangway. The lake was quiet and minnows were jumping into the mist.

Jess MacKinnon gazed over the water. She wore a soft blue sweater. The sweater was a shade lighter than the sky. It was the color of her eyes, too, he realized as she turned in his direction.

"Looks like Mike's out fishing?" She gestured across the lake.

"Uh-huh." Scott stood next to her. "He's got a guy with him from Portland who comes every year. Four years ago, he caught a twelve-pound lake trout, and every year since then he's been back. But then, those fish are hard to catch."

The sun had not reached the dock yet, and the air felt chilly. The skiff was clear across the lake, near the mouth of Old Chuck Creek.

"Are there less lake trout—" She blushed and bent her head. "Are there fewer lake trout now than there used to be?"

"Yeah. Seems like it, anyways." So she was embarrassed about speaking correct grammar. Scott and Brian got that a lot, coming from a family of literary fanatics. But Jess, she seemed so . . . unapologetic. *It's all right!* he wanted to say, but that would have made it worse. He was tired. He wanted to sit down, but the dock was beaded with rainwater.

"You said Mike keeps records of what he catches? I'd like to see those."

"They're in the store room. I can ask Mike." The skiff wasn't moving. "Maybe they're having some luck, or else they'd be heading back by now."

Jess turned her back on the lake and took a step closer to him. She pointed to the dory tied next to her, rocking in the ghostly mist. "Where does the name come from?" she asked.

Mike had stenciled the name, "*Tamkaliks*," on the dory's prow. Mike was fond of that boat, kept it out after all the other boats were stowed for the winter.

"It means 'the place where you can see the mountains,'" he told her. "It's the name the Nez Perce gave to the Wallowa Valley."

Jess looked all around. He followed her gaze with his, wondered what the place would look like if he hadn't grown up here, had never heard of Jonathan Monticola. On all sides of the valley the jagged mountains stood guard.

"I can see what they meant," Jess said. Her eyes were as soft as the fuzzy yarn of her sweater and he had a startling impulse to rest his cheek on her shoulder.

Instead he looked across the lake. The skiff was heading back, cutting smoothly through the silver water. The sun glanced over the mountains and light spilled onto the dock. "As soon as Mike gets back I'm going to the gym."

"There's a gym?"

He laughed as her eyes lit up. "No, sorry. It's the weight room at the high school. Brian wants to work out. That's my little brother." The boat was close enough that they could hear the purr of the electric motors.

"You play football? You and Brian?"

"*Brian* plays football. He's this super-athlete. I mean, he's probably going to be in the NFL. Or NBA. He's excellent at everything. He wants me to play, too, but then, I'm not really that good. They stick me on the O-Line and I basically get crushed." The thought of dressing down to attend even one football practice filled him with such weariness that his skeleton wanted to fold up like a lawn chair.

The skiff drifted dockside. Mike threw Scott a line and Scott wound it around a cleat while Mike helped the Portland customer out of the boat. The man, big and bearded and grinning broadly, had his finger hooked in the gills of a glistening trout.

"Finally got this beauty into the boat, Scott!" Mike's voice was high with excitement. "Ms. MacKinnon. Good morning. Scott, take Kyle inside and let's get this fish weighed and measured. We'll get a picture, too. No, leave the tackle. I'll get that later."

Scott admired the trout as they moved toward the gangway. He heard Jess's voice behind them, asking Mike about the fishing records.

"Those records are confidential," said Mike, and Scott looked back. Mike jogged after them, leaving Jess at the end of the dock, her puzzled face rinsed in sunlight.

30.

At Still Lake High School, Scott found Brian doing push-ups on the painted concrete floor of the weight room. "Hey," said Scott from the doorway.

"Hey." Brian sprang to his feet. "How're you feeling?"

"I feel tired just watching you. God, it stinks in here." Scott made a face. Brian punched him in the arm. "Ow," Scott said, but it didn't hurt.

"Come on. Let's see how much you can bench after a summer of fishing." Brian walked over to the bench press and stood behind the bar in the spotter's position.

"Coach said we should start with squats," Scott said, but he stretched out on the bench and spread his hands on the bar, which was loaded with forty-five-pound plates.

"I hate squats. Anyways, I did them yesterday."

"Whatever." Scott lifted the barbell off its rack and lowered it to his chest, then pushed it back up with a grunt. "That feels very heavy." He managed eight repetitions and racked the weight. He and Brian switched places. Brian did twenty reps. Scott rolled his eyes. His younger brother was so superior in all things athletic it hardly even rankled anymore. He added a twenty-five-pound plate to each side of the bar. Brian slid off the bench. They heard laughter and two loud voices from the locker room getting closer.

"Oh, great," said Brian. "MacKenzie and Letterman."

"Hi, guys." Two seniors swaggered in. Nate Letterman wore a knit cap and a black muscle shirt. His arms were bigger than Scott's neck. Randy MacKenzie followed, pale and wiry with stiff black hair sprouting from the collar of his T-shirt. The two of them crossed to the dumbbell rack on the opposite wall.

Brian and Scott traded off at the bench press. They chatted about the Outfitters and the fishing. Fishing was dicey; merchandise sales were down; Scott knew Mike worried about the future. Shouting erupted from across the room. "Two more! Two more! Yes! Come on, come on, come on, *come on!*" Randy was curling forty-pound dumbbells, Nate crouched in front of him shouting encouragement.

"Oh, yeah!" said Randy loudly, dropping the weights into the rack. He flexed one arm, then the other. "Curls for the girls! Right, guys?" He looked over at Brian and Scott with a tight smile.

Brian shrugged. "Sure, Randy. Whatever." He slid under the bar and placed his hands wide.

"Or maybe not," Nate sneered.

Brian lifted his head. "What?"

"I don't think your big brother is interested in doing curls for the girls. Are you, Cleveland?"

"My name is Scott. And you're interrupting my workout." Scott stood behind the bar and tightened his fist around it. Brian sat up.

"You have a *point*, Loserman, or is it just your usual bullshit?"

"Yeah, here's my point: Your brother's a fairy, Kittridge."

Brian stood and took a step toward Nate. "Take it back, Nate. You've got one chance to do it."

"Let's just leave, Bri," Scott said. "He's not worth the trouble."

"Take it back, Loserman." Brian took another step.

"Bring it, big guy," Nate sang. "Your brother's queer!"

Brian charged, surprising Nate with a head-butt and landing a flurry of punches as the larger boy staggered backwards. Scott trudged into the fray, pulling Randy off his brother's back and punching him in the eye. Randy went down hard and stayed on the floor, clutching his face. Brian had lost his early advantage and was bleeding from his nose and lip as Nate pummeled him. Scott shoved Nate as hard as he could and moved behind him, trying to wrestle him into a headlock. Brian bent over, panting. When he straightened, he looked as furious as Scott had ever seen him. Brian sent a left jab into Nate's face, followed it with a right hook and an elbow to the chest. Scott used the momentum to hurl Nate to the floor. "Let's go!" he yelled, and they ran together out of the weight room, through the locker room, and out the double doors of the school with a crash of metal on metal. They sprinted side by side down Fourth Street.

"The cave!" shouted Brian as they reached the trailhead. They ran to the old sawmill, jumped across North Creek, and slid down to the edge of the lake. The "cave" was a hollow on the steep bank beside the waterfall. They threw themselves onto the sand, gasping for air. "Were they following us?" Brian stood and looked past the falling water.

"I don't think so." Scott's lungs burned. He grinned. "You were amazing, Little Brother. Let's always be on the same side, okay?"

"Okay, you got it." Brian was grinning, too. "Did you hear Loserman hit the floor? Splat! There's probably a crack in the concrete."

"No doubt." Scott found a seat on a boulder. He sat forward, elbows on his knees. The green rush of the waterfall roiled the lake, by the white boulders with their rusty watermarks. "The thing is . . ."

"What?"

"Well, MacKenzie and Letterman. They really do think I'm gay." Scott's head vibrated, and he felt like the waterfall was churning at the bottom of his gut.

"Forget it, Scott. They're jerks."

"But—"

"That's just what you say to a guy. When you're a stupid jerk."

"I know. But here's the thing." He took a breath. Held it. Was he going to say it?

"What? What thing?" Brian wiped the blood under his nose, smearing it across his cheek.

"I am."

"What?"

"I am. You know. Gay."

Brian laughed and punched him on the arm. "No, you're not!" Scott watched his brother's face as the smile waned. Brian's upper lip was starting to puff up. "That's not all that funny, Scott."

"I'm not trying to be funny. I'm serious."

"You're *gay*?" whispered Brian. "Are you sure?"

Scott dropped this eyes to the pebbly ground between the boulders. "Yeah, I'm sure."

"You've never really had a girlfriend."

"I'm *sure.*"

"Okay, okay." Brian stared at him for a long moment. Then he jumped up and scrambled to the top of the bank.

"Brian! Hey!" He squeezed his head with both hands and looked down at the mosaic of pebbles until they blurred and swam. Brian was *always* on his side. Scott's brain held a crystallized memory: the two of them at six and seven years old, in the meadow by the creek. Their father was screaming. Scott sobbed but Brian stepped right up to Cleve, squaring his tiny defiant shoulders.

Scott hauled himself to the top of the bank. On the other side of the creek, Brian reached into the stones of the sawmill's foundation and lifted out the peavey pole from the museum. He walked onto the bulwark that separated the shore from the old wharf where they used to boom logs for the mill. He used the spike end of the pole to tap the rotten planks, testing them before stepping off the stone. Scott jumped the creek. "What are you doing?" he called. "Where are you going?" Tapping and stepping, Brian made his way to the wharf's edge. The lake was choppy, steel gray. Brian tapped another plank and the pole broke through, spitting splinters into the water.

He looked back at Scott, standing on the bulwark. "Come on, then," he called. There was something in his voice—a challenge. Maybe this was some crazy, stupid, macho game. Scott stepped down. The wood creaked and snapped as he put his weight on it. He slid his foot to the left and eased himself onto the first plank. Brian sat and swung his feet over the water. He leaned back on his hands to watch.

Scott took another tentative step. He tried to remember where Brian had stepped with the pole. The wharf was a good forty feet out over the water. Halfway to the edge, the wood felt solid and Scott grew bolder. "I've got this," he muttered. Then a plank cracked like a bone and crumbled under his foot. His sneaker broke through and he pitched forward onto his hands and knees with a cry. He crawled the last fifteen feet to his brother, who turned away as though disappointed.

Scott swung his legs over the edge to sit beside Brian, the peavey pole between them. He picked it up and ran his hand down the handle, feeling splinters in his palm from his fall. "Mom's been looking for this," he said casually, as if they were sitting down to breakfast at home instead of five feet over Still Lake on a crumbling, ancient wharf. As though he'd never spoken words to break the spell of brotherhood and masculinity.

"I'll take it back. I like to sit out here sometimes."

Scott set the pole down.

Brian glanced at him. "Does she know? Mom?"

"No." Scott inspected his palms, pierced with splinters. "I'm still your brother." He pictured six-year-old Brian in the meadow, his shoulder blades, shielding him from Cleveland Kittridge.

"Well, Goddammit, Scott. How can you be gay?"

"I don't know. I just am."

"How do you know? *When* did you know? Why didn't you tell me?"

Scott laughed, a hard, bitter sound. "Which question do you want me to answer?" They watched a red canoe slither across the choppy water from the Outfitters dock. "Remember Roxanne in seventh grade?"

"Foxy Roxy? She was my first girlfriend."

"Is that when you knew you were straight?"

"What kind of question is that? I've always been straight." Brian kicked his feet. "I don't even want to ask this, but—" He poked his puffy lip. "Is there someone? Someone you—"

The words escaped before he could think it through. "Jonathan Monticola."

"Oh, Geez, Scott!" Brian flopped backwards onto the planks. "Jonathan's not gay."

"I know. It's been a barrier in our relationship."

Brian laughed. "Jonathan Monticola. That's funny."

"It's not funny! Not to me."

"Don't take everything so *personally*." He sat up, looked at Scott, then away, across the water. "Please tell me you haven't said anything to Jonathan."

"No." He fixed his gaze on Brian's profile, the hard line of his jaw. Brian wouldn't turn, wouldn't look at him. Scott's eyes burned. He lowered his head and blinked. He and Brian could always talk about anything. Why did this have to be different? "But I wrote this letter." He shifted to the side and pulled the paper from his back pocket, held it out. "Tell me what you think, okay?"

Finally, Brian looked at him, narrowed his eyes. He took the letter and unfolded it, lips moving soundlessly as he read. "Jesus, Scott."

"You think I should give it to him?"

"God. No. Scott, you cannot give this to Jonathan. Promise me you won't do it."

"Why not?"

Brian held the page over the water. "I should throw this in the lake, right now."

Scott grabbed for it. "I stayed up all night writing that!"

The page hung suspended. "Promise me."

"Okay, okay. I promise. Give it back." He snatched the letter and folded it along its well-worn creases, tucked it into the safety of his pocket.

"Okay, I'll explain it to you. One. Straight or gay, doesn't matter. You can't go around confessing your true feelings to people who have zero interest in you. Two. Basically we won that fight. So Loserman and MacKenzie are embarrassed. That means they'll either keep quiet and hope we don't talk about it, or they'll spread it all around school that you're gay. I put my money on number two."

"I don't care. Let them. Anyways, there's nothing I can do about it." Scott folded his arms across his stomach, which was churning again.

"Yes, there is. And you do care. If you don't care about yourself, think about me. Maybe I don't feel like getting teased for having a brother who's a—who's gay." Brian jumped up and grabbed the peavey pole, and for a crazy second Scott thought he was going to hit him with it. "You're hopeless! You always think you're in a badminton match and then—Pow!—you get tackled." Brian thumped the pole onto the dock, snapping a plank in two.

Scott scrambled back. "Watch it!" His throat was closing. He couldn't quite swallow.

Brian turned and began tapping their path back to shore. "Let's get out of here."

Scott stepped where Brian stepped. They tapped back to the bulwark, never speaking. Brian slid the peavey pole into the foundation. Scott wanted to say something, but what? Brian jumped onto the stones and walked the foundation to its corner, then leapt down to the trail. Not once did he look back. Scott kept him in sight until the forest closed behind him.

31.

Jess took Moses to Keeler's Counter for a late breakfast and then sent him on his way home. She promised to keep a close eye on Mayor

Sammy Branch. Then she returned to Still Lake Outfitters. Inside, she found Mike Branch collecting checks from beneath the cash drawer, telephone trapped between his shoulder and ear. There was no one else in the store. He saw her and lifted his eyebrows, then he hung up the phone, bundled a stack of checks with a rubber band, and slapped them down beside the register.

"What can I do for you, Ms. MacKinnon?" he asked, scratching his goatee. He did not smile.

Jess stepped up to the counter. "I'd like to talk about the kokanee."

"Kokanee? There haven't been any kokanee in the lake for a long time."

"How long? Do you know what happened to them?" She spoke softly, as though they were sharing a secret. But Mike's face closed.

He shook his head. "Afraid not."

He was lying. Jess's hands tightened into fists. She rested them on the countertop and forced her fingers apart. "Aren't you interested in recovering the fish population?" She kept her eyes on her hands, willed them to relax, willed her voice to stay calm.

"I'm wondering why you're here, frankly, after what happened to your predecessor."

She looked up. An edge had crept into his voice. "He wasn't exactly my predecessor," she said.

"No? Well, that's a good thing. He behaved like an ass. Puffing himself up, throwing his weight around, talking about how he'd blow open this terrible scandal, this 'crime against the environment,' as he liked to call it."

Ben had never had much tact. Nor could he be bothered to think through the consequences before he opened his mouth. This wasn't the first time she'd paid the price for *that*.

32

Ben showed up at the flat on a January evening after Moses was born. Jess was happy to see him—he'd been back in Oregon over winter break—so she didn't notice at first how ill at ease he was acting. He bounced fussy Moses on his knee and dropped his pacifier, fumbled to pick it up, and knocked over a glass of water.

"What the hell's wrong with you?" Jess said, jumping up to fetch a towel. "Why you got to be so nervous?"

He gave a shrill laugh. To Jess's ear it sounded forced. "How did it go with your folks?" she asked. "Did you talk to them about a car?" Lathrop Homes, the low-rise public housing project where her mother had lived since 1969, was an hour's bus ride from campus. Ben tried to come over every day after his classes, but sometimes, Jess knew, he couldn't face the long, cold wait at the bus stop and the dark trek across town.

Ben nodded. "They said yes. I'll find a used car. They'll pay for it."

"That's great!" Jess wiped up the spilled water, put the glass in the sink. Priscilla hadn't owned a car since her ancient Ford Taurus had laid down and died on the way to work four years before. Jess pictured them buying boxes and boxes of diapers, even a highchair, stuffing everything into the trunk.

"There's something else." Ben's face was so white his freckles stood out like scabs.

"What?" Moses whimpered and scrunched up his face. Jess hoisted him off Ben's knee and gave his bottom a sniff. "What is *wrong* with you? A car's going to make everything so much easier."

Ben put his elbows on his knees and looked down at the floor. "I told them," he whispered.

"What?" Jess asked, but she had heard him.

"I told my parents about Moses. I had to." He scuffed his high-tops on the worn-out carpet. He wouldn't look at her. They had agreed to keep the baby a secret until Ben "figured everything out," as he put it. To Jess, this meant they would get married, find jobs, and move into a place of their own.

Moses wailed. Jess kept her eyes on the top of Ben's head as she backed to the sofa and sat down. She pushed up her T-shirt. Tucked Moses into the bend of her elbow. "Well?" she said when he didn't say anything.

"They're coming here. To visit, to see Moses." He raised his face, drained of color. "To Chicago," he added, as though this were unclear. "They want to help." He tried to smile.

Moses had been more tired than hungry. He stopped sucking and fell asleep. Jess smoothed her shirt down and held him against her chest, where he fit right in between her swollen breasts. She squeezed him too tightly and he woke up, mewed, gave a delicate burp, and fell asleep again. "All right, then," she whispered.

33.

At Still Lake Outfitters, Jess leaned into the counter, staring Mike down. "Crime against the environment," she said. "What do you suppose he meant by that?"

Mike stepped back. "No idea." He picked up the bundle of checks and swatted them once against his palm. "We finished here?" Mike dropped the checks into a bank pouch and zipped it up as though dismissing her.

"Not quite." Jess threw back her shoulders and straightened to her full height, which admittedly only brought her even with his collarbone. She slid her hands off the counter and into her pockets. "I'd like to rent a rowboat, please."

"What for?"

Good. She'd caught him off guard. "I want to take some samples."

"Samples of what?"

"Whatever's there. How much to rent a rowboat for a couple of hours?" Jess tugged her wallet from her pocket.

Mike turned away. "They're not available at the moment. Sorry."

Bullshit, thought Jess, but she managed not to say it aloud. "They're tied up at the dock. Do me one favor, all right? Don't jerk me around."

Mike stared at her. She stared back. She tried to arrange her face into a mild and inoffensive expression. He looked away. Abruptly he strode past her, locked the front door with a key from his pocket, and flipped the sign to "Closed." Jess's muscles tightened, her body on full alert as her brain raced to catch up. What was he doing? A rank of oars stood propped against the wall. He grabbed one. *Jesus H. Christ, he's going to kill me*, said her brain. She backed up, turned to calculate the distance to the door. Which was locked. *Fuck*. Mike grabbed a second oar and faced her. The goatee made him demonic.

"Come on," he said.

"What?" She took another step backward.

"Come on. I'll take you out myself. You can collect all the samples you want, and I'll keep an eye on you. You have equipment?"

Her body went limp. She stumbled and caught herself. "I put it out on the dock already."

"Bold move."

For some reason, she giggled. "Fortune favors the bold," she said, her voice squeaky. She thought he smiled before turning to lead her through the back door.

She was quaking like a jackhammer as she followed him outside to the deck and navigated the gangway to the boat dock. She gathered up her plankton net and clamped it to her chest, where her heart pounded in double-time. He pointed to a seat in the bow of the *Tamkaliks.*

She eased herself into the boat. He tossed aside the mooring line, sat in the stern, and stowed the oars along the gunwales. He switched on a motor and they slid away from the dock.

The seat swiveled. She swiveled away from Mike and closed her eyes against the sweep of the wind. He might still smash an oar into her head and toss her over the side—maybe he had done exactly that to Ben Fletcher. Her heartbeat slowed. She opened her eyes. She would take her chances. The lake shimmered. On all sides of the valley the Wallowa Mountains loomed. *"Tamkaliks,"* she whispered into the wind. *The place where you can see the mountains.*

"Let's stop here," she said when they neared the lake's center. Mike switched off the motor and they drifted. His face had changed. Inside the store, he radiated tension, a thrumming bass line for his near-constant fidgeting. Here on the water he seemed to absorb the stillness of Still Lake until he became placid. He did not look like a murderous maniac. She stretched the net across her knees. "How deep is the lake?" They both leaned over the port rail to peer into the water. The boat tipped.

"At least a hundred feet, up to one-twenty in places."

His voice sounded different, too. His tone had lost its brittle edge; the cadence of his words slowed. She marveled at the transformation. "And you know where the deeper spots are, I suppose?"

"Yes." He looked across the lake while she rummaged in her pack. "You have kids?" he asked. The question made her fingers shake. She fumbled with the equipment, screwing a container onto the net's tapered end.

"No." The expedient answer stung her, then the tug of memory and regret. "How about you?"

"One son, Sam. He's at U.C. Santa Cruz."

Jess held the net above the water's surface and watched its reflection waver. Moses was driving his pickup west on Interstate 84. He'd promised to call her when he got home.

"How does that thing work?" Mike was actually smiling.

"It's called a plankton net, but it can be used to collect samples other than plankton." She let herself settle to the task. Her hands were steady now. She pointed to the white container suspended above the water. "This is a 500-micron bucket, for collecting larger organisms." She ran her fingers up the fabric mesh that tapered down from an aluminum ring. "This is the net that funnels the sample into the bucket." Her fingers traveled above the ring, along a funnel to a smaller ring at the top. "This is called a reduction collar. It helps with the accuracy of the sample and reduces the drag on the net as you pull it up. You have to pull it up fast. I'll show you."

Jess lowered the net, hand over hand, into the water. As the smaller ring reached the lake surface, she nodded to a white rectangle set with an aluminum hook. "That's the release mechanism. See how the line feeds through that hook?" She lowered the rectangle into the water. They watched the net descend. As the line uncoiled, Jess reached a second mechanism, a green plastic square. "And that's the messenger."

"The what? The messenger?" Mike strained forward to see as it passed through Jess's fingers. "What's the message?" He laughed.

"The message is: Stop collecting." She glanced at him, then back to the sinking net. Mike was a riddle. Out here on the water, all his hostility had dropped away.

"So if my collection point is forty meters, at about thirty-five meters I release the messenger and it travels down the line and hits the release mechanism. The line comes out of the hook, the top of the net flops over, and sampling stops. Here we go." She released the messenger and it clattered down the line and into the water, where they both watched it sink toward the bottom. She felt the net topple. She hauled it back up quickly. She was breathing hard as the net cleared. She rinsed it, then pulled it into the boat and unscrewed the bucket. She and Mike peered inside.

"What's in there?" Mike asked. "It looks empty."

"It *is* empty," said Jess. "Let's go about three hundred feet that way and take another sample."

Mike took out the oars and rowed them into position. Jess lowered the net to depth, released the messenger, and pulled it back into the boat. She relished the rhythm of her task, the ingenuity of the device, her little collected fragments of the world. She unscrewed the bucket. Coiled in the bottom was a tiny, white creature, black eyes bristling from the curl of its body. She held it out to show Mike.

"Looks dead," she said. She shook it into a specimen jar.

"What is it?"

"I don't know yet, but I'll find out." She stowed the specimen jar in her pack and swiveled to face him. He pulled on the oars with his strong hands and powerful shoulders, long, even strokes, the blades cutting in and out of the water without a sound, as though all his nervous landward energy had funneled itself into this choreography of rowing. "Do you?" she asked.

"Do I what?"

"Do you know what it is?"

"No idea."

His answer had been too quick. He was lying to her. Again. She decided to let it go. She spun to the front. The prow of the dory cut through the lake's green skin. "The water really is still," she said. "Is that where the name comes from?"

"I don't know who named it. It's been called Still Lake for as long as I've been alive. My grandmother called the lake '*Klip Chuck*,' which means 'deep water.'"

"In Nez Perce?"

"No, in Chinook. Chinook jargon." Mike gazed across the lake in the direction of Old Chuck Creek, but his eyes had traveled even further away. "My mother was German. Sasha Beck. She called it '*Stille*,' with an 'S-H' sound. It sounded gentle when she said it. She said it to me, too. I was always tearing around. She would say to me, 'Michael, *bleib stille*.'"

"What happened to your mother?"

"She died in childbirth. I was twelve."

"I'm sorry."

"It was a long time ago."

34.

Mike Branch swam daily, though in winter his "swims" were thirty-second, heart-clenching plunges that left him gasping. The cold-water plunges began in Old Chuck Creek on the morning after the terrible night Mike's baby brother was born, lived his twenty-minute life, and departed the earth as their mother bled to death in her bed. Mike had not slept; no one had. Jack knelt beside the bed, keening and wailing and holding Sasha's limp hand. Sammy was there. Mike ran out of the house and pelted to the creek, pulling off his shirt and kicking away his shoes as he stumbled down the bank. He took two steps into the freezing water and then threw himself face down into the deepest part of the current.

The water numbed his pain. He stayed numb in the weeks that followed, entrained in a nightmare. If only he could wake himself, then surely his mother would be in the kitchen, frying potatoes in a sizzle of oil. His loss felt deeper than Still Lake, bigger than the Wallowa Mountains. When the worst of it ran through him, in its wake a monstrous anger rose.

Jack Branch was to blame for his mother's death, with his foolish traditional ways, his indifference to modern medicine. When Mike came into the front room early each morning to find Jack in a chair by the window, staring at the creek with tears on his face, the monster reared up and spread its leathery wings and threatened to consume them both. After a year he could not bear the sight of his sorrowful father, so he left Jack all alone in the big house and moved in with his Uncle Sammy. He had an idea that he could go into business for himself. He was good with people (except his father). He wanted to be a fishing guide.

35.

Scott laid his hand on the counter and Sammy bent over it. "The splinters are deep, and the wood is rotten," Sammy announced.

"Maybe he can soak them out." Mike peered over Sammy's shoulder.

Scott pulled away. "I'm fine," he said, but he enjoyed being fussed over. Bertie LaFrance, the Wallowa County sheriff, shoved through the Outfitters front door. He gave Sammy a one-armed hug.

"Is crime penciling out this year, Bertie?" Sammy asked; it was an old joke between them. Scott recited Bertie's response in his head.

"Nope. Crime still don't pay."

"All right. I will stay on the straight and narrow for another year. Can you join us for supper?"

"Not tonight. Another time. Got to get going." He took off his hat and wiped his forehead. "I heard there's another scientist up here, a female."

"That's right," Mike said.

Bertie held the hat in both hands, thick and meaty like the rest of Bertie. Scott felt for the folded piece of notebook paper in his back pocket, but the letter to Jonathan wasn't there; he had changed his pants. What had he done with the letter?

"The kid who drowned—Fletcher. His folks've hired their own investigator," Bertie told them. "Her name's Bishop, Riley Bishop. Has she been up here?"

"She was here on Monday. With the scientist." Mike opened the door and reached into his pocket for the keys, motioning them out. Scott followed Sammy and Bertie outside. The air was cool; fog had drifted in. The maple branches clawed from the mist. A tall man with curly hair stood up from a park bench and ducked behind a tree. Was it Jonathan? Why would he hide? What if Jonathan had gotten hold of the letter somehow? Panic detonated in Scott's brain. That was impossible! Wasn't it?

Bertie planted his hat on his head. "Is the new scientist going to stir things up as bad as the one who drowned?" He left them on the sidewalk and walked to his patrol car.

"Probably," Mike said.

Bertie grunted. He pulled the car door open, waved once, and ducked inside.

"She seems very intelligent." Sammy frowned at Mike.

"I like her," Scott said. "I think she's nice." He pulled his eyes away from the darkness between the maple trees and walked ahead and opened the door to Keeler's Counter. He was tired of all the drama. What had he done with the letter?

They settled at their usual table beside the windows. Fog floated down to the water. Mike cleared his throat. "Scott, you'll be coming to Sammy's birthday party tomorrow, won't you?"

Scott turned his eyes back into the bright restaurant. "Sure."

"Do you intend to bring a date?" Sammy asked.

"Not really." They were both staring at him, faces grave. He burst out laughing. "This is another one of those 'talks,' isn't it?"

"You should not take this lightly, Scott," Sammy said. He put a hand on Scott's arm. "We know you are shy."

"And there's not a thing wrong with that!" Mike added.

"Of course not. However, at times you must take risks. Ask someone on a date, for example."

Scott blushed and looked down at the table. He should tell them. Now Brian knew. Wasn't that enough for one day? It hadn't exactly gone well. He raised his head and started to tell them he would find a date for the party, but the door opened and Jess MacKinnon came in. She charged across the room with her head thrust forward. It was the way she always walked, but today she looked harassed. He waved, and she veered in their direction.

"Oh, great," Mike said under his breath. Mike had gotten his hair cut, his goatee freshly clipped. His voice was clipped, too, and his eyes walled off whenever he saw Jess MacKinnon. It had something to do with the fish.

"Good evening, Jess," Sammy said, smiling.

"Good evening. May I join you?"

"Of course!" Sammy said.

Mike grunted.

Jess sat down. "Does Jack ever join you for dinner? I'd really like to talk to him."

"Not often," Mike said.

"Jack is not particularly sociable," Sammy told her.

Scott wished he could talk to Jess alone. In Portland, right before the flood, gays and lesbians were allowed to get legally married. He had seen it on the news.

"Do you have other brothers and sisters, besides Jack?"

"Three sisters, three brothers, including Jack. I am the youngest. As well as the most attractive." Sammy's smile broadened. "I believe our parents planned on repopulating the tribe single-handedly." His smile faded. "Now only Jack and I are left."

"Were both your parents Nez Perce? You said the other night your mother spoke Chinook jargon."

"Our father was Nez Perce. Our mother was from a tribe near the coast, the Takelma. That tribe is almost extinct. I don't think anyone speaks the language anymore. Even my mother spoke only a little."

"What happened to them?" Scott asked. He smiled to himself as Uncle Sammy straightened and placed his palms on the tabletop—his storytelling posture. He loved to get Sammy talking about old times. Maybe he would walk Jess back to the Lodge after dinner, ask her about the marriages. That would be the same as coming out, wouldn't it?

"The Takelma lived along the Rogue River in Southern Oregon. My mother's father was killed during the Rogue Wars in the 1850s, which is when the white settlers moved in to that area. There was gold in the Rogue River and the Europeans were crazy for it. My mother, who was just a baby, and her mother and a sister got 'relocated' to the Siletz reservation. Her mother and sister both got sick there and died. She was raised by Takelma and Siletz women on the reservation, but she had no blood relatives left."

"I suppose this is part of your research?" Mike said to Jess as they ordered their dinner. Scott asked for a burger. Sammy ordered a bottle of wine, but Jess made a face and asked for a beer instead.

"What was your mother's name?" Jess asked Sammy.

"They called her Mary Riffle. She was smart, and also shrewd. By the time she was twenty she had connected with some white missionaries and traveled all over Oregon and Washington and Idaho with them. She was a nanny to their three small children. She knew Chinook jargon, so she could communicate with the tribes around the Columbia River, and she learned English from the missionaries."

Scott squirmed on the hard wooden chair, his fingers traveling to his back pocket. But of course the letter to Jonathan wasn't there.

Their drinks arrived. Sammy tasted the wine and nodded. "Not as tasty as Birch Stukel's red blend," he told the server. "But it will do nicely." He filled Mike's glass, then his own. "You don't like wine?" he asked Jess.

"Can't stand it." She lifted her beer. "Cheers."

Scott tapped his water against her beer glass. He thought he might have left the letter on his desk at home.

"When did Mary Riffle meet your father?" Jess asked.

"She was twenty-eight. She met Cap Branch on the Nez Perce reservation in Idaho. He was eighteen, a member of the Wallowa band that had lived in this area before 1877."

"Isn't that when the Nez Perce tried to go to Canada and got captured?" Scott asked.

"Exactly so, Scott, but that is not what happened to my father. He was born in 1865, two years after the second treaty with the government was signed. There were two treaties. The 1863 treaty shrank the Nez Perce reservation down to a little piece of land in Idaho, but not all the Nez Perce leaders signed it. The Wallowa band, led by Joseph—that was Chief Joseph's father—did not sign. They went back to the Wallowa Valley. From 1863 on, the Nez Perce were divided into two sides: The bands that accepted the new treaty, and the ones that did not. My father's family was part of the nontreaty band, but my father was raised on the new reservation, by his oldest sister. So in 1877 when the government chased down the Wallowa band, he was in Idaho."

"He didn't have to go to Oklahoma, right?"

"That is correct. He met Mary Riffle and they returned to the Wallowa Valley together."

Scott looked out the window. The mountains and the lake had darkened and fog eased down into the valley. He was almost certain he'd left the letter on his desk. Jess was looking at the mountains, too. His burger arrived; he doused it with ketchup. Mike took a bite of his tuna sandwich and wrapped the rest up in his napkin. Scott knew Mike had no patience for "folklore," as he called it. But to Scott, it gave Still Lake a place in history, a place to belong.

Mike excused himself, but Sammy laid a hand on his arm. "I hate to bring this up again," Sammy said.

"What now?" Mike looked around the room, as though scanning for exits. Scott hoped they weren't going to talk about his dating habits again, not in front of Jess.

"I believe you promised to fix my kitchen sink. It does not drain anymore. Not at all."

"Yes, all right. I'll look at it tomorrow." Mike stood up. "But my pipe wrench is at the Outfitters, in the storeroom. Could you fetch it over to your place, please?" Mike hurried to the door without waiting for an answer.

"Do you know the story of Chief Joseph?" Scott asked Jess. The front door closed behind Mike and he felt the charged atmosphere settle.

"Not as well as you, I'm sure." She smiled, and he noticed her blue eyes again. "Do you know Chief Joseph's famous speech?"

In fact, he had memorized it in third grade. He finished chewing and recited the last line, trying to make his voice as deep as Uncle Sammy's: "From where the sun now stands, I will fight no more forever."

Jess said in a quiet voice, "Sometimes I would like to stop fighting." The way she said it made Scott shiver inside, as though her words were a hub in the center of everything. She looked out the window; she seemed to be speaking more to herself than to them.

"What do you fight about?" Sammy asked. He was staring at Jess, mesmerized.

Her attention wandered back into the room and she smiled at them. "Well, your nephew's fishing records, for one thing. I would like to have copies, but he tells me they're confidential."

Scott bent over his plate, hiding his smile as Uncle Sammy promised to find out where the records were kept, then continued to stare at Jess dreamily, his head propped on one hand. He had never gotten married but he was famous for always falling in love. Outside, a skateboard squealed on concrete. "Watch out!" Mike's voice.

The front door opened. Cold air swept in and with it, Jonathan Monticola. Scott's breath caught and his eyes followed Jonathan across the dining room. He wore a green flannel shirt, untucked, and blue jeans. His hands hung loosely at his sides, the skateboard suspended from his left hand, the sleeves of the shirt too short for his arms. He bounced to the table. "Dad wants you to stop by the Millworks," he said to Sammy.

"Why is that?"

"We made you a porch chair for a birthday present. He wants you to sit in it to see if it feels comfortable."

Sammy chuckled and stood. "I see. You need to measure my ample backside." He turned to Jess. "Would you like to come along to the Monticola Millworks?"

"I'd love to."

Outside the restaurant, Jonathan offered his skateboard to Jess, who hesitated. But then she took the board, rolled it down the sidewalk, and jumped on. She picked up speed, caught some air off the curb, and did a one-eighty. She ground to a stop in the middle of Main Street and landed a kick flip. Sammy applauded. Jonathan hooked his hand on Scott's shoulder and they fell into step together.

"Have you decided to play football this year?" he asked.

"No. I'm retiring." The physical contact made his pulse race. He dug his fingers into his back pocket but of course the letter was not there. What if it had been? The thought of giving it to Jonathan made him breathless.

"Brian still bugging you to play?" Jonathan's hand dropped away.

"No." Scott remembered Brian's retreating back at the sawmill that morning. "He doesn't care."

"Where's your mom tonight? At home?"

"Yeah." Scott glanced at Jonathan's face but his eyes were shielded by a curtain of curly hair. The fog shrouded the streetlamps along Main Street. He felt a rush of something for Jonathan—sympathy or kinship or maybe it really was love—and reached out to touch his arm. But Jonathan hurried ahead to catch up with Sammy, and Scott tucked the hand into his jacket pocket.

36.

At Monticola Millworks, Jess edged away from the others to study the wall of sketches outside Paul's office. She found the drawing dated March 1902, the pair of platforms and ladders. She squinted and leaned closer. There was another scrawl above the date that could have been the word "install," then three capital letters, "NIT." Nit? No, the middle letter was an "L." NLT: "No later than." The mysterious platforms were due to be installed in March 1902—but where? Maybe they had something to do with the log drives. She stepped closer until her nose almost touched the paper. Now she saw "Ipsootchuck" in tiny print underneath "CAP BRANCH." Thanks to Sammy's storytelling, she knew that the Ipsootchuck was a well on the Branch property and that Cap Branch was Sammy and Jack's father. Maybe this platform still existed at the Branch place, where Jack lived. Somehow it seemed important; she couldn't say why. She had to speak with Jack, but time was running out. The meeting with the Consortium was set for ten o'clock on Friday morning. She had to leave town tomorrow to be back in time.

Scott asked what she was looking at. He didn't recognize the drawing, but he nodded when she asked about Jack Branch. "In September and October, you'll find him at the mouth of the creek every morning," he said. "Early." He didn't think Jack would mind her company.

Jess delivered a general farewell and hurried out the front door. "Did you call your mother?" Paul shouted after her.

Jess stopped at Keeler's Counter. The restaurant looked empty and inviting, and she didn't think she could sleep until her brain stopped humming. The sketch on the wall next to Paul Monticola's office. Jack Branch at the creek. The Big Sink. Chief Joseph. Moses, who was home by now but had forgotten to call. She claimed a stool at the redwood counter. Maybe she would have something to drink.

"Mind if I join you?" said a man's voice.

It was Cleve Kittridge, who the day before had called her a "brainless bitch." Jess wavered. She could tell him off and then stomp out of the restaurant, or she could cut right to the stomping out part. She was about to spring off the stool, but she remembered that Scott Kittridge was his son, and that kept her seated long enough for Cleve Kittridge to slide onto the neighboring stool. He folded his hands in his lap and cocked his head to regard her with an expression that looked like embarrassment. "I was rude to you yesterday. I want to apologize." The ends of his moustache drooped morosely.

Jess was about to tell him off anyway when a thin woman with tired eyes walked up from the kitchen, wiping her hands. Cleve smiled, contrite. "Tell you what," he said. "Let me buy you a drink." He nodded to the woman. "Evening, A.D."

A.D. tucked the towel into the belt of her apron. "Evening, Cleve. Ma'am."

"What's your drink?" Cleve asked Jess.

She ordered a beer.

"Beer for me, too," said Cleve. "And a shot of Maker's Mark."

A.D.'s lips made a seam. "You sure about that, Cleve?"

Jess watched defiance rise into Cleve's features. When he spoke, his voice dropped into a deeper register. "Just the one. Don't hassle me, all right?"

When A.D. left to pull their beers, he leaned in closer. "What set me off was, you asked about my job." He looked down at the counter, between his hands. "Truth is, I got riffed back to fifty percent in July. Didn't see it coming."

Maybe they only needed a part-time asshole, Jess thought, but their drinks arrived and she hoisted her beer. He tapped it with the rim of his shot glass. Her mother was a whiskey drinker. The smell reminded her of their flat, of Chicago. "All is forgiven," she said. What a diplomat she was.

"Good." He sipped the whiskey. It softened his eyes and his voice. "Twenty years working for the state! They hired some kid right out of college, no experience."

"I'm sorry to hear that." She watched as Cleve Kittridge tossed back the whiskey, saw the tender tremor in his lower lip before the rim of the glass made contact.

"Me, I never went to college. I ain't fancy. But I work hard." He picked up his sweating beer and gulped it. "Don't know what to do," he whispered, looking into the glass. "Haven't even told my wife." He scrubbed the back of his hand across his mouth. "A.D.!" He held up one finger.

A.D. slid another shot of whiskey across the counter. "That's it, Cleve, and I'm cutting you off. I know you're fixing to drive home."

Jess didn't want to linger for the second round. She drained her beer glass. "I've got to get going," she said.

Kittridge threw back the shot, chugged the beer, and slid off his stool. "I talked to Karl Luder. He's back from Pendleton, says you should stop by the farm as early as you want tomorrow. Says he'll be up by five-thirty at the latest." He tucked a bill under his glass. "So. No hard feelings?" Now his voice was jubilant.

"No hard feelings," Jess said.

37.

"I ain't high class," said Priscilla to the Fletchers. They sat in the front room of the flat. "But I got a good heart, and so does my daughter, by golly!" She patted Jess's head on her way to the back bedroom. Jess batted her mother's hand away. She wished Priscilla wouldn't say "ain't" in front of Ben and his parents.

Priscilla came back into the room with the baby, wrapped in a blanket, asleep. "Well, here he is!" she announced to the room in a stage whisper. "Oh, ain't you the star of the show!" She smiled at Moses. Jess looked down at the carpet between her feet. She never thought about her mother's bad teeth—crooked like her own, black patches showing between them, gaps where she'd had a bad one pulled out. Jess's hand shot up to cover her own mouth.

Becky peeled back the blanket, ran a palm over Moses's thin hair, smiled at her husband. "He has your hair," she murmured.

Rex didn't smile back.

38.

The letter to Jonathan was not on his desk. Scott looked under the desk, under the bed, under the pile of dirty clothes he was supposed to put in the laundry. Oh, right: the laundry.

Everyone else was asleep. Scott hurtled down the carpeted stairs to the washing machine, in the mud room at the back of the house. His eyes adjusted to the darkness. The full moon brightened the fog and made an eerie light. His jeans lay spread eagled on top of the overflowing hamper. He felt in one back pocket, then the other. Then he checked the front pockets. No letter. He flung all the clothes onto the concrete floor, swept his fingers across the bottom of the hamper, and replaced the dirty towels and garments, one by one, giving each a shake, expecting any moment to see a folded sheet of notebook paper flutter to the floor.

"What are you doing?"

"Aaah!" Scott leaped back and tumbled into the pile of clothes. He flung his arms out, hit his elbow on the concrete, felt a damp washcloth soak into the back of his pajamas. It was Brian, shirtless and radiant in the moonlight. "Don't sneak up on me like that!"

"Kind of late for laundry, isn't it?" There was an edge in Brian's voice—taunting, hostile.

"The letter I wrote to Jonathan. I can't find it."

"That's a hell of a thing to leave lying around."

"I know." Scott scrambled to his feet. Brian stood with his thumbs tucked in the waistband of his sweatpants. Was he smirking? Scott stepped closer, trying to read his brother's expression. He whispered. "Do *you* know where it is? You didn't take it, did you?"

A shrug from the glowing torso. "Maybe."

This was too much. Scott wanted to scream, but their parents were asleep so he growled instead: "Don't mess with me, and stop being an asshole!" He shoved Brian with both hands, pressed in, shoved again, knocked him down, and threw himself on top, trying to pin him to the floor.

"Get off me!" Brian heaved up and Scott flew backwards, back into the pile of laundry. "Just get off me, you—" Brian sat back on his heels, staring at Scott.

Scott stared back. "You *what?*" he shot back. "*What*, Brian?"

Brian stood, turned, looked back at Scott with his hand on the doorframe. "Nothing. Go to bed. I didn't take your goddamned love letter."

Thursday, September 30, 2004.

39.

She missed the turn to the Luder farm, or she wouldn't have noticed his pickup, stuffed into the forest. She parked the bike. The truck's rear wheels were dug deep into smears of mud at the lip of the pavement: stuck. She scanned the red sunrise between the trees. "Moses!" she called. She walked deeper into the cold red forest and called again.

"Over here!" Moses's voice. She followed it, tripping over brambles.

Her son was sleeping in the forest. He had a tent set up and squatted over a campfire, feeding sticks into its flames. "What the hell, Moses?" She marched up to the fire.

"Got stuck," he said. His face glowed in the firelight. "Had to spend the night."

"That is completely not the point." His hair was mashed flat against his skull on one side, flying away on the other. None of this made sense. "What are you *doing* in Still Lake? Why are you not at home?"

"Calm down," he said, which made her furious. He stood.

She folded her arms. "Start explaining." The air felt icy. She shivered and squeezed her midsection. Between the trees, the red light yellowed.

"I went home. Then I came back." He held up his hand. "No, listen. This is more important than school. I've been following the mayor."

Inside his unzipped tent she saw the crumple of a sleeping bag, a water bottle, a pack. Moses had been sneaking around town and sleeping in the woods. Sudden weariness weighed her down and she looked for someplace to sit. She perched on a log and held her palms to the fire. "Sammy Branch is not a murderer," she said.

He gave her a grim, knowing smile. "You might change your mind when you hear what I saw."

The first sunlight shot through the trees and lit the contours of his face—so like hers, and so different. The red hair he'd gotten from Ben's family. All the Eatons, her mother's family, were small and dark. Her father, Kevin MacKinnon, had dark brown hair, the same color as hers. He'd left before she could remember him. "We wasn't married, not official," Priscilla had told the Fletchers during their visit. Jess had wished, then, that she could vanish and reappear elsewhere, in a more dignified family. And that was months before everything else had happened. She nodded at her son. "I'm listening," she said.

"He went to Still Lake Outfitters. I followed him inside and watched from behind some skis." Moses squinted in the sunlight. He looked feverish with excitement. "I was in disguise."

"Disguise?" Jess shivered again. The fire was going out.

"Just a cap and scarf. Man, I was sweating like crazy in there!" He grinned. "So Mayor Branch goes back into a room that said 'Employees Only' and he comes out with this giant huge wrench and puts it on the counter and wraps it all up in a towel. Then he carries it out of the store and back to his own house." He nodded again, triumphant. "Bold as fuck!" he added when she didn't respond.

The campfire was out. Moses crouched in front of her and put his hands on her shoulders. He shook her, too hard, before he seemed to realize what he was doing. "Aunt Jess, don't you get it? That's the murder weapon! He was hiding it!"

She bent her head and blew out the breath she'd been holding. He had to believe she took him seriously. Her job was to get him home and convince him to stay there. She had planned to speak with Karl Luder and then with Jack Branch. Those talks would have to wait. She raised her eyes, took his hands. She made a sandwich of her hands with his between. He wanted to be Ben's hero. Maybe that's what he'd always wanted. "Okay," she said. "We'll take my motorcycle back to town. We'll make two phone calls. First, we'll call Riley Bishop and tell her to take over." He started to protest and she shook her head. "You've done good work on this but it's time to turn it over to the professionals, Kiddo. Riley will get the police involved. We have to let them do their job." She squeezed his hands and stared him down until he closed his mouth. "Second, we'll get your truck towed out of the ditch so you can get home."

"But what if he gets away? What if he gets rid of the murder weapon?" Moses shifted from foot to foot, lifting his hands from hers so he could wave them around.

"It'll be all right," she said. She steered him toward the tent. "One thing at a time. We'll get your truck out of the mud. Pack up your stuff." She kicked dirt over the ashes of the campfire.

"Put this on." She handed him her helmet. He held it over his rusty, wild hair. It was too small. He handed it back. "Try it again," she said. "It might feel tight at first." She pushed the helmet back at him.

"It's too small, Aunt Jess." He shook his hair out, swept it out of his eyes, laughed. "That thing is not going on my head. Not unless I cut off my ears. You wear it."

She couldn't let herself wear the helmet if Moses didn't have one. She tossed it onto the front seat of his pickup on top of his camping gear. "We'll just make sure we don't crash, how about that?" She threw her leg over the bike and laughed, but she felt naked without the helmet.

40.

Her mother's ex-boyfriend, Ernie, had given Jess her first motorcycle when she left Chicago in 1987. "I ain't got enough to pay for this," she told him. "Used it all up on that lawyer." She'd been helping in his motorcycle shop all summer, the summer after Moses was born.

"I know," he said. "It's a birthday present. Go ahead and try it out."

"Nice try, Ern. My birthday's in December." But she threw her leg over the bike and took a few turns around the parking lot.

"Like it? Put this on." He thrust a helmet at her, shook it for emphasis. "Every time, okay? You wear this. Promise me. You got a good brain in that head, girl. Don't splatter it across the road."

41.

The curvy canyon road was a challenge with Moses on the back of the bike. "Hold on tight and move *with* me!" she shouted when he shifted his weight and almost sent them toppling. She shifted down and took it slow.

They were almost back to the caved-in curve above the Big Sink when she heard someone behind them. She eased to the broken lip of the road to let them pass, glanced in her handlebar mirror. A pickup's silver grill filled the mirror, bearing down. She had time to scream "No!" before it knocked into them and the bike went down and slid. The frame squealed across the asphalt, shooting sparks. "Jump!" she screamed to Moses, but she couldn't get her own leg free. She and the bike skidded into one of the stanchions. The truck tore past, a flash of white and a smear of orange. The stanchion uprooted from its moorings and she flew into the canyon.

She kicked away from the bike. Slammed into a tree trunk and scraped down its bark to the ground. She heard the bike crash into rocks, then a splash. The sounds careened around the canyon and her breath rasped in her ears. Where was Moses? She lifted her head from the dirt and tried to look around. Her body was pinned against the uphill side of a fir tree, the only thing that had kept her from plummeting into the Big Sink.

"Moses!" That hurt. It hurt to breathe. She tried to move. That hurt, too. She clenched her teeth and wriggled her way to a sitting position. Craned her head around the tree to look down into the canyon, to the scour pool at the base of the waterfall. No sign of Moses. "Moses!" she screamed again. She pushed herself around the tree, scrabbled for a foothold. She held her breath against the pain that knifed through her.

She collapsed on a rock, clutching her side. Her breath was shallow and there was grit in her mouth. Down in the Big Sink, something splashed. Moses. She yelled his name again, then clenched her gritty teeth and held her breath and slid to the next rock. The granite blocks made a staircase down to the water. He couldn't hear her over the waterfall, she knew that. But she couldn't stop calling his name. Her voice echoed around the canyon. Between the rocks, vine maples grabbed out at every angle, and ferns, and shrubs. She clutched at them and slid to the next block and then the next.

Moses made it to the edge of the pool. He was not drowning. She slid to the next rock. Forty feet below, Moses dragged himself out of the water and sat hunched, facing away. "Moses!" she called. "Are you hurt?" But he didn't move. She half-fell down to the next block of granite. Called to him again.

By the time she reached the water, she was shaking and her legs wouldn't hold her up. She thrashed down into the moss beside Moses, who shot up like a rocket when she touched him. He was soaked, shivering. She got her jacket off and dropped it around his shoulders.

She had to shout over the roar of the waterfall. "You fell into the pool?" He nodded. "Are you hurt?" He stared at her. "Moses!"

"I don't know." His voice was high and thin.

She rolled onto her hands and knees, waited out the pain and lurched to her feet. She ran her fingers over his scalp. No obvious head injury at least. She gave him her hand. "Try standing up." He got to his feet and swayed. She put her arm around his waist. She looked up at the edge of the road. *What the hell?* Whoever was driving that truck had hit them on purpose.

The bank was too steep. They would pick their way down the canyon and find help. "We've got to follow the creek," she shouted. They took a step together. Rested. Then another. Twenty yards down the canyon, she spotted her bike on the rocks of the far shore, mangled.

42.

Further downstream, the creek narrowed and the walking got easier. Moses was glassy-eyed and slack-faced. Jess kept her arm around him, shouted questions into his ear until the pain in her ribs took away her voice. *How do you feel? Where does it hurt? Are you okay?* He answered in grunts, when he answered at all.

Fifty yards above Still Lake, the creek left the forest to fan onto a cobblestone delta, where sedges and rushes gave way to open water. Jess and Moses stumbled over the cobbles toward a solitary figure standing near the lake's shore. Jess called and he hurried toward them.

Moses slipped from her arm and crumpled onto the stones as Jack reached them. "I'll get help," Jack said and he ran surefooted across the delta.

135

An ambulance came. Moses breathed in shallow, open-mouthed gasps and wouldn't open his eyes. The medics loaded him into the ambulance and told Jess he would be all right. They handed her a blanket. She sat down hard on the rocks beside the road and began to cry. Jack patted her shoulder. "I'm sorry," she said. She covered her face. *He'll be all right*, she told herself, reciting it inside her head. *All right, all right, all right*. When the tears passed, she looked up. Jack's face was as brown and crinkled as old leather but he wore a small smile. From the open ambulance, the medics spoke in low tones. Moses was hypothermic. They were stripping off his wet clothes and piling him with blankets. "Someone ran us off the road," she told Jack.

They sat on the rocks in silence. From the corner of her eye, she saw Jack watching her, holding his knees to his chest, his body compact against the gray stones, so still he could have been a stone himself. She had never met her own grandfather. Had he been small, like her? Like Jack? He might have had a kind smile. Lively eyes. "What brought you to the creek so early?" she asked, but it wasn't early anymore. The sun hung high over the mountains. She looked at her watch. The face was cracked, the hands frozen at seven-twenty-two—the moment she'd sailed into the tree.

"I watch the creek where the fish used to swim up. Your hand is bleeding." Sure enough, her left fist spattered blood onto the stones. She opened her palm and found a gash. Jack gave her a piece of gauze from the medical kit the paramedics had left on the ground.

She pressed the gauze against the cut. The pressure steadied her, or maybe it was having a task to focus on. Apply pressure. Staunch the flow. "Who would do that?" she said. "They tried to kill us!" Jack said nothing, but his lips tightened. She supposed the answer was obvious: Someone had killed Ben. Now that someone wanted to kill her. And maybe Moses, too.

"Could it have been an accident?" Jack asked.

"Maybe. I don't think so." Could it? A driver barreling down the road, taking the curves too wide, not paying attention? Could it have been Cleve Kittridge, already drunk at seven in the morning?

"How does your hand feel?"

"I'm fine," she said, which was not the exact truth. If she kept very still, the pain faded to a low throbbing. She drew the blanket tighter while she studied his profile, his eyes that looked out across the water. She could see in his lips a resemblance to Mike. "You miss the fish. That's why you wait by the creek."

He bent his head.

"We're ready to go, Ma'am," said one of the medics, the sandy-haired one with sideburns and blue eyes. He helped her up. Jack followed them to the back of the ambulance. The medic with black hair and glasses was adjusting the IV that dripped into Moses's arm.

She climbed inside. Moses opened his eyes and smiled at her. She bit her lip to hold back more tears. "How're you feeling?" she asked him.

"He'll be just fine, Ma'am," said the dark-haired medic. He glanced up at her, then looked more closely. "Are you his mother?" She stared at him and gathered the blanket together at her throat. Her mouth moved but no sound came out.

"She's my aunt," Moses said in a croak. The sandy-haired medic took her elbow and made her sit down. He jumped to the ground and started to swing the doors shut, but Jack stepped into their path.

"About the fish," Jack said.

"Yes?"

"They've seen a lot of trouble in the last hundred years."

"Are they gone? The kokanee. Are they extinct?" She started to stand but the dark-haired medic pushed her back onto the bench and tightened a seatbelt around her hips, trapping her arms in the blanket. She pulled them free and gasped with pain.

"We need to get you to the hospital," the medic said. His partner tried to nudge Jack out of the way, but Jack might as well have been a block of granite cemented to the ground.

"Jack. Are they gone?"

"They've seen a lot of trouble," he repeated. "No surprise if they're hiding." He stepped back.

"What do you mean, 'hiding'?" The doors slammed shut.

43.

Sammy Branch buttoned his shirt to the neck and swung open his closet door, where thirty-eight bolo ties hung, each on its own brass hook. The tiger's eye and the jasper were his favorites, but the jade would look good with the green stripe in his shirt. He unhooked the tiger's eye anyway and looped it around his neck. His birthday party was at seven o'clock at Mike's place, which he shared with his second wife, Race Stukel. He supposed Race was his niece-in-law. In any event he could count on at least one more tie, probably three. This was inevitable, like the birthday itself. No use to tell folks that he already had plenty of ties, and plenty of everything else, too.

His nephew's voice called from the kitchen. "I'm here! Where's my pipe wrench?"

Sammy trudged downstairs to find Mike staring into the cupboard below the sink. The sink held an inch of scummy water and a rime of baking soda. He lifted a flap of the bath towel on the counter to expose the wrench, which was filthy and had probably stained his towel. Mike found a bucket, shoved himself half inside the cupboard, and began wrestling with the pipe.

"Thank you, Mike," said Sammy.

138

Mike grunted. "Well, happy birthday." He braced his foot against the baseboard and pulled at the wrench with both hands. "This thing is really stuck."

Sammy set a jug of orange juice on the counter. "Would you like some orange juice?"

"No, thanks." Mike hauled on the pipe wrench, then flew backwards, out of the cupboard. "Ow!"

"Are you all right?"

"I'm fine." Mike rubbed his knee. "The new fish biologist is gone, finally. I took her out on the lake. I was helpful and polite. So you can stop harassing me."

Sammy sat down at the kitchen table and watched Mike work. "I wish I were sixty years younger." He cupped his cheek in his palm, smiling. When he'd delivered the file yesterday, he had noticed the fresh smell of her hair, like wind off the water. She was smart, too. Well-spoken, a little brassy. These were all qualities he appreciated in a woman. It was not possible to fall for someone of thirty-three, but it was *almost* possible. For someone so young, though, she seemed tightly wound, and a little sad. Sammy wondered what she was sad about.

"I thought being a bachelor was kind of a religion with you, Uncle." Mike shifted onto his knees.

"I suppose it is like any other religion. I practice it because I cannot think of an alternative."

Mike laughed. He pulled the P-trap free. Gray, greasy water cascaded into the bucket; Sammy could smell its stench from the table. He wrinkled his nose. The insides of pipes and the undersides of sinks should, in Sammy's opinion, remain hidden. Mike angled the P-trap toward the light and peered inside. "You can't pour grease down the drain and expect it to keep draining." Mike stood and shook the P-trap over the sink. He took a butter knife from the counter and poked inside.

"I did not pour grease down the sink!" Sammy thumped his juice glass onto the table. He joined Mike at the sink as a mass of greasy sludge fell out of the pipe and plopped onto the porcelain like evidence of foul play. "That is disgusting," Sammy said, staring at it.

Mike wagged his finger. "No more grease down the sink." He smeared something white over the pipe threads.

Sammy sat down at the table again. "Did you tell Jess about the opossum shrimp?"

Mike pushed the P-trap into place and began tightening it down. "No. But she found one in the lake. She'll figure it out soon enough."

"Yes, she will. She's very smart." Sammy cupped his cheek again and propped his elbow on the table. "Did you give her the catch records?"

"No."

"Why not? Maybe she can bring the fish back."

"There are no more kokanee. Nothing to bring back." Mike turned on the faucet and peered under the sink.

"It was not your fault."

"Mm-hmm." Mike turned off the water.

"It never was your fault." More than anyone, Sammy knew Mike's shame, how it sat lumped across his shoulders like a forty-pound bag of chicken feed, no place to set it down.

"Your sink is fixed."

"Thank you."

"I've got to go. I'll see you tonight."

Sammy lifted his hand and let it fall.

44.

Riley parked at the entrance of the Earl J. Grayson Medical Center and waited for the tinted glass doors to spit out Jess MacKinnon. MacKinnon had been discharged with two broken ribs, a laceration but no stitches, and contusions. She wanted a ride back to Still Lake to get her motorcycle hauled out of the canyon—as though it would be worth the effort. Riley could tell from their phone conversation that MacKinnon held on to a desperate fantasy that her bike had survived its plummet onto the rocks, possibly carried by angels. Riley knew what they'd find—a pile of crumpled steel—but she needed an excuse to be elsewhere when the Fletchers arrived, and anyway there was Moses's truck to pull out of the ditch.

Here was MacKinnon now, being pushed out the entrance in a wheelchair. Riley shoved the passenger door open and MacKinnon clambered inside, holding a white paper bag that Riley hoped contained some potent pain medication, because MacKinnon grimaced as she twisted to latch her seatbelt. Her left hand was bandaged. The car door slammed shut, trapping the smell of the hospital inside. MacKinnon was saturated with it. Riley rolled down her window.

Hospitals all smelled the same, a nasty stench, sickness and death. Like frogs in formaldehyde, rat poison, embalming fluid, and roadkill roasting in the sunlight. Riley avoided them.

"You talked to Rex and Becky?" MacKinnon asked.

"I talked to Rex," Riley answered. "He's angry."

"At Moses?"

"Yes, but mostly at me. And you." Riley stuck her elbow out the window and leaned into the cold breeze. The stink was dissipating as they picked up speed on the highway into the mountains.

"So they know I was with him."

Underneath the stench of hospital, Riley caught the bite of citrus that was Jess MacKinnon's smell—that questing, sharp as a searchlight. What was the woman searching for? People yearned for love or for power, in Riley's experience. Usually one or the other. It wasn't power for Jess MacKinnon, she speculated—though MacKinnon wanted to be taken seriously and to appear invincible. "Of course," she said. "Otherwise it might be difficult to explain how he flew into the canyon on the back of a motorcycle."

"I suppose so." MacKinnon slumped in her seat.

The pickup had already been rescued from the mud when they arrived, and the tow truck sat nosed up to the side of the road. The winch on its front bumper whined as it wound up cable. The sheriff waved them around the operation, but Riley pulled over and got out of the car.

"Hey, Bertie!" she called. "Is that the motorcycle? I've got its owner right here." He tipped his hat as she approached. "You look good," she said, putting out her hand. "You been working out?"

"No use to butter me up," he grumbled, but she thought he looked pleased.

"Any leads on who ran into them?"

"Stand clear!" yelled the tow truck driver at Jess MacKinnon, who was trying to see into the canyon.

"No leads yet," Bertie said. "We're on it. Top priority." MacKinnon wandered over. "Is one of you planning to drive that pickup over to the hospital?"

"She can do it," Riley said, nodding at Jess.

"What about the motorcycle?" MacKinnon said. "It might be rideable."

Bertie stared at her, then at the ground. "Ma'am, I don't think so," he said. "That bike's pretty well beat up."

The expression on Jess MacKinnon's face—Riley had seen it plenty of times. It was a mixture of terror and eagerness, frequently worn by parents hoping for good news about their offspring.

With a screech, the bike jumped onto the asphalt and the driver switched off the winch. The frame was bent, handlebars twisted, gas tank crumpled. The driver unhooked the cable and Jess fell to her knees beside the bike. She rested her bandaged hand on the seat, then moved it up to the gas tank, tenderly. Riley and Bertie stood back to give her a moment. The tow truck driver joined them. "That her bike?" he asked, and Riley nodded. Jess bent her head. The smell of sorrow traveled across the pavement: empty as open green water. Riley teared up and had to turn away.

45.

Rill Kittridge had staged a laundry boycott. But now she had nothing to wear to Sammy Branch's birthday party. She settled on a business suit, too formal for the occasion but rescued, she hoped, by a lavender T-shirt and a purple scarf. She found Scott, Brian, and Cleve waiting at the dining room table in a fog of uncomfortable silence. Cleve looked tired and tense. Rill guessed he was having trouble at work, not unusual. Scott and Brian avoided eye contact. They were feuding, but she did not know why. Abruptly, she dreaded the evening.

But she waved her arms toward the door. "Let's go!" she said cheerily. They shuffled outside.

Scott blocked her at the top of the steps and she bumped into him. He dangled a set of car keys. "Can you guys take the truck so I can borrow your car?" he asked, low-voiced. "I need to run an errand."

Cleve and Brian stood beside the little green Mazda, waiting. "Let's take the truck!" she called to them.

"Thanks." Scott tucked the keys into his pocket.

She couldn't read his expression. "Wait just a minute," she whispered. "What kind of errand? How long will it take? What about Sammy's party?"

"I'll be back tomorrow."

"Tomorrow!"

"Jess MacKinnon crashed her motorcycle. She needs a ride to Portland. Tonight."

"What?" The fish scientist was a complete stranger. This was deranged. Had the whole family come unhinged? A Kipling line floated into her brain, her father's voice: *If you can keep your head when all about you. Are losing theirs and blaming it on you.* "You'll be driving all night!"

"I *want* to go to Portland, Mom. Jess has an important meeting. I can sleep at her apartment."

"That's not appropriate!" Now he looked angry. Was he *sleeping* with the fish scientist? She grabbed his arm.

"She'll be at her office all night." He pulled away. "I'll pay for the gas."

"But what about school?"

He hopped away, down the steps. "No big deal," he called. "I'll take care of it." And then, just like that, he was backing the car out of the driveway.

Her sister Race had festooned her house with streamers and lined the walls with tables of food and *three* crystal punch bowls. Rill suffered a burst of little-sister inadequacy. What kind of person owned three punch bowls? But then Rill had not thrown a party since she married Cleve. She left him stuttering to Race at the door and cut through the crowd to get to Sammy, who greeted her as he greeted everyone, with a warm hug and then a kiss on the fingers.

Birch arrived and cornered Sammy, cutting Rill adrift. She found a wall and backed herself into it, looking wildly around at these people she had known all her life. What had happened to her? She was having an affair. Her parents were dead. Her marriage was dead. She watched Cleve approach and tried to remember why she had ever loved him.

Cleve stood next to her with a plate of food. He gestured with his elbow and spoke with his mouth full, strands of chicken in his teeth. "That fish biologist. Race says she crashed into the canyon on her motorcycle. Got taken out of town in an ambulance."

"There's a little drama to break up the monotony," Rill said. He hadn't asked about Scott's "errand." *Was* Scott involved with Jess MacKinnon? She smelled alcohol on Cleve's breath. "What have you been drinking?" She side-stepped away, kept her back to the wall.

"The punch bowl nearest the door has rum in it."

"How much have you had?" To her right, she spotted Jonathan Monticola heading their way, trying to catch her eye.

"A couple. You should try it."

"I'll be back in a minute." She hurried into the hallway. Jonathan caught up to her as she pushed open the bathroom door.

"Rill! I have to talk to you!" His speech was slurred; he'd apparently found the spiked punch.

"Not now, Jonathan." She edged into the bathroom. He blocked the doorway, holding the door open.

"Yes, now! Please!"

She put her hand on his chest. "Jonathan," she said slowly in a fierce whisper. "Cleve is here. This is not the time or the place. You need to stop drinking. Have some water, have some coffee. Are you listening?" She yanked the door from his hand and pushed it shut, forcing him into the hallway.

"Rill!" She threw her weight against the door as he pounded against it. "Rill, please!"

"What's going on here, Jonathan?" said a voice outside. Rill peeked out the door. It was Karl Luder. She stepped into the hallway, which fortunately was empty except for the three of them.

"Karl, Jonathan's had too much to drink. Can you get him out of here, maybe take him for a walk?"

"I expect I can do that." Karl put his arm around Jonathan's shoulders and steered him away. "Come on, Jon, let's get some air." Jonathan twisted to look at Rill with his pleading eyes.

"Rill! You know how I feel! Please!"

Karl looked from Jonathan to Rill but said nothing. He guided Jonathan to the end of the hallway and toward the back door. "Would you let Lydia know where I am?" he said from the doorway.

"Of course. Thank you, Karl." Their eyes met and an understanding passed between them: Karl would not say anything to Cleve, his best friend. She stepped into the bathroom and locked the door and sat on the cold edge of the tub and put her head in her hands, trying to erase what she'd seen in Karl's eyes: pity.

The air had chilled by the time Rill found Karl in the backyard, alone. He was propped against a tree, smoking his pipe. "Jonathan?" she whispered.

"He was sick. I sent him home with his mother."

Lydia banged out the back screen door. As she closed in, Rill stood on her toes to put her mouth by Karl's ear. "I've got to get out of here. Now."

Karl nodded. "Understood." He took Lydia's hand and they laced their fingers together, a gesture that made Rill's mouth taste bitter. Karl pointed across the yard to a giggling cluster of teenagers. "Brian's over there. Brian!" he called. Brian joined them under the tree. "We're heading home, and we're giving your mother a ride. Want to come along?"

"I'll go home with Dad. What happened to Jonathan?"

Karl tapped his pipe against the tree to empty its spent tobacco. "He got into the spiked punch and made himself sick."

Rill took her son's arm. "Brian, you should come with us now. Your father's been drinking too and he might not be okay to drive."

Brian shook her off. "I already took his keys. I can drive us home. See you later." And he was gone.

In the back seat of the Luders' Oldsmobile, Rill watched Karl and Lydia hold hands as Karl drove. This made her so irritable she could not speak. She mustered monosyllabic replies to Lydia's small talk about the newspaper and nearly groaned with relief when they pulled up to her house. But Karl followed her to the door. He stepped inside, uninvited, and spun her around.

"What in God's name are you doing?" His face was rigid with fury. "Are you sleeping with a nineteen-year-old *boy*?"

"He's twenty." She saw in Karl's face how ridiculous it sounded. There was nothing to say. She looked at the floor.

"Karl?" Lydia called from the car. She tapped the horn, a polite bleat.

"I don't know, Karl." She met his outraged eyes, then looked down again. "I don't know what I'm doing."

"Well, *stop*." The horn beeped again. He backed out of the house.

"I will." Her voice sounded small.

46.

Almost two a.m. in downtown Portland. The building was empty, even the janitors long gone. Jess sat in a pool of lamplight at her desk. She looked up from Sammy's file. The window cast back her reflection, her face a muddy foreground for the tops of the trees and the streetlights fifteen floors below.

A ringing blow, metal on metal, jolted her upright. Then another sound, like a chain dragging, link by link, along the floor. She rose and put her face next to the window, peering into the darkness outside. Her office was cold. She thrust her arms into the sleeves of her sweater and pain shot through her side. She had dosed herself with coffee instead of painkillers. A car passed on the street below. The sound must have been the gate of the parking garage jerking open, then closed. The empty building groaned, popped, and fell quiet.

Jess eased herself back onto her chair. She knew, now, what had happened to the kokanee. But she still didn't know whether they were gone forever. The goal of any species is persistence, she had said to Paul Monticola. And Jack Branch seemed to think they *had* persisted. "No surprise if the fish are hiding," he'd said. Hiding. What did he mean?

She picked up the minutes from the Still Lake City Council meeting in June 1962. In 1962, the kokanee thrived.

Wednesday, June 6, 1962

47.

At twilight in the spring of 1962, sixteen-year-old Mike Branch hopped lightly onto the dock and tied off his skiff. Arn Randall stepped out behind him, but Dirk Muhling stood stiffly at the thwart until Mike reached back to help him out of the boat. Thin, densely freckled, and sunburned, Dirk wore a canvas fishing hat and a smear of sunblock across his nose, though the sun had disappeared behind the mountains to leave Still Lake in shadow. Dirk's grip was sweaty, and Mike scraped his palm on his pants as he bent to retrieve fishing rods, tackle box, and the bucket of fish they had caught.

"Hey, that was fun! Did you have fun, Dirk?" Arn slapped Dirk on the back and he stumbled. The two men headed together up the gangway to the rocky lake shore. Mike followed, juggling four rods in the crook of his arm. In his right hand he carried the bucket, sloshing with lake water and nine live kokanee. His feet made squelching sounds and left wet prints on the planks of the dock.

"Yes, fun," Dirk answered without enthusiasm. Dirk's voice was high and piercing, a little nasal, but Arn's was deep and Mike did not hear his reply. Arnett Randall had been Mike's first real, out-of-town customer. Mike wasn't sure how he made his living—he seemed to spend all his time fishing and hunting and, as he explained to Mike, searching the west for remote, little-known spots just like Still Lake—but he knew Randall was very rich.

Randall stopped to wait for him, his teeth flashing white between his tanned cheeks. He was tough and lean and well groomed. Randall set a heavy hand on Mike's shoulder and with the other slid a Polaroid photograph from his shirt pocket. "Take a look at this, Mike." He propelled Mike forward and they walked side by side toward Mike's "Still Lake Fishing Tours" kiosk. "That's me." The photograph showed Randall standing in a boat holding up a large silver fish. "And that's a six-pound kokanee."

"Six pounds? Are you sure it was a kokanee?" Mike set the rods and tackle box inside the kiosk.

"You bet I'm sure." Randall and Dirk Muhling sat down on a bench. Mike set the bucket on the rocks and opened the fillet counter that unfolded from the side of the kiosk, admiring as always its laminated hardwoods and its perfect pair of oak hinges. The woodworker, Casey Monticola, had built the counter for him, and the kiosk, the bench, and the skiff. As payment, Mike kept Casey's family supplied with kokanee, even in winter if he could catch them through the ice. Mike drew a knife from his belt and a spiral notepad from his back pocket and placed both on the counter. He pulled a thrashing silver fish out of the bucket, rapped the back of its head on the rocks to kill it, then stretched it out against a ruler built right into the rear of the counter. Eight and a half inches. He pulled a pencil stub from the spiral of the notepad and recorded the measurement inside. With the knife, he sliced the fish open, belly to chin, as Randall and Muhling watched. He scooped out its innards.

"That was in Canada earlier this month," Randall continued. "I stay up in Nelson, in British Columbia. You been up there?"

Mike shook his head. He grabbed a second fish, killed it, stretched it on the counter.

"That's Kootenay Lake." Randall continued. "That fish is six pounds, one ounce. The world record is not much more than that."

"I've never seen a kokanee that big." Mike cut open a third fish.

"How big are these kokes we pulled out of the lake tonight?"

"Eight and a half inches, eight and three-quarters, nine and three-quarters." The fourth kokanee was just under eight inches. "This one's seven and seven-eighths." Mike recorded the measurement in his notebook.

Randall smiled at him. "This is what I was telling you, Dirk. He keeps exact records of everything that comes out of the lake. Knows where the fish are. Knows every move they make."

Mike felt his face get hot.

"It's a small lake," Muhling said, dismissive.

Randall ignored this, directing his attention to Mike. "You have no scales, right? You really should be weighing these fish."

"The kokes weigh about a pound apiece. I do weigh the macs, over at the post office." Mike rinsed the fourth fish.

"Macs?" Dirk Muhling frowned.

"Mackinaws. Lake trout," Randall said.

"Ah. *Salvelinus namaycush*."

"Dirk here is a scientist," Randall told Mike. "Studies fish, and lakes. What's that called again, Dirk?"

"Limnology," Dirk answered in his shrill voice.

Randall zipped up his expensive wool jacket. The light behind the mountains was fading and the air turned cold. "Okay, so you don't know how much the kokanee weigh. But what's the longest you've ever pulled out of Still Lake?"

"Fourteen and a half inches. That was a nice fish." Mike smiled as he planed his thumbnail up the spine of the fifth fish, chasing the pocket of blood that was trapped there.

"The kokes are good eating," said Randall. "They taste just like salmon. In fact, they *are* salmon, aren't they, Dirk? Technically?"

"*Oncorhynchus nerka*."

Randall shot him an irritated glance. "Would you mind speaking English, Dirk?"

"Kokanee are a freshwater species of *Oncorhynchus nerka*, sockeye salmon. They rear in the lake instead of migrating to the ocean."

"That's right." Randall nodded. He watched as Mike pulled a sixth fish, thrashing, from the bucket, and rapped it sharply against the counter. "But the Still Lake kokanee are for meat, not for sport. It's the trophy anglers who spend money, Mike. That ought to be your customer base."

"Okay," said Mike. He couldn't see what Randall was driving at.

Dirk Muhling pulled off his fishing cap. The last light from behind the mountains made his bald head glisten. He swatted the cap on his knee and put it back on his head. "The kokanee are fine for the meat fishermen," he said. His eyes were hidden under the brim of the hat but his lips were twisted in what Mike decided was a smirk. *Smirking Dirk*, he thought to himself. *Smirking Dirk the Jerk*. He cleaned the sixth fish and rinsed it in the bucket.

Arn Randall rested his elbows on his knees. "Here's the deal, Mike. There could be six-pound kokanee in Still Lake, just like Kootenay. Still Lake could become one of the best kept secrets in Oregon. And you'd be in charge of it all. Think about that. You'd make so much money you wouldn't be able to spend it all."

Mike held the seventh kokanee in both hands. It was twelve-and-a-quarter inches, a beautiful fish. A beam from the setting sun glanced over the mountains and caught the silver symmetry of its scales. "How is that going to happen?" he asked, addressing the fish.

"I was waiting for you to ask that." Arn Randall chuckled. "We give them shrimp—a species called opossum shrimp. They're about this big." He held up his thumb and forefinger, less than an inch apart.

"*Mysis relicta*," mumbled Dirk Muhling. Mike stared at him.

"What?" he said. "Shrimp?"

"Yes, opossum shrimp. They're called mysids. They introduced them into Kootenay Lake thirteen years ago. The kokanee started eating them and they've been getting bigger ever since."

"Where do you get the shrimp?" Mike sliced open the seventh fish.

"Dirk can have them up here in a week." Randall swatted his companion on the back. "Enough to stock the whole lake. They'll start breeding and then they'll be on their own."

Dirk made a coughing sound. Randall looked at him, then back at Mike. "Interested?" he asked.

"Sure, I'm interested." Mike set the fish aside and made himself look directly into Randall's light gray eyes.

"Good. Here's what I want to do: Dirk and I get the shrimp and you take us out on the lake to spread them around. When the kokanee start growing—it could take a few years, a couple generations—you give me three years of fishing before you start advertising to the rest of the world. Right now on Kootenay you can barely get a boat into the water where the kokes are, it's so crowded. Meanwhile, you set yourself up in the general store building, which you can buy for a song, it's been empty so long. How much money would you need to build that out as a guide headquarters and equipment shop, including your inventory?"

Mike's head was buzzing. "I have no idea."

"Let's say twenty thousand dollars, another thirty to buy the building. I think that's in the ballpark. I give you a long-term loan, no interest, maybe set you up with another boat and expand the size of your dock. By the time the anglers start coming here in droves, you'll be ready for them."

"Except you have to drive seven hours to get here," Dirk interjected. "And then there's no decent place to stay."

"The mayor wants to build a lodge over on Second Street." Mike pulled the second-to-last fish from the bucket but it squirmed out of his fingers, flopped and jackknifed on the dusty rocks. He trapped it in both hands, blushing. He looked over at the men and found Dirk studying him, his face shaded and unreadable under the hat.

"How old are you, Mike?" Dirk asked him.

"Sixteen." Mike turned back to the fillet counter.

"You look like you might be part Indian."

"Half," said Mike. He stretched the eighth fish out along the ruler.

"Which half?" Randall chuckled.

"What tribe?" Dirk asked.

Mike sliced the fish open and briskly pulled the guts away. He reached into the bucket for the last fish, which was already dead, and cleaned it before he decided to answer this question that was none of Dirk Muhling's business. "My grandmother was from the Siletz reservation. My grandfather was Nez Perce." He rolled the nine gutted fish into a brown waxed paper bundle, rinsed his knife and wiped the blade dry. He scraped the pile of innards onto the rocks and poured the water out over the fillet counter. He felt Dirk's shaded gaze on his back.

He handed the bundle of fish to Randall, who stood up. "Caroline Keeler will pan-fry these for supper if you ask her." He ignored Dirk Muhling, who continued to scrutinize him from under the fishing hat.

"Sounds great." Arn smiled at the package with affection—either for the fish or for Mike—and tucked it under his arm. He walked up the slope toward Main Street. Dirk caught up with him.

Mike closed up the kiosk. He let his gaze travel over the mirror of the lake to the jagged mountains with their spring patches of snow. His head still buzzed; it was a lot to take in. He started up the hill.

Arn Randall and Dirk Muhling stood talking on the sidewalk in front of the boarded-up building that used to be the Still Lake General Store. Dirk's shrill voice carried across the park: "I can't believe you want to do this, Arn." Mike placed a maple tree between himself and the men. If Arn answered, Mike couldn't hear it. Dirk's voice, then: "Some dumb Indian kid who doesn't know shit from Shinola." And Arn's voice, angry: "Shut the hell up, Dirk. It's my money and I'll do whatever the hell I please."

48.

Mayor Colby Stukel had been elected to build a bridge. For the Nez Perce, he was a steward of the natural environment, the quiet mountain lake, the forest, and everything wild and pure. For the white settlers, he was a visionary. He would grow the town's infant economy into a fine, strapping youth—strong, resilient, and rugged. Still Lake would become a destination for sportsmen and families across Oregon, the nation, the world. His bridge connected stewardship to vision, offering up Still Lake's unspoiled beauty to create prosperity.

The men seated before the council table had just laid at his feet the timbers for his bridge. He did not trust himself to look at the city councilmen: Sammy Branch and John Luder to his right, young Casey Monticola to his left. He held the even gray gaze of the wealthy Sacramento fisherman, Arnett Randall, and waited to speak until he was sure no trace of adolescent delight would escape into his voice. The simpering limnologist, Dirk Muhling, picked at something on his forearm. Colby ignored him. He was a minion of the man with money.

"Let me make certain I understand your proposal," he began, and he paused to let his stentorian tones echo across the polished floor of the City Hall he had commissioned and built. "First, you want to put these opossum shrimp into the lake as a food source for the kokanee, which you tell us will create trophy-sized fish in Still Lake within a few years. You're volunteering to fund this yourself." Behind Randall and Muhling, the hall was packed with townspeople. Mike Branch sat in the front row, his knee bouncing.

Behind Mike, Casey's father Tony Monticola sat with his wife, Harriet, the third of the seven Branch children. Three of her brothers—the fourth, Sammy, sat beside him at the table—had lined themselves along the back wall, though there were still empty seats and Colby had opened the meeting by inviting everyone to sit down. Charley Branch, the oldest brother, nearly seventy now, wore his white hair long in two braids with a beard too sparse to hide the white scar that ran from his left eye to his chin. He kept his hands tucked in the bib of his overalls and his gaze jerked around the room as though taking inventory. Tucker and Jack, younger than Charley and only a year apart, were both small men—runts of the litter, Jack liked to say— and stood in the same posture, leaning against the wall with their arms folded across their chests. The Branches could be an obstacle to his bridge building. He searched their faces for signs of disapproval. Charley, with his scar, always looked severe unless he was smiling, and he wasn't smiling. Tucker and Jack wore no expression. Colby looked directly at the three of them as he resumed speaking.

"Second, you are offering a no-interest loan to Mike Branch and his uncle." Colby motioned toward Sammy, aware that all his gestures, every movement, must appear decisive. "You propose they purchase the vacant general store building and remodel it as a retail outdoor store and a base for Mike's fishing guide business, which you view as ripe for expansion." He watched Jack Branch, Mike's father, as his expression grew stern, almost a scowl, the cross of his arms impenetrable. Things hadn't been right between Jack and his son since Sasha Branch's death. "Sir, you are aware that Mike Branch is only sixteen years of age?"

Arnett Randall smiled and glanced over his shoulder at Mike, who fidgeted in his seat. "I have every confidence in Mike." His deep voice filled the hall to its glass chandeliers. "He's man enough for me."

Mike's knee stilled and he sat up taller. Colby suppressed a smile. "Very well," he said. "Your third proposal is a loan to the City of Still

Lake, to fund and be secured by a new hotel in the style of a sportsman's lodge, at Second and Elm Streets." Murmuring erupted in the audience. Colby frowned it into silence, then shifted his gaze back to Randall. "Do I understand your proposal, Mr. Randall?"

"You do indeed."

Colby spread his arms to embrace the room. "The floor is open for public testimony."

Amos Keeler was the first to speak. He supported all three parts of Randall's proposal. His family's restaurant relied on tourism, and a hotel would bring more tourists. He, Amos, was only twenty-three. He wanted to stay in Still Lake, not be driven away to a bigger city to seek his livelihood like so many of his friends.

Following Amos's lead, several young citizens spoke in favor of the proposal, praising the opportunity for economic growth. Councilman Luder's nineteen-year-old daughter, Alice, was among them—but his oldest son, John Junior, who had married Tucker Branch's daughter, remained in his seat.

After the youth of the town had spoken, the Presbyterian minister rose and reminded them all—not briefly—that God had given them dominion over the creatures of the sea, which included the fish of Still Lake. In all, more than twenty citizens testified in support; but still no one from the Branch family had come forward. In the lull after the last speaker, a hum of conversation rose and Colby was about to announce the close of public testimony. As he opened his mouth to do so, Sammy Branch put a hand on his arm and jerked his head in Mike's direction. In the second row, Harriet Branch Monticola had struggled to her feet and was limping toward the podium on her bad hip. The crowd fell silent and shrank apart to let her pass.

She gripped the sides of the lectern, pulled her white hair away from her face, looked all around the room, and nodded to her brothers along the back wall. "Yesterday was my seventieth birthday," she said, and a murmur of appreciation and some scattered applause traveled around the hall. "So I am just a young woman." Laughter. She smiled with her lips closed. "My mother died two years ago. She was one hundred and four."

Harriet turned toward the council table and Colby set his face into a pleasant expression, mildly expectant, but he wondered whether she had a point and, if so, when she would get to it.

"I want to tell you what my mother would say if she were here. She would say, 'Everything has its count.' Which is hard to explain." Harriet moved her gaze to Sammy, her brother, and Colby glanced to his right. Sammy Branch frowned in concentration. Would Colby lose one of his votes?

"It means there is an order. Everything has a place where it belongs. The lake, the Klip Chuck, belongs in the valley next to the mountains. The kokanee belong in the lake." She paused. The hall was so still Colby could hear the clock ticking on the wall behind him.

"The opossum shrimp belong somewhere else. Not here. That's all I have to say." Harriet's husband, Tony Monticola, hurried to the front of the room to take her arm and help her back to her chair. No one moved or spoke until Harriet and Tony were seated; then Colby heard a shuffle from the back of the room. The three Branch brothers walked single file to the podium and Charley Branch stepped behind the lectern.

"We agree with Harriet," he said, and nodded once.

Colby groaned inwardly. Sammy looked down at the table, his face inscrutable. Colby closed the testimony and called for an immediate vote from the council. His instincts told him the less time the councilmen had to mull over Harriet's speech, the better. The vast majority of the town supported the Randall proposal; that would carry the day, he felt sure. Reasonably sure.

He collected the votes on folded slips of paper. He opened and read them, building in a dramatic pause each time to ratchet up the tension. But the vote was unanimous, or nearly so—Sammy Branch had abstained. The tension leaked away, the citizens rose and milled about, and Colby sat back in his chair, drained.

"Congratulations. Nicely done." Arnett Randall shook his hand.

Colby stood. "How soon can you have the shrimp up here?"

Randall passed the question to Dirk Muhling with his eyebrows. "Middle of next week," Muhling answered in his irritating voice.

"Perfect." Colby smiled broadly. "Ring out the old, ring in the new!"

"Wordsworth?" asked John Luder, slapping him on the back.

"Tennyson," Colby answered. "*In Memoriam*." And he was so giddy that a giggle escaped before he could stop it.

Thursday, June 14, 1962

49.

At five-thirty in the morning, Mike Branch bounded off the end of the dock and launched himself into the lake. He swam as fast as he could, chopping his arms, out a hundred yards and back again. He pulled himself onto the dock in one movement as though the lake had spit him out, and there was Jack Branch sitting cross-legged on the planks.

"Papa! What are you doing here?" He hugged his bare torso, goose bumps erupting. Jack placed a broad, veined hand beside him on the deck, then rested it again on his knee, and Mike sat down. Jack pulled off his jacket and offered it. Mike shook his head. In the east, the mountains were dark with the sun behind them, tops glowing orange.

"The opossum shrimp, Michael. It's a bad idea to put them in the lake."

Mike took a deep breath and blew it out. "I don't agree with you. The shrimp will give the fish more to eat."

"These shrimp don't belong here." Jack had been sitting with one hand splayed on each kneecap. Now he turned his left palm upward and looked toward his son.

"What are you saying—that nothing should move around? What about Mama? She came here from Germany. Was that wrong? Did she not belong here?"

"That's different." Jack's hand flipped back over and he stared down at his knees again.

"No, it's the same."

"This is not about your mother. It's about the fish."

It *was* about his mother. Everything between them was about his dead mother. The sunrise lanced over the mountains and hit them both in the face. Mike stood up. "It's not a good enough reason, Papa, that you want everything to stay the same all the time. Things don't stay the same, they change." He took a step toward the shore.

Jack stood. "You're making a mistake."

"The City Council decided. We're going out this morning to put the shrimp in the lake."

"What gives the City Council the right to decide?" Jack grabbed Mike's wrist.

Mike shook him off and straightened to his full height, half a foot taller than Jack. He glared at his father. "Don't treat me like a kid, Papa. I'm my own man now." He turned and set off, leaving wet footprints on the dock.

Dried and dressed, Mike walked from his uncle's house to Monticola Millworks. On the front porch, he found two boys sitting against the wall, each with a block of wood and a knife, their laps littered with wood shavings. The bigger boy was twelve-year-old Karl Luder. Mike didn't recognize the other boy.

"Hi!" said Mike. "I need to talk to Casey. Is he inside?"

"He's not here," Karl answered. "He said he'll be back in five minutes." He held up the knife and wood block. "He's teaching us chip carving!"

"Looks nice."

"This is Mike Branch," Karl told the smaller boy. "He's a fishing guide. He has his own business. He took me out fishing in his boat and I caught a fish as big as a mule!" The boy grinned. Karl was a good, solid kid. Mike was fond of him.

"That's right," Mike said. "Karl here holds the record for the biggest kokanee out of Still Lake. Aren't you going to introduce your friend to me, Karl?"

"Oh, right. This is Cleve. He and his brother just came to town last Sunday. They have no parents, but now Cleve's brother is eighteen and he's allowed to take care of Cleve. They moved here from Washington, by themselves!"

The other boy seemed nonplussed by Karl's stream of disclosures. He set the knife down and held up his hand. Mike shook it. "Cleveland S. Kittridge," he said gravely. "And we do have parents, but they're drug addicts. And I can take care of myself."

"Nice to meet you," said Mike. "Do you and your brother like fishing?"

"Sure."

"Well, I'll take you out fishing on the lake sometime, then, how about that?"

Cleveland S. Kittridge smiled for the first time. One of his front teeth was missing. "Thanks!"

"You boys interested in helping me this morning for a couple of hours? I'm going out with some men to put live shrimp in the lake. We could use a hand."

"Sure," Cleve said, but Karl Luder shook his head.

"My mother wants me home by eleven. Sorry."

"Let's go, then, Cleve."

The boy jumped to his feet to follow Mike.

"Karl, would you tell Casey to meet us down at the dock?"

"Sure thing, Mike. Leave the knife here, Cleve."

Cleve Kittridge turned, started to hold out the knife, then lunged at Karl with the blade, sudden wildness in his eyes.

"Hey!" Karl scrambled away.

Cleve set the knife down, laughing. Mike and Karl stared at him as though he were a fatal car crash, and his smile faded. "Sorry," he mumbled.

"Yeah, okay. Let's go." Mike hurried down the steps to the street, letting the strange new boy run to catch up.

Mike sat with Casey Monticola and Cleve Kittridge at the end of the dock, waiting for the men from Sacramento to arrive with the mysids. They swung their legs over the water and ate cinnamon rolls from a paper sack.

Casey stuffed the last half of a roll into his mouth and licked his fingers. "What's the plan, Mike?" he said with his mouth full. "We just go out in the skiff and dump the shrimp in the lake?"

"I guess so." Mike flattened a napkin across his lap and peeled apart his roll, lining its curled sections along his thigh.

Casey reached over and plucked a curl from Mike's leg. "What did Jack say?"

Mike slapped Casey's hand. "He said I shouldn't put the shrimp where they don't belong."

"Who's Jack?" Cleve asked.

"My father."

"I thought Sammy Branch was your father."

"He's my uncle." Mike gathered up the fragments of cinnamon roll and pushed them into a sticky ball.

"Why do you live with him and not your father?"

"My father and I don't get along." Mike watched the kid swing his legs, one knobby knee poking from a tear in his blue jeans. The kid looked up and met his eyes. Cleve's eyes were the color of steel.

Four sharp cracks echoed across the lake, rock on rock. Mike squinted along the bright water. From the talus slope at the water's edge his gaze lifted up the gray mountainside to the high crags against the blue. Another four cracks traveled over the water, and Mike spotted a fuzzy white shape moving slowly across the sheer face of one of the peaks, the source of the tumbling rocks. He put a hand on Cleve's shoulder and pointed. Under his fingers, he felt the boy flinch and shrink away. "Mountain goat," Mike whispered.

The three of them watched as the goat eased into a depression in the rock and lay down. A fish jumped, quick flash of silver, and sent circles widening over the water.

Friday, October 1, 2004

50.

Jess arrived early for the meeting on Friday morning. Darrin was already there, dressed in a dark suit, fussing with coffee cups on the credenza.

"Morning." Jess slapped her sheaf of papers onto the table and tried to remember whether she'd ever seen her boss in a suit before. She poured coffee and gulped it, checked her reflection in the window. She wore the emergency skirt and blazer she kept hanging on the back of her office door. Considering everything, she looked pretty good. After yesterday, she could have used a solid night's sleep, but she'd only managed an hour's nap in the car with Scott. She smoothed down the free-wheeling strands of hair that always escaped from her braid.

Darrin pointed to her bandaged hand, asked how she was feeling. "I'm fine," she answered. She wasn't. Her side ached. She hadn't taken any pain medication.

"Are the fish extinct?" Darrin asked her. "Are we looking at reintroduction? Or restoration?"

"Not clear. I'll cover both."

The clients arrived in a clump: from the Bonneville Power Administration, a ruddy, strapping scientist dressed in khaki and a red fleece vest; a blustery blonde woman from the governor's office, wearing a pants suit; and the Nez Perce tribal representative and his lawyer, both in suits.

The blonde woman—Dolores Capfield, whom Darrin had once described to Jess as a "policy wonk"—interrupted Jess halfway through her rehearsed introduction. "How can we not have an answer yet on whether these fish are extinct? Why can't you just stun all the fish with a big electric current? What's that called, Hobbs?" She turned to the BPA scientist and the look they exchanged told Jess they knew each other well. With coffee, the jumping in her gut had gone into double-time, so she pictured them naked, in bed together, Dolores on top with her long hair cascading down her back to the spread of her generous hips. The image was so vivid Jess felt herself blush. She bent over her papers.

"It's called electrofishing, Dee," Hobbs said. "And I know you're picturing a big jolt that sends all the fish in the lake floating to the top, but that's not how it works." He turned to Jess, who hastily dressed him again in her imagination.

"Here's my question: If the fishing guide thinks all the fish are gone, shouldn't we assume they are? When's the last time someone caught a kokanee out of the lake? You said the guide keeps records."

"I wasn't able to obtain the records," Jess said. She could not tell them the real reason she believed the kokanee survived—Jack Branch's cryptic message at the open doors of the ambulance. *No surprise if the fish are hiding.*

Dolores began a renewed tirade, but stopped when the tribal representative, Lewis, held up his hand for silence. "I'd like to hear the answer to that question," he said. He folded one hand over the other and leaned toward Jess with a small encouraging smile.

"Thank you, Lewis," Darrin said.

"Let me back up a step," Jess began. "Remember that the goal of any species is persistence." She looked around the room. Dolores scowled. Hobbs looked bemused. "A species will adapt, adjust—anything to ensure survival." Lewis and his attorney caught each other's eye and smiled.

"I'm sure the Still Lake kokanee were originally anadromous sockeye—say ten thousand years ago, when they could have had a passageway through the Columbia Basin to the ocean."

"Excuse me a moment." Dolores huffed and spread her palms on the table. "When you said you were going to, quote, back up a step, unquote, I didn't realize you were referring to geologic time." She looked at her wristwatch. "The governor has a schedule. *I* have a schedule. Let's cut to the chase. Are these fish extinct or not and how can we find out?"

"I don't think they're extinct." Dolores's pants suit was pale green, her blouse fresh and pressed and flawless. Jess glanced down at her lap, the wrinkles in her skirt.

"Why is that?"

"I'm trying to answer that question." Jess caught the sharp edge in her tone and regretted it. She made herself smile at Dolores. No one cared about the wrinkles in her skirt. Probably.

Dolores's mouth opened, but Hobbs put a hand on her shoulder. "Let her finish, Dee."

"Please go on, Ms. MacKinnon," Lewis said.

She focused on Lewis and made her voice louder. She wanted it to fill up the conference room. "An anadromous sockeye population will, as a species, hedge its bets. Some of them stay in freshwater rather than migrating to the ocean. Those are called resident sockeye. That way, if the passage to the ocean gets blocked or becomes too difficult, the species can stay alive. When that happens, as it did at Still Lake thousands of years ago—" Jess glanced at Dolores "—the resident sockeye developed into kokanee, a freshwater fish."

Dolores looked at her watch and folded her arms.

"So that brings us to 1962." Jess stood and stepped over to a white board on the conference room wall. "The Still Lake city council and the fishing guide, Mike Branch, stocked the lake with *mysis relicta*—opossum shrimp—as a food source for the kokanee."

Lewis frowned. "Why would they do that?"

"They wanted to promote sportsfishing. Mysids had been introduced to a lake in British Columbia and the kokanee did use them as a food source and developed into a much bigger fish."

"I take it that's not what happened in Still Lake." Hobbs nudged Dolores, who was looking at her watch again.

"No. In Still Lake the mysids became a food source for the lake trout, and the kokanee were extirpated—or severely compromised. That's the question we're trying to answer." Jess found a blue marker and drew a bathtub-shaped basin on the board. "Here's a cross-section of the lake." She drew a dotted line three inches from the water surface, then put fish shapes above and below the line. She tapped the line with the marker. "This is what's called the thermocline, basically the area between the cold and warm layers in the water column. The line moves downward as the weather gets warmer, so it'll be closer to the surface in the spring, deeper at the end of summer. Kokanee typically feed near the thermocline."

"Thermocline," Dolores muttered. She looked at her watch, then out the window as if plotting an escape. Jess ignored her.

"Also, kokanee are sight feeders, so they feed during the day." She used a red marker to draw squiggles along the lake bottom. "Here are the mysids. They're sensitive to light. They stay low in the water column during the day, right near the bottom, and they move up toward the surface at night. But kokanee don't feed at night, so they miss each other." She found a black marker and drew some larger fish shapes near the bottom. "But lake trout feed on the bottom, so *they* eat the mysids."

"But why does that make the kokanee die out?" the lawyer asked.

"It's a food chain issue, predators and prey. Mysids eat zooplankton. They compete directly with kokanee alevin and fry for the same species of zooplankton. And mysids have the edge because they feed all the time, day and night, and they reproduce like crazy." She drew more red squiggles on the lakebed, then pointed to the larger fish shapes. "Also, lake trout eat kokanee, so as the lake trout began to thrive on the shrimp, it was a one-two punch for the kokanee—not enough food to eat, and more predation."

"Just like that," Lewis said, and the room got quiet.

Dolores uncrossed her arms and slapped her palms on the tabletop. "We should prosecute those people."

Hobbs laughed. "Then you'll have to prosecute several state resource agencies along with them. They were throwing mysids into lakes all over the west after what happened in Kootenay Lake. And, yes, the kokanee were extirpated from some of those lakes, too." He nodded at Jess. "Or compromised."

Lewis spoke. "That's what I don't understand. Why would the kokanee get bigger in Kootenay Lake, but in other lakes be destroyed? Do we know the answer?"

"We do know the answer," Jess told him. "There was a popular kokanee fishery in a part of Kootenay Lake known as the West Arm. In the West Arm, a stream enters the lake." She drew a blue arrow on the left side of her lake diagram, then some swirling lines below it. "We think the stream caused upwelling in the lake and mixed the mysids all through the water column, where the kokanee could find them and eat them. It's not that the kokanee don't want to eat mysids, it's just that the mysids aren't usually there at dinnertime. But if they are, presto! Bigger kokanee."

"But that's unusual," Hobbs added.

"Right." Jess tucked the marker into its tray. "Kootenay Lake was unique. In some lakes, the kokanee survived after mysids were introduced. In others, they didn't."

"And in Still Lake, we don't know yet," Hobbs said. "So what's the plan?"

Jess passed everyone a sheet of paper, pain stabbing each time she extended her arm. "These are the options. One: restoration. Two: reintroduction. If the kokanee are extinct, we can use a donor stock to rebuild a population. The Lake Whatcom kokanee would be a viable candidate."

Lewis and his lawyer looked up from Jess's paper. "The tribes do not support reintroduction," the lawyer said.

"Yes, I know." Jess rested her hands on the back of her chair and kept her gaze on Lewis, his clear eyes and calm face. He was in his forties or fifties, she guessed. The lawyer was older, his hair nearly all white.

"It might be the only way," said Darrin. "Are there no circumstances where you could endorse transplanting a donor stock?"

The lawyer looked over at Lewis and raised his bushy white eyebrows. "We'd go to one of the alternative sites first," said Lewis. "Maybe Warner Valley. We know we can do restoration there."

Dolores looked agitated again. Jess braced herself for another outburst. Hobbs looked amused. Dolores huffed out a sigh and turned her palms to the ceiling. "Why all this ecological purism? How is that even appropriate in this day and age? Hasn't that ship sailed already?"

The lawyer gave her a sharp look. "You mean, like in 1492?"

Dolores opened her mouth and closed it. Hobbs turned to look at the door, and Darrin folded his fingers on the table and stared at them. The silence started to feel dangerous.

"Tell you what," Jess said. "Let me have another week in Still Lake to see whether there's a remnant of the native population. That's still a possibility." She heard Jack's voice again: *The fish are hiding.* But where?

"We support another week in Still Lake," Lewis said quickly. He waved at the white board, held up the paper. "I'm impressed with you, Ms. MacKinnon. I'm happy to have you on the project."

"We had reservations about your inexperience," the lawyer added. He nodded at Darrin. "You were right. She was the best choice."

Dolores cleared her throat. "Sorry to interrupt this chapter meeting of the Mutual Admiration Society," she said loudly, "but I don't think the governor will be on board with another week. In my opinion, it's time to stop researching the site and move forward with one of these options." She slapped the paper. "Or scrap Still Lake and go to the alternative site. Fish or cut bait, so to speak."

"So to speak." Hobbs gave Dolores a crooked, sideways smile. "BPA will support another week in Still Lake. You're outvoted, Dee."

"I'm the State of Oregon. I have all the votes." She pushed him playfully and Jess saw the vaguely sexual charge pass between them again.

"One more thing I'd like to bring up," the lawyer said. "The Fish and Wildlife Service employee who drowned. Is it true they've reopened the investigation into his death?"

Jess sat down and opened her file folder, lines of type swimming across the pages.

"Not officially," Darrin told him. "The parents have hired their own investigator."

"Is there any reason for concern?"

Jess could feel the lawyer's stare on the top of her head as she bent over her papers, tidying their edges with her fingers. She couldn't let this project go, not now. She'd told Darrin the crash had been an accident, and here in the bright fluorescent conference room, she half believed it herself. Besides, she had promised Moses. She put a smile on her face and lifted her head. "No reason at all," she said, and the lawyer seemed satisfied.

"Another week, then?" Darrin asked.

"Oh, fine." Dolores stood up, opened her briefcase, and tossed the sheet of paper into it. "But there'd better be a written report and a concrete proposal one week from right now." She snapped the case closed. "Agreed?"

Jess got to her feet. "Agreed." She found Darrin watching her as the clients spilled into the hallway. She blew out a breath.

"That went reasonably well." His hazel eyes bored into hers.

"Christ on a stick, Darrin. Don't you ever smile?"

"No, MacKinnon. I do not ever smile." Then he did smile, a flicker across his closed lips. "Nice work in there."

"Thanks." Instead of a wide, ridiculous grin, she gave him a small professional nod, gathered her papers, and tapped the stack on the table.

51.

In her office, Jess stared out the window at the lead-colored sky. Another week in Still Lake, another week to find the hiding fish. How could she get Jack to talk to her? How could she get her hands on Mike's catch records?

After the client meeting, she had spent two hours in Darrin's office, and then he'd called her twice more with questions. The phone rang. "Jesus H. Unbelievable Christ!" she shouted, snatching it up.

"Now what?" she said.

Silence on the other end of the line, then an unfamiliar but cheerful male voice spoke. "I was thinking coffee, actually, if you've got a few minutes."

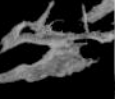

Jess shut her eyes and rubbed the bunched-up skin between her eyebrows. "I'm sorry," she told the caller—not Darrin Woodruff. "I meant to say, 'Hello. This is Jess. Jess MacKinnon.'"

"Jess, I'm Sam Branch. I'm on my way to Seattle. My grandfather suggested I stop in Portland and make your acquaintance. But if this is a bad time—"

"No, this is fine. I'd love to meet you, Sam. Where are you?" Jess stood up and looked out her fifteenth floor window as though Sam Branch might be hovering outside. Sam Branch, son of Mike, might help her get the fishing records. "Have you had lunch?" she asked.

She picked out Sam Branch at a table for two beside a window, reading a newspaper. He raised his head when Jess sat down and his dark eyes came to rest on her face for a long moment. She surprised herself by blushing.

Then he smiled, sincere and sweet; the graceful curve of his lips, the merriment in his eyes, pierced her. *Holy shit!* she thought, *he's adorable.* She smiled back.

They ordered lunch. She drank more coffee. He wanted iced tea. Rain peppered the window. He pushed his fingers up into his bangs, scraping them to the side over his forehead. Jess looked outside as a wind gust sent rain drumming across the window. A passerby on the sidewalk grappled with an umbrella that threatened to blow inside out. Sam asked about the restoration project and, still looking out the window, she caught the musical quality of his voice, a baritone ground for the drumming rain. She almost lost the content of his question.

Her gaze drifted back to his face, then to his hands on the table. "The goal is restoration of a native fish population in Still Lake," she said.

Their food arrived and they busied themselves with utensils and condiments.

"The fish population that was decimated after my father stocked the lake with mysid shrimp?" He poked a stray curl of lettuce back into his sandwich. "What?" he said when he saw her expression.

She laughed. "It's just that I thought it was a big secret. Apparently it was only a secret from me."

He smiled and she had to look away. This was what people meant when they talked about "chemistry." Out the window, the sun sent weak shafts of momentary light onto the sidewalk and across their table.

"It's true my father won't talk about it. No one does."

Light from the window bathed the side of Sam's face, accenting his lips. Something squirmed giddily under her aching rib cage. "Why is that?

He put down his sandwich and looked out the window, biting his lip. Then he met her eyes. "Shame," he said. A muscle in his cheek twitched as though flinching away from the word.

"Shame?"

He nodded. "The kind of deep shame that changes the culture of a community." He lifted his glass of iced tea and set it down again without drinking, gazed beyond her as though he were looking into the past. "The town's own government supported the project. Still Lake Lodge was financed with money from the sportsman who wanted to grow trophy-sized kokanee in Still Lake. For his own entertainment."

"And they helped your father expand his business?"

His eyes returned to her face and his mild features hardened. "They *used* my father. He was only sixteen."

She nodded, looked down at her plate, which was pale yellow and chipped on the edge. She rubbed her finger over the chip, testing the sharpness, and waited for the anger in his face to subside. She wiped her fingers with the paper napkin. "Did Mike tell you what happened?"

"My grandfather. Jack told me." The tension was gone from his face. He resembled Mike, in the set of his dark eyes, his forehead—the placid Mike of the dory and the lake.

Jess folded her napkin in half, creasing the edge, then into quarters. "Jack said to me the fish were 'hiding.' But your father believes they're extinct. What do you think?"

Sam steepled his fingers and tapped them on his lower lip. "It's true that my grandfather talks about the fish in the present tense. And he becomes mysterious and cryptic when the subject comes up." He pushed his fingers into his hair, chuckled. "But he's frequently mysterious and cryptic."

"I've noticed."

"You know, he still goes to the mouth of the creek every morning in September and October. As though he's waiting for them."

Jess nodded, remembered Jack hugging his knees to his chest, folded into the cobbles of the streambank.

"How can you determine that? Whether they're truly extinct?" He pushed his plate aside and leaned forward.

"Still working on it." Sam's proximity was causing some kind of rift in space and time where the edge of his white collar against his brown skin became a portal for every meeting of dark and light. It made her dizzy. She pushed her chair back and looked down at her hands, folded her napkin into eighths and tucked it under her plate. She was tired and punchy, that was all. Plus, she hadn't had a date in more than a year. She had no interest in being part of a couple, or sharing a household—but sharing a bed for a few nights, that was another matter. She fixed her gaze upon his chin. "Your father has kept records of all the fish caught in the lake since around 1960. He hasn't been willing to release them to me. It would help if I had them, if I knew the last time a kokanee came out of Still Lake."

"Well, I can answer that. The last time anyone caught a kokanee was 1975, the year I was born. Does that help?"

"Oh. Well, sure. It helps to know that." She felt the information bludgeon her. Almost *thirty years.*

"You're disappointed." He touched her hand, drew away.

A thousand emotions burst into her throat and swelled there. She was losing it. Everything tumbled into a pile—the pain in her ribs, sleep deprivation, her attraction to Sam, lost fish, flying into the canyon. Moses, who could have been broken on the rocks. She put her fist against her mouth. She would *not* burst into tears in front of Sam Branch, who after all was a complete stranger.

He watched her kindly with his hands in his lap. The server came to take their plates.

She steadied herself. "Well, yes," she said. "That's a long time."

"I've never seen them, you know. The fish." He drank from his glass and the ice cubes rattled.

"No, I suppose not." She tossed a bill onto the table and followed him to his car. The sunlight gained strength against the heavy sky as they faced each other and he held out his hand and told her it had been a pleasure to meet her. She wished him safe travels. He climbed into his car and pulled away from the curb with a wave.

She bounced on her toes, hugging herself, pressing her palms against her tender ribs, holding herself in. The sun broke out of the clouds, then ducked back behind them. She watched his brake lights at the next intersection, and the next. He turned left, and she stared down the empty street until the clouds closed and the rain began again.

52.

At four-thirty Rill Kittridge locked the museum. The sky was cold and heavy. A pall crept over the bark and spent leaves of the vine maples, the lichen on the stones of the sawmill's foundation, everything drained of color. She crossed into the forest and heard a sound, a footfall. In the trees she saw a glint of gold and around it, what looked like a face. She stepped off the trail and froze, listening. "Cleve?" she called. "Cleve?"

Now she saw nothing, heard her own breath. Fog filled the gaps between the trees. Cougars lived here and sometimes attacked. She should stand her ground, not run. She wheeled back onto the trail and ran anyway, uphill, until her breath came in gulps and her chest burned. At the top of the canyon, clear of the trees, she slowed to a fast walk and looked over her shoulder. Nothing there. At the Monticola place, the doors of the shop building stood closed, no bandana tied to the handle. Just as well, she told herself, retracing her steps to the main trail. She was still breathing hard when she flung herself through the back door of her house, slammed it shut, threw the deadbolt, and leaned against it with her eyes closed.

This had to stop, all the sneaking around. She, Rill, had to end it. In the kitchen, she pulled a pan from the cupboard and dropped it on the counter for the clatter it made in the empty house. She dreaded the silence of winter. The fog made it worse. When the snow fell, quiet would fall with it, so deadening that thinking about it made her want to scream until her throat turned raw.

By the time Brian banged through the front door at six-twenty, Rill had buried the silence with Emmy Lou Harris. "Right on!" Brian shouted. He dropped his gym bag by the door and danced into the kitchen.

"Two hours of football and you can still dance!" Rill said. "Have you seen your brother?" Rill's car had reappeared in the driveway, so Scott was back from Portland.

"He's at work." Brian snapped open the refrigerator. "What's for dinner?" he asked.

"Quiche. Squash." She heard tires on the gravel outside. "Turn off the stereo, will you?" She gave the squash a final stir.

"But I like it!"

"Your father's home. He won't want it on." Brian pursed his lips at her but he walked to the living room to turn off the music as Cleve came inside. He kicked Brian's gym bag.

"What's this?" he said, and Brian scooped up the bag and took it upstairs. Without another word, Cleve sat at his place at the table and Rill began ferrying dishes from the kitchen. She set the table, twisted two white tapers into the brass candlesticks that had been her mother's. The candlesticks were too tall, heavy and ungainly, tarnished. Rill hated them. She lit the candles. Cleve liked the candlelight, the formality of their family dinners. Every evening. Six-thirty, sharp.

When Brian came back downstairs, Cleve's voice turned jovial. "Well, Brian, any news?"

"What do you mean?" Brian asked. Cleve was not normally cheerful and Rill watched him warily as she cut the quiche.

"Have a seat! You must be tired from football." Cleve gestured insistently at the chair to his left. Brian sat. "You *are* playing football, right? You're not, say, telling us you're at practice and then sneaking off to do something completely different?" Still the jovial tone.

Was Cleve joking around? Had he been drinking? Rill stood in the kitchen doorway with two bowls, one of green beans, the other butternut squash.

"What are you talking about, Dad? Of course not!"

"I mean, Brian, I am just wondering if you have any secrets you'd like to share with us. Anything at all."

Cleve's lips were smiling but Rill saw that his eyes were hard as steel. It wasn't alcohol behind his mood. It was something else. Her abdomen clenched. She stood motionless with the steaming bowls. Did he know?

"How about you, Darlin'?" he asked her. "Any secrets? Anything new to report? Where was your car this morning, for instance?" He rose and took the bowls out of her hands. "Mmm. That smells good." He sniffed the squash. "Why don't you sit down, Rill?"

Rill perched on the edge of her chair. "Scott," she said. "Scott borrowed it." Her heartbeat thumped in her ears, faster and faster.

"I see." Cleve spread his hands wide on the table and his smile broadened under the bristly black moustache to reveal his gold front tooth. "Oh, I remember, that's right: *I* have some news, something I forgot to tell you. As of July the thirty-first, my job got riffed to fifty percent. Budget cuts. So ever since then, I've been getting off work at two o'clock. Don't work at all on Tuesdays now. I forgot to mention that, didn't I?" He scooped a spoonful of squash onto his plate. "Twenty years I've worked for the state." He shrugged and chuckled, his voice hollow. "But loyalty don't go both ways, does it?" He passed the bowl to Brian. "Course, I've got no college degree. I'm not no . . . sci-en-tist." He divided the word into pieces and spat them out like seeds. "Just a working stiff."

Rill's spine turned fluid and lost its ability to hold her upright. Could Cleve have found out about her dalliance with Ben Fletcher? With Jonathan? She gripped the table's edge to keep from sliding right out of her chair.

Cleve piled green beans on his plate. "But I did make use of my extra time. I parked in town and followed you home, Darlin', on Monday, and yesterday, and again today. On Monday an interesting thing happened: I saw you go into the Monticola's woodshop and come out an hour later with your hair all messed up. Isn't that interesting?"

Brian set the bowl of squash down with a crack on the oak table and Rill's eyes followed the sound. Brian's face was flushed, his mouth slightly open. Cleve continued in his cheery tone.

"Oh, and I did have time to help out with the laundry, which is something you mentioned you'd like me to do." Cleve stood and reached into the front pocket of his jeans. "And look what I shook out of the cuff of your pants!" His fist came out clenched and as he slammed it on the table, his smile vanished. He lifted his hand to reveal a pile of wood shavings.

"Cleve—" Rill said quietly.

"Shut up!" he barked. "This is all very, very interesting, isn't it?" His voice had hardened to match his eyes. A vein throbbed in his temple. He turned toward Brian. "Son, if I have forgotten to tell you this, I apologize. Because you need to know. There are two kinds of women in the world. There are good, decent women, and then there are whores. Lots of times you can't tell the difference, not at first."

"Cleve, for God's sake!" Rill pushed her chair back.

Cleve pointed his finger at her. "You're a whore!" he screamed. Brian stood up fast and knocked his chair over.

"You shut up!" he shouted. He took one step toward Cleve with his fists clenched at his hips. There were voices on the porch, then the door burst open and Scott and Jonathan walked inside together. They pulled up short at the edge of the dining room, taking in the angry faces, the fallen chair, the untouched food. Paul Monticola followed them inside and closed the door, his smile and greeting fading as he turned toward the table.

"Well, speak of the devil!" Cleve's voice was low and dangerous. "Here's the very man who's been playing me for a fool!"

Rill locked her gaze to Jonathan's in a silent plea, willing him not to say anything.

Cleve stepped away from the table. "Here's the S.O.B. who's been screwing my wife!" He grabbed the wood shavings off the table, crossed to the door in two steps, and threw them in Paul's face, on which there was nothing but astonishment. With two sharp cracks of bone on bone, Cleve hit Paul twice. Rill screamed, and Paul went down, hitting the back of his head on the door jamb.

Jonathan rushed at Cleve with a shout, spun him around, and punched him. "Stop it! Stop it!" Rill repeated in a shriek. Brian wrapped Jonathan in a bear hug and pulled him back.

"Rill!" cried Jonathan, straining toward her. Brian pinned his arms from behind.

Rill stood. The room shook like a filmstrip, misfed. She sat down hard and her face swelled and heated until tears spilled. Scott fell to his knees beside Paul, helped him sit up. Blood streamed from Paul's nose onto the front of his shirt and coat. His head wagged groggily. Cleve stood over them, fists clenched and face contorted. Jonathan wrenched himself free of Brian's grip and ran to his father; he and Scott pulled Paul to his feet.

Paul touched his face and looked down at his fingers, then at Cleve. "For the record," he said thickly. "You've got the wrong guy." He leaned on his son as Scott opened the door. "You can talk to Sheriff LaFrance about it."

Blood dripped from his face onto the carpet. Rill kneaded her eyes with the heels of her hands until she heard the door shut. She took a long, shuddering breath.

At the other end of the table, Cleve sat down, his movements rigid and his face hard with fury. Brian and Scott pressed against the wall near the door.

"Scott, you were late for supper, so you missed the first part of our interesting conversation." Cleve cut into a slice of quiche with the edge of his fork. He took a bite.

"I'm sorry," said Scott.

"We were talking about secrets, getting a few things out in the open. Anything new with you, Scott? Any secrets?" Cleve took another bite and chewed slowly. The room vibrated with tension.

"No, I don't think so," Scott answered.

"Because, as I was telling Brian and your mother earlier, I have been catching up on the family laundry." Cleve set down his fork and wiped his mouth with a napkin. He pulled a folded piece of paper from his pocket. He unfolded it and cleared his throat. "This letter was in your pocket. I think we'll all enjoy hearing it. 'Dear Jonathan.'"

Rill's mouth opened in surprise. She looked at Scott, against the wall. Panic rose like daylight in his eyes.

"'I hate how people talk and never say anything real.' Blah, blah, blah. Oh, here's the interesting part: 'I know it sounds crazy, but—'"

Scott ran at the table and lunged for the paper. Cleve jumped up, holding it out of reach. He pushed Scott in the chest, shouting now. "'I know it sounds crazy but I think I've fallen in love with you.'"

"That's private!" Scott screamed. Tears streamed across his face as he wrestled the paper from Cleve's fist.

Rill's brain felt addled. It was an Escher drawing, all of it, where none of the strands could meet. Paul, Jonathan, Scott. Shame burned behind her eyes. *Her* fault, all of it.

Cleve laughed, low and cruel. "Well, obviously." He pointed a finger at Scott. "Is it true? I have a homo for a son?" All traces of laughter flew away. "My own son. You're a *faggot*?" He sputtered, a vulnerability flashed into his steel eyes, disappeared. "Is it true?"

Scott's lips flattened. "It's true," he said loudly. "I'm gay."

"Oh, Scott!" Rill cried. Cleve shot her a look of warning.

Scott backed up into the wall, next to his brother.

"And are you proud of that, son?" Cleve asked in a tight voice.

"I'm not ashamed." Scott wiped his cheeks.

Cleve's voice broke into a shout. "You should be!" They all flinched. "Men with men—it's repulsive! It's against God, it's against nature, and you *should* be ashamed!" He took a step toward his sons, and they edged together away from the wall, circling Cleve as though he were a rabid animal. They moved in tandem past the stairs toward the back door. Cleve spun to face them. "Get the hell out!" he screamed.

"No!" Rill stood up, bracing herself against the table. Darkness swirled into her peripheral vision. She willed herself not to faint.

"Yes!" Cleve shrieked, pointing at Scott. "No goddamned queer lives under my roof! Get out!"

"No!" Rill yelled again.

They reached the back door and Brian pushed Scott through it, into the mud room. "Mom, come with us!" Brian called through the doorway.

"No, this can't be happening!" Rill stumbled toward them.

"Get out now!" Cleve screamed, his face red, fists tight.

"Come with us, Mom—we're leaving!" Brian pleaded, but the room was lurching and Rill braced herself against the table again.

"Get out of my house!" Cleve stomped toward them. Scott opened the back door and they ran outside.

She needed to leave, but her body trembled uncontrollably. Cleve whirled on her. She saw his raised hand an instant before the back of it cracked across her face. She swayed. He hit her again. The blows seemed to jar the haziness from her brain, though her face was numb when he backhanded her a third time. She collided with the edge of the table and bent backwards, landing on her elbow. She moved into the pain, sliding her arm across the polished oak. The candles were still burning, guttering insanely. She closed her fingers around the candlestick. Hot wax seared the back of her hand as the candle toppled away, but that pain cleared her head, too. The pain and the violence were beautiful in their clarity, primal. Her fingers crept to the rim of the candlestick and glued themselves into the melted wax as Cleve stepped closer and raised his hand. With all the strength of her arm and shoulder and torso and thighs, she swung the candlestick into the side of Cleve's head.

She rushed him as he staggered backward, brought the clumsy, ugly thing around, and twisted her whole body into a backhand that hit him in the jaw. He crumpled and lay still. The spilled candle ignited a paper napkin. It leaped in a fireball to the floor and sprouted a lawn of flames.

The smoke alarm shrieked. Rill tossed the candlestick into the middle of the fire and wondered whether she should let the whole goddamned house go up in flames, with Cleve in it. But there were her children to consider, and this house was the Stukel homestead. The roof over their heads was *her* roof, not Cleve's. She stepped over Cleve to the hall closet, pulled a quilt from the shelf. She stepped over him again as she shook out the folds and spread it soft as falling snow over the flames. The fire had flung an emissary to the curtains. Rill tore them down and stomped it out. The flames died. The quilt smoked. A pity about the quilt: Her mother had sewn it by hand.

On her way out the back door, she paused to stare at Cleve's face. His eyes were wide, his lips bleeding, pulled back in a grimace. He might be dead. She felt nothing.

53.

Deep in the forest, they stopped running. Scott braced his hands on his knees and tasted vomit. He shut his eyes and the forest lurched. He opened them and looked at his brother.

"We have to go back," Brian said. The last of the daylight threw his features into relief, leaving black sockets where his eyes should be.

"What? Are you nuts? He'll kill me." Scott straightened.

"There are two of us. It'll be okay." Brian grabbed his forearm, squeezed.

"No. It definitely won't." Scott's throat constricted. The vomit taste bloomed on his tongue. He tried to swallow, couldn't.

"Well, I'm going back. We can't just leave her there." Brian turned. Scott stepped into his path.

"No. No, look—we'll call the sheriff from Jonathan's house."

Brian bit his lip. "What if it's too late?"

"We'll call Sheriff LaFrance, then we'll go right back to the house. Okay?"

An owl called, long and low. Brian turned his head, a silhouette in the last light. Scott shivered, hunched, drove his hands deep into his front pockets. "*Okay*, Brian?"

The owl called again, from somewhere else, down toward Old Chuck Creek. Or maybe a different owl, answering. Finally, Brian nodded. "Let's hurry."

Saturday, October 2, 2004

54.

The acrid smell of singed cotton invaded Rill's nostrils all night and interrupted her sleep on the bench beneath the trees, though she shifted and twisted the quilt every which way to escape it. Finally, as the eastern edges of the mountains began to glow with a seam of orange light, she plunged her face into the burnt fibers and inhaled, as though seeking out danger. With the smell, the terrible clarity returned, and her thoughts organized themselves like typeset columns on a long clean page. She sat up on the hewn log, lifted her fingers to her cheeks to probe the swelling.

With the burnt quilt hanging heavy over her arm, she had walked last night to the end of the trail, near the headwaters. Here, between three lodgepole pines, Jonathan had mounted a frame of poles, had woven saplings into lattice for a roof. With his chainsaw, he'd carved a bench and placed it underneath.

Rill stretched her legs and looked up through the lattice to the orange and pink sky. She and Jon had made love here, sprawled naked on the long brown needles. Less than one week ago, she'd sat in this exact spot with her legs draped over his shoulders and her fingers in his hair, guiding his mouth, while animal sounds tore from her throat.

She stood, her face hot. She had been cavorting with a twenty-year-old. Had stayed married to a man she detested. Had failed to register that her son was trying to come out of the closet, that he pined for young Jonathan. *Her* lover. She squeezed her palms against her ears, clamped her eyes shut as though she could keep from seeing the truth.

When she opened her eyes, she saw Jonathan through the trees, a flash of his red flannel shirt, heading up the trail with a rucksack. She realized she had been expecting him.

She waited on the bench with the quilt wrapped in a sloppy pile around her. He broke into a run when he saw her, the rucksack bouncing on his back. He flung it down inside the shelter and slid onto the bench beside her. He took her swollen face between his hands and whispered, "He hurt you."

His touch made her flinch. She put her hands on top of his. "I left him there. Is he dead?"

"Not dead. In jail. Where he belongs."

"Scott and Brian?" She dropped her hands to her lap. They were shaking. Jonathan gathered them together and held them, his hands large and square and strong.

"They're fine. They came to our house. Sheriff LaFrance was already there. We all went back to your house together, but you were gone."

"Is your father badly hurt?"

"He has a concussion, from hitting the door when he fell."

"Is Cleve? Hurt?"

"Who cares?"

Rill snatched her hands away and bunched the quilt up under her chin. Jonathan's dark eyes, his smooth, tanned face, the postage-stamp of a black beard tucked beneath his lower lip: abruptly, he seemed menacing.

"He was still unconscious when we got there. They took him to the hospital. Now he's in jail. My father is pressing charges. They think he ran that fish scientist off the road, too. On purpose. She could have been killed."

"Is she all right?"

"Bruised up. I heard she broke some ribs."

Rill nodded, squeezing the quilt at her throat.

"There's a rumor they're going to charge him with murder."

"Murder! Whose?" The burnt cotton smell pealed into her nostrils.

"Ben Fletcher. They don't think he drowned by accident. Cleve's been yelling about 'prissy homos with science degrees' taking his job." Jonathan's lips were tight.

"Cleve's not a murderer." But was he?

"Maybe, maybe not. He's definitely a son of a bitch." He pried her hand loose from the quilt and trapped it in his fingers. "Rill. You're not going to stay married to that bastard."

She shook her head slowly. It thudded with a steady, rhythmic pain. "No."

He clamped her hand between both of his. "Then come away with me. We can be together, somewhere else. We'll just leave. You and me."

"That's impossible."

"Why?" The word flew at her like a bullet.

She was still shaking her head and the pain was getting worse. "Don't do this, Jon. Not now."

But his eyes glowed, reckless. "What if he *was* dead? Then would you come with me?"

He was squeezing her hand too hard. She pulled it away. A bristle of violence beneath his questions made her think of Cleve. She shuddered, twisted away, stood and steadied herself with her palm on the pine tree. "No. Anyway it doesn't matter." She fixed her gaze on her hand, splayed her fingers on the puckered bark. The hand did not seem to belong to her. She touched its fingers to her face again, felt the swelling below her right eye. Pressed. Winced.

From the bench, behind her, Jonathan said, "Why not? I don't get it. I never get it. I never know where I stand with you. What the hell."

She did not turn around. "Jonathan. I'm forty-two. You're twenty."

"So what?" His voice got louder. "How old was that scientist you were fucking, Ben Fletcher?"

She set her hand on the tree again and braced herself, not turning. Her words were even and slow. "Don't talk to me like that."

"How old? Did you sleep with him? I just want to know."

His tone had sharpened to a dangerous edge, and suddenly she registered what he'd said about Ben Fletcher. The summer's events meshed together like gears: Jonathan had seen her in Ben's truck. Jonathan wanted her. Then, Ben had drowned.

Rill had learned something about violence: It was easy and it was natural. She kept her gaze on her hand and her words even. "Did you kill him?"

He rose to stand behind her. "Did you sleep with him?" Outrage in his voice.

Still she didn't turn. "Did you kill him?" Her voice rose an octave. "Why don't you answer the question?"

"Why don't *you*?" he yelled. "Did you fuck him?" He put a hand on her shoulder, pulled her around to face him, not gently.

Something burst behind Rill's eyes bright as a camera flash. She spun, swung, hooked him on the side of his head with her open hand. They stood glaring at each other. A mark on his cheekbone reddened, faded. "Don't touch me like that," she spat out. "I'm done being manhandled."

"I'm sorry." His eyes softened.

She looked away. She'd slept in her bra and now it cut into the skin under her breasts. She picked at it, folded her arms across her chest. This had to end. She took a breath. "Look, Jonathan, this is too much. I'm done. I'll tell you exactly where you stand. It's over."

He reared backward as though she'd struck him again. He mouthed the word "No" again and again. He said it aloud: "No, Rill. Please. No."

He bent his head and began to cry. He was just a boy. Not a murderer. *She* was the monster. She wanted to tear herself in half, expose her ink-black heart. She wanted to comfort him, cradle his head to her shoulder, take it all back. She let the quilt slip from her shoulders like a husk of dead skin and stepped past him into the forest, stumbled on a root, caught herself. Kept walking.

Sunday, October 3, 2004

55.

The milk had gone sour. Scott sniffed it and took a cautious sip. The sour taste bit his tongue and he spat into the sink. He soaked his cereal with half and half instead and carried his bowl to the table.

Brian and Rill sat there like zombies. Brian's cereal bowl was empty, but for a white puddle at the bottom. On Rill's plate was a single piece of toast, untouched. Her hands were folded in her lap and she looked old and beat up, with one black eye swollen shut, her lip split open, the bruise on her other cheekbone lumpy and spreading. Her fingers kept wandering from her lap to her face, poking at the bruises.

"Mom, I made coffee. Would you like some?" Scott set his bowl on the table.

She turned her unfocused eyes in his direction. "Yes. Thank you." He slid a mug next to her plate. She groped for the handle. Lifted the cup to her lips.

Scott looked down at his cereal. "Did you use milk?" he asked Brian. "It's spoiled."

"Didn't notice," Brian said. He stirred his spoon around the puddle in his bowl.

The three of them sat in their usual places at the round dining table, now scarred with a burn mark. Rill's chair was nearest the kitchen; Scott to her left and Brian to her right. Cleve's empty chair, at the far edge nearest the front door, sat at an angle away from the table. No one had touched it.

From the table to the front window, a scorched path led across the carpet, the curtains in a blackened heap next to the door. Scott moved his eyes back to the bowl. The half and half tasted sweet, sweeter than milk. Colby Stukel, his grandfather, used to eat Raisin Bran with half and half for breakfast. When Scott and Brian were grade schoolers, they stayed with him overnight every weekend, shuffling to his big dark trestle table in their pajamas, hair sticking up in all directions, glass bowls and silver spoons and dimpled paper napkins arranged on linen placemats.

First, they passed the cereal box: Scott, Brian, Colby. Then the carton of half and half: Scott, Brian, Colby. Then Colby would hold up a glass pitcher like a ball of morning sun and boom, "Orange juice?"

They spoke in chorus. "No, thank you." Neither of them liked orange juice, especially in the morning, when it felt like acid in the throat and spoiled the sweetness of the raisins and the cream. Which was special. Which filmed their spoons and could be licked free like the memory of a dream.

On Friday morning, in Portland, he'd taken himself out to breakfast at the Rainbow Café. Two men sat nearby. Scott was sure they were a couple. He must have been staring, because one of them, a white guy with a trim brown moustache, said, "How's it going?"

"Fine," he'd managed to answer.

"You're visiting?" the other asked. He was Asian, a big smile on his round face. The smile looked like it belonged there, like he smiled a lot.

Scott nodded. They introduced themselves as Mark and Robert, shook his hand, paid their tab but lingered. They asked where he was from and agreed that they'd never heard of his tiny hometown. The white man, Mark, asked, "How is that working out for you?"

Scott knew what he meant. "Not that great," he'd answered, and, with no warning, he'd had to swallow back tears.

When they got up to leave, Robert, with his easy smile, rested his hand on Scott's shoulder. "Hang in there," he said. "It gets better."

"Not just better," Mark said, lisping on purpose. "It gets fabulous!"

And they kissed, on the lips. Right in front of Scott and everybody. The wonder of it chattered in his brain like a buoyant travel companion all the way back to Still Lake.

Brian took his bowl to the kitchen and returned with a mug of coffee. "The half and half is gone," he told them.

"I used it on my cereal. Sorry." Scott swirled his tongue on his spoon. Sweet. He remembered the sweetness from ten years before, when he and Brian spent the night at their grandfather's house. Colby's bathrobe was made of brown corduroy. His slippers matched. He would set the pitcher on the table with a clunk as his bushy white eyebrows drew together in dismay, every time. How could his grandsons not want orange juice?

Colby Stukel had a Ph.D. in English Literature from Indiana University, a bachelor's degree in journalism. The Stukels were high class, reasonable, cerebral. How had his mother ended up with their dad? Scott had never wondered about it before.

"You know, Mom," he said, and waited for her to look at him. Brian looked up, too, setting his cup down. "Maybe you should've kept your own name when you got married. Lots of women do." He could only think of one, his Aunt Race, married to Mike.

"Mmm." Rill sipped from her yellow cup.

"Why did you? Change your name?"

Rill's voice came out gravelly, as though it hadn't been used and had rusted. "Your father never felt he belonged in a family. It was important to him that we all be Kittridges."

Scott tried for a light tone. "We could have been Stukels. He could have changed *his* name."

Rill smiled, deepening the lines around her mouth. Brian wrinkled his nose at him as if to say, *Where the hell are you going with this?*

Scott didn't know where he was going. He regretted bringing Cleveland S. Kittridge into the conversation. He felt lightheaded, giddy almost, the way he'd felt when he floated out of the Rainbow Café. He could not seem to drop the subject. "Still, *you* could have kept your name." His spoon rattled as he chased the last bit of cereal around the bottom of his bowl.

"We fought about it, actually. I lost." She sagged in her chair. "I'm so tired of fighting."

Scott remembered Jess MacKinnon at dinner, the conversation about Chief Joseph. *I would like to stop fighting*, she'd said, her eyes illuminated like bright blue stained glass. "Why don't you stop, then?" he said to his mother.

She deflated like a punctured balloon and her head dropped into her hands.

"Jesus, Scott," Brian hissed.

They sat, silent. Brian spun his empty cup on the table. "So, Mom?" he said.

Rill raised her head. "Mmm?"

"What's going to happen now?" Brian ran his fingers through his light brown hair, which was already standing up. His hair was wavy and unruly, as though he'd inherited Rill's curliness tempered by Cleve's hair: straight, tame, always clipped. Scott had Cleve's hair. At least his *hair* was straight. He laughed, giddy again. They stared at him. He pretended to be coughing.

Brian pushed his bowl away and bent across the table toward Rill. His gray-blue eyes matched their father's. They shone across the table like headlights trying to pierce the fog that surrounded their mother. "I mean, Dad's in jail. Scott's kicked out of the house for being, you know . . ." Brian trailed off.

Scott watched Rill, glanced at his brother, then back to his mother. Rill's bruised face remained slack and expressionless, but then her features firmed themselves and she sat up straighter. "No, Scott is *not* kicked out of the house," she said loudly. "This is *my* house, not Cleve's. Your father won't be coming back here. He's not going to live with us anymore." She gulped her coffee, dribbling some down her front.

Scott and Brian stared at Rill as she brushed at her shirt. She asked for more coffee. Brian refilled her cup. "The half and half is gone," he said again. Rill nodded, slurped the black coffee, dribbling again. Scott had never seen her like this. His mother was not sloppy.

"I used it on my cereal," Scott said, as before. He had the sensation of being caught in a time warp, some crazy loop.

Rill set her cup down. "Scott. You tried to tell me about being gay. I didn't listen. I am so sorry, so very sorry."

Scott's throat closed. He bent his head, scraped his empty bowl with the spoon, waited out the hot surge of tears. "It's okay, Mom." He looked at his brother, then back at the cereal bowl.

Brian cleared his throat. "It's fine with us if you're gay," he said. "Right, Mom?"

"Of course it is." She reached over and patted Scott's shoulder.

"No more secrets. Right?" Brian folded his arms. He stared at Rill. "Right, Mom?"

Rill's lips parted. Her fingers wandered to her cheek, poking at the bruises. "What do you mean?"

Scott frowned at his brother. "What are you talking about, Bri?"

"*Your* secret, Mom. That he hits you. This isn't the first time."

Rill's eyes filled. She covered them with her hands.

"You thought we didn't know," Brian said.

Scott's spoon fell from his fingers. His eyes followed the burned path across the carpet to the front door. *Had* he known? He had seen bruises on his mother's face before. He'd seen his father, taut as a rattlesnake, raising an open hand. Could you know and not know a thing, at the same time?

Rill nodded, hands over her eyes. Scott could tell she was crying.

Monday, October 4, 2004

56.

"We got us a situation, Cowpoke," Riley said when Jess MacKinnon arrived on Monday. MacKinnon sat on the edge of the chair. She looked all right but she held herself tight and her movements were tentative, the way a person navigates with two broken ribs. Barely noticeable, but MacKinnon usually stomped about like a rhinoceros. Plus, she had a new smell, now, beneath the citrus scent and subtle. Riley looked down at the desk and closed her eyes: It was oil. No, tar. Asphalt burning under the sun.

"What situation?" MacKinnon said.

"Moses is missing. Again. Rex and Becky are very upset. In addition to finding out how Ben died, it is now my job to find Moses."

"Dammit." MacKinnon spat out the word.

"Not to worry. He checked into a room at the Enterprise Motor Hotel, not far from here." She chuckled. "To be fair, nothing in Enterprise is very far from anything else. He's not there now, but they'll call me as soon as he comes back."

MacKinnon smiled quickly at the small-town joke, then bit her lower lip. And there it was again, the smell of tar.

"Tea?" Riley sprang up without waiting for an answer. She left the door open while she ran downstairs to the restaurant, though she knew no amount of airing would make the smell go away. She enjoyed MacKinnon's baseline scent: fresh lime, sour and sharp and a little bit sweet. To Riley it smelled like eagerness but also like longing. Where did the tar smell come from? She trudged up the stairs, holding the cups steady so the tea wouldn't slosh.

She set the tea on the desk and took her seat. MacKinnon was rooting around in a backpack. No duffle bag today, no helmet. Of course: no more motorcycle. "How'd you get here?" Riley asked.

"Rental car." MacKinnon shrugged as though it didn't matter but the tar smell rose between them. MacKinnon slid a notepad onto the desk and asked Riley for the phone number at the Enterprise Motor Hotel.

Riley gave her the number. "I predict he'll show up there before dark. There's snow in the forecast tonight." She bent over the tea and let the steam fog her glasses and carry the smells of pepper and cinnamon and cloves into her nose. Olfactory scents were different from the smells that came from the short-circuited gadgetry in her neuroatypical brain. A case in point was her rancher client, Bob, who showed up for his appointment two days after being sprayed by a skunk. The memory made Riley's eyes water. She inhaled the steam from her cup: cardamom.

"Are you going to Still Lake to look for him? As soon as I get to town, I'll check the place I found him before." MacKinnon tapped her fingers on the top of the teacup.

"I doubt he'll be there. And please be careful." Riley pushed her cup to the side. "To answer your question, I'll head up there this afternoon." She folded her arms on the desk and leaned over them. "We need to talk about last Thursday. There are fourteen white pickup trucks in Still Lake. We know that one belongs to Cleve Kittridge. Another belongs to Karl Luder, who is on the city council."

MacKinnon nodded. The smell rose, sun-baked asphalt. It was fear, Riley decided. And a vulnerability MacKinnon felt without her motorcycle. Which was odd. Riley felt safer with the steel of her Subaru around her, but it wasn't the same for Jess MacKinnon.

"How sure are you that the pickup hit you on purpose?"

"Pretty damn sure," MacKinnon said, not sounding sure at all.

"Give me a percentage."

"Ninety." Uncertainty crossed her face. "Eighty-five."

"So you're not positive."

MacKinnon bent her head. "It happened so fast." Her fingers did a tap dance around the rim of her cup. "Cleve Kittridge bought me a drink and apologized for begin rude. Otherwise, I'd be sure it was him." She wrinkled her face in concentration, then pinched at the skin between her eyebrows. Riley let her eyes fall shut as the scent rose all around them, a thousand limes sliced open. "He's married to the woman who runs the newspaper," she added when Riley didn't respond.

"I know who Kittridge is. He's in jail right at the moment."

"Jail? For what?"

"He punched someone. Punched his own wife, too. He seems unstable."

MacKinnon pinched between her eyebrows again. "Maybe it *was* him." She sipped her tea.

"Tell me more," Riley prompted.

"He works for a state agency and he's angry about 'college kids' getting hired while his job got cut back to part time. He considers me one of those college kids." She smiled as though this was funny. It made her look younger and less worn, the crooked teeth oddly compelling. Then the smile dropped away. "He would have considered Ben a college kid, too. Maybe he's the one who killed him."

Riley added it up. She took off her glasses and wiped them with her shirt tail. It didn't make sense. "You think he murdered Fletcher for having a college education? That doesn't sound like much of a motive."

"Well, he's angry. He drinks. He's violent. And he does drive that white pickup. How many did you say there are?"

"Fourteen."

MacKinnon shrugged. "I'm sure you'll figure it out." She stood. "Thanks for the tea. As for me, I have to go find out whether there are any fish left. Please find Moses."

Riley saluted. "Those be my marching orders, Ma'am." MacKinnon closed the office door and the bright smell of limes left with her.

57.

The ring of keys had been hanging in the Outfitter's storeroom and they felt like ice. Sammy found one labeled "Boat Storage" and jiggled it into the padlock. Where were his gloves? It was unseasonably cold. The sky hung low and the air tasted like December. The first snowstorm was heading their way, early this year.

The lock sprang loose and Sammy opened the double doors of the storage room under the back deck. He stepped clear and looked out over the tin-colored lake. Mike was on the dock, hauling boats and canoes out of the water with help from Sheriff Bertie LaFrance, who had been pressed into service until Scott arrived for work. Sammy blew on his hands and stowed them deep in his coat pockets. Cleve Kittridge, the brute, had thrown Scott out of the house for being a homosexual. Had punched his wife for sleeping with Paul Monticola. Sammy shook his head. So much drama! He wondered how much of it was true.

He ducked into the storage area. There was no electricity and no lights, but sunlight slanted through the slatted walls, striping the dirt. Sammy found a broom in the corner and swept away the cobwebs around the racks where the boats would wait out the winter. Mike would want the hulls dried, too, so they would not ice up. Sammy brushed cobwebs from his shoulders and took the stairs up to the deck to look for towels.

When he entered from the back door, someone was knocking at the front entrance and looking through the window: Karl Luder. Sammy let him in. "I've got a favor to ask," Karl said.

Birch Stukel thudded up the steps in her cowboy boots and shoved into the room wearing a pink beret and matching scarf, the fringed end of which she tossed over her shoulder before plunging her index finger into Karl's chest. "What the fuck, Karl?" she sputtered.

Karl raised his hands in surrender and took two steps backward.

"What is troubling you this afternoon, my dear?" Sammy asked her.

She rounded on him, red-faced. "He posted bail for Cleve! The fucker is out there right now, asleep in Karl's truck!" She put her hands on her hips. "Or I suppose he's passed out drunk, correct? What were you thinking? Can't we leave his sorry ass in jail and have a few days of peace?"

Sammy did not point out that Birch's voice had risen to a shriek and that she, not Cleve, was the one currently disturbing the peace. His, at least.

"Have you *seen* my sister's face?"

Karl hooked his thumbs in his belt loops and looked at his boots. "Cleve and me are friends. From way back. You know that."

"What I know is you stick to Kittridge like a fly on shit. Get a clue, Karl! He's a bad, bad man!"

Karl looked up. "He's not, though. He's rough around the edges, sure. But decent underneath it all."

"Decent." Birch shook her head. "I haven't known him as long as you have, Karl, but I've known him plenty long enough, and I have yet to see this decent underneath part. What are you planning to do with him? He sure as hell is not welcome at Rill's place."

Karl spread his hands, sent a small, rueful smile in Sammy's direction. "I was hoping he could spend the night in the storeroom. I think Mike keeps a cot in there."

Sammy felt for the ring of keys in his pocket. "The storeroom is cold," he said. "Although there may be a space heater. Can he not stay with you?"

"Lydia won't have him in the house," Karl answered. Birch snorted. Sammy heard footsteps out back, and Mike and Bertie came in, bringing a cold gust with them.

Birch opened the front door, inviting another gust inside. "Well, gentlemen, that's your problem." She stepped outside, closed the door, and opened it again. "But I'll see you for dinner, won't I?" Sammy nodded, wishing she would shut the door, for pity's sake!

"What's happening?" Mike asked. "What problem?"

"Cleve," Karl said. "He's passed out in my truck."

"We'd better go get him, then," Mike said. "Before he freezes solid." Mike's face was flushed with exertion and also excitement, Sammy supposed. Mike loved the boats. Sammy remembered the towels he'd come for.

"I came in for towels," he said. "To dry the boats."

"I took care of it." Mike put a hand on Karl's elbow. "Come on, Karl. Let's get your buddy inside." He opened the front door and frowned down the street, scratching his goatee the way he always did, and bouncing on his toes. Where he got all that energy from was a perpetual mystery. "I wonder where Scott is. He should've been here by now."

The clock on the wall said three-forty-five. Scott arrived after school, usually at three-thirty. Sammy's chest clenched: What if Scott had resorted to self harm? What if he were dead, swinging from a rope in some dark, hidden place? It happened to gay kids. Tears leaked from his eyes, summoned by his own over-active imagination—only that! He followed the others out to Karl's white truck, wiping his face.

Cleve revived when Karl pulled him from the cab. He clutched the neck of a bottle of Jack Daniels. "Hello, gents!" he slurred cheerfully, taking a swig.

"That's an open container," Bertie said. "Shall I write you a ticket, Karl?"

Cleve fumbled in his pocket and found the cap. He twisted it onto the bottle, triumphant. "There. Now it's closed."

Karl snatched the bottle and put it in the truck bed.

"Oh, come on!" Cleve whined. "Rules, rules, rules." He groped for the bottle.

"Yes. Rules." Sammy shoved Cleve back against the truck, harder than he meant to. The image of Scott hanging from a rafter had turned into fury at this father who did not deserve such a fine son. "You should try obeying them."

Cleve laughed. "I make my own rules," he said merrily, pushing Sammy's hand away. The movement unbalanced him, and he flopped onto the pavement like a landed fish.

Mike helped Karl half-drag Cleve into the storeroom and stretch him out on Mike's Army cot. Sammy watched as a muscle under Cleve's eye twitched. Scott resembled his mother, thank goodness. Except for the hint of dimples when he smiled: Those were Kittridge's. Scott hadn't been smiling as much lately. Sammy chastised himself for not noticing. Cleve's eyes closed, his mouth fell open, and he began to snore softly.

"Cold in here," Karl said.

Mike nodded. "Feels like snow. I stowed the boats for the winter, except the *Tamkaliks*. For emergencies."

Emergencies. Where was Scott? Sammy hung the ring of keys on their hook and pictured young Scotty walking into the frigid lake, stones in his pockets. Like Virginia Woolf. It was after four o'clock.

Karl found the space heater and plugged it in. He spread a gray wool blanket over Cleve and tucked it around his shoulders. With the blanket under his chin and his moustache shaggy and blowing with his breath, Cleve looked vulnerable. But Sammy couldn't shake off his anger. "Cleve is lucky to have you, Karl. No one else has any use for him."

"I make allowances." Karl straightened. "He hasn't had an easy life."

"I suppose that's true," Bertie said.

Mike grunted. They followed him out into the store, where they surprised someone peering into the front window. Mike flung open the door. "Come on in!" he said. "Can I help you find something?"

The interloper leaped back. "No! That's okay." His voice sounded young, muffled though it was by a scarf around his face. Coils of red hair flew loose from his cap. Sammy peeked over Mike's shoulder to get a better look. "You!" the boy shouted, pointing his finger. "Is that your truck?"

Karl elbowed past them and put out his hand. He and the boy were the same height. "Karl Luder. The truck belongs to me. Is there a problem?"

Instead of shaking hands, the boy stumbled down the steps to the sidewalk. The scarf fell away from his angry mouth. His pointing finger drew a bead on Karl. "You knocked me off the road!" he shouted.

"You're wrong about that, son," Karl said, calm as always.

The kid was hysterical. Sammy edged around Mike and looked down from the top of the stairs.

"And *you*!" The finger pointed back toward Sammy. "You killed my brother!"

"Excuse me?" Sammy said.

Bertie pushed through the human knot on the landing and clumped down the steps. "You're Moses Fletcher. You should be at home, young man."

The boy backed away. "You're going to pay for that!" he shouted as Bertie closed in. "An eye for an eye! I'll take you out myself! You're going to pay for killing my brother, Mayor Branch!" Bertie grabbed for the boy's arm but he spun out of reach and sprinted down the street.

"What's going on?" said another young voice and one Sammy knew well. "Who was that guy?" Scott joined them on the landing. "Sorry I'm late," he said. Sammy wrapped his arms around the boy and squeezed until his bones cracked.

58.

At Keeler's Counter, Sammy half-listened as Birch railed on about Cleve Kittridge and Karl's misguided loyalty. He had already filled her in about the installation of half-conscious Kittridge on the cot in the storeroom. "Someone should take this opportunity to put a pillow over his face and hold it there," Birch had observed—a shocking comment, even for her.

Now she was complaining about the "goddamned lawyers" in her patent infringement lawsuit. Birch lived comfortably off license fees from her software inventions. She fueled her reputation as a recluse and eccentric by staying home and mixing mysterious home-grown concoctions—including the bottle of fermented tea she had just given him, which Sammy was saving for a half-baked plan later in the evening.

They ordered their meals. Birch droned on. Sammy wondered about the odd young man who believed Sammy had killed his brother, Ben Fletcher. Sheriff LaFrance had promised to investigate.

Birch changed the subject. "I'm concerned about this fish restoration project. Why is there another scientist here, after what happened to the last one?"

He assumed the question was rhetorical. He imagined himself walking arm in arm with Jess MacKinnon, on whom he had an unmistakable crush. His imagination made him fifty years younger, forty pounds lighter, and perfectly charming. There would be moonlight, of course.

"Is the Outfitters in financial trouble? Don't you do the books? Why are you smiling?"

Sammy pulled himself back from the moonlit stroll. It took him a moment to replay Birch's last few sentences, to cull some fragment he could latch on to by way of a satisfactory response. "Yes, I do the books. After a fashion." He tried out a smile, but Birch wore a scowl, which seemed perpetual. She had turned brittle since Colby Stukel's death. Colby had doted on Birch, the youngest of his three daughters, in particular.

"Well, if they stock the lake with kokanee, that sure as hell won't mean more fishing. Those fish will be protected."

Sammy saw their dinner plates approaching. He unfolded his paper napkin and smoothed it over his thighs, securing the edge under his ample belly. He had ordered chicken stew. He started to answer her, but her face jerked, her eyes squeezing shut and her lips pulling back into a grimace. It lasted less than two seconds. She had developed this tic after Colby's death, involuntary and, he was sure, unconscious. As though loss had destabilized her tissues.

Sammy tried his stew, a spoonful from the edge of the bowl where it would be cooler. There were three dumplings, half submerged, packed together like ice floes. They would be molten. "It would help us all to have kokanee in the lake again," he said. "Think how Colby would feel."

Birch slammed her fork down onto the table so loudly that conversation in the restaurant halted. "What do you mean?" she spat. Why was she bristling up at him?

"I am certain Colby felt some guilt about what happened, as does Mike. Even now."

Birch hid her face behind her napkin but Sammy saw the tic again, drawing her features closed. "My father had no reason to feel guilty." Birch leaned across the table.

She had more to say, clearly, but Sammy interrupted with a gesture toward the door: Jess MacKinnon had arrived. She strode across the restaurant, waving. Sammy thought about the moonlight and blushed. What a schoolboy he was! Completely inappropriate for a man of his advanced age. Still, he stood and took her hand and kissed it. Saw Birch roll her eyes, wicked woman.

"We were just discussing your project," Sammy said when Jess had settled next to him at the table. "Have you made progress?" He tried and failed to dampen the effervescence in his voice. Birch was smirking into her napkin.

"Some." Jess opened the menu and thanked the server who had delivered it.

Sammy pointed to the chicken stew, with dumplings. Would Birch ever stop smirking? Even the tic would be preferable.

Sammy turned to look out the window as Jess ordered the chicken stew. Low clouds, the lake a vast black emptiness. As he watched, the first snowflakes fell, arriving like tiny ghosts out of the darkness. "It is snowing," he announced, and he felt a downy sweep of emotion, something like nostalgia, equal parts gratitude and longing. He turned back to his dinner companions, held up his hand in a gesture that made a circle of the window, the lake, the restaurant. All of Still Lake, really the whole world. "First snow." He looked into Jess's summer blue eyes and smiled.

She smiled back. "You know," she said, "I would really like to see Mike's catch records. Can you convince him to show me?"

The spell was broken but Sammy's smile bubbled into laughter.

"What records?" asked Birch.

"Mike has kept notes of all the fish caught in the lake since 1962," he told Birch. "Measurements, weights. Other details."

"What other details?"

Sammy watched while her face contorted into the grimace. "Contextual details." He patted Jess's hand, felt the tingle of the contact.

"Like what?" asked Birch.

Why was Birch focused on Mike's records? Sammy frowned at her and turned back to Jess. "The records are in the storeroom at the Outfitters," he told her. "I will get them for you myself."

"Thank you. You're sweet." She kissed his cheek. He pretended to swoon.

"For God's sake," Birch muttered.

59.

After dinner, Jess went back to her room. Riley would call her the moment Moses showed up at the Enterprise Motor Hotel, at which time he would be escorted home by his parents, who were lying in wait.

She sat on the edge of the bed and stared at the phone, willing it to ring. What could Moses be thinking? Maybe this was his way of dealing with Ben's death. Death made you feel helpless. Moses was running away and skulking around because he wanted to *do* something. That must be it.

Jess sprang to her feet and crossed to the window. The snow fell in earnest, crowding the darkness outside her window as it floated down to cover the lake and the town. Portland didn't get much snow and Jess missed it. As a girl she had loved waking up after an all-night snowstorm—to the ethereal quiet, the white softness that erased all the harsh, dark edges of Chicago. But now she scowled at the storm. What if Moses was out in the forest? "Come on!" she yelled at the phone.

Six days from now, Moses would be eighteen, and that would make it harder for Rex to swoop in, gather him up, and cart him back to the Fletcher ranch. At twenty, Ben had allowed Rex to push him around, but Moses was less compliant. More like her, if she were honest.

60.

"He's starting to look more like you," Ben had said on the Kid's twelfth birthday. They were standing beside her motorcycle, late afternoon, the sun already slanting into twilight. "His face has the shape of yours." He smiled.

"I don't see it," she said, but she *had* noticed.

"Look, Jess, we can undo this thing."

Ben's face wore its solemn, earnest expression. It took her a minute to realize what he was talking about: this "thing" with their son, he meant. "No, we can't," she said. "I signed the papers. So did you. I talked to a lawyer about it, years ago." She flicked the kickstand up and whipped her leg over the seat. With the bike under her, she felt bolder. She was stronger than Ben and always had been. "I won't risk it, not being allowed to see him. Once a year is better than never. Anyway, I promised."

"He'll be eighteen in six more years. Then he can decide for himself."

"I suppose. Six years is a long time."

"Not that long. Let's tell him, together. On his eighteenth birthday. We'll talk ahead of time, we'll decide what to say." He stepped up closer, his shoes crunching on the gravel.

She looked down at the handlebars. "Your parents won't like that."

"Doesn't matter."

"Doesn't it?" She reached for the ignition switch but he cupped his hand over hers.

"No. Jess. I was wrong to side with them when Moses was born. I was scared. But wrong. I hope it's not too late to be on *your* side, now. Because I am. Really." His eyes had moistened, his face still tanned from summer and his freckles like a sprinkle of stars flung across the night sky. She turned up her palm and squeezed his hand. She couldn't speak. She pulled the helmet over her head, turned on the engine, and tore down the gravel road.

61.

When Sammy ventured outside again at nine o'clock, snow clotted the sky. Several inches had accumulated on the street. He trudged through it, urging his slow feet forward. With each step, his boot sole creaked as it compressed the snow; as his weight released it, the snow gave a soft crunchcrunchcrunch, as though grunting to acknowledge his passing. Creak, crunchcrunchcrunch: it was the only sound in Still Lake. No one else was about. Two wine goblets clinked in his coat pocket. He halted, reached inside, adjusted the handkerchief that kept them apart.

In his right pocket, its neck poking out as if to brave the cold, he carried a bottle of Birch's mint-infused cherry blossom tea, lightly fermented. Birch had assured him it tasted nothing like wine. In his mind, he carried the unformed beginnings of a foolhardy plan.

The light inside Still Lake Lodge was gray and a pinewood fire crackled in the big stone fireplace. The desk clerk had pulled one of the wingback chairs close, propped her feet on the hearth. She glanced up from her comic book to nod at him as he shuffled through the lobby.

At Jess's door, he raised his hand to knock. But he heard her talking. Lowered his arm. Someone was with her; no, she was talking on the telephone. He stepped back, but her voice floated into the hallway. "Then where the hell is he?" she nearly shouted. She sounded upset. Well, it would not do to eavesdrop. He removed his cap, wiped the melted snow from his face. He would come back later. He would bring along the fishing records. She would be finished with her phone call then. He pulled his cap down tight over his ears, which compressed the feathery flakes of his disappointment into a ball behind his Adam's apple.

Downstairs, the clerk had fallen asleep in her chair, the comic book splayed across her chest. He pushed out into the cold and started toward Main Street. But the snow had blended the sidewalk with the road. His boot landed on the curb's edge and he stumbled and went down. As he landed, face first, he heard the wine glasses shatter inside the wool of his coat. He rolled to his back and watched the snow spooling from the dark sky. Fear tingled through him, and he began his inventory: neck, spine, ribs, limbs. Hips. He was not hurt.

Then the creak-crunch of running feet, and Scott Kittridge knelt beside his head.

"Did you fall? Are you hurt?"

"I am fine. Just making a snow angel." Sammy swept his arms feebly.

Scott helped him sit up, then stand. He gestured toward the Lodge. "Sammy! Are you stalking Jess MacKinnon?" He pointed at the bottle in Sammy's coat pocket. Which, thankfully, had escaped intact.

Sammy brushed the snow off his thighs. "Not at all." He wiped at his shoulders, his snow-crusted front. "Well, a bit perhaps. One loses one's head when a beautiful woman comes to town." He poked a finger into his left pocket, felt the edge of broken glass, snatched his hand away.

Scott's smile held a hint of shyness in it, always. It made you want to cup his cheek in your palm. Sammy might have gone ahead and done that had he not remembered the fracas at the Kittridge house. "Or a beautiful man, for that matter," he added, patting Scott's shoulder.

But Scott's smile disappeared and he looked down, chewing his lip.

Sammy put a hand on his arm. "What is it, Scotty? No one minds one little bit if you are—if you love men."

"My father minds."

Sammy sighed. "Your father will evolve. Someday."

"I don't think so."

Sammy leaned into the boy and held on. "Help me over to the Outfitters, my lad." Scott wrapped an arm around his waist. Sammy tried a step. Then another.

"Are you okay? Are you sure you're not hurt?"

"Finer than frog's hair, my lad." But he leaned on Scott as they walked. A gray weariness had settled in his limbs and he could not catch his breath. If he could breathe properly, he would tell Scott that who he loved did not matter, male or female; it was *that* he loved that mattered, and how well. If he, Sammy, were forty years old again, he would swing his heart open like a big barn door. He felt he had been too cautious in love. He would tell Scott not to be cautious, that it was better to throw yourself open and let your heart break into a million pieces if it came to that. But now they had reached the Outfitters.

Sammy hunched behind the counter, picking shards of glass from his pocket, when groaning from the storeroom made him stiffen in alarm. Now, only silence. He picked another shard and heard a soft growling, barely audible. Could an animal have gotten in? A bear?

Then he remembered Cleve Kittridge, asleep on the cot. He threw open the storeroom door. Kittridge slept on, reeking of whiskey. The blanket twisted around his ankles and fell to the floor, brushing against the glowing space heater. Well, that would not do. Sammy moved the heater away and switched it off. He decided he did not care whether Cleve Kittridge was warm enough.

Sammy stepped in closer, watching Kittridge's lined, angular face, the shaggy black moustache. He remembered Birch's mean-spirited suggestion that someone should smother the man with a pillow. In the absence of a pillow, he supposed the blanket might suffice. It would be easy to take the bastard out of Scott's life forever. Sammy shook his head. What a strange and evil night it had become. He tucked the blanket around Cleve's torso, moved the heater further away from the cot, and switched the heat back on.

In the far corner of the storeroom, Sammy found the banker's box where Mike stored the catch records. He carried it back inside the store and slid it onto the counter. The box felt heavy. He doubted whether he could carry it back to Still Lake Lodge in the snow.

He drew the bottle from his pocket and stood it next to the box. Damn! He had taken the wrong one. This really was an ill-fated evening. He cradled the bottle in his hands: Wild Berry Wine, sporting a hand-drawn label of a woman in a red dress. This would not do to foster companionship with Jess MacKinnon, who did not like wine.

He would drink alone, then, and to hell with it. He snatched a paper cup from next to the coffeemaker. Above the coffeemaker's little table, framed photographs lined the wall, some quite old. Most were pictures of men holding large trout for the camera. Many included Mike, his arm draped around the customer or cradling a fishing pole. The photographs were sequential from Sammy's right to his left, Mike's image aging from one side of the room to the other. Sammy paused by the oldest photographs, fuzzy black and white pictures of Nez Perce men paddling flat-bottomed boats on the lake. Most had long, braided hair. Some wore blue jeans and plaid shirts; others traditional Nez Perce leggings, vests, ponchos. Sammy's eyes roamed to a photograph of two men. They stood on the lake shore holding between them a pole hung with a dozen silver kokanee. The smaller man wore a straw hat that shaded his face, but Sammy knew it was his brother, Tucker Branch, dead twelve years. The other man, bareheaded, face to the sun, was his other brother Charley. A scar ran from his temple past his left eye—an accident with an explosive that had happened before Sammy was born. Charley had died year before last. They were all dead, his brothers and sisters, all except Jack. Who might be immortal, since he drank water from the Ipsootchuck every single day. In the background, a boy sat in the stern of a boat, his hand on a sculling oar: Tucker's son, Simon, who was seventy-one now and lived in San Diego.

Sammy felt his eyes get wet. Where had they all gone? Still Lake and the kokanee had held them all together like the pole strung with fish, an unbroken link to the past and future, ancestors and descendants. Sammy was in danger of falling victim to a foul mood, so he nodded to his dead brothers and shuffled outside to the back deck. He plunked the wine bottle and the paper cup onto the rail, patted his pockets for his corkscrew.

Still Lake, iron black, fretted in the snowstorm. Sammy longed for the past, for the fish. Jack and Mike feuded, the rest of the family dead or scattered across the earth, after his parents had used all their money and determination to return to the Wallowas. He twisted the cork from the bottle and filled his cup. What happened to the fish had evil in it. To the Nez Perce, the fish were like brothers and sisters, but they—Colby Stukel and Arnett Randall and the city council and even Mike, though he had only been a boy—they had treated the fish as commodities. And now they were gone. Sammy raised his cup to the lake, to the spirits of the kokanee, and to Jess MacKinnon. She would bring the fish back.

He tasted the wine: not one of Birch's best vintages. He tipped back the rest and its bitterness made him shudder. Then he felt the cold and began to shiver. He refilled his cup, corked the bottle, and parked it on the deck next to the rail. He carried the cup into the storeroom and settled himself on a crate beside the space heater, sipping the bitter wine while Cleve snored on.

62.

Moses did not return that night to the Enterprise Motor Hotel. The snowstorm left the roads impassable, so all Jess could do was wait for Riley to call again with news. She paced from the bathroom to the window, where white flakes filled the square of darkness, and she paused to glare at the silent telephone. Then back to the bathroom. Seven steps. She told herself he was fine, almost definitely, that even if he was out in the forest he had good camping gear. She fell asleep in her clothes at two in the morning, then woke to the wail of a siren.

It was still dark outside; her breath made a circle of fog on the window. Three police cars blocked the street, sweeping the snow with blue and red. People were shouting. Pillows of smoke rose above Still Lake Outfitters. Someone ran by, slipping in the snow. Jess pulled on her boots and hurried downstairs.

The rear of the Outfitters building was in flames, orange against the snow-choked sky. Jess pushed into a crowd by the back deck. Her eyes slid from face to face, scanning for a mound of rust-colored hair. As their owners exhaled into the frozen air, the faces clouded and blurred, then sharpened. It occurred to Jess that she might still be asleep, and dreaming. Two brown-uniformed officers guarded the stairs. The onlookers stamped like restless horses and trampled the fresh snow. Jess found a space between a maple tree and a park bench crammed with teenagers. She squeezed past the tree until she had an open view.

Flames jumped out of the double doors and the two big windows glowed. Another officer—Sheriff LaFrance—knelt at the top of the stairs with a megaphone braced on his knee. Past the bench of teenagers, Jess spotted Mike. He shouted at a deputy, chopping the air with his hands. Then Riley Bishop appeared next to her, like a wraith from the darkness and smoke.

"What are you doing here?" Jess asked her. *Am I dreaming?* she almost added.

"Followed the sheriff."

Was Moses really missing or was that part of the dream? "What about Moses?" she asked and saw the answer in Riley's expression.

"Nothing yet." Riley reached across her shoulders and patted her. "I'm sorry."

Jess teared up. She bent her head. One of the windows burst, spraying glass. "Is someone inside?" she asked Riley.

"The sheriff thinks Cleve Kittridge is in there," she answered.

"Cleve Kittridge!" the sheriff shouted on cue, pointing his megaphone. "Can you hear me?"

"I thought he was in jail."

"Out on bail." Riley's glasses glowed orange. "No one can get in. We're waiting on the fire truck."

Again, on cue as though Riley were directing a dream sequence, a fire truck pulled up on Main Street, lights flashing and tire chains clanking. Men poured out and began unwinding the hose.

"Some say the world will end in fire, some say in ice," said a low voice at Jess's elbow. Birch Stukel smiled at her grimly, her face and her bright pink parka illuminated by the fire's glow. "Robert Frost. Come to watch the show, my love?"

Jess's mouth fell open and she found she couldn't speak. A piece of the building fell, an explosion of sparks. Someone in the crowd screamed, and Cleve Kittridge backed out of the burning doors. He was dragging something, or someone.

At the front of the crowd, Jess saw Mike's face in profile against the orange sky. He mouthed the word "no" and pushed past the deputies.

Cleve eased his burden onto the deck and spun around, coughing. Flames leaped from the back of his shirt.

"Drop and roll, Cleve!" the sheriff shouted. He grabbed Kittridge's arm and twisted him onto the deck. Mike and a deputy ran up the stairs, blocking Jess's view. A murmur traveled through the crowd: *It's Sammy. Sammy Branch. Dead? Dead.* Birch cried out, ran up to the deck, weaved and bobbed behind Mike and the deputies as they bent over Sammy. Was it possible? Jess felt dizzy, felt herself sway. She longed to wake up. Riley pressed a hand into her back.

"You all right?" she asked.

Jess could only stare at her. Riley pivoted, guided her to the park bench, ordered the teenagers away. Everything started spinning and Jess dropped onto the bench's cold wooden slats. Wind blew by, carrying the noise of the crowd and the fire away from her, and she heard the water of Still Lake, sucking against the rim of ice at its shoreline. *Death. Death. Death,* it chanted.

63.

From the top of the stairs, Riley Bishop surveyed the scene. Due east, a cold dawn began to lighten the sky behind the smoking frame of the Still Lake Outfitters building, about one-third destroyed. Possibly rebuildable. Two deputies occupied the deck with her, stringing up their yellow "police line" tape; so far they tolerated her presence. She leaned against the rail and tried to look unobtrusive.

Her gaze moved northeasterly, where a solitary figure plodded down the middle of Main Street on snowshoes. Riley raised her hand to shield off the rising sun. It was Jack Branch. Brother of the deceased. Jack joined the cluster at the ambulance's rear doors: one paramedic, Scott Kittridge (son of Cleve Kittridge, who had been treated for burns and refused transport), Race Stukel, and Mike Branch—Jack's only son and half owner, with the deceased, of Still Lake Outfitters. Riley's eyes narrowed to watch Mike, talking to the others and waving his hands. The fire had been quick and vicious and Riley suspected it had been set. Mike Branch might have torched the place to collect the insurance money—it was not an uncommon method to wrap up a business venture and fund an instant retirement plan. Had he killed his uncle, too, to collect both shares of the proceeds? Much less likely. But possible.

Jack bent to unstrap his snowshoes, then the paramedic helped him into the back of the ambulance. The boy, Scott, began to sob— Riley saw his shoulders bobbing. Race gathered him up in her arms. She shook her head vigorously to something Mike said. Jack stepped out of the ambulance, slipped and stumbled in the trampled snow. Mike took Jack's shoulders to steady him. Now Jack was shaking his head, and Mike's gesturing shifted into double time. He took his father's arm and led him down the snow-covered slope to the park bench (north) where Jess MacKinnon sat with an unfocused stare.

Riley twisted to look west down the gangway to the dock and the lake, slate gray and frozen at the edges. Her eyes followed the sudden rise of the mountains, along the milky horizon and back to the deck. Her survey paused at the rail: a green wine bottle sat on the deck fifteen feet away. She looked around. At the bottom of the stairs, the deputies were arguing with a woman in a pink parka and blue cowboy boots, bright yellow hair. They were trying to use their police-line tape to block the stairs; the woman appeared determined to ascend them.

Riley crept along the rail toward the bottle. It was corked, half full. She pulled her sleeve over her fingers and lifted it. Cute homemade label, a drawing of a woman with long dark hair. Riley smelled candles. Wax, melting.

"I'll take that, my love." The yellow-haired woman spoke to her and the parka produced a gloved hand, reaching for the bottle. The deputies flanked her. They did not look happy.

Riley stepped back, gripping the bottle. "Who are you?"

"I'm the wine maker." She reached for the bottle. The candle smell again.

Riley put one of the deputies between herself and the advancing pink parka. "Good to know. You have a name?"

"She's Birch Stukel," said the deputy.

Riley said, "You can't grow grapes way up here in the mountains, can you, Ms. Stukel?"

"It's made from berries." She reached. Riley pivoted around the deputy. "I reuse the bottles. May I have that, please?"

"Sorry. It's evidence." Riley handed the bottle to the deputy, who was wearing latex gloves.

The woman crossed her arms. "Of what?"

Riley lifted her palms to the leaden sky. "Well, we don't know that yet, do we?" She turned to the deputy and put a hand on his shoulder. "Richard, right?" He nodded. He was no more than twenty. "Make sure this gets tagged. I want it tested. Have Bertie call me if he wants to talk about it."

"Yes, Ma'am."

Birch Stukel hovered. The burning wax smell sharpened, a blown-out flame, thread of smoke rising. The woman's eyes squeezed shut, and her lips pulled back. What the hell? She was seriously weird.

Riley gestured to the second deputy, pointed down the stairs, mouthed "crime scene." The deputy nodded.

"Ma'am?" he said to Birch Stukel. "We need to secure this area. You'll have to come with me." He took her elbow and escorted her off the deck.

She steered Richard away, putting distance between the wine bottle and the winemaker, who was shouting at the other deputy. Richard smelled like freshly cut grass, a summertime smell. "Where is Bertie?" she asked.

"He's looking for that kid, your client. Moses Fletcher."

Riley found this surprising, though she had begged the sheriff to help her run the kid to ground. "That's great," she said, "but what about the crime scene? You don't think that fire was an accident, do you?"

"Yeah, well." Grass clippings, sunshine. "Maybe I shouldn't tell you this." She smiled at him, waited. "Moses Fletcher could be a suspect. He threatened the victim yesterday. Right in front of Sheriff LaFrance."

"Really?" Riley rolled her eyes. "What a clusterfuck."

The deputy laughed. He was young, he didn't know what to make of her. She was used to that.

Riley left Richard on the deck and crossed to the park bench to check on MacKinnon. She found Jack Branch sitting stiffly beside her, his lips pressed together. The snowshoes leaned against the maple tree. Mike Branch stood in front of the bench, bouncing on his toes. The woman next to him turned in Riley's direction. She was Race Stukel, sister of the winemaker, married to Mike. She smelled like apples and so when she smiled, Riley smiled back. Race laced her fingers through Mike's and whispered to him.

Most of the onlookers had trudged away. They had mashed the new snow into dirty powder; over it floated the bitter smoke, the smell of wet wood, and a metallic scent that Riley tasted on her tongue.

Scott Kittridge walked down the hill. His nose and eyes were red. Race held out her hand and Riley took it. "You're the private investigator," she said. The apple scent sifted through Riley's brain and the taste of metal faded. She nodded. Race put her hand on Scott's shoulder. "I'm going to take Scott home. Mike needs to follow the ambulance. We need someone to look after Mike's father."

Jack stood, bracing his hands on his knees. "I do not need to be looked after." He shuffled around the bench and took the snowshoes, one in each hand. "I'm going home."

"Papa. I don't think you should walk all that way, and I don't think you should be alone," Mike told him.

"I noticed you have chains on your car," Race said.

"I can give him a ride home, no problem," Riley said. She would not refuse a favor to anyone who smelled like an apple orchard.

Race bent down. "Would you be willing to stay with Jack until we get back?"

MacKinnon flattened her hand on her chest. "Me?" she asked. She looked up the hill, as though to locate the person Race was really addressing.

"We don't think he should be alone."

Jack seemed ready to protest, but MacKinnon gave him a weak smile. He grunted and tucked the snowshoes under his arm. "All right," MacKinnon said slowly. "Of course."

She stood. Jack offered her his arm. Riley led them up the hill to Main Street.

"Sam's on his way, Papa," Mike called after them. "He'll be here tonight."

64

On Jack's front porch, Jess stared up through the branches of a towering Ponderosa pine, dusted with snow and sparkling in the mid-morning sun. It made her think of the winter light on Lake Michigan, of bleak distant shores and mortality. The tree was older than any of them. Older than Jack.

Inside, the house was cold. Jack removed his boots. She and Riley did the same. None of them had spoken since leaving the Outfitters. What was there to say? A big ginger cat took a run at Jess's leg, arching his back. Jess reached down to scratch behind his ears. "What's your name?" she asked the cat, her voice deafening across the silence.

Jack looked embarrassed. "Cat. His name is Cat." He crossed to a woodstove in the far corner of the long room.

"Very appropriate," said Riley. She stood by the front window with her coat still on, looking outside. Jess dropped to her knees to stroke Cat, who purred and butted her hand. She watched as Jack built a fire. To her left, a grand stone fireplace and hearth occupied nearly the entire wall. Before it, a braided rug, a sofa, two heavy chairs. Jack stood and brushed his hands.

"This is not good," Riley said, and Jess saw a black SUV park next to Riley's Subaru. The Fletchers. Riley grimaced and backed away from the window. "Should I hide?" She laughed. "Should *you*?"

"Probably," Jess said.

Then, footsteps on the porch, a hard rap on the door. Jack crossed the room to answer, but Rex—the arrogant fuck—pushed the door open and shoved his head inside. "Hello!" he called.

"Please come in." Jack pulled the door wide, throwing Rex off balance. Becky squeezed past him, thanking Jack and introducing herself. Jess eased herself backward to the stones of the fireplace. She *did* want to hide. Too late for that, obviously.

"Sorry to intrude." Rex towered over Jack, not looking sorry. He gestured toward Riley. "We need to have a word with Miss Bishop. It's urgent."

Jack nodded. He returned to the woodstove, poked at the fire. The room was still cold. Becky had her hands in the pockets of her puffy down coat. Jess could tell she was balanced on some dangerous edge, close to full-blown panic. But Rex—he was furious. His neck swelled like a bullfrog's when he got angry. He folded his arms and stepped into Riley's personal space. "Are you aware that Moses is being hunted by the sheriff's department *and* the state police? They say they want to 'question' him about this fire."

Jess could only see Riley's back, not her expression, but she thought Riley stiffened as Rex took another step in her direction. "Where is he? Why are you not looking for him?"

Jess could not hear Riley's answer. She pressed her back into the round, smooth stones. Rex and Becky still had not noticed her. "Here?" Rex's voice was too loud for this room, this house, this little town. He swung his arm around. "Moses is not *here*, obviously. Why are *you* here? I absolutely need you to find him before the police do!"

Jack stepped into the configuration, making the Rex, Becky, Riley triangle into a square. "She's here because she was kind enough to see me home," he told Rex. He wasn't shouting, but Jess had never heard him speak so loudly. "My brother was killed in the fire."

Becky looked horrified. She put her hand on Rex's arm. "We're intruding," she said.

Jess snorted, an involuntary response. "Ya think?" she muttered to herself. Becky heard her.

"Oh!" She pivoted out of the square, blushing. "It's you!"

"What are *you* doing here? Where is my son?" Jess thought he'd put a tiny emphasis on "my." She pushed off the fireplace stones and folded her arms. Why had she ever, for one minute, put up with this bullshit?

Riley set her hand on Rex's shoulder and steered him toward the front door. "Let's go for a walk, Dr. Fletcher," she said. She picked up her boots and shoved him out onto the porch. Jess heard his protests through the closed door, then his angry thumping down the steps.

Becky bent her head. "I'm so sorry," she said.

"Would you like coffee?" Jack's voice had softened to its usual volume.

Jess smiled at Jack. "I would absolutely love some coffee," she told him. "May I help?"

Jack waved toward the sofa. "No, thank you. Please make yourselves comfortable." He walked around a corner past a blue table and into what must have been the kitchen. Above the table, the ceiling was lower: a loft. Jess settled into a corner of the sofa. She heard water chime into a kettle. The sun poured through a window in the back door, sent a beacon across the room. Jess ran her fingers along the sofa's arm, through the light. Becky pulled off her sneakers and set them by the door with the other shoes. She sat down next to Jess and began to cry.

"We are so worried!" Becky's voice wavered, muffled beneath her hands. "That's why he gets that way, so demanding. He doesn't mean to be rude." She raised her head and wiped at her eyes.

Jess watched her. She felt only anger; her voice was icy with it. "He doesn't care whether he's rude or not."

Becky's eyes widened. Jess usually made an effort to remain civil. "His birthday is only a week away," Becky said. "Moses."

"I know," Jess said. She sure as hell didn't need to be reminded.

"He'll be eighteen." Becky reached out to touch Jess's arm. Jess flinched and pulled away. From the kitchen, she heard the teakettle whistle.

"Yes," she answered. "I know." Then, because Sammy was gone and Moses might be frozen somewhere, dead, and because it didn't matter anymore, she heard her cold voice say, "Ben and I planned to tell him the truth. On his birthday."

Becky gasped. Her fingers flew to her mouth. "But … you didn't? He doesn't know?"

Jess shook her head.

"We—Rex and I—we were wrong. The way we treated you."

Ya think? Jess wanted to say, again. But Becky's face had crumpled and her body shook with fresh sobs and Jess looked down at the furrows of the braided rug. She watched a tuft of Cat's orange fur travel across the floor, gathering momentum like a tumbleweed in the draft from under the door. "You were mean. Heartless," she said to the rug, because there were no more reasons not to say it.

"Yes." Becky's voice trembled. "We were mean." More sobbing; her hands went back over her face. "But, oh Jess. I love that child so much." Her shoulders jerked. "My two children. I've lost them both!" She dropped her hands to look at Jess, her face streaked with make-up, tears, and snot. "You know about Ben's little sister? Baby Isabelle?"

Jess nodded. The baby girl they'd lost to SIDS when Ben was eight. Ben had told her. Becky had told her. Some of her iciness thawed. She spotted a box of tissues on the blue table by the back door and she almost collided with Jack as he bore a serving tray from the kitchen.

Becky stood when Jess presented the tissue box. "I do treasure him. Your son," she whispered.

Jess blinked. She'd never heard Becky or Rex acknowledge her as Moses's mother. Jack set his tray on the stone hearth. He had added a plate of apple slices, radishes, bread, and butter. Jess realized she was famished. She accepted a mug of coffee and buried her face in its steam.

"I know that," she told Becky. She buttered a slice of bread and perched on the hearth. The stones were cold.

65.

The first two years were the worst. She worked in the detail shop of a used car lot in Portland, vacuuming and polishing the insides of Toyotas and Hondas. When she finished her work day, an emptiness settled, so heavy she thought it could split her body open. In the endless span of hours between work and bedtime, the emptiness seeped down into her fingers. She would walk through her plain apartment and pick things up—a hairbrush, a pair of scissors, a bowl—and weigh them in her palm, brush them with her fingertips.

She'd fall asleep as midnight came on, thrash in the blankets with restless dreams, and wake to find the emptiness had traveled to the bend of her elbow, where Moses had slept in the first months of his life. If the moon was out, she'd find it from her apartment window. She liked thinking that the same moon hung in Baker City, over her son. She liked knowing that she could ride her motorcycle from Portland to Baker City in less than five hours. Even though she wouldn't, not that night. That she could climb through his bedroom window. That she could scoop him from his crib.

After his second birthday party, she and Becky sat on the sofa in the Fletchers' ranch house. Becky had offered her the guest room for the night; she had declined. She would ride back to Portland in the dark, no matter how cold it was. If it snowed, she'd hole up somewhere with her sleeping bag and tarp. She'd rather sleep on the highway median than accept the Fletchers' hospitality.

"I know this is difficult for you, and I'm sorry for it," Becky had said. The twilight dwindled and the room darkened to leave Becky's face in shadow. Jess tried to sort out the woman's expression. She responded with a noise of neither assent nor denial. Becky picked up a

228

spent birthday candle and set it next to the remains of the cake, wiping a spot of brown frosting the candle had defecated onto the glass coffee table. "You know we lost our daughter, Isabelle?"

Jess made another sound: "Mmm-hmm." Becky's face was hidden but a path of the last light illuminated her fingers as she plucked more candles from the glass, scraped a dime of melted wax with her thumbnail.

"Ten years ago. It seems like no time at all." She piled the candles on a paper plate and wiped her fingers with a napkin. "Losing a child, that kind of grief. There's a way it throws you outside time. You never get over it. Truly, you have no idea."

Jess stared at her in disbelief. She damned well *did* have any idea. She could have slapped the woman, but Rex walked in from the kitchen and flipped on the light. She saw in Becky's widening eyes that she realized what she'd just said. Becky busied herself stacking paper plates. "So you see how important Moses has been to me. A gift."

Jess felt her outrage flare into every corner of her body. She imagined hurling the last wedge of chocolate cake into the center of the immaculate living room, grinding it into the cream-colored carpet with her heel. She could almost feel the frosting soak into her sock— no shoes allowed in the house, especially not motorcycle boots—and the ecstasy of watching Becky's horror, Rex's fury. Rex strode into the center of the room, right where Jess's imagination had thrown the cake. She said, in a vicious whisper so only Becky would hear, "I know how important Moses is."

"What are you two doing, sitting in the dark?" Rex said.

66.

Rex stomped into Jack's house, leaving wet footprints across the floor. "Miss Bishop is checking all the hotels and motels within a 60-mile radius," he announced. "Becky and I will go back to our hotel. I'm going to make some calls, line up a private search and rescue team to go through the forest. It's time to take control of this situation. Past time."

"What?" Becky said. She stared at her husband with no sign of comprehension. Jess gathered up the cups and carried the tray past the blue table into the kitchen. She would leave Rex to bluster and "take control of the situation" without her. She washed the cups and studied the contents of Jack's refrigerator. At last she heard the door bang shut.

When she returned to the living room she found Jack at the front door, shrugging on his coat. "I'm going to fetch water," he told her. He buttoned his coat and picked up a galvanized pail.

The telephone hung on the wall outside the kitchen: the only way Riley could reach her with news about Moses. But Jess was tired of waiting for the phone to ring. And she was supposed to look after Jack, who after all was a hundred and two years old.

"May I come along?" she asked, and he nodded. She followed him outside, where afternoon sun brightened the snow. He helped her strap on snowshoes and together they walked, flat-footed and wide-legged, to the bank of Old Chuck Creek.

When they cleared the forest, Jess followed Jack upstream until they reached a bend in the creek where the current gushed through a gap beside the cleaved face of a boulder the size of a Volkswagen. The boulder wore a beret of snow.

Jack pointed. "When I was born, the settlers were cutting trees and driving logs down the creek and building up the town with lumber from the sawmill. I remember the dynamite explosion that blew that boulder apart."

"Will you tell me the story?" Jess moved closer, stumbling on her snowshoes.

Jack set the pail in the snow. "The explosion made the house shake. I may have been only three years old. My mother grabbed me out of bed and our whole family ran down to the creek. This boulder used to make a dam, and the timbermen had a lot of trouble getting logs to float past. They would jam up and spread onto the banks, right here. The men would have to loosen them with pike poles and sometimes with dynamite. They loved to blow things up. They had cleared a lot of the creek channel with dynamite further upstream, but never beside our house." Jack turned to look upstream and Jess followed his gaze up the canyon and into the mountains, snow-covered now with rock jutting out like the fractured ends of bones. Jack's words seemed to have broken free like the logjam in his story.

"On this day they were determined to blast apart that boulder. Albert Monticola was the one who set the charges—sticks of dynamite tied together. He would stand on a boulder, light the fuses, and tuck the dynamite in by the rock. Then he and the others would take cover in the trees and wait for the explosion.

"My family ran to the creek just as Monticola set a second charge in front of the boulder. My mother was carrying me. There were at least ten sticks of dynamite in that bundle. He hopped back to shore and saw us and yelled, 'Stand back!' and my mother and father pressed us back into the forest."

"How many in the family then? How many children?" Jess asked. She pictured children scurrying away from the stream bank.

"Six children, including me. My mother shielded me between her body and a cedar tree. I remember the smell. The dynamite exploded and the tree vibrated and pieces of the boulder went flying around everywhere. One piece caught my brother Charley on the side of his head and knocked him down. He was flat on his back, a lot of blood down the side of his head dripping onto the pine needles. My father was shouting at Albert Monticola and my mother got Charley to his feet, pressing a cloth to his head, and Monticola walked over to

Charley and my mother was shouting at him, too. I don't know what they said but the men left and never tried blasting any more boulders in that part of the creek.

"My mother sewed up Charley's cut herself right there in this house, on the blue table. It was a different color then." Jack picked up the bucket, leaving behind a ring in the snow. "He had a scar down the side of his face his whole life."

Jess drew the sharp air into her lungs, a taste of pine. The edges of Old Chuck Creek were frozen. She stared at the sheared-off face of the boulder, heard the explosion in her imagination, the shouting, running to the house with a bleeding child. It wasn't her memory, but it sent a tremor through her, leaving her breathless with something that felt like fear. She saw Mary's fingers, slippery, red, gathering the edges of the wound. Her hands would have been steady, her face set. But her heart was knocking and her blood raging through her veins.

Jess jerked her head, looking all around them, listening—for Moses, she realized. What if he was hurt, bleeding, unconscious, dead? She closed her eyes and breathed in the cold air, the pine smell, and wrestled her thoughts away from their ledge of panic. She opened her eyes. Everything was still, muted by the new snow.

Jack looked upstream again. "This will be a high flow year." His eyes rose to the mountains. "Like last year, when the creek flooded. Some years the creek fills and everything gets cleaned out. Not every year."

Jess let out the breath she'd been holding, feeling her heartbeat slow. "A flushing flow," she said.

Jack turned toward her, repositioning his snowshoes. "Pardon?"

"Fish biologists call it a 'flushing flow'—a heavy spring flow that scours sediment and silt out of the gravel and clears the good holding pools. It makes the creek better habitat for fish."

"Yes," said Jack. "A flushing flow, yes." He seemed to taste the words for flavor and Jess noticed him muttering them to himself as he turned to walk uphill. He struck off westward through the forest.

She slogged after him, lifting her feet high to clear the powder, scanning the trees for movement. By the time they reached a meadow and began angling back toward Old Chuck Creek, she was sweating and panting. She rested against a snag, bleached and weathered smooth as porcelain. Her exhalations made a cloud around her face.

They stopped at a dry stream bed and a mound of cobbles. Jess's gaze followed the gully west. This was the side channel she'd noticed before, when she and Moses staggered down through the canyon. She pressed her palm against her side. Her ribs still ached; the exertion made it painful to breathe. The side channel drew away from Old Chuck Creek below the scour pool, the Big Sink.

A coil of rope hung from a rusty nail on a fir tree. Jack unhooked the coil and knotted the end of the rope around the bucket's bail. The other end was tied around the tree. He carried the tethered pail to the mound of stones and moved six skull-sized cobbles to the side, crouching on his snowshoes. Jess opened her mouth to offer help, but there was something ritualized about Jack's movements that kept her silent. The displaced cobbles had exposed an opening in the rocks, into which Jack lowered the bucket, hand over hand, a long distance. The line grew slack, then pulled taut, and Jack raised the pail, took it from the rocks, and set it, full, on the ground.

"This is the Ipsootchuck." He untied the rope from the bail. "The water is medicinal." He coiled the rope and hung it on the nail, lifted the rocks back into their places. Again, Jess let her eyes trace the dry bed's path. This branch channel must seep into a groundwater aquifer, leaving piles of alluvium, like this mound of cobbles, at each place the surface water slipped underground. She could see two other mounds along the bed, humps of snow-covered stream debris.

Jack carried the bucket and they walked in silence back to the house. They removed their snowshoes and Jess followed Jack into the kitchen. He set the water on the counter and opened the refrigerator.

"It's almost time for supper," he said, closing it again, empty-handed.

"Why don't I make something?" she said. "You can rest."

"There should be something on the porch by now," said Jack. He smiled at her puzzled expression. "I'm quite old. A lot of people have died. When someone dies, this is what we do. The neighbors. There's always a casserole." He walked to the front door and returned with a foil-covered pan and a small brown box. Beneath the foil was a lasagna. Inside the box, a carrot cake. Jack opened the card that was taped to the top of the box, then rested it on the table, next to a radio. He turned on the oven and slid the lasagna inside.

"The others will be here soon," Jack said when the lasagna was heated. "With my grandson, Sam. But not in time for dinner." He cut squares of lasagna and ladled water from the pail. He filled a glass for her, and one for himself.

She thanked him. He picked up his water glass and set it down. She asked about Sam. He busied himself with his lasagna until she wondered if he would answer. Then he propped his elbows on the table and regarded her over his clasped hands.

"My grandson was born in 1975. Michael married a Nez Perce woman from the Colville reservation, Amanda John. They divorced when Sam was only five years old. Later, Michael married Race Stukel. But Sam was almost grown by then."

She drank from her glass, water from the Ipsootchuck. The cold numbed the back of her throat. It tasted like winter and snow and the jagged mountains. "I enjoyed talking to him in Portland." She remembered her attraction to Sam and her cheeks got hot.

"He goes to graduate school. He studies ethnography and linguistics." Jack picked up the glass and drank the last of his water. "He's writing a book."

"What about?" she asked.

"Language. Indian languages. The book is his Ph.D. dissertation but it has already been accepted by a publisher."

"You must be proud of him." It was getting dark outside. Where was Moses? Jess drank the cold water.

"He has never married."

Jess cut through the layers of lasagna with her fork, watching the furled edges of the noodles compress against the ricotta. "Is that right," she murmured.

"You are not married?"

She smiled and pointed the fork at him. "I think I see where this is going."

Amusement rose in Jack's eyes. "Well?" he said.

"Not married. No." She finished her water and Jack refilled her glass. Ben Fletcher remained her longest relationship, all nineteen months of it. She had loved him, and he had betrayed her—there was no other word for what happened. Maybe she'd get over it one day, but so far she had never been interested in anything but the most casual liaison.

The telephone rang. Jess jumped up. Jack rose from his chair—excruciatingly slowly, it seemed to her—and answered it. He held out the receiver. "It's for you," he said.

"I found him," said Riley. Something clipped in her tone made Jess's throat close.

"Is he—" She started to say "dead," then tried to say "alive." She couldn't get any of those words out.

"He's fine," Riley said quickly. She chuckled. "Doing quite well, as a matter of fact."

67.

The young woman was maybe 20, scrawny, eyes defiant. Her hair looked like a home-cropped-and-dye job and erupted from her scalp in black spikes. Which was wholly consistent with her attitude, Riley thought, amused. She and Moses and the woman waited in the parking lot of the Jefferson Motel, adjacent to the Jefferson Truck Stop and Diner—a complex known locally as "The Jeff." The woman held Moses's hand, their fingers interlaced.

The Wallowa County Sheriff's truck pulled up beside them. "Have you called the parents?" Sheriff Bertie LaFrance wanted to know. The deputy, Richard, was with him. Riley shook her head and thought Bertie looked relieved. He probably didn't want to deal with Dr. Rex Fletcher any more than she did. And Moses had told her straight out that he would run away again if turned over to his parents. She *had* called Jess MacKinnon, even before notifying the sheriff. That was a breach of protocol, but not a serious breach, and she saw no reason to mention it.

"That's Rhonda Johnson," she told them. "She's a waitress at the diner. The kid went there for dinner about nine p.m., stayed until her shift ended at midnight. She came back here with him and spent the night." Moses did not want his parents to know about Rhonda. Riley left that part out, as well as her supposition that Rhonda had helped him lose his virginity. In her periphery, Riley saw the kid lift Rhonda's hand to his lips and stare at her like a puppy. Sweet, but nauseating. "She has to be at work in half an hour. I'm hoping you can let her go in time."

Bertie coughed. His face was broad and florid, so Riley couldn't say for sure he was blushing, but she thought so. He always smelled steady, like oilcloth or canvas. Very fitting for a county sheriff, in Riley's opinion. As per usual he took his time answering. He always liked to think things through before he spoke, which was something else she appreciated about him. "So she's his alibi for the fire last night, correct?" Bertie finally said.

"That's right." They'd want to take Moses to the station, but there wasn't any point. Several of Rhonda's co-workers had seen them leave together at midnight. There was no way Moses had navigated the icy roads back to Still Lake—a two-hour drive in the best of conditions— in time to set fire to the Outfitter's store room. She saw that Bertie had figured that out. "Look, I need to call Dr. Fletcher," she said. "Why don't you go ahead and talk to them here. Maybe we can let Rhonda make it to her dinner shift. Before the Fletchers get here." She glanced at Richard, who was trying not to smile. "It might be a little early in their relationship for her to meet his parents. If you see what I mean."

"Right," Bertie said. He took out his notepad.

By the time the Fletchers arrived, Rhonda had left for work. "I'm very sorry I made you worry," Moses said, in what was clearly a rehearsed speech. "But I'm not going home with you. I'm going to stay here for a few days." His voice broke, and Riley saw his hands shaking before he shoved them into his jacket pockets. But his eyes held the same piercing belligerence she had seen in his mother, Jess MacKinnon.

"You'll do nothing of the sort!" Rex wasn't quite shouting, but it was close. "Sheriff!" Bertie LaFrance, having announced that Moses was free to go, was edging toward the squad car where Richard waited for him, engine idling. "Some assistance from law enforcement, please! This is a minor child. He needs to come with us."

"I'm not going with you," Moses said. "You can't make me. And I'll be eighteen in exactly one week."

Bertie spread his arms wide as though to embrace the entire ridiculous situation. "What would you like me to do, Dr. Fletcher? Hog-tie him?" Fletcher brightened, as though that might not be a bad idea, and Riley made a note to look up "hog-tie" on the Internet, in aid of a more precise mental image. "What about you?" Bertie was gesturing toward her and staring.

"Excuse me?" she said.

68.

As night fell, Jack's front porch filled with footsteps and voices. Sam, Mike, and Race filed in and hung their coats on pegs inside the door. Since the news about Moses, Jess had felt so buoyant with relief that she hardly seemed to inhabit her own body. She let herself be hugged and patted and praised for watching over Jack.

Sam and Jack embraced. Sam kissed Jack's cheek and whispered something that might have been Nez Perce. Jack answered in the same language. Sam chuckled, and they both turned in her direction, wearing smiles that struck her as mischievous. She felt her attraction to Sam whistle across her collarbone, a primitive thing.

Sam got a blaze going in the big stone fireplace. They drew seats around the hearth, Jack somehow contriving to place Sam's chair between Jess and the fireplace. Jack sat on the sofa to her left, Mike next to him. Race made a pot of tea that tasted of maple and nutmeg, and Mike passed around slices of carrot cake. Race spoke first, into the silence. "He would love this." She was talking about Sammy. "He always wanted us all together." She turned toward Jess. "You, too, Jess. He really liked you. He would want you here."

Jess made a sound of acknowledgment, acutely uncomfortable. Sam put his hand on hers, smiled when she looked at him with surprise. Another wave of giddiness tore through her body. She pulled her hand away but compensated with a small smile. As the room grew dark, they stared into the flames, silent. At last Mike cleared his throat and scratched his goatee. "Sam. Did you show Papa the book?"

"Not yet." Sam stood, tossed another piece of wood onto the fire, and retrieved a softcover book from his coat pocket. "It's an advance copy." He passed the book to Jack, who held it reverently, his hands framing the edges.

"*Indian Culture and Language in the Pacific Northwest*, by J. Samuel Branch," Jack read.

Jess bent over to see. "What does the 'J' stand for?" she asked.

"Jackson," Sam answered. "After my grandfather."

Jack was bent over the book, but Jess saw his expression—astonishment.

Mike saw it, too, and raised his eyebrows. "What, Papa?"

"His name is Jackson Samuel?" Jack said loudly. "His first name is *Jackson*?"

"Well, of course, Papa." Mike chuckled. "You know that. I personally liked 'Samuel Jackson,' but Amanda pointed out that was already taken. We always called him Sam."

"Well, I *know* what we called him. I definitely did *not* know . . ." Jack trailed off. He rested the book on his knees. His hand made circles in the firelight, groping for words.

Sam slid off his chair to kneel on the rug before his grandfather. "You didn't know I was named for you, Grandfather? All this time? How is that possible?" Jack shook his head. Then there were tears on his face, vanishing into the creases there.

Mike cleared his throat. "There's no need to get dramatic, Papa. It's always been his name."

Sam sat back on his heels. Mike reached across the back of the sofa to grip Jack's shoulder. Jack was now weeping profusely. A tear dripped off his chin and splashed onto his leg, soaked into the denim. Mike stretched his arm across Jack's shoulders and pulled him close.

Jack grabbed him in a hug and Mike reached around to cradle the back of Jack's head and guided it to his shoulder. The book slid to the rug. Sam picked it up. Jess was tearing up. She blinked fast and held out her hand. Sam passed her the book. She scanned the table of contents, angling the print toward the firelight.

Jack wiped his face with his shirtsleeve. Race offered him the box of tissues and he blew his nose. "You are right," he said to Race, "about my brother wanting us all together. When we were children all of the family would sit here in the evenings, talking and telling stories. He missed that."

"What language did they speak?" Jess asked, looking up from the book.

Jack considered. "There is not just one answer to that question. My mother spoke English, and Chinook jargon, and some of the Takelma language and some Nez Perce. My father's language was Nez Perce but he spoke English and he could understand Chinook jargon. At home we spoke a mixture of all those languages. My mother also made up names for things, usually from Chinook or Chinook jargon, and of course I couldn't tell the difference between the names she invented and the other names."

"What did your mother call Old Chuck Creek?" Jess asked him, remembering Birch Stukel's story. "The creek is Old Chuck," Mary Riffle had said, a hundred years before.

"We called the creek Olo Chuck. In Chinook jargon, '*Olo*' means 'hungry.' '*Chuck*' means 'water.' So '*Olo Chuck*' means 'thirsty.'"

"That must be related to the name 'Old Chuck.' Isn't it?" Jess brushed her fingers over the pages of Sam's book. He was watching her, the side of his face glowing with the firelight as though illuminated from within.

"Orion Stukel was the first mayor of Still Lake and the first newspaper publisher. I believe Orion Stukel wanted to give the creek an Indian name, so he asked my mother what it was called and she told him. But when Stukel's newspaper assistant set the type, he mistook the 'o' for a 'd' and printed the name as 'Old Chuck.' 'Chuck' was what Charles Stone was called, so the misprint made sense to the settlers and it became the creek's name."

"Why did your mother call the creek 'Olo Chuck'?" Somehow the name was important to the mystery of the kokanee, how and where they were hiding. She felt it strongly but couldn't say why.

"That was her name for it." He was staring into the fire. "Jack," she began, but he didn't turn his head. Still, she had to try. "Why did you tell me the fish are 'hiding'?"

"So many questions." He rose and set another piece of split pine on the coals. The flames caught and leaped. He brushed his hands on his thighs. "Tell the poisoned bear story, Grandson." He patted Sam's knee, then sat down again.

"What's the 'poisoned bear story'?" she asked.

Jess sipped her tea and looked at Sam, waiting.

"I'm not sure I remember all the parts." He smiled at her. The fire grew warmer and brighter.

"Of course you do," Race said. "Don't be coy."

He laughed at this. "Shall I tell it in Nez Perce?" He raised his eyebrows, his head backlit by the flames.

"Do you speak the Takelma language?" Jess asked.

"I studied it. I would like to learn it—there is no one left to speak it now."

"Is that in here?" Jess's fingers slid down the open pages of *Indian Culture and Language*.

"Yes." He straightened in the chair and tapped his chin with a forefinger, professorial. "In Takelma, body parts are used metaphorically. So the word for 'leg' would be incorporated into a verb when someone was talking about an action happening low to the ground. One of the ideas I explore in the book is that in native languages and cultures there is less distance between the speaker and the natural world."

"Fascinating," Jess said. He smiled at her. The giddiness swept through her, leaving her head light.

"Are you ever going to tell the bear story?" Mike's knee bounced.

Sam perched on the hearth, backlit, his face in shadow. "My great grandmother's people, the Takelmas, lived at the confluence of Cow Creek and the Rogue River. They fished for salmon in the rivers. At salmon festivals the people would roast the fish at the fire pits.

"Then Old Man Bear came to that place. And he was greedy and thirsty and he would go to the Rogue River and he would drink and drink until the river was empty and the boulders were dry in the riverbed, and he would drink in all the salmon that were swimming in the river, as well. Three times he did this, and the salmon festivals stopped and the people were hungry and discontent.

"Coyote saw what had happened and he said to the people, who had always treated him kindly, 'I will help you.' He ran down the dry river bed to the ocean and there he found twelve seabirds and told them his plan. Coyote returned with the seabirds to Cow Creek.

"Old Man Bear was asleep by the dry river bed, his stomach bulging with water and fish. As Coyote had instructed them, the seabirds flew to the forest and gathered baneberries. They woke Old Man Bear and gave him berries to eat and then he fell asleep again. Taking his fur in their beaks, the twelve seabirds lifted Old Man Bear into the sky and flew with him to the headwaters of the Rogue River in the Cascade Mountains. They flew over the Cascade Mountains and they continued to fly for a long way and then they dropped Old Man Bear into some mountains far off from the land of the Takelmas. And those mountains were the Wallowas, the *Wal' wáapo*, and the place they dropped him became the basin of the lake, which is in the shape of a bear's backside.

"When Old Man Bear woke up he was sick from the baneberries the seabirds had given him, and he thrashed about. With the claws of one arm he carved the channel of the long creek to the west and with the claws of the other arm he gouged out the channel of the short creek to the north. Then with his hind foot he made a hole in between the two creeks.

"Then Old Man Bear vomited all the water and the fish in his stomach. The water filled the lake and the creeks and the hole in between. The fish swam around and were happy to be free from the darkness of the Bear's stomach.

"Old Man Bear staggered off into the forest. After that he lived by the creek and ate the bodies of the fish after they had left their eggs in the creek bed. He never returned to the land of the Takelma.

"The waters of the creek to the west were named *Olo Chuck Chuck*, Thirsty Creek. The waters of the lake were called the *Klip Chuck*, Deep Water. And the waters inside the Bear's footprint, between the two creeks, were called the *Ipsootchuck*, the Hidden Waters."

Jack had been gazing off toward the front window as Sam told the story, but now he smiled at him.

"Thirsty Creek." Jess frowned. "Because of the bear?"

"I suppose so," Jack answered.

Jess peered at him. Again she had a sense that the name was significant. "You suppose so?"

Jack leaned over to look into her cup. "Would you like more tea?" He gathered their cups and the teapot and took them to the kitchen.

Jess heard a car in the gravel, then a knock at Jack's door. Mike answered. "You!" he shouted. It was Moses and Riley.

69

"For God's sake, Mike. Let them in." Race stood. Jess followed her to the door. Race pulled Mike out of the doorway and invited them inside. "Take off your shoes," Race told them. "And your coats. Come join us by the fire."

"And start explaining." Mike scowled. "Explain how it is you're here on my father's doorstep after you threatened his brother's life and then torched my store!" His fury and his voice rose together and flushed his face. He blocked Moses's path. Jess saw his fists tighten. "My uncle is dead. Dead!"

Riley nudged her boots aside with one foot and took Moses's arm. "He came here to apologize," she told Mike, her voice low and calm.

"*Apologize?*" Mike shouted.

"I didn't start the fire, Mr. Branch," Moses said. "Tell him, Aunt Jess!" Jess stepped around Mike and pulled Moses into her arms. He bent his head to her shoulder. He was shaking.

"It wasn't him," Jess said to Mike. Moses was crying now. She knew this would embarrass him, so she led him to the kitchen, where Jack was assembling a tray of tea and bread. "Can we have a moment alone?" she whispered. He nodded to a bench against the far wall, then hurried out with the tray.

"I was wrong, wasn't I?" His face was buried in her shirt, his voice muffled.

"Sammy didn't hurt anyone, Kiddo," she whispered. "But neither did you. It's okay now. Where are your folks?" She stroked the back of his neck, smoothed the untidy hanks of hair that poked from his head.

He lifted his face, wiped his eyes. "I wouldn't go home with them," he told her, smiling a little. The two of them had always shared this, the camaraderie of rebels. "The sheriff said I could stay with Riley. I'm 'remanded into her custody' until I turn eighteen."

Jess brushed the hair out of his eyes. "Which is in one week."

He nodded. "Riley said one week of parenting was about the longest commitment she was willing to make." Jess laughed.

He laughed too. The grin stayed on his face. "I met a woman at The Jeff. Rhonda." He blushed. "She spent the night."

Jess looked away so he wouldn't see her smiling. "Oh?"

"It was nice. Private to me, and special. I didn't want them to be part of it, especially him. He would have changed it. Do you know what I mean?"

"I do indeed." Wherever he went, Rex occupied all the available space. Even when he wasn't speaking, he was loud.

Moses's lip trembled. "I'm so sorry, Aunt Jess!" He put his face back down on her shoulder and she pulled him close. In her body she felt the memory of all the times she'd held him like this, even back to the weight of his infant self, when he'd still belonged to her, the weight that settled and grew heavy when he fell asleep.

70.

As soon as school was out, she and Ben flew to Oregon with Moses, only eight months old. Ben, excited, chattered through the whole flight about what his parents might have meant by "wanting to help them out" and how their lives were likely to improve. A house, maybe. A monthly stipend from Ben's trust fund, which was otherwise locked away until he turned thirty. A better, newer car. A highchair for Moses, a proper crib.

"Mmm," said Jess. She stroked Moses's cheek. He slept in his car seat between them, his chin wet with drool. She tried to share Ben's enthusiasm. It bubbled up and covered all three of them, swept out into the aisle, filled the plane. But she couldn't shake a feeling of foreboding.

At the Fletcher ranch, late in the evening, they settled into the guest room. There was a double bed, and a white crib made up with matching sheets and blankets of sky blue. From the whispered exchange between Ben and his mother, Jess understood that the crib had been "hers"—Ben's dead younger sister, Isabelle. Moses fussed. He was overtired. She nestled him down on the soft sheets. Becky watched, wiping her eyes, as Moses fell asleep. Ben said he was hungry. He and Becky went downstairs. Jess collapsed face first on the bed and was asleep.

She woke and heard voices: Ben and his father. She followed the voices to the end of the hallway. The door was ajar; she could just see into the kitchen. Rex and Ben sat at the yellow table. Ben's voice, low and subdued: "It's been hard. I admit that." Jess eased herself backward into the bathroom doorway, her socks silent as they left the carpet and crept onto the tiles. Where was Becky? She heard water running, the clink of dishes. Becky must be standing at the sink, her back to the table. She couldn't hear Rex's response over the running water. The faucet shut off. She caught Rex's voice, then, rising at the end of a sentence: ". . . untenable situation, son."

She peered through the gap in the doorway. It framed Ben's face, his expression sweet and earnest. "But I love Jess. We could get married!"

She smiled. Her breath spread across her collarbones and seemed to lift her from the floor. A fist slammed down onto the table—Rex's, she assumed, followed by his voice. "Are you completely deranged?" The faucet turned on again. A metal pan clanged onto the porcelain.

Ben's voice: "If we had enough money to live in a nicer place—" Jess had imagined it; she could see it all now: a house in Edgebrook, bright rooms, an apartment upstairs for her mother; springtime walks with Moses to his elementary school, holding his tiny hand. Ben, a doctor, would wear a white lab coat, switching it out in the evenings for a cardigan, like Mr. Rodgers. Maybe without the singing.

"Let me give you just three reasons that is out of the question," Rex said. "The first three of a very long list. Number one. She is fifteen years old. For Christsake!" The fist slammed down again. "Not eighteen, like you told us. Not a college student. Like you told us. You lied to us, Benjamin."

"No, listen!"

"Listen to what? Your mother asked Priscilla." Rex switched to a falsetto. "I ain't high class, by golly. But I got a good heart." Jess folded her arms across her stomach, holding herself in.

"Stop it, Dad. Just stop it. Okay, yes. She's sixteen, actually."

Again, the high, thin, mimicking voice: "She's sixteen, actually." Jess pressed her arms into her abdomen. She squeezed her eyes shut. "Are you that fucking clueless, Ben? That's statutory rape. In Oregon *and* in Illinois. I checked. You could be arrested. You could be convicted. Prison. How does that sound? Your life would be functionally over. No, I'm not finished. Number two. You need to stay in college. If you have any prayer of getting into medical school, you'll have to stop screwing around—literally, I'm afraid—and do something about your grades." Ben sputtered. Jess stepped backward into the bathroom, hardly able to breathe. She held herself with her arms, feeling as though she might spill onto the floor. Rex raised his voice. "Number three. And the most important. This girl is a zero. A fifteen-year-old inconsequential piece of white trash. Let me be absolutely clear. She is not, under any conceivable circumstances, going to be welcomed into this family. Understand? She's nothing but a shitty little tramp from the projects, just like her pathetic hillbilly mother." The words hit her like fists in her gut, left, right, left: Shitty. Little. Tramp. She bent over her crossed arms as though the punches had landed. She trembled.

"But what about Moses?" She heard tears in Ben's voice.

"Moses is another matter," Rex said. "We'll take care of that."

Jess unfolded herself, dropped her arms, her body rigid. Moses! With a sharp involuntary cry she ran down the hall to the guest room. He was asleep, on his back. His two plump arms made a frame for his face. She touched his cheek, the shock of soft orange hair on his scalp. She pulled his blanket up to his chin, though the room felt warm, and smoothed the bedclothes. Shitty little tramp: the words ricocheted off the inside of her skull like escaped bullets. She felt them slicing through her brain. She squeezed the sides of her head, watching Moses sleep. His lips moved, made a sucking sound. She cupped his cheek. She backed up until her legs hit the bed. Sat down hard. Then stood up. Sat down again, held her arms across her midsection, and rocked back and forth. Shitty little tramp. Tramp from the projects. Pathetic, a zero. Just like her mother.

But Ben loved her. She loved him. That was enough. Wasn't it? They would be together, a family. Without Rex and Becky. Dr. Rex Fletcher, what a fucker he was! She jumped up. "Fuck you, Dr. Fletcher!" she said in a vicious whisper. Moses opened his eyes, two circles of the summer sky. She bent over the crib. "Hello, sweetheart," she said and he smiled at her. She put her forefinger in his hand and he squeezed it.

71.

On the bench in Jack's kitchen, Moses lifted his head from her shoulder. "Okay now, Kiddo?" she asked, and he nodded. "Shall we go sit by the fire with the others?" He nodded again.

"All right." He dug his knuckles into his eyes, his movements so childlike that Jess's own eyes filled up. She stood and patted his shoulder.

Mike and Sam rose when they came in. Mike reached for Moses's hand and pumped it up and down, which Jess took as the universal masculine "everything's fine between us now" gesture. Sam led him to the sofa and Jess sat beside him, in case he needed protection.

Race took Mike's elbow and led him to the door. "It's late," she said.

Jack stood, the fire blazing behind him. "There's room for everyone to spend the night here." His arms spread to take in the house. "There are four beds upstairs in the loft, and you and Mike can have the back bedroom. The roads will be icy." He nodded to Riley. "You won't have an easy time getting down out of the mountains. Best to stay over."

"Then where will you sleep, Papa?" Mike put an arm around Jack's shoulders. His voice held a tenderness and affection Jess hadn't heard before. Some reconciliation had come about, deep, a tectonic shift that closed a rift between them.

"Right here in this chair. Most nights I sleep here. By the fire. Because I'm old."

"Old and gray and full of sleep. And nodding by the fire," Race said.

"Are you quoting someone?" Jess asked, and Race nodded.

"A poem. William Butler Yeats. One of my father's favorites. After my mother died, he used to recite it and then get very quiet." She gave a little laugh. "Listen to me! How maudlin." She switched on the radio that sat on the blue table. "Let's find a weather report." An announcer's tinny voice cut across the silence, warbled then sharpened. Then music started, a country song. Race started to move the tuner but Riley held up her hand.

"Wait!" Her voice sounded urgent. "Just a minute. If you don't mind." Guitar chords and banjo picking filled the room, and Race stepped back. A woman's voice sang.

"That's 'Shaniko,'" Moses said. "It's on all the time. Nan Cherise."

"*Fran* Cherise," Riley said. "It's Fran, not Nan."

"Shaniko, Shaniko, prairie winds and blowing snow," sang the voice on the radio.

Jess had never seen Riley so animated. It made her curious. "You know her?" she asked. "You know the singer?"

Riley looked around the room. "Yes." Some wash of vulnerability crossed her face, vanished. She gave a firm nod. "We're together. She's my . . . partner. You know. She's from Shaniko. This is the song that made her famous. It's a big hit."

"I didn't know anyone was *from* Shaniko," said Race, apparently taking this revelation in stride. "It's a ghost town, isn't it?"

"You mean you live in Enterprise, you and Nan? You're a couple?" Unlike Race, Moses appeared scandalized.

"Fran, not Nan. And no, she lives in Nashville. Because of her career. Temporarily."

"Nashville. That's a long way for a long-distance relationship," Jess said. She put a hand on Moses's leg, willing him not to say anything rude. "How often do you see her?"

"It's been eight years." Riley looked around the room again. Every shadowed face, glowing in the firelight, was turned in her direction wearing a look of puzzlement. "What?" Riley's glasses danced with the reflection of flames.

"It's great that you support her career," Sam contributed. "She's very popular. Very talented. Big name in country music."

The others nodded. The song ended. They listened to a weather report: tomorrow the temperature would rise into the forties. Jess had hardly slept the night before. She felt her eyes closing. Moses toppled over and rested his head in her lap. She stroked his hair, a rusty tangle.

72

"It's time for us to have a talk," Rex said, the day after they arrived at the ranch. Becky cleared the breakfast dishes. The yellow table had a scalloped chrome edge. Becky put a hand on Jess's plate, her stack of untouched pancakes, and raised her eyebrows in a question. Jess shook her head: no, she could not eat. She had hardly slept, after the conversation she'd overheard. Becky stacked the dishes on the counter, ran water in the sink. "Becky, please sit down." Rex pushed away from the table, crossed his legs, and clasped his hands on his knee. Now that the dishes were gone, Jess noticed a stack of papers at the end of the table, where Rex's plate had been. She could see that he, Rex—Dr. Fletcher—was in command. But Ben had promised her last night that nothing bad would happen; that he, Ben, would not let anything bad happen to the two of them, or to Moses. Rex turned his cold tight face in her direction. "We can all agree, I think, that you and Ben are not equipped to be parents."

The bottom dropped out of something in her gut, something it was vital to hold on to. "What?" she cried. "That's not true! We *are* parents. We've *been* parents. Ben!" Across from her, in the seat next to his father, Ben looked at the table and was silent. He would not raise his eyes. Something was very wrong. She had an impulse to run, gather Moses in her arms, flee. Later, she wished she had followed it, this first and most correct instinct.

"You're overreacting," Rex said. "That's not helpful."

"Think of what's best for Moses," Becky said. "Not those nasty little apartments! Do you know I saw rats by the garbage dumpsters? Rats!" Jess stared at her. What was happening? Ben fidgeted in his chair.

Rex uncrossed his legs and planted his palms on the tabletop on either side of the papers. "We will take sole custody of the child. It's all right here." He splayed his fingers across the typewritten page. "If

you fight us, we'll go to court. You'll never see him again, I guarantee
it. If you accept this situation, right now, you can see him every year,
on his birthday. That part is not in the paperwork." His fingers tapped
the papers. "That part is between us. There are conditions. The most
important is that you will not ever tell Moses—or anyone else—that
you're his mother. Ben is his brother. We are his parents. You can be
a family friend." He shoved the stack of papers across the table. "If you
tell anyone, it's over. You'll never see him again." Jess watched his
mouth, his angry, thin lips. She looked down, tried to decipher the
print that marched across the page, but she could not bring it into
focus. In her staggering brain, fear and rage battled each other for
control.

"You could be an aunt," Becky said. "'Aunt Jess.' That sounds
nice, doesn't it?"

Jess's hands were shaking. So she slapped her palm down onto the
incomprehensible papers, making everyone jump. "This is bullshit!"
she shouted. "We don't agree to any of this! Ben!" She snapped her
fingers in front of his face. He seemed to be in a trance. "Ben! Back me
up, here!" He lifted his head. His eyes were hard and his face stone.
Like his father's. Side by side, in fact, the resemblance was uncanny.
She swallowed hard, swallowed whatever she had planned to say next.
Its edges felt jagged in her throat.

"I know you're not terribly bright." Rex smiled with his lips
closed. "But I did think you'd catch on by now. There is no 'we.' I'm
talking to *you*. Ben has already signed the consent forms."

73.

Jess woke to find Sam watching her from the hearth. Moses and the
others had gone to bed; Jack slept in his chair. Sam held his book,
Indian Culture and Language, open in his lap. He seemed to be
caressing the pages, but stopped when he saw she had woken. He

smiled at her. From outside, yelping and a long howl echoed down through the canyon. Jess shivered. "Is that a wolf?"

"Coyote." His smile widened, his teeth white in the shadow of his face. "Coyote, the trickster."

74.

Jack's loft was open to the main part of the house and the ceiling pranced with shadows from the fire downstairs. The room smelled of pine smoke and peppermint. Riley had the bunk nearest the far wall, Moses in the next bed—her charge for one week. Riley Bishop, a child's guardian! If only Fran could see her now.

Fran. Riley should never have mentioned her. Now she was out, as a lesbian and—the part that really stung—as a loser who would wait around for eight years for her lover to return. As for the homosexuality disclosure, most of this crowd wouldn't care. Riley would place bets that Race's nephew was gay, the one who worked at Still Lake Outfitters. What was his name? Scott.

She listened to Moses breathing, with a little delicate snore every few breaths. In the next bed over, MacKinnon slept on her back with her arms flung out. The fourth bed was empty. Downstairs, Sam whispered with his grandfather and dropped a log onto the fire. The sparks flew up and the shadows on the ceiling danced faster.

Fran would come back when her record album was finished. She didn't like telephones and never called. Riley wrote letters, one every week. She'd gotten six in return, four in the first year they were apart. That was because Fran was famous and busy with her music. She might come back any day. When Riley went traveling, she left a note on the front door. She kept a key hidden under a rock in the flower bed. Fran would remember where it was.

Fran smelled like roses flexing their petals in the sun. Good God. How could Riley have kept herself from falling for the woman? They'd met in Riley's own neighborhood in Brooklyn, at a bar where gender was unimportant and anyone could dance with anyone. Fran stood out because her long brown hair was plaited into two braids and she wore a dress—some kind of loose hippie thing made of cotton or linen or possibly hemp—and Birkenstocks with fuzzy wool socks. She was alone, so Riley sat down without asking, told her she looked like Laura Ingalls Wilder, and offered to buy her a drink, the overpowering fragrance of roses having gone to her head. Fran spoke in that long, slow way they talked in the West, smiling a lot and laughing for no reason. Riley did her best to keep Fran talking and laughing long into the evening, then the night. The next day, at Fran's apartment where two guitars and a mandolin hung on the bedroom wall, Fran sang her a song. Riley was lost in a forest of rosebushes blooming, she was plunging into a tub of petals. And that was that. Almost before she realized what was happening, Riley had packed up her belongings and closed down her business and followed the woman to Oregon.

Eight years: she'd seen the startled looks around the room last night. But what did they know about it? Eight years was no time at all to wait for a woman like Fran. Riley would wait eight more; she would wait eight hundred years. She fell asleep and dreamed about Brooklyn.

Wednesday, October 6, 2004

75.

Jess dreamed she was back in Chicago, skateboarding at the lakefront in her baggy T-shirt, blue jeans, black high-tops. With her hair in a bowl cut (executed by her mother), everyone mistook her for a boy. At the bottom of a flight of steps, her mother's boyfriend Ernie spread his hands as though in welcome or benediction, his long hair floating in the wind. She balanced on the board, felt the delicious wobble, the flexing of her ankles. "What should I do?" she called to him.

He spread his hands wider. "Fall into the arms of God!"

She nodded. This seemed (in the dream) the correct answer. She pushed off, launched out over the steps, free falling.

76.

In June of 1987, the Fletchers put Jess on a plane back to Chicago. She called her mother, but it was Ernie who picked her up at the airport. "I thought you guys broke up," she said when he poked his head out the car window and waved.

"Hello to you, too! I'm just dandy, thanks." He took her duffle bag and threw it in the back seat. "We did break up. I can still give you a ride, can't I? Get in." He slid behind the steering wheel. Stared at her, frowning. "Where's the baby?"

"They took him." She stared back at him, pressed her lips into a seam of stone. Her eyes were also stone, her cheeks, and her chin. Like

Ben's face. Like his father's. On that last morning, she remembered running into the bedroom at the Fletcher ranch, running up to the crib. Moses was gone, leaving the imprint of his tiny body on the sky blue sheet. She put her palm in the center and felt his warmth.

Ernie started to say something and stopped.

"You still working evenings?" he asked when they were on the expressway. "Waiting tables down at Cookie's?"

"Yeah."

"And Baby Daddy—what's his name?"

"Ben."

"He's not in the picture anymore?"

"He's staying in Oregon. Transferring to another college. He's got to be right under his father's thumb. Chicago's too far away." Jess turned her stone face to the window.

Ernie laughed, then blew out a long breath. "Oh, boy," he said. "So, you interested in another job during the day?"

She looked at him then, his long brown hair that fanned across his shoulders in waves, his bushy sideburns. He had a cleft in his chin and an old scar that ran from the side of his nose across his lips. A knife fight, he'd told her. "What you got in mind?" she asked.

"I need help at the motorcycle shop. That boy I had working for me decided to hitchhike around the world or something. I'll pay you better than the restaurant, and I'll teach you to work on motorcycles too, if you want."

"I got to take those bikes on test drives, right?" He glanced away from the road and caught her grinning.

"Definitely." He tapped his thumb on the steering wheel and hummed. He played bass in a rock band and was always writing new songs in his head.

"You got yourself a new employee," she told him.

77

In the morning, Jess found Jack in one of the chairs by the hearth, wrapped in a blanket. The fireplace glowed with embers. He pulled a tissue from its box and blew his nose. From the back of the house, Jess heard a door open. She rubbed Jack's back. "It's good you can cry."

"I suppose." His body shook, then stilled.

"There." She patted his knee. "Is that better?"

"Yes," he answered. "Better, I think so." He put a hand out, touched her head. His fingers sent warmth across her shoulders like a shawl. The warmth made a bundle around them. "I suppose this is like a flushing flow, yes?"

She smiled. "Yes, exactly like that."

Mike bustled into the room, switched on a lamp. "Morning, Papa. Ms. MacKinnon." He tossed a piece of pine onto the embers in the fireplace, carried a second piece to the woodstove. "Sure is cold in that back bedroom. Where's Sam?"

Jess blinked in the lamplight. They heard boots stamping on the front porch, the door swung open, and Sam stepped inside, chased by a flurry of snow powder.

"He's right over there," Jack said.

"Thanks," Mike said dryly. "You shouldn't go off by yourself, not without telling someone."

"Didn't go far." Sam hung his coat.

"How deep is the snow?" Mike asked.

"Half a foot, maybe. It's warming up, though. Won't last."

"It'll be a Chinook wind tonight," Mike said. "Thaw the whole valley." Out the front window, dawn sent pink fingers through the trees, the snow resplendent.

Sam crossed to Jack's chair, gathered his grandfather's hand, and pressed it between his own. His hands were large and square, like Jack's. Jess's breath caught and staggered. She turned to watch the fire.

"Rough night?" Sam asked.

Jack answered in what Jess assumed was Nez Perce, the response lengthier than the question seemed to demand. Sam squeezed Jack's hand and laughed. He looked up at Jess with laughter in his eyes. He answered Jack in the same language. Mike grunted in irritation and retreated to the back of the house, muttering.

"My grandfather believes that, to be gallant, and in the interest of safety, I must walk you back to the Lodge," Sam told her. The laughter had moved into his voice.

"Is that right?"

"You'll need this." He held out a hat, a green plaid, fur-lined affair with ear flaps.

She held up her hands as though to ward it off. "I don't think that's my style. Thanks anyway." She checked her watch. It wasn't there. She'd broken it flying into the canyon.

"I disagree," he said, smiling. "And you do need a hat." He pulled on a knit cap to demonstrate. Then he shoved the plaid cap over her head. She let him do it.

"I'm glad you're here," she surprised herself by confessing. They picked their way down the trail along North Creek. Sam had pronounced snowshoes unnecessary. At dawn, he had tramped all the way to the sawmill, packing the snow into a track. She chided him for going so far, and for fibbing about it. But she was thankful all the same.

The track was slippery where the sunlight slipped through to melt it, and Jess slid on a wet patch and went windmilling down to land on her backside. Pain shot through her side, and she sat in the snow, eyes closed, to wait it out.

Sam pulled her to her feet and kept hold of her hand, though it meant he had to walk outside the track in the deeper snow. At the edge of the forest, she heard the crash of the waterfall. Still Lake spread like a sheet of tin, the mountains swaddled in white.

Sam yanked her back and shushed her. Across the creek, a big brown and white cat threaded its way along the shore, lifting its paws high to clear the snow, the long swoop of its black-tipped tail swinging.

"Cougar," Sam whispered. He took her arms and backed her into the trees. Jess stumbled and the cat froze, its head jerked up, black eyes fixed in their direction.

Jess stared back, transfixed. The cougar stepped toward them very slowly until only the narrow creek lay between. Jess's heartbeat thumped in her ears. The muscles in the cat's shoulders bunched; it drew down into a crouch.

Sam stepped in front of her, unzipping his jacket. "Go away!" he shouted. He spread his arms, holding the jacket open. He was trying to look bigger, Jess realized, like a predator instead of prey. The cougar rose out of its crouch. Sam shouted again: "We are *not* breakfast! Go away!"

The cougar's ears twitched; its head turned to look beyond the clearing where the sawmill's foundation stood. At last, smooth as poured milk, the long, lithe body glided across the clearing toward the forest.

"Whew!" Sam deflated like a punctured balloon.

"Jesus H. Christ on a sled!" Jess cried with a nervous laugh.

Sam turned to look at her and started to say something. Over his shoulder, Jess saw the cat halt and whip around. In the time it took her to scream Sam's name, the cougar bounded across the creek and sprang at them.

Sam ducked and butted his head into the cat's white belly as the cougar folded over him, knocking him down. Its front claws shredded the back of his jacket.

Jess's instincts brought her arms up to shield her face. They also urged her to run for it. But, flat on the ground, Sam grappled with the cougar, shoving its head as its jaws snapped for his neck. The cat was maybe a hundred pounds: muscle, claws, teeth, fur. Jess staggered backwards for a running start and then she slide tackled the cougar, clenching her teeth against the pain in her ribs. Her left boot made contact and the cougar rolled. Jess scrabbled after it, feet first, kicking out with her boots as she scooted through the snow. Three more solid blows, and the cat had had enough. It scrambled to its feet and loped up the hill into the forest. Jess collapsed onto her back and stared up at the white sky, hugging her ribs. Her breath made a cloud of vapor around her head.

Sam knelt over her. He had sticks and pine needles in his hair and a cut below his left ear that dripped blood onto the snow. His hands were cut and bleeding, too. "Are you okay?" he asked.

"More or less." She sat up. "I escaped without a scratch, which is more than you can say." She nodded at his face, his hands. The plaid cap had fallen off. She picked it up, brushed off the pine needles.

He touched his neck, inspected the blood on his fingers. "How deep is it?"

She pushed his hair back to see the cut. "It's bleeding but it's not too bad. About three inches long, maybe a quarter inch deep. Missed your jugular vein, apparently." His head smelled of wood smoke and cedar and some musky pheromone that made her tingle. *I'll kiss it and make it better*, she barely kept herself from saying aloud. Then, as though the effort had depleted her impulse-control reserves, she pulled his chin around and kissed him on the mouth.

He seemed to like it. He drew her in with his hands on the sides of her head, opened his mouth, darted his tongue along her lips. When the kiss ended, he kept his fingers in her hair and smiled at her.

Holy shit, she thought, pulling away. "So," she said. She stood and brushed herself off. "I have a first aid kit with me, back at the Lodge. Why don't I clean up those cuts for you?"

"That's it? That's your pick-up line: 'Come to my room and see my band-aids'? Do you use that a lot?" He grinned from his seat on the ground.

"All the time." She gave him a hand up. They made their way past the sawmill and through the empty streets of the town with their arms wound around each other, for protection.

Once his wound was cleaned and dressed, she kissed his hairline, inhaling his scent of cedar and musk. His hands were decorated with iodine and bandages. He pushed them under her shirt as their mouths met. He rubbed her breasts through her bra and she groaned. Her shirt came off, then his. They tumbled onto the bed.

Her body became a creature of yearning. The air itself thickened until she glided through a pure distillation of pleasure. She breathed it in and clutched the blankets. They were naked, his skin against her skin, his hands everywhere. He kissed her neck, her breasts, her stomach. Now his head was bobbing between her thighs. Her fingers wove into his hair. Her cries grew urgent. She pressed his head. Her body strained, undulating.

Then she plummeted, pitching in a torrent of delight. He raised his head, his face wet and eyes shining. He lifted himself onto her and inside. She held his shoulders and rode out the sensation of falling. At last she plunged into shade and deep stillness. Her body went rigid and then quiet. Sam collapsed next to her and she tucked her head beneath his chin.

78.

Her head nestled on his shoulder, she listened to his slow breathing. On its own, her arm slithered across his ribcage and squeezed him.

Jess MacKinnon didn't want or need intimacy and she did not seek it out. Sex was fine for occasional entertainment. Most men were willing to leave it at that. Sam might be an exception. Even as he slept, she felt him trying to creep closer. She lifted her arm and flopped onto her back, stared at the knotty pine ceiling as though she could decode a message there, in the dark sockets that used to grow branches.

The phone rang.

79.

Riley felt irritated, but her irritation dissipated when Jess MacKinnon answered her telephone. "Hello?"

"Four things. One. Moses is fine. I've appointed him my assistant. It's helping him stay calm."

"Can I talk to him?"

"I sent him out for bialys. Two. Ben Fletcher's toxicology results are being re-examined this morning. Nothing yet."

"Does he even know what a bialy is?"

"I don't think so. Nor do I believe he will find any in Enterprise. At best, I expect onion bagels."

"When will you know anything about the toxicology?"

"Not until Friday. Three. That fire was set deliberately. Could have been Mike Branch, of course. Prime suspect is always the owner. Four."

"What? Why would Mike burn down his own business?"

"To collect the insurance money. Four."

"I'm sure Mike wouldn't do that!"

I'm sure you were born yesterday, thought Riley, rolling her eyes. "Four," she repeated. "Sammy Branch did not die from smoke inhalation. He was dead already by the time the fire started." Silence on the other end of the line. She could hear Jess breathing. Then a voice in the background, a male voice, asking a question. "Am I interrupting something?" she asked.

"No, it's okay. What did he die from, then?" The voice asked another question, more insistent, and MacKinnon shushed him. That sounded like Sam Branch's voice. Maybe they were sleeping together. Riley found that disturbing. Actually, she found it infuriating. She wanted to hurl herself through the telephone line and throttle the man. MacKinnon had been through enough.

Riley stood up and paced across her office, tethered by the phone cord. A nasty scent gasped from the carpet and saturated the room: burning tires, burning trash. Riley recognized it. It was the smell of her own outrage. She'd smelled it in her own house, on her own body as she stepped out of the shower, mixed with the floral shampoo. It happened the whole first year after Fran left for Nashville. "Won't know for sure until the lab tests come back," she said into the telephone. She relaxed her hand, which on its own had turned into a fist. The fury passed, the smell faded, leaving her queasy. "His pupils were dilated. That's all we've got."

"When?"

"Friday. I'll be in touch. Answer your phone. Check your messages." She hung up. Shook her head, puzzled at herself. "The plot thickens," she muttered. She loved saying that.

80

"Let's walk over to Keeler's and get something to eat." Sam had his fingers interlaced behind his head and lay stretched across the bed, naked, half covered by the sheet. He looked as languorous and lithe as the cougar, and Jess edged away, bumping against the desk. Her braid had come undone. She pulled her hair band free of the tangles and looped it around her wrist. Her brain was a muddle; she had a sensation of rushing headlong into danger. Her underpants were wadded on the floor. She pulled them on, then smoothed her hair, combed it with her fingers, parted it into three strands. Jess knew he was watching her. She looked out the window while she braided her hair.

Her jeans were draped over the desk chair. She found her bra on the floor, then her shirt. "I've got to go," she said. Where were her socks? She opened a drawer and found another pair.

"Go? Where? What about breakfast?" He sat up.

"Not hungry." She balanced on one foot, then the other, putting on her socks. Shoved her feet into boots. She was dressed. She bolted for the door. Closed it firmly behind her.

"Jess!" Sam flung the door open and stumbled into the hallway, wrapped in a blanket. "Wait!"

She ran down the stairs. The desk clerk put down her comic book as Jess speed-walked through the lobby. "Is there a problem?" she wanted to know.

"Not at all," Jess told her. And she was out the door.

She walked the paved trail around the lake to the mouth of Old Chuck Creek, shushing through the melting snow. The sex had been nice; her body felt light. Even the pain in her ribs had softened. She hoped there would not be complications. She thought of Riley, waiting for her lover to come home for eight years. They were alike in a way—she had been waiting for Ben, even knowing they would never be together again. She always had this feeling of waiting for something to happen. But what? For Ben to come to his senses? He'd admitted he'd been wrong; that hadn't changed anything. She dipped her head and watched her boots march over the wet asphalt through the piles of mushy snow. Was it different now that Ben was dead? It didn't feel different. Like Riley, she was still waiting.

Jack stood at the fringe of the forest. He was waiting, too, watching the water. He held out his hand. She took it. He helped her over the shifting cobbles. Her palm was sweaty from walking, but his was cool and dry. Steady. "I would like to show you something," he said.

"Oh?" Their hands dropped.

His eyes, dark, were the same as his grandson's eyes. Her feelings about Sam were jumbled together with her affection for Jack, and with the mystery of the fish. "I would like to show you where the fish are hiding," he said.

"Great!" She could hardly stop herself from shouting. "When? Right now?"

He stepped further into the forest. "This afternoon. Come to the house before two o'clock. You and my grandson."

"Sam?" Her excitement took a sharp turn back into anxiety.

"Yes. Bring Sam along with you."

81.

Jess had seen the behavior before: the soft puppy eyes, the nervous forays onto the threshold of a room where awkward professions of True Love peeked from behind the furniture. Then, when she acted cool—never rude, not quite dismissive—there were forced attempts at humor, cavalier gestures and remarks ("*Well, anyway, we had some fun. Didn't we?*"). Sam was struggling, obviously, with the transition to Phase Two. As they walked uphill through the forest to Jack's place, he took her hand. She allowed it for twenty seconds. Then she stepped away and pretended to examine scratch marks on a Ponderosa pine.

"Bear?" she asked him.

"Probably that cougar," he answered, reaching up to touch the cut on his neck.

"Yikes." She chuckled and jogged ahead up the trail, leaving him to follow.

Jack greeted them at the front door. He carried a propane lantern. Jess frowned at the lantern—it was broad daylight. The three of them walked west to the dry creek channel, where a mound of cobbles marked the Ipsootchuck. A breeze blew, the warm Chinook wind. It delivered the ragged, sweet smell of alpine wintergreen.

Jack knelt and lifted cobbles out of the creek bed. "I brought you here once when you were small," he said to Sam. "Do you remember?"

Sam looked puzzled. "Did you bring me here at night?" he asked. "I remember it being dark."

Jack dropped his shoulder against a low, broad stone, braced his palms against it, and pushed it back. Beneath it, the rock was scored.

Jess's breath quickened as Jack lit the lantern. His movements appeared ritualized, as before. She could hardly keep still. "What are you doing?" she asked. "Where's the water bucket?"

"We won't need the bucket today." Jack unhooked the rope from the tree and motioned to Sam. He looped the rope under Sam's armpits and knotted it at his sternum. "You won't need the rope, unless you slip." Jack tested the knot, then patted Sam on the chest. "I suggest you don't slip. The rope is old."

Sam wore an expression of bewilderment and excitement. Jess squatted at the edge of the streambed. The afternoon light sent shadows down the hillside. "I have the impression you are planning to lower me into the well," Sam said, smiling at his grandfather, then at Jess. Her attraction to Sam rattled her bones like a booming bass line beneath the thrill of it. Where were the fish hiding? She was about to find out.

"No, you can climb into the opening." Jack pointed at a space between the rocks. "There are places for your feet on the sides. Then, when your head goes under, you will feel a platform, with your toe. You can stand there, and I'll pass you the lantern."

Sam looked down into the hole, then up to Jess's face. She gave him a shrug and a goofy smile, then turned away, embarrassed. Sam lowered his feet into the darkness. His body descended and vanished. Jack passed down the lantern.

"There's a ladder," he called. "Should I climb down?" Something tugged at the hem of Jess's memory: the sketch in Paul Monticola's workshop. A platform, a ladder.

"Yes," Jack answered. "Go down the ladder. But untie the rope first and leave the lantern on the platform." The rope slackened. Jack pulled it into the light. "Would you like to go down?" he asked her. She found she couldn't speak. She nodded. He looped the rope under her arms. She held her breath. "Not too tight, please," she whispered.

Jess swung her feet into the opening. The lantern sent a rinse of light up into the well shaft. Her toes found indentations in the rock, then handholds. She reached with her foot. There was the platform. She released her grip on the rock walls.

She was standing in the lantern's puddle of light. The well shaft had widened and grew wider still below the platform, which was only about a yard square—rough-milled planks, moist. When she knelt and held out the lantern, she saw the ladder, descending into black. She loosened the rope and let it fall. She raised her face toward the jagged circle of daylight above. "Are you coming down?" she called to Jack.

"Yes. Leave the lantern." The opening filled with Jack's foot.

"Hallo!" Sam's voice echoed off the rock walls, far away. She felt with her foot for the first rung. The ladder's wood was slick but the rungs felt solid. As she descended the air grew colder. Without the lantern, she could see nothing, not the walls of the shaft, not the ladder. After a few moments of climbing the air felt different, the dank smell changed, and she sensed that the shaft was broadening again. She heard the tinkle of water.

With a jolt, her foot hit a second platform. The ladder changed direction, a quarter turn to her right—exactly like the Monticola diagram! She continued down. Jack's voice echoed in the shaft above her, tinny and brittle against the rocks: "All right down there?"

"All right!" she called. The glow of the lantern began descending toward her in jerks. Again her foot hit something flat and solid: stone. She stepped down and shifted her feet. She stood on a rock floor; Jack and the lantern far above; the opening to the well shaft a pebble of daylight. Within the darkness, she sensed an expanse, a chamber. She reached her hands out, groping, found a cold stone wall. Everything damp.

"Hello, there," said a voice next to her, and she yelped. It was Sam, of course. "I'm sorry," he said, and he steadied her with a hand on her back. She let herself lean into his palm for a moment, saw the flash of his smile.

Jack stepped down beside her, turned, and held up the lantern. "Oh!" Jess cried, and her voice flew away and sprang back, watery echo. They stood in an immense cavern with a thirty-foot pool at its center.

The lantern light spilled over the walls. They glimmered—yellow, green, streaks of white. Bulbous stalactites hung from the ceiling, dripped into the pool. On the narrow shore, stalactites met stalagmites in sleek wet columns, a moist stone forest with an understory of knobs and tongues of gray-green limestone.

She turned toward Sam. "Did you—" She pressed back against the moist wall and shut her eyes against the sensation of falling. She looked at Jack. "Is this—" she started. She laughed then and spread her palms. "Jesus H. Christ with a headlamp!"

"I couldn't have said it better myself," Sam said.

"Follow me, please." Jack strode briskly around the lake and they followed. "What time is it?" he asked. Jess checked her watch, which wasn't there.

"Two o'clock exactly," Sam said.

Jack pointed to the ceiling, but all Jess could see was dark stone and the yellow glint of stalactites. "If the sun's out, it shines through a crevasse for a few minutes each day, about two o'clock in October. Come over here." They trailed Jack and his lantern to the far side of the pool. The sound of gurgling water intensified. A stream entered the pool through a stone ditch. Jack walked ahead.

Jess brushed her fingers along the wall. "It's a solution cave," she whispered. "This is limestone."

"How do you know?" Sam whispered back.

"Limestone is made of calcite." She turned in a circle. "It dissolves from acid in the groundwater. If the water is even slightly acidic, it can carve out passages, caverns like this one." She tried to make out his face in the darkness. "Did you know about this, Sam?"

"No. I think he took me here, but I don't remember."

She nodded. It was this way with all deep secrets. You could walk across the surface in daylight, again and again. Never knowing.

Jack and the lantern were twenty feet away. The lantern light disappeared and reappeared again and he called back to them in a voice hollow and reverberating. "Over here."

Jack retrieved a dip net from a sculpted ledge. A shaft of sunlight poured into the cavern and the walls grew radiant. A brilliant road streaked across the lake. Jack eased the net into the pool and guided it up the stream against the current. He pulled it free of the water and held it up into the light.

A red fish thrashed in the mesh. Jack held the net out to Jess. "Is this—" She could hardly breathe. It *was*, she knew it. "It's one of the kokanee."

"Yes," Jack said.

"From Still Lake?" Her fingers brushed the twisting fish, slipped over its dorsal fin.

"Yes," Jack repeated.

Jack lowered the net into the lake and freed the fish. "How is this possible?" Her voice came out so softly he didn't hear her. "Does Old Chuck Creek connect to this lake?" she asked more loudly.

Jack rose and returned the dip net to its place on the ledge. "These are the same waters. But there is no passage for the fish from Old Chuck Creek."

"Then how did they get here?"

Jack sat on the stone beside the lake, resting his back on the cave wall.

"Sit down," he told them. "I'll explain." The sun passed over the crevasse and the light disappeared.

Jess sat beside Jack. Sam took his seat beside her, close but not touching. Jack set the lantern on a stump of rock. It illuminated his face as he spoke.

"My mother named the creek *Olo Chuck Chuck*, Thirsty Creek." He smiled at Jess. "Not because of the bear, but because the ground drinks the creek. The water leaks into the ground along the side channel when the creek runs high." He gestured toward the stream mouth, where the fish had been. "This stream goes west a quarter mile, underground."

Jess could picture it. The passage would begin right below the Big Sink. The limestone must lie underneath the granite. "But the fish—" she said.

Jack held up his hand. "I was born in 1902. The log drives were at their peak. Chuck Stone and Albert Monticola could not be stopped from driving and blasting logs down Old Chuck Creek to the Luders' sawmill. My mother and father were very worried that the fish would not survive. So every year our family trapped small kokanee in the creek and carried them here in buckets, to the Ipsootchuck. We lowered the buckets into this lake, where we let the fish go. Some of the fish we carried up the stream and released them in the current. We did not know whether they could survive here, but the small kokanee swam in this lake, just as they swim in Still Lake, and they grew and turned from silver to red and swam up this stream again to spawn. They have lived here for a hundred years.

"We stopped moving the fish in 1910. I was eight, and I had been big enough to carry the buckets up the hill for two summers. My youngest brother was born that year." He paused and they sat in silence until Jess felt as though the moist air had thickened with grief.

"Sammy didn't know about this?" Jess asked.

"He knew about the cavern and the lake. We told stories about the fish and the log drives. I don't know how much he remembered."

"And my father?" Sam asked. "He doesn't know?"

Jack looked down at the rock in front of his shins. "No."

Jess pushed off the polished wall and lurched to her feet. "What do they feed on?" She was no longer whispering. "Are there cladocerans—plankton? Kokanee are sight feeders. How do they see? They must have adapted somehow. I need to do some sampling. We could probably get a small raft in here."

Sam laughed.

She spun to face Jack. "How many are there? Do you know?"

"I don't know," he answered. "Enough, I think." The lines in Jack's cheeks split into a grin, his face lit with lantern light. This changed everything.

Thursday, October 7, 2004

82.

By Thursday morning, the new edition of the *Still Lake Gazette* was stacked in newspaper boxes across town. Fifty copies were piled on the table in the Museum, fragrant with ink. To Rill Kittridge, they smelled like the breath of the earth and the plants when the rain came after a long dry time.

She took a fresh *Gazette* with her into the print shop to finish cleaning up from yesterday's print run. She was rummaging through a bucket of clean rags when Jonathan Monticola walked in. She stepped to the door and handed him the newspaper. "Hello, Jon," she said.

"Thanks." He pulled a stool away from the wall and sat down. Rill went back to the bucket and pulled out a rag.

"I came to let you know I'm leaving," he said, thumbing through the pages of the *Gazette*.

"Where are you going?" Rill wiped ink off the press. She unclipped the chase and set it on the counter.

"Amsterdam."

"Really?" She looked up. "For how long?"

"For a while, at least a year. I have a relative who's a boat builder there. I'll work as his apprentice."

Rill smiled and tried to meet his eyes, but he was staring down at the newspaper. "Jonathan, that's wonderful! When do you leave?"

"Monday." He folded the *Gazette* in half and tucked it under his elbow. "I'll save this and read it on the plane."

Rill pulled the plate from the chase and began removing the type. "You know, if you give me an address I could mail you the *Gazette* each week. You could keep up with what's happening in town."

"No, thanks." Jonathan pulled the *Gazette* from under his arm, folded it a second time, swatted it against his knee. "I'll have plenty to do."

"Okay, sure." Rebuffed, Rill reached into the bucket for another clean rag.

"The idea is to leave Still Lake, not take it with me."

"Right. I see." Rill felt her chest tighten as a new surge of guilt broke through.

"I want to ask you a question," he said, his voice clipped. "Two questions, actually. And I hope you'll give me an honest answer instead of a bunch of super-polite bullshit." Now she heard anger in his voice and the constriction in her chest tightened another notch, like a belt.

"All right." She tossed the rag aside and turned to face him, her left hand resting on the marble next to the plate with its half-cleaned type. "Fire away."

"Was it just sex for you or did you care for me at all?" Jonathan's eyes were hard and shining. She kept her gaze on his face, though she had to fight the urge to look away. If nothing else, she supposed she owed him this, an answer.

"I did care for you, Jonathan." Her voice was quiet. "I care for you still. Of course I do."

"But you weren't in love with me." Still the anger, a brittle defiance, the hint of a tremor in his voice. In his place, she realized, she would not have the courage for these questions. Was it youth that made him brave? Or perhaps she was a coward. It had taken her twenty years to stand up to Cleve Kittridge.

"Love is a complicated word, more complicated when you're forty-two than when you're twenty."

"That's a bullshit answer, Rill. Give me a real answer." He slapped the twice-folded newspaper against his thigh.

She tried to take a breath deep enough to quell the anxiety that had wedged itself under her diaphragm, but the tightness in her chest would not allow it. She raised her left hand, started to speak and fell silent, then lowered her fingers to a block of clean type and flipped it absently. How could she compose words all day, and print words, and read words, and not be able to speak a simple, truthful sentence to this young man who sat in her print shop peeling back the skin of his heart? That you could love someone desperately and they might not love you back—that was a truth so harsh that Rill did not want to give it voice. She closed her hand around the piece of type until it bit into her palm and she shut her eyes for a moment and blurted it out: "No, I wasn't in love with you."

He turned his face away.

"That doesn't mean I don't care for you."

"I know."

"It doesn't mean, obviously, that you're not lovable, or that someone else won't fall in love with you. Someone suitable." She walked toward him and he stood and pushed the stool back against the wall.

"Right," he said.

"None of that helps, does it?" She wanted to comfort him. But he was using anger now to stay afloat, as though anger were a smooth canoe he would build to slide away from her.

"No. But thank you for being honest. I needed that from you." His voice was calm now and steely. He had already slipped away.

She lowered her arms to hang empty at her sides. "You said you had two questions."

"I was going to ask about Ben Fletcher. But it doesn't matter now."

"We never slept together," she said, but he was right. It didn't matter anymore. *Did you kill him?* she wanted to ask. But that didn't matter either.

He turned and left the print shop. She heard his footsteps cross the Museum.

83.

Jack had kept the cavern and its transplanted fish population a secret from everyone; still, Mike Branch looked affronted when he heard the news. The Outfitters was ringed with yellow tape and closed until further notice, but most of Mike's inventory had escaped the fire. He presented Jess with a box containing a new inflatable raft. In curt tones, he instructed Scott to help with her investigation.

Jess and Scott loaded the *Tamkaliks* with testing equipment and they were out on Still Lake by noon, measuring temperature profiles in the water column and gathering samples with the plankton net. They would climb down into the Ipsootchuck with the raft and spend the afternoon and evening taking samples and temperatures in the underground lake.

"Mike had no idea about the cavern, did he?" Jess asked Scott, lowering the plankton net hand over hand into the deep water.

"No." Scott sat in the stern. "He's a little bit mad, I think."

"Which is understandable." Jess released the messenger to close the net at thirty meters and began hauling it back up, taking care to keep her speed constant. The task, the gathering up of little pieces in the puzzle of the lake environment, kept her hands and her mind busy. She had no time for her thoughts to stall on Sam. She had agreed to meet him for dinner, but she had also agreed to send her boss a finished report by the end of the day Friday, as in tomorrow. Dinner would have to be brief. The plankton net emerged from the water and she unscrewed the bucket from the bottom and poured its contents into a specimen jar.

Scott bent to see the jar. "Is there anything in there?"

"All kinds of stuff. Organisms." Jess swirled the jar gently, revolving its cloudy contents. "You can't really see them without a microscope." She stowed the jar under her seat. There was water in the bottom of the dory. She pushed her backpack higher into the bow, where it was dry. Her laptop was inside. "Let's try that direction." She pointed south.

Scott eased the boat into motion. "Did you talk to your boss yesterday?" he asked her.

"Yes. He's pretty excited about the fish. He's driving up here himself on Saturday morning."

They drifted into position. Jess screwed the 64-micron bucket onto the end of her net.

"Will your report be done?"

"It has to be. I stayed up until one in the morning working on it." Jess lowered the net, leaning over the rails and tipping the dory.

Scott grabbed the sides of the boat. "Careful! That water's freezing. If you're going to tip us over, please do it closer to shore."

She glanced at him. He wasn't joking. It probably hadn't been the best idea to bring her laptop, with the only copy of her report inside it. She nudged her pack further into the bow.

The plankton net reached its depth and the release mechanism clattered down the line to swing it shut. Jess hauled on the line. She held the net above the water and rinsed it, unscrewed the bucket. Scott reached down to the floorboards for an empty specimen jar and handed it to her. He started the motors and she pointed west, toward Old Chuck Creek.

She turned and bent to look down into the water, clear and cold, rippling with the boat's passage. She touched the block letters stenciled on the bow: *Tamkaliks*. She shifted her gaze to the scored gray mountains that seemed to rise out of the lake, spreading their talus skirts.

"The boat's name," Scott said, watching her. "Do you remember what it means?"

"The place where you can see the mountains," she said, repeating what he'd told her on the dock—was it only a week ago?

Scott nodded, smiling his approval. "Sam says in Nez Perce there's a feeling of reverence that doesn't come through in English. He says a better translation would be 'the place where you stand up and take notice of the mountains.'"

"Well, then," she said, looking at her knees. Dinner was at six.

"Well, then," he answered.

84.

Scott saw him first, a familiar shape sitting on the edge of the dock. He was the absolute last person on the earth Scott wanted to deal with. Jess leaned over the bow. "Is that your father?"

"Yep," he answered. Jess knew nothing, probably, about their family drama—his mother's beat-up face, the scorched carpet, the note to Jonathan. Scott shuddered as he remembered his father at the dinner table reading the note aloud in his stupid, mocking voice. He cut the engines and cranked the tiller around. "Are you sure you don't want to take some more samples?" He tried to keep his voice light, like he might be joking, but she turned around and wrinkled up her forehead.

"The two of you aren't getting along?"

Shoot straight and speak the truth, Scott recited to himself, though the terminology was less than perfect. It was one of Colby Stukel's lines, from a poem. His grandfather would not have minded that his grandson was gay, Scott was sure of that. He had better get himself used to telling people. And the shame that stood in that doorway, leering, wearing his father's face: he had better learn to shut the door on *that*. "I came out," he said. The three words echoed across the water and bounced off the mountains.

"Ah," Jess said. She didn't seem surprised. "How did that go?"

"Not great. I'd rather not talk to him right now." He steered the dory in a wide arc away from the dock, heading nowhere. But Jess was folding up her plankton net.

"I'm sorry, Scott, but we've still got to get down into the cavern and take samples. And then I have to finish my report." She crammed the plankton net into her duffle and zipped it closed like the final word. "Tell you what. I'll run interference. As soon as we dock the boat, I'll send you up to my car so we can load up. I'll deal with your dad."

Scott felt dubious, but what else was there to do? He couldn't drive the boat around in circles all afternoon. He swung the tiller and looped back toward shore.

All the other boats were in storage, so he put the *Tamkaliks* on the far side of the dock from his father. Cleve lurched to his feet and spread his arms as though to welcome them. In one hand he held an open bottle of whiskey by its long neck. Scott's brain shifted into high alert. He jumped onto the dock and tied off the bow line. He kept his eyes down, watched his fingers looping the rope around the cleat in figure eights.

"We need to talk, son." Cleve's words ran together, sloppy and soft. Abruptly, Scott was furious.

"Do we?" He straightened up and took a step toward his father, who staggered backwards. "Because I thought I wasn't your son anymore. Or don't you remember saying that?" He took another step. Now it was Cleve Kittridge's turn to be struck off-balance, to run.

His father performed a drunken pirouette, barely keeping his feet. He laughed and took a pull from the bottle. "That's right! Yeah, you really had me going there for a minute! Gay! Hah!" He laughed again, throwing his head back. The movement sent him off kilter and he lurched toward the boat, where Jess sat watching. "What're you looking for out there on the lake?" he asked her.

Jess squinted against the sun. "Mysids," she told him. "Opossum shrimp." She slid her backpack onto the dock. "I'm afraid we're in a hurry, Mr. Kittridge. You'll have to excuse us." She tossed the duffle. Scott caught it, cradled it against his chest, a strange comfort. Beneath it, his heart pounded. "Would you take that, Scott, please?" she said. He nodded, caught a movement to his left. Mike was loping down the gangway.

"Opossum shrimp! I sat right here on this dock with Mike Branch and Casey Monticola the day they dumped those things in the lake. I was twelve years old." He took a long swig of whiskey, then another.

"I remember," Mike said. "What's going on, Cleve? What're you doing out here?" Scott clutched the duffle and side-stepped around his father. Jess stood up and the boat rocked.

"Well, I'm just getting me some fresh air, Mike!" Cleve inhaled dramatically. "I'm staying over at the Lodge." He waved his arm, staggered. "They gave me a discount, too—seeing as how my wife kicked me out. Just having a drink. Want to join me?" He held out the bottle.

The rest of it happened like the steps of a horrible dance. Cleve lost his balance, tipped, and fell toward the edge of the dock. Mike grabbed for him and missed. Cleve's foot hooked the shoulder strap of Jess's backpack and he pinwheeled into the water, dragging the pack behind him.

Jess yelled. She scrambled onto the dock. On her hands and knees, she stared down into the water. Scott let the duffle fall. He knelt beside her. Cleve surfaced twelve feet away, sputtering and laughing. "My pack!" Jess shouted at him. "Do you have it?"

"What's going on?" Mike asked.

"Her laptop's inside. Her report." His father thrashed to the dock and Mike helped him out of the water. Cleve flopped onto the planks like a walrus. No backpack, of course.

"Whew. That's cold!" Cleve hugged himself and rolled around. Jess was about to jump in. Scott put a hand on her shoulder.

"I'll go," he said, and before he let himself think he toppled headfirst into the lake.

The cold felt like it would stop his heart. Twenty feet deep through the clear water he saw the orange pack bedded into the silt. He kicked down and snatched it, kicked back up, and threw it, then himself, onto the dock. He watched Jess unzip the pack, pull the laptop free. She opened it. Water streamed out. Scott started to shiver. "Will it be all right?" he asked her, his voice shaking like the rest of him. But he knew the answer. Laptop computers were not amphibious.

"No," she said. She closed the laptop, stood, grabbed the pack in her other hand. "No, it will not be all right." Her mouth twisted; she was trying to smile but wanted to cry. "But thank you, Scott. Come back to the Lodge and we'll get you dried off." She walked toward shore and Scott followed her. He heard his father calling to him but he didn't look back.

85.

At Keeler's Counter, she found Sam waiting in one of the booths by the windows. She slid in to face him. "I don't have much time," she said, by way of a greeting.

He wore a sweater vest over a white T-shirt. His fingers were folded on the table. She blushed and looked away. She propped the menu in front of her face, quelled the memory of his hands on her skin.

When she looked up Sam was watching her. He motioned to the window. "I sat here so we could see the lake." A thin margin of sky had cleared along the mountains. The clouds bunched above their peaks were tinged with orange and the lake caught the color.

"It's beautiful," she said.

"Yes. And deep, and mysterious." He smiled. "Not unlike my dinner companion."

Jess bowed her head. "I don't mean to be mysterious." She lifted her eyes. His lips closed and his smile turned tender. He was a sweet man. She would be gentle with him.

His arm moved as though to take her hand, but A.D. Keeler appeared. She wrote down their orders.

"Thanks, A.D." Sam smiled at her.

A.D.'s tired eyes brightened. "Nice to have you back, though I sure am sorry about your uncle. Will you stay for a while?"

"Not sure."

A.D. looked from Sam to Jess and back again. She dropped the order pad into her apron pocket.

"So," he said, when A.D. had gone.

"So." She pinched at the skin between her eyebrows. "You heard about my report? The laptop?"

"Yes. I'm really sorry. My father says you're welcome to use his computer, as long as you need it. Race said she'd make you a pot of coffee."

"That's really generous." It was. Jess was touched. "I can't tell you how much I appreciate that."

"Will you be able to finish in time?"

"Maybe." Would she? Her notes were dimpled and damp, but decipherable. She had written the report once, most of it. Would she remember? All at once she felt exhausted. The table seemed to pull her shoulders down, bending her neck.

He took her hand. "You're tired. What can I do to help?"

She shook her head. Her face heated up with emotion. She felt tears threatening, a current that would knock her down and pull her under. For a moment she longed to give in, let everything go, and let herself be swept away. Maybe she could accept his offer of help. But what could he do? She hardly knew, herself, where to begin.

Enough. It was lack of sleep, and stress; that was all. She tugged her hand out of his fingers, turned, studied the counter for evidence that their dinner was coming. Without him touching her, it was easier not to cry.

"I'm a decent proofreader." He smiled. Refolded his fingers. She could see in his eyes that she'd hurt him by pulling away.

Jess drained her water glass. It made a wet ring on the table. She skated the glass back and forth in the moisture. "That's a good offer," she said, watching the glass, noncommittal.

"Right." He tapped his folded fingers on the table as a long uncomfortable silence hovered between them. "Let me ask one question, Jess, please," he finally said.

Inwardly, she grimaced. *Here it comes*, she thought. She turned again and looked for their food. Turned back, arranging her face into what she hoped was a casually expectant expression.

"I had the impression the attraction was mutual. Was I wrong about that?"

She looked out the window at the lake, fiery in the day's final light. "You are not wrong." She chose her words with care. "I *am* attracted to you. Obviously, there's chemistry between us. That's the issue." She could see he didn't understand.

He pushed his bangs back, puffed his cheeks, and blew out a shaky breath. She hoped he wouldn't cry. "Are you being deliberately vague?"

"No." The last light swept down the mountains, their tops lost, now, in clouds, their flanks seething with strands of mist that wove through the trees. Her eyes moved back to Sam. Her attraction tugged at her, insistent. She wouldn't mind going to bed with him again, but there seemed no way to keep things casual.

He spread his palms upward on the table. "I'm trying to understand. It feels like more than chemistry between us. What about intimacy? A relationship?"

"Sam." She sighed. "I don't do relationships. I just don't."

"Never? Never ever? You've never been in a relationship?"

"One time." And there was Ben's freckled face in the sunlight, dropping into the bowl of her mind like a girl on a skateboard. "I was very, very young. Let's just say it didn't end well." She turned toward the kitchen again. A.D. was stacking plates on a tray. At last. "So that was it for me. You know?"

"No, Jess. I do not know." He sat back, clearly frustrated. A.D. delivered their food. Jess stilled the churning in her gut by gobbling half her sandwich. Sam picked at his omelet. Finally he dropped his fork onto the plate, making her jump. "Explain it to me."

"What?" She kept her eyes down, selected a French fry, swept it through a pile of ketchup. Then she set it down.

"How being hurt once makes you decide never to try again."

"It was more than being hurt." She pushed her plate away. "Much more." Sam stared at her as though she, Jess, were a specimen in a jar. He pushed his fingers into his hair again. He looked angry.

"It was a long time ago," she said.

86.

Nineteen eighty-seven. Jess worked at Ernie's motorcycle shop, slept at her mother's place, waited for October and Moses's first birthday.

She spent her paycheck on a lawyer, Charles Fenster, who was two years out of law school and told her to call him Chip.

"Yeah, I could try to unwind that consent, file a motion, get a judge to look at it. Maybe we could get some traction. Maybe not. You signed it. The father signed it." Chip leaned back in his chair. His desk had a glass top that reflected Jess's face when she put her elbows on the edge and held her head between her hands. Chip had straight brown hair and sideburns, a mole under his left eye. Her mother would have called it a beauty mark. His hands looked soft, his fingernails trimmed into tidy white squares. "Thing is, I'd be billing you by the hour. You could easily spend ten grand and have nothing to show for it but an empty bank account."

Jess's bank account held a balance of seventy-two dollars. Chip's sixty-minute consultation was costing her fifty bucks.

"There must be a way to get him back!" her mother said when Jess told her the news. Priscilla's face wore a little grim smile, as though losing Moses were annoying but expected, like misplacing your car keys.

"The lawyer said it would cost ten thousand dollars." Jess wanted to be alone. She wanted to lie on her bed and stare at the ceiling while night came on and the sky darkened. Her mother didn't have ten thousand dollars. No one they knew had ten thousand dollars.

"Oh, lawyers!" Priscilla said, waving her hands. Jess wanted to grab her mother's shoulders and shake her, hard. "You just got to accept it, my girl. Dr. Fletcher, he's rich. Could be better this way." Priscilla chuckled and reached out to pat Jess's head, but Jess swatted her hand away, more enraged than she could ever remember feeling. The fury dropped low into her gut and turned cold, a chunk of scraped-off road snow, filthy with gravel. She hated everything about her mother right then: her hoarse voice, her too-bright fingernails and lips, the stoop of her shoulders and her low-cut blouse.

"No, I don't got to accept it!" she snapped. "And I'm not your fucking girl!" Her mother's mouth fell open, a lipstick red O of surprise. Jess pushed past her to her bedroom and slammed the door so hard the wall rattled.

87.

"Tell me what happened, Jess. Please." Sam leaned over the table, closing the distance between them.

She felt herself bristle, but then she thought, why not? Maybe she could tell him about Moses. The deep, hundred-year secret of the Ipsootchuck was out in the air now; maybe her secret was a fair exchange. She could offer it up as proof that she wasn't a monster, that she didn't take his feelings lightly. But he would never understand. To her, it made sense. To everyone else it would be incomprehensible— how losing Moses had forced her to protect what remained. What remained was the shallow imprint of his little body on the mattress of the crib at the Fletcher ranch. That empty place held, and would always hold, all of her tenderness, every gram of devotion that she, Jess MacKinnon, had to give. There was nothing left over for Sam. She was sorry about it—for him and for herself—but that didn't change anything. The secret would do neither of them any good. She would feel exposed beyond nakedness and that would leave her furious. He would only be confused. The fantasy of telling him retreated. She gathered it back up and pulled it close. "Can't you just accept that I'm not ready for a relationship?" she said. "It's not you. It's not personal."

"It doesn't get much more personal than this." He fixed her with a pair of stubborn eyes that reminded her of Jack's.

It was dark, the quick darkness of a valley between mountains. She looked away from him, out the window, but all she saw was the inky sky over the lake, and her own reflection.

Sam interlaced his fingers and rested his chin on them. "Was it so horrible, what happened? So horrible you don't want to talk about it?" His face was tender, his voice low.

"Yes, it was horrible." She looked down at her folded arms. Her knuckles had gone white. She dropped them to her sides and collapsed against the seat back. "I'm sorry. I shouldn't have gone to bed with you. It was unprofessional."

"*Unprofessional?*"

She understood his incredulity. It was a cold word, and she had delivered it coldly. She said it again. "Unprofessional, yes."

He threw his napkin onto the table and stood up. "All right," he said. He was stung, she could see that in his brusque movements. There were tears in his eyes. She assumed that was why he wouldn't look at her. "All right," he said again. "I'm going to storm off dramatically now." He glanced her way and smiled, but she saw his lip tremble. "But that doesn't mean I'm giving up. Fair warning." She watched him cross the room, open the door, step outside.

88.

By the time Jess left Keeler's Counter, the darkness had thickened and the wind was picking up. In her pocket, she found the green plaid hat that Sam had loaned her. She pulled it over her ears. She leaned into the wind. The Sam situation was dealt with. Now the report had to be written. Again. She would go to Mike and Race's house and stay there all night if that's what it took.

A gust of wind slapped her face and blew off the hat. She chased it down Main Street but lost it in the darkness. She scanned the ground. Another gust hit her face.

"Looking for this?"

Birch Stukel materialized like an apparition, astride her mule, holding the borrowed cap in her hand. As she passed it over, the fringe of her bold-striped Mexican poncho tickled Jess's neck. Jess fixed the cap back on her head. Birch dismounted.

"It's lucky I ran into you." Birch's mass of yellow curls blew across her face. "Will you still be in town on Saturday?"

The gusty wind roared by. Jess held the cap onto her head. "Yes. Why?"

"There'll be a small gathering at my place at noon. A memorial for Sammy. The Branches will have their own rituals. This is for his friends. I think he counted you as a friend. I know he appreciated what you're trying to do." The wind whipped Birch's poncho and the curls of hair around her face.

"Thank you." Jess's eyes watered from the rising wind. "I'll try to be there."

Birch swung herself onto the mule's back. The mule stamped and brayed. "Settle down, Socrates." Birch patted the brown neck and looked up the Old Chuck Creek canyon as the wind gusted by again. "There's a storm coming. Whenever the pressure changes, the mountains act like a funnel, pushing wind down through the canyon."

Her next words were partly lost in the wind; Jess heard, "Watch your back, my love."

"What?" Her head jerked up. She moved closer and strained to bring Birch's face into focus through the shadows. "What did you say?"

"I said, watch your hat. See you Saturday." She and the mule disappeared into the dark.

89.

By midnight, Mike and Race were asleep, leaving Jess hunched over a keyboard in their tiny home office. She had reconstructed most of what she'd already written. But now she found herself at an impasse as it occurred to her what would happen to the Ipsootchuck when her report was released to the state and became a public document. She would repay Jack's trust by opening his family's home to a swarm of tourists clamoring to inspect the only known solution cave in northeastern Oregon. She stared at the screen, the white page with its marching regiments of type. There was a way around the problem, she was sure of it. She padded to the kitchen to refill her coffee.

It was past three in the morning when she got back to her room. She and Scott would meet at the Ipsootchuck at eight for more sampling. They would trap a live adult fish, too, and haul it up the ladders into the daylight. By afternoon, she would have enough data to finish her report. She peeled away her clothes and left them on the floor. Her pillow smelled faintly of woodsmoke, the smell of Sam's hair. No use to turn her thoughts in that direction. She flipped the pillow over and fell into a black sleep.

90.

As Rill passed the spur trail to the Monticola place, her listlessness threatened to ripen into full-blown depression. Part of this was the publication cycle. The paper came out on Thursday; Fridays always felt aimless. The other part was Jonathan. It was true, she wasn't in love with him—if she even knew what love was—but she missed him terribly. And, prancing like a mantis around the undusted corners of her mind was the troubling knowledge that she had committed a grave wrong.

The trail forked; she veered right, toward the house, though she dreaded going home. The house would be empty. Before long it would be permanently empty and she would rattle around like the loose piece of a machine. No husband, because she had chosen badly. No Scott, the tender gay son she had failed utterly to love and protect. And no Brian. After the fracas at the house, Brian had pieced together what was going on between her and Jonathan. He hadn't spoken to her since.

A crow dropped from its high perch and landed in front of her, in the center of the muddy footpath, derailing this depressing train of thought and stopping her in her tracks. It flapped and scolded, hopping on its spindle legs. Then, message delivered, it launched its ungainly black body back into the trees.

Rill took it as a sign. She doubled back to the fork and took the trail south to the footbridge. *Back into my chamber turning, all my soul within me burning*, she muttered, remembering her father at the dinner table, reciting "The Raven," all of it, from memory. She would visit her sister. Birch would invigorate her.

But Birch did not seem to be home. Rill called her name and rapped on the front door. She tried the knob. It was not locked, but no one in Still Lake locked their doors. Rill debated with herself about going inside—a breach of etiquette, but she had done it before. She dropped her hand. What was she thinking? Her moral compass seemed to have spun awry. She trudged back to the yard, where the trail began. Socrates brayed from the barn. That meant Birch probably *was* around here somewhere. Rill performed a little dance of indecision at the trailhead. Then she followed the sound to the barn.

The barn doors were wide open. *That* was unusual. Unlike the house, the barn was always locked tight. Rill stood in the door frame, smelling hay, manure, a sour scent from the rabbit hutches, the sweet stench of fermentation—each odor familiar, but disturbing in concert. The mule nibbled from a trough in the dim rear of the building. Birch's cat, Meno, crept out of the darkness and sat watching her, his face strangely human in the half light.

A feeble whimper drifted from the far corner, then a whine. She saw movement, heard a rhythmic thumping. She moved closer. On a pile of straw in the corner, a dog lay on a blanket, tail swatting the ground. She reached out a hand, bent down, made soothing noises. The dog whined again, as though it recognized her, tried to rise to its feet. It tottered and landed in the nest of its blanket and straw. An old dog, failing.

The dog was familiar, a gaunt brindle mutt with a Labrador face. Rill bent closer, scratched behind the dog's ears, scanned the plank wall for a light switch. Instead she found a rust-colored field jacket hanging on a nail. Frowning, she pulled it down. The collar, forest green flannel.

"What are you doing here, snooping around?" Birch rushed into the barn carrying—no, brandishing—a shovel. Behind her, the door to the backyard made a rectangle of daylight.

Rill held the jacket in front of her. "This is Dad's jacket." She pointed to the dog. The shaft of light from the door illuminated a white star on its head. "And isn't this Rascal?" At the sound of the name, the dog lifted its head. The tail thumped once, twice.

Birch advanced without responding. The back light from the doorway left her face inscrutable. Five feet away, she set the shovel's blade in the straw and hung on the handle as though her body had grown too heavy to bear. "Yes. That's Rascal." Her voice was weary. The tail thumped.

Rill's mind whirred. "How can this be Rascal? Did he not drown? When did you find him? Why didn't you tell me?" She shifted sideways to change the angle of the light. She peered into her sister's face. "Why is Colby's jacket here?"

"Rascal was never in the lake." Birch's voice was hoarse now. "I made that up."

"What?" Rill felt dizzy. "Why?"

"Dad's death wasn't an accident. I just wanted everyone to think so."

"I can't understand what you're saying." But a horrible thought landed in the maelstrom of Rill's spinning brain. Birch had inherited full ownership of her house at Colby Stukel's death. Birch did not need money. But she did crave roots, a place to belong. Rill blurted it out before she had time to think. "Did you *kill* him?"

Birch sprang, swinging the shovel. "I'll kill *you* for saying that, you hateful bitch!"

Rill dodged. The shovel hit Rascal in the head. Rascal yelped. Birch's momentum flung her around, the shovel flew out of her hands, and she collapsed in a pile. She threw her arms around Rascal's neck and sobbed into the old dog's shoulder.

Rill knelt beside her in the scattered straw.

"There's an envelope in the jacket pocket," said Birch, her voice shaking.

Rill sat cross-legged on the cold barn floor and pulled the jacket across her lap. In the pocket, her fingers found the envelope, the word "Girls" printed in Colby's perfect handwriting. Inside, a folded half-sheet of paper, eggshell white. "From the desk of Mayor Colby Stukel," it said across the top, in forty-eight point Helvetica. Her father's stationery—he had printed it himself on the Chandler & Price. Below, three lines in Colby's script: "It seems I have outlived my usefulness to Still Lake. I am too old and too full of shame. I love you and I'm sorry to leave you, but it is time." At the bottom of the page he had written something else, but scribbled it out. Then an apparent biblical reference: "Genesis 1:20."

Rill brushed the words with her fingers as though that could make sense of them. She felt numb. The barn was so quiet she could hear Socrates chewing.

Birch broke the silence in a whisper. "You know what night it was: March Seventh. We were sandbagging the museum. I noticed Dad was missing. I went looking for him, found Rascal tied to a tree near the sawmill. Next to Rascal, a garbage bag. Inside, his jacket, folded, with the envelope on top."

Rill desperately wanted her to stop the tale. It was all coming at her too fast. Her father, a suicide? She could not take it in. She left the letter in her lap, covered her face with her hands, and began to cry, chanting "Stop. Please stop." But Birch went on.

"I read the note. Couldn't think what to do, where to look. The rain was coming down in sheets—you remember. North Creek was out of control. It was impossible to see or hear anything. I decided to check the house. But when I untied Rascal, he started lunging for the lake, so I knew that's where Dad had gone." Birch began to cry. "I saw his white shirt in the water. He was floating, face down. I was sure it was too late but I was taking off my raincoat, getting ready to swim out there. That's when the sawmill came down, right on top of him. The noise was deafening." Birch stroked the dog's neck, tears streaking her face. "So I brought Rascal here. He's not that old, he's ten. But he's been dying of grief, dying in little increments, ever since Dad left him."

Birch's eyes held such raw pain that Rill wondered if her sister, too, was dying in increments. "Why didn't you tell us?" she whispered. "Does Race know?"

"No one knows. Only me." Birch's fingers continued their absent stroking but her eyes traveled all around the barn, to Socrates, lipping up grain from his trough, to the open door. She wiped her face. "A secret has to have a keeper," she said at last. "I decided to keep his secret. The note, the suicide. I didn't want his legacy to end that way. He was already so ashamed."

"But *why*?" Rill beat on her thighs with her fists. "And what in God's name does this mean?" She held up the letter and pointed to the bottom. "Genesis 1:20?"

"You know why, if you think about it. The fish, of course. He blamed himself for their extinction. In Genesis chapter one, verse twenty, God creates all the creatures in the water. On the fifth day. That's when he made the fish."

91.

Jess was dead on her feet by Friday afternoon. She and Scott had spent the day on Still Lake and in the cavern, but there was no time to pause. She sprinted across the lobby of the Lodge. The front desk clerk waved a slip of paper as she passed.

"The P.I. from Enterprise called four times. She said it's important."

Jess snatched the paper and ran up the stairs.

In her room, she tucked the message slip beside the phone, picked up the receiver as she kicked off her boots. She sat down and peeled away her wet socks, in which her feet had been marinating for eight hours. No dial tone. She pressed down the receiver with her finger, held it for a count of ten, released. The tone stuttered, then blared onto the line. She squinted at the message slip. Picked it off the table, held it inches from her face. No number.

She hung up the phone. Her pants were soaked to the knees. She stripped them off. She had Riley Bishop's phone number written down somewhere. She couldn't think where.

She had promised to send her finished report to Darrin by email no later than four o'clock, so he would have time to read it this evening before his long morning drive from Portland to Still Lake. She checked her watch. Three-thirty-five. Fuck. She pulled on her last dry pair of pants and slipped her wrinkled feet into sandals, no socks, though the weather had turned cold again. Frostbitten toes: she would take one for the team. She grabbed her pack and ran downstairs.

"Did Riley Bishop leave a phone number?" she asked Bethany, the desk clerk. Bethany looked up from her comic book with an expression that suggested she had never considered taking a message that included a telephone number. She shook her head. "Well, if she calls again, would you please get her number?"

"Sure," said Bethany.

It was past nine when she sent the report. Race asked her when she'd eaten last and made her a sandwich. She sat Jess down at the table and poured each of them a glass of milk. "Maybe you'd rather have a glass of wine?" she asked, taking the chair across from her.

"No, thank you." Jess's stomach lurched at the thought. She drank the milk.

"You know, my stepson is a really good guy."

Jess's sleep-deprived brain could not find a context for this remark. She nodded and hid behind her sandwich, cheddar on whole wheat with tomato slices. Oh. She meant Sam. Word traveled fast in a small town. "I couldn't agree more," she told Race.

When she got back to her room, another message slip was scotch-taped to her door. She yanked it free. She could hardly bring the desk clerk's handwriting into focus. "P.I. called twice more," it said. "More" was underlined three times. There was the phone number.

She sat on the bed and pulled off her sandals, tucked her freezing cold feet under the covers. She would just lie down for a moment.

The phone woke her at five-thirty. She sat up in the darkness and swatted for the phone. By the time she fumbled the receiver to her ear, the ringing had stopped. She left the phone off the hook and went back to sleep.

Saturday, October 9, 2004

92.

Jess's meeting with Darrin Woodruff was set for ten-thirty at Keeler's Counter. She woke at nine-forty in the grip of deep apprehension. She'd sent her report off, late, without reading it through one last time. Why hadn't she proofed it again? Everything depended on that report: funding, her role as project manager, client approval, the project itself. What if the report was bad? Unorganized? Unintelligible? She stripped and stood in the shower to let needles of water stab her in the face. Every new classroom, every standardized test pelted her with the shower spray. A number two pencil in the clutch of her sweaty fingers. A sea of bubbles on the answer sheet. *Read the directions silently while I read them aloud.* Squirming in that molded plastic chair, she was an imposter. A tramp from the projects.

"I read your report," Darrin told her. "Which arrived at nine-twenty last night." He slapped a bundle of typewritten pages onto the table between them.

"Sorry about that," Jess said, gulping coffee. She didn't elaborate. Darrin didn't like excuses. After four months at C.E.C., she'd been twenty minutes late to a meeting, and had kept clients waiting. He'd interrupted her explanation—an accident on the highway, backed-up traffic—and had started the meeting with an apology to the clients. Later, he told her, "I'm not interested in excuses, MacKinnon. I'm interested in performance." He wasn't mean, he wasn't even unreasonable. But he was demanding, and she knew where she stood. She had to prove herself.

"I've got a few questions." She looked at him carefully. Darrin was a solemn man. She braced herself for the worst. *I expected better, MacKinnon. I can't give the clients this kind of work product.* Why hadn't she read it again? Why hadn't she given it to Sam? He had offered to proofread. They ordered food. A.D. Keeler refilled her coffee cup.

On her first day of college at Portland State University, she sat in the front row for her eight o'clock class, Writing 101. The instructor told them to turn to Chapter One and Jess discovered she had her history textbook, not the writing textbook. She looked around in a panic. The instructor, a young graduate student with a bushy black beard, asked her what was wrong. "Sorry," she answered. "I brung the wrong book." Three beats of silence and then a soft titter flew across the room like a bristle of hard rain on concrete. Her face burned. She bent her head. The wrong textbook rested, heavy, on the desk. "I mean, brought. I brought the wrong book," she whispered, but the instructor had shifted his attention to another, more competent student. There was nothing to say. You had to get it right the first time. Shitty little tramp, exposed.

"You said you had questions." She massaged her eyes with her fingertips.

"Four questions. First, direct transplantation versus captive rearing. You recommend no hatchery propagation. Why not do both? We could build up the population faster if we captured spawners and stripped their eggs and hatched them in a hatchery."

Jess had discussed the hatchery idea with Jack, who had fixed her with a look of incredulity. "What does that mean, 'strip the eggs,'" he'd asked, folding his hands primly on his knee.

She held Darrin's gaze over the rim of her cup, inhaling the coffee-scented steam that rose like a promise of redemption. "There are disadvantages to captive rearing, that's why I recommended against it.

Higher potential for disease transmission. Direct transplantation will work if we take fish from the donor stock at different life stages. It may take longer to build up the numbers, but the Ipsootchuck is small, so we can trap fish efficiently." She stared at the stack of pages. Darrin had tabbed it with sticky notes. It was too late now to correct her mistakes. You had to get it right the first time.

"That may be all right. But you'll have to transplant in high numbers, fry and sub-adults, maybe fertilized eggs. No spawners?"

"Spawners are too vulnerable to handling stress. But we can collect them near the mouth of the stream before they go up to spawn."

"Are you prepared to stay up here for a year or more?"

Did he mean the report was all right? Or was this all hypothetical? Maybe he was testing her. Anyway, there was only one right answer to this question. She'd have to find a place to live, maybe in Enterprise. Maybe Moses would move there. Once he turned eighteen, he'd be free to leave the Fletcher ranch. Maybe he'd want to be closer to his new girlfriend. Before she had time to spin out that fantasy, she remembered she hadn't returned Riley's call. A shadow fell across her hands: A.D. had crept to the table to refill her cup. She gulped the fresh coffee, burned her mouth, and nodded yes to Darrin's question.

"For several years? Driving back and forth from Portland? Six hours each way?" He held up his hand as she opened her mouth to answer. "Let's be clear, MacKinnon. I need to know your level of commitment. I need to know you're ready to stay with this project over the long haul."

But did that mean the report was okay? Jess kept her eyes on Darrin's stern face. She could read nothing there. "I'm committed to the project," she told him. If there *was* a project. He might give her another chance, let her rewrite the report. He might assign someone else to manage the project, someone more competent.

"Okay." Darrin opened the report to a page he had tabbed. "Second question. Could you transplant adults this year? Or is it too late already?"

"I saw them in the lake. They're in the middle of their migration. We can do it this year. We can start right now."

"All right." He sounded noncommittal. He nodded, then nodded again as A.D. arrived to set their plates down. "So if they spawn in Old Chuck Creek this fall, their mature offspring should return in 2008, right?"

"That's right. That will be the first generation that has hatched in Old Chuck Creek in at least thirty years." They were talking about the project as though it were going to happen. Jess pictured bright red fish at the creek mouth. She felt a little better. Maybe she could eat. She sliced off the hind end of her omelet with the edge of her fork.

Darrin thumbed through the report to another tabbed page. "I have a question about the mysids. You say they're all but gone from the lake, but I don't see any explanation in here." He tapped the report with his fingertips.

"I don't have an explanation, just a theory." The mysids were gone, that was the important thing.

"What's your theory?" Darrin propped his chin on one hand and waited.

"You remember the catastrophic flood back in March?" He nodded. "I think the flood acidified the lake enough to weaken the *Mysis relicta* population. Then the lake trout took care of the rest, by predation." She lifted the fork to her lips. The smell of eggs made her gag. She let the piece of omelet slide back onto the plate.

"Interesting. You think the lake became acidic enough to take out the mysids, but not the lake trout?"

"Yes." She poked at the omelet's skin with her fork. "*Mysis relicta* are acid-sensitive. They start to disappear if the pH falls below six. Lake trout can survive at pH five-point-five. Also, I think the acidification was brief—a few days or weeks in the spring—and an organism like a fish would have more staying power than a mysid." Jess watched Darrin's face. She saw evidence in the pinch between his eyebrows that he was dissecting her theory and examining its components. Darrin had an analytical mind, sharp as a scalpel. She rummaged in her backpack for her notebook and began flipping through water-wrinkled pages of handwritten notes.

"What happened to your notebook? Looks like it went for a swim."

"It did." She hadn't told him about the accident with her laptop, the loss of her report. It had been stupid to take it with her in the boat. And Darrin wasn't interested in excuses.

"What's the pH of the lake water now?"

"Above six-point-five."

Darrin folded his hands at his chin and scrutinized her. "What caused the lake to acidify in March?"

Jess scanned through her notes. "Acidity in the lake will always be higher in the spring," she began, meeting his eyes. "That's because its alkalinity depends on bicarbonate, which mainly derives from calcite—the limestone aquifer. When the water moves slowly through the limestone, the bicarbonate buffers the acids and keeps the pH high.

"But when the water moves quickly, in the spring during the snowmelt, then it picks up acid from the soil—from the forests, which are full of organic acids and spodosols. So, less buffering." She took a deep breath and glanced down at the notes. "The March flood was big. I think the flood carried so much acidic organic material into the system that Still Lake lost its ability to buffer acids and that, however, briefly, the pH in the lake water dropped low enough to compromise the *Mysis* population."

Darrin nodded and the pinch between his eyebrows softened. "But not low enough to affect the lake trout."

"Correct." Jess closed her notebook and waited.

Darrin nodded again. "That's a good theory, MacKinnon. I like it."

Jess cut another square of omelet and scooted it around the plate. She couldn't stand it anymore. "What about the report?" she asked.

"What about it?" He tapped the pages. "The mysids are gone. That means we won't have a repeat of what happened in 1962."

"That's not what I mean."

"What, then?" He raised his eyebrows. She couldn't speak. He'd worn this same expression when she'd waited for his opinion about her very first report, the first she'd ever produced at C.E.C. She'd endured a silence as long as this one, then Darrin had tapped the pages with exactly the same gesture. She'd noticed that he'd circled two words in red on the first page. "You've misspelled several words," he'd told her, as though delivering news of an untimely death. He tapped the first circle. "'Sallow-water habitat'? That should be 'shallow.' Correct?" She'd shrugged, smiled. "Yes, of course," she'd answered, as if to say, *So what?* "How can I trust your work product?" he'd asked. "How can I trust your research?"

"Darrin!" she cried, finding her voice. "The report! Is it all right?" She swept her hand toward the stack of pages and knocked over his milk glass. They both threw paper napkins into the spreading puddle.

"Well, sure," he said, as though this were obvious. He looked around for A.D. "It's fine. More than fine. The clients will be pleased." A.D. appeared with a rag and wiped the table. Then she brought another glass of milk. "I agree with you—this basin is ideal, now that we have a donor stock."

She felt like a punctured balloon. All her anxiety hissed away, leaving her limp with relief. Her breakfast was cold, but she tore into it. "And there's another thing, too, about the mysids," she told him, waving her fork.

"What's that?"

"The kokanee have been living underground for the last one hundred years. I'm willing to bet they've altered their feeding patterns so they're less dependent on light and will feed all through the water column."

"You think they'll eat the mysids now, if there are any left?"

"That's right." Jess grinned—she couldn't help herself—at this prospect of ecosystemic justice.

To her surprise, Darrin returned the smile. "Okay, one more issue. I have questions about the donor stock." He found another tabbed page. The yellow tabs curled up from the edge of the stack like question marks. How many more were there? It looked like a lot. "What's the water called again?"

"The Ipsootchuck."

"You call it an 'unnamed' water system, I think?"

"The name is not official." She tried not to answer with her mouth full. The report was 'more than fine'! But she would do her best to avoid spitting food on her boss.

"Okay, the Ipsootchuck. Unofficially. Are you taking me there this afternoon?"

"That's the plan, but first you'll go out with Mike Branch for a tour of Still Lake." Jess looked at her watch, but it wasn't there. "What time is it? We'll try to get to the Ipsootchuck before two o'clock."

"Ten after eleven. You told me on the phone you'd found a groundwater system and a cave network in the Martin Bridge Limestone." He picked up the report and opened it to another page, another tab. "But all you say in here is that the donor stock originates, quote, 'from a small, isolated, unnamed spring-fed pond and stream system located entirely on private property but hydrologically connected to the Old Chuck Creek surface water through a regional groundwater aquifer.' Unquote. And your report has no location information for the donor population."

Jess had been expecting this question. "The report will be a public document," she said, "because state and federal agencies are involved. But the cave has to stay a secret. You'll see it this afternoon: It's a unique resource. Fragile. I don't know of any others in this part of the state; do you?"

"No. But that's exactly why it *should* be public. The cave needs to be protected and managed. It should be a public resource. I know that's what we'll hear from the governor's office. Dolores Capfield."

Had Darrin almost rolled his eyes? She ate the last chunk of potato and washed it down with the lukewarm coffee. "I know, but I don't agree," she said. Darrin waited.

"The Branch family have been stewards of that resource for a hundred and twenty years. The cave is virtually untouched, the formations are intact. Compare that with the caves in Southern Oregon that have been open to the public for that long. The stalactites are broken off, the air flow's all screwed up because the Park Service blasted tunnels through the rock, there's algae growing in there because of the lights. For God's sake, Darrin, there's glazed-over graffiti on the flowstone."

"Obviously there's a downside to public access."

"There's no graffiti in the Ipsootchuck." She planted her palms on the table and leaned over her plate, which was empty. She didn't remember tasting the food.

Darrin crossed his arms and narrowed his eyes at her. "No one knows about it. No one gets to see it."

"And that's the way it has to stay." She folded her napkin into a tiny one-inch cube. She locked her gaze on Darrin's face. He had to understand. "Bottom line, the property owner won't consent to this unless we agree to keep the existence of the cave confidential. He's not going to let us onto the property. No access, no fish, no project." That wasn't really the bottom line. The state could condemn the Branch property, the feds could designate it a national monument. But not while Jack Branch was alive, she hoped. And not before the fish came back. She pushed her plate away and clasped her fingers into a resolute ball. The rigidity in Darrin's face softened and she saw that he had given up.

"But your report is inaccurate," he said, tapping the stack with his long fingers.

"How is it inaccurate?"

"You characterize the unnamed waterway as surface water, and it's not; it's technically groundwater."

"Read it again," said Jess. She unfolded the napkin cube and spread it across her thighs. "I never say the Ipsootchuck is surface water." Darrin scanned the tabbed page again, then flipped through the rest of the report as Jess watched. Finally he set the report down and spread his hands to signify capitulation.

"Fine. You win. You have yourself a project. Congratulations." He smiled for the second time.

"This is going to be great!" She felt like jumping up to hug him, but the impulse passed.

"What's great?" Mike Branch stood at her shoulder. She hadn't seen him come in. Darrin got up and shook his hand.

"Darrin Woodruff."

"Mike Branch." He pulled up a chair.

"You must be the fishing guide. The one who's taking me on a tour of Still Lake."

"That's me." He waved as Sam came inside. "Over here!"

Sam scooted onto the bench beside Jess. He introduced himself to Darrin. "So, we're all going out for a boat ride," he said.

"Not me," Jess said. I've got some other stuff to do." She glanced at her watch. It still wasn't there, just a band of paler skin where her watch used to be.

Darrin excused himself to visit the bathroom. Mike left to get the boat ready. Sam slid closer. Jess moved her thigh away from his, but not before the rush ran through her body. She felt his breath on her cheek as he spoke, and smelled the woodsmoke in his hair.

"My grandfather would like to supervise the visit to the Ipsootchuck this afternoon."

"Of course."

"He also has invited you to lunch beforehand. Can you come by at noon?"

More matchmaking, Jess thought. She tried to think of a graceful way to decline. Then she remembered Birch Stukel's invitation. "Oh, I can't. I've agreed to go to a ... gathering."

"A gathering? Of people?"

She laughed. "That's my assumption. Excuse me. I should go change."

He stood, freeing her. He took her arm as she edged toward the door.

"Are you finished with me, Jess?" he whispered. "Because I can't quite accept that."

"I really do have someplace to be at noon today."

"Where? In town?"

"Birch Stukel's place. She invited me."

His arm fell to his side. "I'm not giving up on you."

She blew out a breath and left the restaurant. He *would* give up. Eventually. He followed her outside, hands in his jacket pockets, head bent as though deep in thought.

Out on the dock, an overcast sky sealed the valley, mountain to mountain, black-bottomed thunderheads massing in the west. A strange, warm wind gusted, wrinkling the water. Sam joined her but stood at a distance.

Mike looked from her to Sam, noticed the space between them, said nothing. He stowed a pair of oars in the *Tamkaliks* and loosened the line from around its cleat. "You'll need more layers," he said to Jess. "It'll be colder out on the water."

"I won't be joining you," she told him. Darrin Woodruff, his yellow rain jacket bright against the low, gray sky, jogged down the gangway.

Darrin asked about the fire as Mike helped him into the dory. Mike had convinced the sheriff he hadn't torched the Outfitters, but who had? Why would Cleve Kittridge set fire to the building, then stay inside? Could Sammy have set the fire, then suffered a stroke? Riley had told her Sammy's pupils were dilated; did a stroke do that? None of it made sense. Again, Jess remembered she owed Riley a phone call.

"You coming, Sam?" Mike called. "We need someone to man the engines." Mike sat in the swivel chair in the dory's bow. Darrin took the seat across the thwart.

"Oh, all right." Sam side-stepped into the boat and took a seat at the transom, freeing the line and tossing it to Mike, never once looking in her direction. He switched on the motor and they slid away from the dock. Mist rose from the lake and the clouds sank lower.

93.

Scott and Brian walked to town before lunch. Brian had his gym bag. Scott had a hunting knife strapped to his belt, which made him feel silly. But their mother had heard about a cougar jumping Jess MacKinnon and Sam Branch, and she had enacted new emergency rules. No one walks alone. Someone carries a weapon. He slid the knife along his belt and pulled his shirttail over it. At least he didn't have to wear a coonskin cap.

They passed the sawmill. No cougar waited to ambush them. They parted ways at First and Main. On Fourth Street, a familiar voice called.

"Scott! Can you give me a hand with this?" It was Jonathan, dragging his canoe through the mud of the mill yard. A cavity opened in Scott's chest.

He trotted over, slipping in the mud, feeling his face redden. He tucked his fingers under the edge of the aft bench and lifted it with a grunt. "Over to the dock?" His voice sounded high and disembodied.

"Yeah." They slid and stumbled through the muck to the street, through the park, down to the dock. The sky was gray, the lake was gray. Scott picked out the *Tamkaliks* a hundred yards from shore, its edges brushed soft in the mist. He couldn't see the mountains. "Why go out today?" he asked.

"It's warm out and it's not raining." They eased the canoe into the water. "I just want to take her out one last time before I leave."

Jonathan stepped into the stern. Scott sat cross-legged on the edge of the dock. "Leave? Where are you going?"

"Amsterdam. On Monday. I'm moving there. Didn't your mom tell you?"

"*Amsterdam?*" The hollow space in Scott's chest grew, deep as a well, and he became a round gray stone plummeting into darkness.

Jonathan pulled a paddle from the bottom of the canoe and laid it across the thwart. He pointed to a second paddle. "Want to come along?"

Scott felt tears damming up behind his eyes. "Guess not, thanks," he managed to say.

Jonathan pushed off and glided away. Scott raised his face to the low sky and let the tears fall. "O love is the crooked thing," he muttered.

94.

Jess wasn't sure what protocol demanded for a "small gathering" to honor the dead in Still Lake. So she opted for what she was already wearing: boots (slightly damp), jeans, a light blue sweater. She did not especially want to attend Birch's gathering, but at least she would not have to endure awkward conversation and matchmaking at the Branch house. She grabbed her pack off the desk, emptied it of papers, and stuffed in her rain jacket. The phone was still off the hook. She replaced it in its cradle.

The desk clerk waved her down at the bottom of the stairs. "Let me guess," Jess said. "Riley Bishop called again."

"Twice, but your phone was busy."

"I'll call her right now."

The clerk dialed the number, then stretched the phone cord over the desk and handed her the receiver. Jess let it ring six times. "Not there. I'll call her when I get back."

95.

The canoe left a slithery wake. Scott watched until it melted into the mist. Footsteps, running, bumped down the gangway. He scrubbed his face with his sleeve and stood. A short, thick person with glasses ran up to him. It was the private investigator, Riley Bishop. The red-headed kid, Moses Fletcher, was a few steps behind.

"I'm looking for Jess MacKinnon. You know where she is?" Riley walked to the end of the dock and back again.

"Sure. She's staying at Still Lake Lodge."

"She just left there. Any idea where I can find her?" She rounded on him, bulky in her black wool coat. She had a funny way of talking, clipped and fast.

Scott pointed across the water. "She might be out on the lake with Mike Branch."

"Can you reach them? It's important." She took his arm, gripping it.

"No way to reach them. What's so important?" He pulled his arm away from the vise of her fingers.

"She's in danger. Serious danger. Can you take us out there?"

Serious danger? The boats were stowed for the winter, except the *Tamkaliks*. Scott turned toward shore, the Outfitters, the storage shed under the deck. It was locked with a chain and a padlock. And no other boats out. Except . . .

He peered into the gap between the rising mist and the sinking clouds. He cupped his hands around his mouth. "Jonathan!" he shouted. "Hey! Jonathan!"

He shouted twice more. Then the canoe's high prow slipped out of the fog. Jonathan was coming back.

96.

Jess parked in Birch Stukel's graveled yard, scattering the chickens. Birch intercepted her at the car door; she wore a brilliant, tie-died Mumu over red long johns, the bottoms tucked into cowboy boots. Her hair was gathered back into a knot, festooned with blue feathers. When Jess stepped away from the rental car, Birch hugged her as though they were best friends.

"I'm delighted you could come. Simply delighted." Jess heard warmth and affection in Birch's tone, saw tears fill her eyes. Birch and Sammy had been close.

Birch swept her arm in a gesture that included the meadow, the canyon, her yellow cottage, the huge gray barn. "It's so warm out, I've set us up in the backyard for now. If those clouds let loose, we'll run inside." She smiled, made another gesture. "We'll go through the barn." Jess followed her across the yard and into the dim, fetid barn.

They scuffled through loose straw on the barn floor, past the crocks of wine, the rows of bottles. Further in, the mule rested on its side, a cat tucked under the curve of its neck. In the far corner, the curl of a sleeping dog.

Birch led her through a side door into the yard behind the cottage, offered her a seat at a white wicker table. Then Birch excused herself and vanished into the house.

The glass-topped table and six wicker chairs were grouped with potted cabbages on a flagstone patio. Beyond the flagstones and a fringe of brown grass, the yard was walled on three sides: behind her, the back of Birch's cottage; to her left, the long gray side of the barn; in front, a row of blackberry bushes, shriveled and black, as tall as Jess. Three trees grew out of the brambles, dangling with ivy. To Jess's right, the yard opened into a meadow that ended at the lip of the canyon. Jess could hear the creek gushing down its channel.

Birch banged through the back door with a teapot and eight cups on a tray. She filled two cups and sat to Jess's left, chattering brightly about the warm weather.

Jess tasted the tea, a jarring mix of mint and ginger and something else, earthy and pungent, that reminded her of walnuts.

"Do you like it?" Birch leaned toward her.

The tea was sweet but left a trace of bitterness on her tongue. A gust of wind tore a few remaining leaves from the branches of the maples, sent them flying like brown rags to a pile drifted up next to the barn. "I do like it," Jess said. She wrapped her fingers around the warm cup, a small Japanese-style basin without a handle. The teapot matched: blood-red blossoms against a dark green glaze. "It's unusual." She checked her watch, which wasn't there. "When will the others get here?"

"Soon. Very soon."

Jess set her empty cup on the table and Birch refilled it.

97.

In the middle of the lake, the fog thickened. Scott rested his paddle across the bow and peered into their thirty-foot radius of visibility. The noon sun made a dime overhead, gray on gray. In the stern, Jonathan kept them moving, slowly. Riley knelt in the middle, between them, clutching the gunwales with both hands. Behind her, Moses sat cross-legged, looking all around. The canoe rode low in the water.

"Hallo!" Scott called. "Ahoy! Mike!"

Scott thought he heard a thin voice call back over the water.

"Did you hear that?" The fog made him whisper. He twisted to look at Riley and Moses.

"Scott? Is that you?" Mike's voice floated out of the mist.

Scott sat up like a bird dog, straining to listen. "Ahoy there!" he called again.

Mike shouted, "Over here!"

Scott yelled back. "Mike! Keep shouting. I can't see you."

"Over here, Scotty! Over here!"

The dory emerged, wraithlike, from the wall of fog. He brought the canoe around with a backward paddle stroke. They bumped

312

broadside into the dory, narrowly missing one of Riley's clutching hands. She snatched her fingers away and sat up, tipping the canoe.

"Whoa!" Jonathan shouted. Moses grabbed the edge of the dory.

"This thing is unstable." Riley tugged her overcoat more tightly around her. "I'm looking for Jess MacKinnon," she told Mike. "She's not with you?" She leaned over to peer into the dory as though Jess might be hiding in the bottom. The canoe tipped.

"Please stop doing that!" Scott yelled.

Sam pulled the canoe closer alongside the dory. "Why are you looking for Jess?" he asked her.

"I'll be brief. Sammy had atropine and scopolamine in his bloodstream. He was poisoned. The same poison showed up in the toxicology results for Ben Fletcher. The levels in Fletcher's body were probably not high enough to kill him. He was hit in the head, knocked unconscious, and then he drowned."

Darrin's eyebrows shot up. "Ben Fletcher was murdered?"

"Damn straight he was," Moses said in a choked voice

"Where is Jess MacKinnon?" Riley said. "I believe she's in danger. The sheriff's on his way."

Mike and Darrin exchanged a blank look. But Sam nodded. "I know where she is," he said. "She's at Birch Stukel's place."

"That's not good at all." Riley stood, tentative, clutching the sides of the canoe. "Can you take me there? Now?"

98.

A choppy wind blew up from the canyon, flattening the meadow grass and parting the curtain of ivy at the back of Birch's yard. Jess glimpsed something white behind the wall of seething green. The wind passed, but the wall of ivy and blackberries and maple branches continued to

313

roil like maggots on rotting meat. Jess shook her head and tried to focus. Her mouth felt dry, as dry as dust. She asked for water; Birch offered her some wine. Jess shook her head. Birch poured another cupful of tea. Jess gulped it down.

"I don't like wine," Jess said. Or meant to say. Had she spoken? Her head felt funny. She looked at her watch. It was not on her wrist. She could not remember what had happened to it.

"Ah," Birch said, pouring more tea. "So that's why you gave your bottle of homemade berry wine to Sammy." She narrowed her eyes at Jess. Her face sharpened, then blurred, then sharpened again. "I don't approve of re-gifting. I don't approve at all."

"I didn't give the wine to Sammy." Jess steadied herself, gripping the sides of her chair. It seemed important to communicate this to Birch, who looked menacing. "I gave it to the desk clerk at the Lodge."

"The point is," Birch said in a low voice, "that wine was meant for you." Her face swam closer. "How do you feel?"

"I don't feel well." Getting the words out required all her concentration.

"Understandable. You've had quite a lot of Jimson weed." Birch lifted the teapot's lid and peeked inside. "Might be enough to kill you, actually. You're small. How much do you weigh?"

Alarms went off in Jess's brain, but they were far away. "I should go," she said, and stood up carefully, leaning on the back of the wicker chair for support. Then she was splayed on the flagstones with no memory of falling. She rolled onto her back. It occurred to her that she might be asleep and dreaming, again. The clouds seethed and the sky whirled. Then Birch's face hovered above her. The tie-dyed spirals in her Mumu were spinning. Birch's lips twisted into a demonic grin.

"You killed Sammy. That put life and death out of balance. It was not his time."

Jess struggled to sit up. "Sammy?" She wobbled, flopped back to the cold stones. They felt hard and real, not like a dream at all.

"It's my humble role to restore balance. You'll have to die to atone for Sammy's death, just as Ben Fletcher had to die for Colby Stukel. It's really not personal." Birch picked up Jess's hand and pulled her to her feet. She tottered; Birch held her up. "It's time to go." Birch kept a firm arm around her waist and walked her across the grass toward the wall of blackberries.

99.

Riley joined Darrin on the bench in the middle of the boat. Moses crowded in next to Sam. Sam's impatient fingers tapped the switch for the boat's motor. He was visibly agitated. "Let's just go!" She heard the hysteria in his voice. So he and MacKinnon had slept together. Apparently, he had fallen for her, hard.

Mike, Scott, and Darrin were arguing about whether it would be faster to return to shore for a vehicle, or to cross the lake and hike to Birch's on foot. Finally they sent Scott and Jonathan back to town in the canoe to wait for the sheriff. Riley resigned herself to the boat ride, as it appeared inevitable. She smelled brackish water. Sam turned the motors on and steered the boat in what they all hoped was the direction of Old Chuck Creek and the road to Birch's house.

Riley filled them in: the wine had been made with Deadly Nightshade berries, lethal, which had almost certainly killed Sammy before the fire began. At the scene, Birch Stukel had identified herself as the wine maker.

"Could she have used the Nightshade berries by accident?" Mike asked.

"Don't think so," Riley told him. "The label had a hand-drawn figure of a woman on it and the word 'Italia' underneath."

315

"What's the significance of that?" Darrin reared back to regard Riley with a frown. He was a stern sort of fellow and smelled like paper.

"Datura belladonna is the botanical name for Deadly Nightshade," she told him. "In Italian, 'belladonna' means 'beautiful woman.'"

No one spoke. Sam bit his lip.

Finally Darrin said, "So. We're going to confront a murderer, in her own territory. What are we going to do when we get there?"

More silence. Mike swiveled to look out over the bow. The mist was clearing as they reached the mouth of the creek. "Veer to port twenty degrees," Mike said, pointing. The boat swerved. Then, over his shoulder, "Do you carry a gun?"

"Me?" Riley swatted her chest. "No, sorry."

100.

Birch steered Jess into a gap in the blackberry bushes, a thorny tunnel of shriveled leaves. Behind the bushes and the ivy, a white pickup rested in the middle of the forest. Birch released her grip on Jess' torso to lower the tailgate; Jess crumpled onto a carpet of wet leaves.

She had to get away. She crawled through the leaves toward the front of the truck. Birch, apparently unconcerned about her slow-speed escape attempt, opened the passenger door and rummaged behind the seat. An emblem on the door made something clunk into place in Jess's addled memory: a picture of blue water, orange sky, a leaping fish, a flying game bird. Jess stopped crawling and strained to get the print into focus: U.S. Fish and Wildlife Service. *Clunk*: the memory surfaced. This was the image she'd glimpsed on the truck that knocked her motorcycle into the canyon.

She sat up, struggling to hold this slippery moment of lucidity. Birch knelt beside her, a plastic bag in her hand, full of snakes. No, zip-ties. This worried Jess but she couldn't think why.

"You tried to kill me. Last week. On the side of the road."

"Yes. I've been trying to get rid of you since you first came to town. You don't belong here, my love. You don't seem to understand that you should leave Still Lake and never come back." Birch pulled a zip-tie from the bag. "It's too late for that now. Now it's different, because you killed Sammy. Your death is a ritual death. There is no other way to restore the balance."

"This is Ben Fletcher's truck," Jess said, concentrating. But the price for her mental acuity seemed to be muscular control: she could only grunt as Birch knocked her over and planted her in the musty leaves with a knee on her back. Birch yanked her arms behind her.

"Yes, isn't it ridiculous? That's the government for you. A truck goes missing, no one notices." Birch cinched the zip-tie around her wrists. "Your tax dollars at work, my love." She rolled Jess onto her back and pulled her to sitting.

Jess twisted against the binding. Her fingers went numb. "That's too tight," she said.

Birch stood behind her and clamped her arms around Jess's shoulders, hauling her to standing. "You won't need your hands anymore, not in this lifetime." She marched Jess to the open tailgate, bucked her on top like a bale of hay, and rolled her into the truck bed.

The tailgate slammed shut with the finality of a cell door. A flock of brown leaves swirled upward. Against her cheek, the corrugated steel of the bed felt frigid and gritty. Her hands swelled. She spat out a piece of leaf and rolled to her side. Through the chaos in her brain a single thought pinged, beacon through the fog: if she couldn't get away, she was going to die. The truck's engine turned over with a long slow groan.

101

The fog dispersed as the dory neared the creek mouth, and all Riley could smell was flat, brackish water. Mike insisted on taking the tiller. He and Sam traded places, stumbling between Darrin and Riley. They all twisted around to watch Mike steer the *Tamkaliks* toward a bank of cobbles. Mike's features were frozen.

"Everybody hold on!" he shouted.

Sam gripped the sides of the boat. Riley braced her feet. They nosed into the weeds. Mike wasn't slowing down.

"What are you doing?" Sam yelled. Riley smelled danger, blood in the water.

"Just hold on!"

Mike steered the boat through the vegetation and into the creek, the keel rasping over stones. Still they were at full speed, though the force of the current slowed them down. Now they were well into the creek and the boat bounced over stones.

"Dad!" Sam yelled.

With a loud crack, the boat splintered and water pooled in the bottom. Riley and Darrin lifted their feet. Darrin's face was pinched with anxiety, but Riley felt herself fill with excitement. Mike had sacrificed his boat to rescue Jess MacKinnon!

"Get ready!" Mike shouted. The keel broke apart. Mike cut the motors and rammed the prow into the bank. Sam jumped and scrambled over the rocks, sliding. They'd made it eighty yards upstream, almost to the road. Sam climbed the embankment to the asphalt. Riley caught up to him, Darrin and Mike and Moses close behind. They started running.

102.

Instead of paddling back to town, Scott and Jonathan had followed the *Tamkaliks* through the fog, keeping their distance. They watched Mike speed up the creek and into the forest. They poled the canoe against the current a few feet past the mouth, then beached it on the cobbles and walked to the road. The others were gone.

"We'd better go back," Jonathan said.

Scott hesitated. He wanted to be part of the rescue operation. What if Jess was hurt?

"Come on!" Jonathan called. "We have to meet the sheriff. He won't know where to go."

Scott jogged back to the canoe.

103.

Jess heard Birch cursing in the cab. The truck wouldn't start. She felt bumps through the cold metal of the bed as Birch pumped the accelerator. Her muscles seemed to be working again. She wriggled to the wheel well, shoved her hips up onto the raised surface. More cursing from the cab, then the engine stuttered and caught. Jess hooked her leg over the side. Lifted her hips. Hooked the other leg. The engine faltered; Birch pumped the gas. Jess poured herself over the side of the pickup and spilled to the ground. The fall knocked the air from her lungs, sent pain stabbing through her ribcage, and dislocated her shoulder. The truck roared and lurched forward. Jess rolled away from the rear tire. She was on the truck's passenger side— there was a chance Birch hadn't seen her. She kept rolling. The truck bumped through the forest.

It was astonishingly difficult to get to her feet with her hands tied behind her. Jess made several attempts, lunging forward and toppling over each time. Finally she rolled to a tree, flung herself against it and inched upright, scraping against the rough bark.

The truck stopped. The door slammed. Birch had seen her.

On her feet at last, Jess started running, stumbling and weaving through the trees. She tumbled to the ground, gasping as her shoulder hit. Dammit. She rolled to a tree, flung herself, inched to standing.

But the vise of Birch's arms trapped her shoulders from behind, and Birch's voice hissed into her ear: "Not so fast, my love." They waddled back to the pickup, Birch's body clamped to Jess's back. "Fletcher was not this much trouble. All he did was roll around and make noise." Birch shoved her against the truck. "We had sex, you know." Jess could feel Birch's spit on her ear. "And I knew when we fucked that I was going to kill him." She laughed. "It's the ultimate aphrodisiac. You can't imagine!" Birch opened the tailgate, keeping one arm tight around Jess's torso. "It's unbelievable, the potency you feel holding someone's life in your hands." She wedged her knee against Jess's hips and bucked her into the truck bed. Another zip-tie tightened around her ankles. She felt consciousness leaking away. The sensation of the cold truck bed against her cheek disappeared, then the pain in her shoulder, her ribs, the numbness in her fingers. The only thing left was Birch's voice, shrill and far away. "It's the flip side of childbirth, I suppose. Have you had a child? Well, never mind. This isn't about you. Yes, you have to die. That's destiny. But you're only a minor piece in a grand game. A pawn." The truck door opened. "Maybe a bishop." The door slammed shut.

104.

Except for Moses (who after all was a teenager), Riley was in the best condition of the five-member rescue team. She credited her iron self-discipline and her gym membership. She trotted easily alongside Sam, who was gasping. They passed the footbridge just as, twenty yards ahead, a white pickup lunged out of the forest and onto the asphalt.

They stopped in the road as the truck bore down. Birch was driving, alone in the cab. She had Jess in the truck bed, Riley was sure of it. She smelled wax, wicks, and flame. "She's in the back!" Riley shouted.

The others reared away from the silver grill plunging toward them. But Moses ran past her as the truck tore by. He jumped, got his arms over the side, twisted his body into the bed. Riley yelled. The truck slowed down. Birch had seen them; had she seen Moses? Well, Riley was in charge of Moses Fletcher while he remained a minor child—four more days. She pivoted and ran a jagged pattern to the rear of the truck, saw that Birch's eyes were still on Mike, Sam, and Darrin. She pitched herself over the tailgate.

There was Jess, bumping like a rag doll. Moses knelt beside her. He was trying to free her ankles. "Get down!" Riley whispered, flattening herself against the truck bed.

Moses stretched his long body out. Jess was curled on her side, arms and legs tied. Riley put her face next to Jess's. She was breathing. Her eyes were open, but her pupils so dilated that almost nothing but black remained. Her hair was tangled with leaves and her face covered with scratches. Riley wiped blood and mud from her forehead with her thumb and smelled limes. The truck bumped as the gears caught. They picked up speed. She heard Sam shouting.

"I've got her feet loose!" Moses whispered.

Jess did not seem to register their presence. The truck lurched and threw them all together. Birch was driving much too fast for this winding road.

Riley found her pocket knife and turned Jess onto her stomach. Jess's wrists were bound with a zip-tie, skin so badly swollen around the binding that Riley could not get the knife blade underneath. She found the place where the tie slipped through its plastic eye. She used the blade to press the tiny tongue that would release it, but the truck careened to a stop, pitching them into the rear window. By the time Riley untangled herself and peeked over the side, Birch was out of the truck.

Riley put her mouth next to Jess's ear, hand on her shoulder. The smell of limes, the smell of tar. "Jess? Can you hear me?" Nothing. "Keep down!" she told Moses. She looked out again. They were parked next to the lake shore, at the waterfall. Gray water chopped against old pilings and the fog hung low. She spotted Birch by the sawmill's foundation. Birch turned; Riley ducked. She watched Birch through the windshield as she prodded Jess's puffy wrists, feeling for the zip-tie. Birch was twenty feet away, carrying something: a pole with a hook on the end. Riley dropped her pocket knife. It clanged onto the truck bed. Jess was utterly limp. "Cut the zip tie!" she whispered to Moses. Birch was ten feet away. Five feet.

Riley sprang from the truck. She'd planned on taking Birch down in a flying tackle, but Birch used the pole to fend her off. She landed hard, rolled to the side as Birch swung the pole at her head. She swung it again; Riley grabbed the end. The hook was iron, forked, sharp. Riley held on with both hands. The weak sunlight made a nimbus around Birch's head, her shadowed face malevolent.

Riley jerked the pole and pulled Birch off balance. She kicked Birch's shin. Birch cried out and Riley scrambled to her feet. But Birch recovered too quickly, yanked the pole out of her hands, swung it like a baseball bat. Riley dodged. Moses ran up to them, yelling. Birch swung the pole again, right at Moses's head. Riley flung her arm up. The iron hook hit and the pain was instant and blinding. She dropped low and rammed her shoulder into Birch's knees.

They went down and tumbled. Moses grappled for the pole. Birch got on top of her, slammed her head back onto stone. The light leaked away to leave her in darkness.

105.

They had almost reached the Outfitters dock when Scott's eye caught movement on the wharf by the sawmill. He pointed, and they turned the canoe toward North Creek, hugging the shoreline.

As they closed the distance, Scott made out a figure picking its way across the deck in a strange, erratic dance. First, the figure tapped the planks with a pole—he guessed it was the peavey pole Brian had taken—then it turned and retraced its path, walking backwards, dragging something long and heavy.

"Hey!" he said when he saw who it was. "It's Birch—she's got Jess tied up! She's going to push her in the lake!"

They dug their paddles into the water and reached the end of the wharf just as Birch arrived there with her prey.

Scott stood up. The canoe rocked. "Birch!" he screamed.

Jess, who had been limp while Birch dragged her, began thrashing and kicking her feet. Birch set one blue cowboy boot on Jess's hip as though trapping a soccer ball. The peavey pole hung like a spear from her left hand.

"No!" Scott shouted. They were close to the wharf, but it was chest high, no way to get up there from the canoe.

Birch pushed with her foot and Jess rolled, still kicking, into the water. Then, incredibly, Birch vaulted into the canoe, which heeled and nearly went over. Scott threw his paddle at her head and jumped over the side.

106.

Riley forced herself onto her hands and knees. She shook her head to clear it and a bullet of white pain ricocheted across her skull. She smelled iron. No, it was blood, fresh. Possibly her own. Keeping her head rigid, she sat up and twisted to one side and then the other, scanning for Moses, for Birch, for Jess. There was Moses, stretched out flat on the wharf. She crawled onto the rotting planks. They left splinters in her hands as she crept toward him. His head was bleeding; he was unconscious. Or dead. She pressed two fingers against his neck, felt his heartbeat. Not dead. That was good. The blood seeped from a gash on his scalp. His hair was matted with it. She combed it aside. The gash wasn't deep. Also good.

She looked up and the pain shot through her head, blinding her. When she could see again, there were Birch and Jonathan, standing in the canoe. Birch advanced. She held the pole with the iron hook across her chest with both hands. The canoe rocked. Jonathan raised his paddle. He used it to block her as she leaped at him—then the canoe flipped and threw them both into the lake.

107.

Jess descended to the lake bottom and landed on her knees. A puff of silt billowed around her. She struggled, jerking her zip-tied hands. She rose to her feet and pushed off, kicking as hard as she could. She could not swim up without her arms. She drifted back to sit on the lakebed.

The compulsion to inhale was overwhelming. But even as her body fought against itself, her mind grew calm. The silt settled. She saw everything at once, her vision wide and sharp. The water, turquoise. Jewels of fine bubbles. Muted sunlight at the surface. Plants waving in slow motion. All complete.

Now it was all right to inhale. The realization made her body thrash to its feet. A silt cloud rose.

Through the cloud a face emerged, cheeks puffed out and dark hair streaming. It could be God. No, it was Scott Kittridge, fumbling with something at his belt. A knife! He swam behind her. The zip-tie tightened, horribly, then released. But it was too late. She couldn't move her arms and she was out of air, out of time.

Scott hooked an elbow under her armpit, tried to swim up. She could see sunlight, dancing on the surface. At last her arms responded, though only one seemed to work. It was enough—she pushed up, paddling and kicking. When her mouth opened to gasp for air, it really *was* air, and the sunlight blinded her.

108.

She was a fish, breathing cold water. She stroked her tail back and forth and waited beside a tangle of twigs. She needed to swim on. Her body floated low, heavy with eggs. Against this heaviness, the need to move pulled her past the tangle, her yearning bright and buoyant, like a woman's voice calling her name.

"Jess? Can you hear me?"

It was her mother. She swished her tail, pushed against the current. *I'm sorry about everything*, she said. *Ain't no call for that, my girl*, Priscilla answered.

Something squeezed her fingers: it was Ernie's hand. She opened her eyes. The creases in Ernie's face rearranged to accommodate his smile. Behind his head, a spray of fine bubbles and turquoise water, writhing with shadows. She floated. He floated beside her. *I wrecked my bike*, she told him. He made a sympathetic sound. His face wavered, twisted. Blurred. Sharpened.

Around his face, the shadows took form, curling and uncurling. Above her, wind wrinkled the skin of the water. When it stilled, she saw three faces peering down, watching her. Ben. Becky. Rex. But Ben was dead. Wasn't he? In her nostrils, the water turned sticky as blood. She clawed at her face. She was drowning. No, she was thrashing, then swimming, then cutting through the current and racing away upstream.

"Hold on—I think she's coming around."

The Fletcher faces were gone. Another face swam by. She struggled to bring it into focus. *You're in big trouble, MacKinnon*, said Darrin Woodruff.

"Hey." A hand touched her shoulder.

The drone of sounds sorted themselves out, murmurs of conversation from far away. Closer, a persistent electronic beeping. Riley Bishop's face loomed closer, her glasses shimmering.

109.

"You're awake." Riley patted Jess MacKinnon's shoulder, the one that wasn't injured. MacKinnon was a mess. Her wrists were bandaged, her relocated shoulder bound to her side. Her face was covered with scratches and her hair looked like a bird's nest. An untidy bird. As per usual MacKinnon bolted upright and tried to swing her legs over the side of the hospital bed.

"Whoa," she moaned, falling back again.

Riley pressed the button that lifted the back of the bed. MacKinnon raised her arm and studied her IV tubes. "Where are the others?" she asked.

"Nobody here but us chickens," Riley answered.

"What?"

"Mike and Scott were here earlier. They'll be back in a few minutes." Riley turned away. "Sam, too," she forced herself to add, even though she would prefer to omit him. Even though she would prefer that he drop right off the planet. At the sink she found a hairbrush. She held it up. "Want help with your hair?" she asked. "Before you have to meet the public?"

MacKinnon felt her head, laughed, and nodded. Riley pulled the bristles through MacKinnon's hair, slowing when they snagged on a tangle. MacKinnon closed her eyes. Riley, who had felt sick all morning from the hospital's formaldehyde smell, bent to sniff her hair. It hadn't been washed but still smelled of soap and rosemary. Underneath was Jess's scent, bright lime. It made Riley think of margaritas, and patio furniture with yellow stripes. Late afternoon sunshine tossing out bands of light and shadow. "Shall I braid it?" she asked. Her voice came out hoarse. She coughed.

"Yes, please."

"What do you remember?" Riley asked her. Jess's hair was dark brown but with reddish streaks. Riley had never noticed them. She divided the hair into plaits, sifting the strands between her fingers. She worked slowly, having had few occasions to develop any hair-braiding skills.

"Birch invited me to her house for a memorial, but no one else came. She gave me tea." MacKinnon's face crinkled in concentration. "It was drugged with something—Jimson weed. Then she had a Fish and Wildlife pickup hidden behind some blackberries. She tied me up. Threw me in back. The next thing I remember I was in the lake."

"We found you unconscious in the pickup. Birch rolled you into the lake." Riley wove the plaits together. Fran had worn her hair long and loose, swinging like curtains over her face when she bent over her guitar. When she smiled at Riley over a mug of coffee in the morning, she would tuck it behind her ears.

"We? Who found me?"

Riley tied off the braid with a hair band. "I did. With my new assistant, Moses." Mike and Race came in through the open door, trailed by Scott Kittridge. Riley dropped the braid and stepped away.

"She's awake!" Mike said. "Have you filled her in?"

"Not yet." No sign of Sam. She decided not to inquire.

MacKinnon bolted up again. "Wait! Where *is* Moses? What day is it?"

Race threw MacKinnon a puzzled look. None of them knew about Moses. Riley put a hand back on MacKinnon's shoulder, half protective, half to keep her from running out of the room with a contrail of dripping IV tubes. "He's on this floor, a few rooms down. I'll bring him by later. He's getting discharged this afternoon."

"He had a concussion," Scott volunteered.

"Courtesy of my little sister, I'm afraid," Race said. "Riley had one, too."

"They were on special. Two-for-one." Riley wanted desperately to make MacKinnon laugh again, but it wasn't working.

"But what *day* is it?"

"Thursday."

"What day of the month?"

"October fourteenth," Scott said.

MacKinnon fell back onto the pillows. Riley understood: she had missed Moses's eighteenth birthday, yesterday. "Well," she said brightly. "Would you like to hear the details? I have autopsy results." She opened her binder. "The new autopsy report on Fletcher is consistent with your scenario: a big dose of Jimson weed, a bumpy ride in the back of his own pickup, splinters from the dock in his shoe soles, a blow to the head from that log-driving pole, and then death from asphyxia and cerebral hypoxia." She closed the binder with a snap. "In other words, drowning. And I should turn in my license for missing the most obvious piece of all: Fletcher's truck. I never asked myself how he got to Still Lake, or what happened to his vehicle." She thwacked herself on the forehead with the heel of her hand. "Must be my urban upbringing. I assumed he took a cab." She was still trying to make MacKinnon laugh. The others obliged, chuckling at the absurdity of a taxicab in Still Lake, but MacKinnon was frowning.

"What about the fire?" she asked. "Do we know who set the fire?"

"I don't think we know that yet," Mike said. "I'm still a suspect, technically, and so is my uncle."

"Sammy? That's crazy!" Race said.

Mike shrugged. "He was my business partner. The business was failing."

"Isn't Birch a suspect?" Jess asked.

"Of course," said Riley. "But she's lawyered up and isn't talking. Anyway, what motive would she have? She didn't want Sammy to die."

Jess looked from face to face. "The catch records!" she shouted.

"What?" Riley reached out to restrain her again, if necessary, but MacKinnon stayed down.

"She wanted to destroy Mike's records."

"But why?" Mike asked. "All they are is measurements and weights. Nothing about Colby Stukel in there."

"Right." MacKinnon tried to lift her hands, one of which was strapped to her torso. She winced. "But she didn't know that. She only knew the records were important to *me*. She was having dinner with Sammy when I asked him to help me."

Riley nodded. "She wanted to destroy you. And everything you were trying to do."

"Did you say 'are'?" Jess asked Mike.

"Come again?"

"Do the records still exist? Didn't they burn up in the fire?"

"Oh. No, Sammy had moved them into the store. Only the storeroom burned." He scratched his goatee. "And yes, you may have them. You've certainly earned them."

"I've never ever missed your birthday." MacKinnon's eyes filled with tears. Riley offered Moses the chair. He wore a hospital gown with a pair of basketball shorts underneath. Riley hovered by the sink, then crossed the room to look out the window, turning her back on what promised to be an emotional conversation.

"I know it." Moses's voice was soft.

"I was there when you were born."

"Really? With my mother?"

Riley turned around. Would MacKinnon tell him the truth? The room was so quiet Riley could hear the fluorescent lights buzzing. MacKinnon reached for his hand, patted it. She looked up toward the ceiling, then back to his face. "That's right, Kiddo," she said. "With your mother."

110.

Late in the afternoon, Jess wheeled her IV stand down the hall to visit Moses. He was dressed, sitting on the edge of the bed. Becky fussed with a vase of flowers on the table. Rex stood by the window, arms folded, his back to the room. Jess stopped short in the doorway. She backed up and turned to leave but Moses spotted her.

"Aunt Jess!" His face split into a grin, which made her smile. He was happy to see her. "We were just talking about you. How you almost died. How you solved the mystery! And you saved the fish."

"You found Ben's murderer," Becky said, her voice breaking on the name.

"That was Riley Bishop," Jess told her. "I was just the bait." She wheeled the IV stand back and forth, watched the wheels swivel against the linoleum.

Rex turned. He wore jeans, loafers, a brown sports coat. His face looked pinched and his eyes tired, but it wasn't enough to still the anger that rose hot into her cheeks every time she saw him, and the attendant impulse to kick him right in the crotch. "We're grateful to Miss Bishop, of course." His voice sounded grave, almost subdued—if Dr. Rex Fletcher could ever be described as subdued. "And to you as well. Thank you."

She met his eyes. He loved Moses. That was the only thing that redeemed him. "You're welcome," she said. She couldn't say, later, what made her blurt out the rest. Maybe it was because Ben was dead. She had survived. She had succeeded where Ben had failed. There was a bitter sense of vindication in that. "Not bad for a tramp from the projects, right?"

He squinted at her. She watched his face. She waited for the flash of recognition. It didn't come. He didn't remember saying it. She wanted to laugh, or maybe to cry. All she could think of for almost eighteen years were those words—and they took up no space in his brain at all. She did laugh then, and felt giddy. She stepped over to her son and kissed the top of his head. "See you later, Kiddo," she said. She flung out a hand in what passed as a farewell wave to Rex and Becky and she left the room, trailing the IV stand behind her. She floated, weightless, down the hall.

Friday, October 1, 2010

Jack Branch stood in the trees near the creek watching the water gush past the sheared-off side of the boulder that Albert Monticola had blasted with dynamite. The afternoon sun poured into the forest, hot for this late in the year, and he could smell sweet cedar and the turpentine scent of pine. On an island of stones, a little water ouzel hopped jerkily in and out of the water, dipping its head and then shedding the moisture with a shimmy of its body and a shrug of its dark wings.

Young Moses Fletcher had married a woman from Enterprise. He and his stepchild, Lucy, walked down the trail and squatted near the creek. Wings twitching, the water ouzel jumped across the stones away from them. Moses pointed into a pool of slack water. He spoke to Lucy, but the rush of the creek overwhelmed every other sound. Jack shuffled forward to see into the water; there were six red kokanee in the pool, their bodies waving over the yellow sand. Lucy squealed and jumped and startled two of the fish. They darted into the faster current then back into the pool again.

One of the fish made a run for the boulders, its body a bright muscle. It thrashed sideways into the froth between two stones and cleared them to rest in the calmer water above. Lucy clapped her hands. She and Moses climbed over the rocks to follow the fish.

Lucy pointed at a carcass wedged into a rock dam on the upstream side. In death, the kokanee's brilliant red had faded to pink, as though color were life, and the eye was empty. Lucy found a stick and poked it, then squatted to examine the carcass, wrinkling her nose. Jack could imagine the rotting fish smell. Blood and bone and rust and shadow.

Jess MacKinnon appeared at Jack's elbow. She was checking on him. Being a hundred and eight meant that folks checked on you. You missed three-quarters of what went on. You lived in the circle of a present moment that narrowed and narrowed and grew more quiet. It was not unpleasant.

His boots rustled in the pine mulch as he shuffled to face her. She carried a galvanized pail. Inside floated the ladle Jack's father had carved from ash. She dipped the ladle and he took it. He lifted one eyebrow, by which he meant, *Ipsootchuck?* She nodded and smiled with the blue sparks of her eyes, by which she meant, *Yes.* He tipped the ladle and drank it all. She chuckled, the sound of water.

His grandson Sam popped up next to Jack's other side and kissed his cheek. "Would you like a chair, Grandfather?" he asked in Nez Perce. Jack nodded and eased himself into the seat. Sam unfolded a second chair next to him and sat down.

His son Michael came with more chairs, bouncing along as Michael did. His crew cut was gray and he had filled out around the middle, but he still bobbed about, quick and nervous as a water ouzel. He opened a chair for Jess and one for himself. He plopped down next to Sam. The four of them, Jess, Jack, Sam, and Michael, sat in a line and watched the five red fish scoot around their pool.

It was time. Jack rested his hand on Sam's knee.

"Have you asked her to marry you yet?" he said in a stage whisper. This was his opening line for the same words they exchanged, in exactly the same way, every time. It was part of how everything fit together.

"Of course. I propose to her on a weekly basis. Usually on Sunday afternoon."

Mike grunted. Jess laughed. The Ponderosa dappled the ground with lacy shade.

Jess rested her palm between his shoulder blades. "Are you hungry, Jack? Do you have everything you need for right now?"

"I have everything I need for right now," he told her.

About the Author

Jennie Bricker is a natural resources attorney based in Portland, Oregon. In addition to her law practice, Jennie works as a freelance writer and editor. She received a Burton Award for a co-authored nonfiction article about the Endangered Species Act. She has also published short stories and micro fiction in *Third Wednesday Magazine*, *100 Word Story*, and a *Writer's Digest* prizewinner's anthology. *Thirsty Creek* is her debut novel.

About the Press

Unsolicited Press is based out of Portland, Oregon and focuses on the works of the unsung and underrepresented. As a womxn-owned, all-volunteer small publisher that doesn't worry about profits as much as championing exceptional literature, we have the privilege of partnering with authors skirting the fringes of the lit world. We've worked with emerging and award-winning authors such as Amy Shimshon-Santo, Brook Bhagat, Elisa Carlsen, Tara Stillions Whitehead, and Anne Leigh Parrish.

Learn more at unsolicitedpress.com. Find us on Instagram, X, Facebook, Pinterest, Bsky, Threads, YouTube, and LinkedIn. Unsolicited Press also writes a snarky newsletter on Substack.

www.ingramcontent.com/pod-product-compliance
Lightning Source LLC
Chambersburg PA
CBHW021021310726
48969CB00006B/1492